FATE OF ELODIA | BOOK TWO

THE *Fortune* OF *Fractured Fate*

AMBER D. LEWIS

Paperback ISBN: 979-8-9921218-1-0

Ebook ISBN: 979-8-9921218-2-7

Cover Art: Jo Lewis

Cover & Book Formatting: Once Upon an Amber Dawn, LLC

Editing and Proofreading: Andi L. Gregory, LLC

For Business Inquiries visit www.amberdlewis.com or write to 4359 Wade Hampton Blvd, #282, Taylors, SC 29687

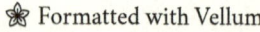 Formatted with Vellum

ALSO BY AMBER D. LEWIS

FIRE AND STARLIGHT SAGA

The Night the Stars Fell

Scars: Alak's Story

The Starlight in the Shadows

Star-Crossed: Cal's Story

The Stardust in the Ashes

Stray: Kai's Story

To Wish Upon a Star (Short Story)

The Stars Amid the Storm

Among the Starlight: Constellation One

FATE OF ELODIA

Between Fate & Failure

The Fortune of Fractured Fate

To Ari, for always being willing to listen to my ramblings and for being a supportive friend, even in the middle of the night

AUTHOR NOTE

This book is meant for an adult audience and contains adult language, adult content, and adult situations.

This book also contains:

- Eye Stabbing
- Non-consensual Drugging (not a main character)
- Teenage girl bound and gagged for a sacrifice
- General violence, blood, and gore
- Dark, murder-y thoughts and actions
- Anxiety and panic attacks
- Dying/Sick Parent
- References to struggles with conceiving (not main characters)
- References to previous suicidal ideation
- *Very* slight consuming of blood
- Accidental drugging of a main character which leads to dubious consent for a brief period of time
- Fire used to cauterize a wound

FROM THE ROYAL STORYBOOK

BOOK ONE RECAP

Once upon a time, but not so long ago, the daughter of a farmer was set to marry the crown prince of Elodia.

Freya was chosen to be the bride of Prince Tybalt—affectionately called Ty—because her blood showed the signs of Fae heritage needed to keep the kingdom's magic intact. Originally, they were to wed when she turned twenty-one, but when the king's health began to decline, the wedding was moved up.

According to tradition, Prince Ty and his bride-to-be went on a pre-wedding tour to gain support and fetch a magical crystal that would seal their marriage and restore magic. Joining them on their tour was Bastion Shamblefoot, the kingdom's top assassin and former lover of the prince. The tour started well enough with a visit to a nearby town, but Bastion—affectionately called Bash—was forced to confront his past. When Freya stepped forward in his defense, Bash's heart softened toward her, and she earned a little of his respect.

That night, Ty and Freya had dinner with a duke that went poorly. Freya left the dinner early, and Ty was verbally assaulted by the duke. Frustrated, Ty drank too much and confronted Freya. They had a falling out that they later solved by talking things through. The following night, they connected beneath a starry sky and thought things might turn out okay.

That's when things went horribly wrong.

The next day, their carriage was attacked by the *cultas draíochta*, and thanks to the efforts of Bash, Ty and Freya managed to escape. The three continued their journey on foot while trying to stay clear of the cult that wanted them dead. As they traveled, the three grew closer. Ty shared his past with Freya, and she accepted him. Little by little, the two fell in love.

Unbeknownst to them, however, they weren't the only ones falling.

Bash also found himself growing closer to Freya and, rather against his will, developed feelings. Like the loyal guard he was, he decided to keep his feelings for both Freya and Ty secret, determined to see them safely back to the capital. As much as it would break his heart again, he decided he could make his peace with them being together as long as they were happy.

Happily ever afters were put on hold, however, when the trio arrived home to discover that the queen had made other plans. At her side stood a new bride for Ty—Princess Amarelia Poshswallow, princess of the Rebel Isles. With her engagement to Ty dissolved, Freya was dismissed and Ty was brokenhearted. When Ty asked Bash to help Freya get over him as Bash had done, Bash confessed that he still loved Ty, but promised to look after Freya and protect her. When Bash went to Freya to comfort her and take her a letter from Ty, he asked her to run away with him to help take down the *cultas draíochta*. Freya agreed.

And now their story continues . . .

CHAPTER ONE

FREYA

I am going to kill Bastion Shamblefoot and make it look like an accident. Unless I die on this little adventure, in which case I'm going to haunt his ass. I push thoughts of murder aside, focusing on saving my own life. The door behind me is locked, but it won't hold. By my estimate I have roughly ten seconds to come up with a plan. I quickly scan the room, looking for anything I can use as a weapon. There are plenty of options, none of them ideal. Shelves of clay vases, figurines, and knickknacks line the walls. An over-stuffed chair sits between a precarious stack of books and a table with a large oil lamp. The most promising thing, however, is a large oak desk, its surface covered in an unorganized scattering of papers and objects. I scoot around the desk, bumping the matching chair out of the way with my hip, and scan the surface for anything weapon-like.

I freeze as I realize the papers could be the information I came for. I look over the scattered documents, shoving papers aside as I assess which ones hold the most promising information.

The doorknob rattles, followed by a body slamming against the door. Time's up. I grab several papers, folding them and tucking them into the waistband of my pants. I'll sort them out later. The door shudders again, followed by the sound of cracking wood. I resume my efforts to find a weapon, my eyes falling on a letter opener. I've worked with worse. I snatch it up just as the girl chasing me smashes through the door, the wood splintering around the now broken lock as the door hangs loose on its hinges. I say girl, but she's probably close to my own age, maybe even a touch older.

"You aren't getting out of here," she snarls, charging toward me.

I can't help the smile that curves my lips as I dodge out of her way. Bash has been teasing that I love danger, and maybe it's a little bit true. Not that I'd ever admit it to him.

"Are you the one who's going to stop me?" I challenge. "Or is someone more competent on their way?"

The girl pulls out a dagger—*my* dagger, oops—and steps toward me, putting herself solidly between me and the exit. I shift the letter opener in my hand and she tracks the movement.

"You chose the wrong house to rob if you think that's all you need to fight me off." She glances to the desk, and her mouth tips into a cruel grin. "And it looks you've seen more than you should've."

"Maybe I was supposed to see it," I counter. "Maybe I'm one of you."

The girl scoffs. "Hardly. There are protocols in place, which you would know if you were one of us. He always sends word when someone is on the way."

He. Who is he?

"Besides," she continues, circling me, "I don't see the likes of you completing initiation. No way you could kill someone with magic to make it into one of our top ranks. And even if you killed someone merely magic adjacent, you wouldn't have come here first. You'd be in Bellshire waiting for final initiation."

"Bellshire?"

Her eyes narrow, realizing she gave something important away. "Well, now I definitely have to kill you. Unluckily for you, I'm well trained. Luckily for you, I can make it quick."

This time she lunges with the intent to kill. My heart jumps into my throat and I force my brain off so I can lean into my instincts—instincts I've had barely a month. Now, how do I make those instincts work again?

"Stop overthinking," Bash says with a chuckle as he offers me a hand up from the floor.

"If I don't overthink, how the Hell am I supposed to know what to do? You have years of training."

Bash tilts his head, a twinkle in his eye as he looks me over. "You need to learn to react in the moment. Go with the flow instead of fighting it."

"I don't know what that means."

"Close your eyes."

I frown. "What? How am I supposed to—"

He takes a step closer. "Do you trust me?"

My heart somersaults for some odd reason. "Of course."

"Then close your eyes."

I hesitate a moment before following his command. "Okay, now what?"

He's stepping carefully but I still catch the slight scuff of his boots against the floor and the rustle of his clothes as he moves closer. Yet, when his breath tickles my cheek, I'm not expecting it.

"React on instinct," he whispers, his lips brushing my ear and sending shivers down my spine.

When he tries to bring me down again, I flip him, winning for the first time. When I open my eyes, he grins up at me, and the warmth flooding me has little to do with my victory.

Memory fresh in my mind, I relax and let my training take over. Fighting this girl in a cluttered room is very different than training with Bash in a nearly empty cabin, but it makes my instincts awaken all the same. I won't let my brain override the movements my body knows are right. I block the girl's first few blows almost effortlessly. She growls, changing up her movements enough that she lands a decent kick to my hip, shoving me into the desk. She rushes forward, and I twist to the side, barely avoiding getting stabbed. I spin around the girl and rush toward the open door.

"No, you don't!" she yells, diving toward me.

She wraps her arms around my waist and we both tumble to the ground. My face smacks the hard floor and blood floods my mouth. I trace my tongue across my tingling teeth, but I don't have time to register more than the fact that they seem to be intact. Before the girl can right herself, I kick back and make contact with her face, a sickening crunch echoing through the room. She swears, but even with a broken nose, she doesn't let up. In fact, it seems to fuel her. She stabs at me with the dagger without landing a blow. I roll away from her, shifting onto my back, but she manages to nick my arm. I hiss at the sting and her eyes widen as golden-red blood bubbles up.

"What? You have—"

I take advantage of the distraction to arch up and stab her eye with the letter opener. She screams and I fight back a gag. I scramble out from under her, grab one of the many vases, and slam it against her head. She crumbles and I snatch up my dagger from where it's fallen on the floor, tucking it into the sheath on my waist.

I lean down and check her pulse. She's still alive. I should kill her, but I can't make myself do it. Instead, I dig through my pocket and pull out a packet of special herbs. I pry her mouth open with two fingers and shove a decent amount of the mixture into her mouth. She'll wake with a horrible headache, a bitter taste in her mouth, and a fuzzy memory too vague to be useful, but she'll wake. Assuming she doesn't bleed out first.

A door opening and closing from the ground floor of the house reminds me that this girl isn't the only person who could catch me, even though Bash told me the house would be empty. The filthy, dirty liar. Though, to be fair, the girl was the only one here when I arrived, but that's clearly not the case anymore judging by the voices floating up the stairs. I quickly shut the lopsided door the best I can and block it with the armchair. It won't keep anyone out indefinitely—I'll be lucky if it lasts two minutes—but it will hopefully slow them down so I can make my escape.

I cross to the desk and quickly sort through the papers to make sure I'm not leaving anything important behind. I'm about to give up and take what I've already grabbed when I spot a familiar seal. I snatch up the paper and shove it in with the other papers. Footsteps grow closer and my eyes dart around the room, seeking an escape. The hall only had one way in and out which means I can't leave the way I came. Thankfully, there's a window. It sticks on the first try, but with a little swearing and the help of my dagger, it squeaks open, cool night air rushing inside. I have it about halfway open when the doorknob rattles.

"Kitty, you in there?" a male voice calls out.

I swear under my breath, attempting to shove the

window up some more. When it doesn't budge, I decide it's now or never. I've never been slight, and nothing is a better reminder of that than trying to squeeze through a partially opened window. The door rattles again, and I suck in my breath and force myself through the gap. I'm on the second floor of the house, but I don't have too far to fall. Of course my luck ran out long ago, and I land poorly, my ankle twisting as I land.

"Shit," I mutter, pushing myself up. I test my ankle but it seems mostly okay, just a little sore. If Bash is where he's supposed to be—I swear to all the gods, he better be—I don't have far to go. I can make it.

A crash sounds from the room above followed by a cry. Shit, shit, shit. I race off into the darkness, only vaguely aware of the man yelling threats from the window behind me. My ankle aches and my lungs burn, but I don't pause until I'm well within the tree cover surrounding the property. I stumble to a stop, sucking in air. I'm about to call out for Bash when he materializes. He's wearing a sloppy grin until I step into a shaft of moonlight shining down through the trees and he sees the blood and tattered clothes.

"Are you okay?"

"You said the house would be empty! Empty, Bastion! Do you even know what empty means? Because that, *that* was not empty!" I thrust a finger back toward the house, glaring at him as fiercely as I can in my winded state.

He steps closer, the intensity of his gaze trailing over me, the slightest flicker of concern in his assessing eyes. "But you're okay?"

"I'm alive, if that's what you mean," I huff, crossing my arms.

His mouth tips back up into a smile. "Good." Several voices echo through the night and Bash grabs my hand, pulling me further into the trees. "Let's get out of here and get you cleaned up. The horses aren't far."

We take a few steps before he glances at me over his shoulder, smiling. "Good job, Princess."

As much as I want to hate him, as much as I want to continue yelling at him, something in me warms, and I'm almost ready to forgive him all his sins. Almost.

CHAPTER TWO

BASH

Freya hasn't stopped yelling at me since we got back to the little room we've been renting the past few days. Which is fair, I suppose, since I sent her in a little blind, but I had my reasons.

"This was my first solo mission. My first," she yells from behind the changing screen, water splashing as she washes. "I deserved to have all the information!"

I grin, appreciating her fervor, but don't reply. Instead I focus on deciphering the letter she snatched. Like previous correspondence, it uses a code consisting largely of key phrases with hidden meanings. Freya was the one to figure out the base code, which is thankfully simple. Even though Freya's only been bathing for a few minutes, I almost have the message worked out.

"And another thing!" Freya says, waster sloshing as she gets out of the washtub. "You owe me a new shirt."

"Why is that?" I ask, making another mark on my paper.

"Because I got blood on my last good white shirt."

I look up and immediately still. I was not expecting her to

step out from behind the changing screen with nothing more than a towel wrapped around her. I do my best not to react as I take in her bare shoulders, long legs, and hints of cleavage where she's gripping the towel. I'm definitely not noticing the droplets of water trailing down her exposed neck or the way the red in her reddish-brown hair seems more prominent. While I always appreciate her attractiveness and am finally starting to get used to the waves of affection I feel toward her, I'm not typically affected . . . physically. Right now, however, I'm definitely feeling a rising wave of desire. I swallow, pushing aside the warmth gathering inside, and force a smirk.

"It's the risk you run when you're doing what we're doing." Is my voice a little hoarse? No, I think I'm fine. I turn back to my paper. "You can borrow one of mine."

"No, I'm *stealing* one of yours," she mumbles, padding over to where our clothes sit in an unorganized heap. "To keep."

I copy out the last line from the letter and lean back in my chair, reading the words over to make sure it fits the pattern.

"Did you overhear or see anything else important while you were there that we didn't already know?" I ask as I read.

"Well, there are the other papers I grabbed, though I'm not sure they're anything more than someone penning a dull novel." The last few words are muffled slightly as she pulls a shirt over her head. "Oh, and when the girl and I were fighting, she said something about an initiation and mentioned the town of Bellshire."

"Initiation? What sort of—" The words die on my tongue as I twist in my seat to find Freya standing mere feet away wearing nothing besides a shirt. *My* shirt. And I thought the towel was problematic. The white material clings to her still damp curves, stopping mid-thigh. She doesn't seem to notice my sudden wordlessness, focusing on squeezing as much water as possible from her hair.

Suddenly, I miss the tiny cabin where we spent several weeks training after our departure from Rosana. Sure, it was drafty as hell and the roof leaked, but we each had our own room. Since it was literally in the middle of nowhere, hidden in a forest, I could go for a long walk when sharing space with Freya got to be too much. I could ignore this attraction, bury my feelings. Sharing this little rented room in a somewhat busy merchant town, however, gives us no space to ourselves. Now that attraction refuses to be pushed aside, gnawing in my chest like a rabid animal and forcing me to face the fact that I am frustratingly in love with this woman to the point of distraction. I'm barely able to function at the moment, my mouth dry as my brain refuses to focus on anything besides her curves and my inconvenient desire.

"I don't know exactly," she continues breezily, unaware of my inner struggle. "She said something about killing someone with magic or someone—how did she word it?—magic adjacent."

"That, um, that would make sense and fit with, uh, what we know."

Damn it. I can do this. I shake my head and force myself to think about anything other than the attractive, half-naked woman wearing my clothes.

"What did you say the town name was?"

"Bellshire."

I pull my map out, happy to have something else to focus on, and scan it over. She steps up behind me and peers down at the map. I repeat the name under my breath so I'm not thinking about the way she's leaning on my shoulder, her breath warm on my cheek as a damp curl tickles my ear.

"Here it is," I mutter, tapping the town's inkblot. "It's not too far. Maybe three days at most."

She pulls away and I can finally breathe. And think. I hear her shuffling behind me, hopefully putting on more clothes. I turn my attention back to the letter, dipping my pen in the ink and circling key words in the text. When Freya reappears at my shoulder she's wearing a loose pair of leggings—hers, thank the gods—and her hair is pulled up in a soggy bun.

"Have you deciphered the letter?"

"I believe so. If it's using the same pattern as before, there should be a carriage heading to resupply one of the more remote groups tomorrow."

"Time?"

"Mid-morning." I frown down at the paper, tapping the last line of the note. "I haven't figured out this part yet. It wasn't in previous communications we intercepted."

She leans closer, squinting at the letter, and I try very hard not to think about all the places her body is touching mine. Gods, I forgot how truly disruptive attraction can be.

"'A bluebird will fly along with a robin and three crows,'" she reads aloud. "They've never mentioned birds before." She straightens. "Any clues in context?"

I shake my head. "Not that I noticed."

"Still want to risk taking it?"

I grin up at her. "Best way to see what the birds mean, don't you think?"

She matches my grin and my heart leaps. "Definitely. Plus, it adds a little more fun to it, not knowing all the details. Keeps it interesting."

I chuckle, carefully folding the letter and slipping it into my bag along with other notes and correspondences we've commandeered. "I never would've guessed you had such a taste for danger, Princess."

She goes very silent behind me and my stomach drops. I take a deep breath and stand, turning to face her. She's twisting the front of my shirt in her fingers, looking down.

"Hey," I say softly, crossing to her and taking her hands in mine. She raises her eyes to meet mine, and I'm not prepared for the shadowed sadness I find.

"Why do you keep calling me that?" she asks, her voice so quiet I wouldn't have been able to hear her if I wasn't standing so close. "I'm not a princess anymore. I never was, really."

I manage a small smile, tilting my head as I look down at her. "And who said you aren't a princess?"

She frowns. "Everyone. I'm not—" Her voice cracks slightly and she takes a steadying breath. "I'm not marrying Ty anymore."

"That's not what made you a princess. It's not why I call you that, though it may have started that way." Her brow furrows and I brush my thumb along her cheek. "You're a princess because you have the fire and pose and strength of a princess. You're stunning and beautiful and can command a room the moment you walk in. You're truly amazing and, even if the queen couldn't see it, fit to be a princess."

She blinks her wide, blue eyes. "Do you really think so?"

"Yes," I say without a breath of hesitation.

Her shoulders relax as a small smile creeps onto her lips. I force myself to step back, to put distance between us before I do something stupid like kiss her.

"Now, if you want me to stop calling you 'Princess,' I will, but I don't know what else I could call you."

She rolls her eyes. "You could always try 'Freya.'"

I make a face and she laughs, her expression turning thoughtful. "Ty did call me 'Frey' once. I didn't hate it."

I bite back a grin, shaking my head. "Too on the nose.

Besides, whatever I call you, I want it to come from me and only me." I swallow and dare to be bold, adding, "You're my princess now, and no one else's."

Her smile doesn't disappear, but it shifts into something else, something I can't quite define, and a fire sparks in her eyes. She holds my gaze for several agonizing seconds, and I don't dare to breathe. She blinks, shaking her head as her smile softens, and relief washes over me.

"Fine. You can call me 'princess' for now, but I want you to think on it." She flashes me a wide grin. "Consider that your homework."

A laugh startles out of me and her eyes shine. "Nuh-uh, Princess. I'm the one who's supposed to be giving *you* homework."

"That was before, when we were training."

"Training never stops. It's an—"

"—ongoing process. Yeah, yeah," she says, waving her hand, and I barely hold back my laugh. "But that also means you have some things to learn, too."

I bite my lip to keep from smiling like a ridiculous, lovesick fool. "Fine, but as I rather like calling you 'Princess' and having made what I feel is a very good argument in favor of the title, I can't promise to come up with another name anytime soon."

"Fair enough." Her smile fades and her attention shifts to the tiny window in the corner of the room. "Do you think he's okay?"

All my previous delight fades, and I do my best to ignore the growing pit in my stomach.

"Ty? Yeah, I'm sure he's fine. He's resilient. It takes a lot to bring him down." I force a smile that I'm sure isn't convincing in the least. "Now, whose turn is it to buy dinner?"

"Yours," she says, plopping down on our bed. "And I expect it brought up and delivered on a tray, given that you lied to me and nearly caused my death."

I don't try to hold back my laugh. "As you wish"—I meet her eyes—"Princess."

CHAPTER THREE

TY

I glare at the empty liquor bottle. Maybe if I concentrate hard enough I can make it refill somehow. Now that would be useful magic. Much better than being able to command flames. I could ring for a servant to bring me more, but I'm pretty sure my mother ordered them to stop bringing me anything besides regular, boring food and tea. Given her constant demands for me to join the evening dinners, I'm surprised she still allows that. I refuse to be forced to socialize with the people ruining my life.

A knock on the door startles me out of my stupor, and I glare toward it. I don't answer, but that doesn't keep Klarissa from bounding inside moments later.

"Go away," I moan, sinking dramatically into an armchair. "Actually," I amend, perking up. "Can you run down to the cellar and get me—"

"No," she says, cutting me off with a sharp glare. "I am not going to get you any sort of alcohol."

"Come on, Rissa," I whine. "You're being unfair."

"And you're being a sullen ass. What happened to the

bright-eyed Ty from when I arrived who was desperate to uncover a conspiracy to steal his throne and magic?"

I close my eyes, my heart clenching. "That Ty had hope. He's dead now."

"Well, revive him."

I sigh and glare up at her. She looks properly cross, and I almost care. Almost.

"I can't."

"Why not? Your kingdom could still be at stake. At first I thought you were grasping at straws, but now I think you may have been on to something. Things at court are shifting in a very weird way, and you need to do something."

"It doesn't matter."

"How can it not matter?"

The muscle in my jaw twitches. "Leave it, Rissa. Leave *me*."

"No," she says, crossing her arms.

"Yes," I say, my voice hard.

"Ty, I know you've been through a lot, but you can't give up. You have to find that bit of you from before."

A harsh, humorless laugh escapes me. "I told you, he's dead."

"Ty—"

"No!" I snap, shoving up from my chair. "He's dead, and do you know why?" She purses her lips but doesn't interrupt, so I plow on. "Because his hope died when the two people he loved and cherished more than anyone else in the world died."

"You don't know they're dead," she says, her voice soft and sickeningly kind.

I laugh bitterly, shaking my head. "Don't I? Don't I? Let's look at the evidence, shall we?" I march toward my desk. "Day one, Freya and Bash are evicted from the palace with a laughable scattering of soldiers for protection." I arrive at my desk and turn to face her. "Mind you, I wasn't allowed to see them off, forced to watch from my window because my mother was afraid I would 'make a scene.'"

"Joke's on her then," Rissa says drily. "Seeing as how you set your curtains on fire to attempt a distraction."

I don't bother to reply, spinning back to my desk and jerking open a drawer with far more force than necessary. "Let's skip ahead a few days to when I receive a letter"—I snatch out a piece of paper and brandish it in the air for effect—"stating they arrived safely in the next town and that the soldiers, their only protection, have returned, their duty fulfilled."

"Ty, I know—"

"No, you don't get to interrupt me now," I snarl. "We're recapping."

She falls silent, her eyes filled with pity. I turn away from her and grab something else out of the drawer. I take a deep breath, holding it over my heart for a moment before I turn back to Rissa.

"And then, several days later I receive word that a royal carriage—their royal carriage—was found battered and broken alongside the road with no survivors." All my previous vitriol seeps from my voice. "All that was among the wreckage was pieces of bodies—*pieces*—and this."

I hold up a crystal on a leather string, letting it swing through the air. It still has splatterings of blood on it, but I can't bring myself to clean it.

"Do you know what this is, Rissa?" I ask, my voice quiet but hard. She nods, but I tell her anyway. "It's Bash's crystal. I know, because I'm the one that gave it to him. I put it on the string myself after stealing it from my father's collection."

"That doesn't mean—"

"No!" I yell, cutting her short. I then repeat in a whisper, "No. Whatever scenario you've conjured up, whatever you think you've worked out—no. Bash wouldn't leave this behind, not with what it means. And even if Freya managed to escape, she never made it home."

I set the crystal back in the drawer and close it carefully, like it could break. Tears burn my eyes as cruel silence fills the room. I force myself to take a deep, steadying breath and turn back to Rissa, all my fight gone.

"Like I said, the Ty you found when you first arrived is dead, and he's not coming back. He doesn't have anything to live for."

For a moment Klarissa is quiet, studying me, and I think she's going to give up and leave me alone. But then she straightens her shoulders and takes on a look I've seen far too many times to believe I could be so lucky.

"You're wrong, Ty." I open my mouth to protest, but she holds up her hand, silencing me. "The Ty from before and the Ty you are now have something in common—you both care about and want the best for Elodia. Giving up now doesn't suit either of you. You were never a quitter, and I don't know why you've given up so wholeheartedly now. You should still be fighting."

"For what? What should I fight for, Rissa? Because I was fighting to get Freya back. I thought if I could prove that something nefarious was going on, I could bring her back and marry her. I thought uncovering some sort of plot could give me what I wanted. But now she's gone. That's no longer a possibility."

"You still shouldn't give up."

I sigh, rubbing my temples. I am far too sober for this conversation.

"Okay, let's play this out. So we uncover a plot that says

Amarelia isn't who she claims. What then? Before I could've whisked Freya back to the palace and married her on the next Fae moon. But now? It took us years to find someone with the right blood who could provide an heir, and, even if my father seems to be recovering, we don't have time to find someone else. With Freya . . . dead"—the word is almost impossible to say, catching in my throat—"I don't have any options besides Amarelia."

"Okay that may technically be true, but that doesn't mean you should give up. You know two people with strong Fae blood, Ty. *Two.* That means there have to be more out there. I actually find it a little odd and somewhat baffling there haven't been more candidates. Furthermore, I refuse to believe that someone as crafty and stubborn as Bastion Shamblefoot let himself die tragically in something as mundane as a carriage ambush."

I shake my head. "I'd like to think that, too, but the crystal says otherwise."

"Damn the crystal!" she yells. She takes a deep breath, composing herself. "I know it looks bad, but Bastion is exactly the kind of person who would know how to make it look as realistic as possible."

"He would have found a way to tell me."

"Maybe he did, but you've been too stubborn to see it. Maybe . . ." She trails off, her eyebrows furrowing as she stares off at nothing.

I take a step closer to her. "Are you okay? What are you thinking? Or are you having a fit of some sort?"

Her attention snaps back to me. "Show me the crystal again."

I sigh, shaking my head. "Rissa . . ."

"Show it to me again," she demands. "Trust me."

I open the drawer and hold the crystal up so it catches the light. Rissa steps closer, her eyes locked on it.

"Ty," she says slowly, carefully. "Look at the crystal."

I frown. "What?"

"Look. At the. Crystal."

I sigh and turn it over in my palm. I don't know what she's noticed but— My eyes go wide and my heart stops beating. For the first time in weeks, hope blooms in my chest. I swallow hard, looking up into Rissa's eyes.

"The blood is red."

A smile curves on Rissa's lip as she nods. "But both Freya and Bash—"

"—have golden blood." I swallow. "This isn't their blood. They could still be alive."

A laugh bubbles out of me and I can't stop it. I don't want to stop it. Rissa grins, her eyes bright as she straightens, giving me her favorite 'told you so' look.

"And what would they think if they are alive and they're out there saving the kingdom while you sit here wallowing?"

I sober and take a deep breath. "I still don't understand why Bash would leave his crystal behind. It—it isn't just a crystal for magic. It means more than that."

Rissa shrugs. "I don't have the answer for that. I don't have very many answers, actually, because I've been trying to figure things out on my own."

Her last few words have bite to them and I barely contain my smirk. I raise my hands in surrender.

"Okay, fine. Fine. I will, at least temporarily, join you in uncovering the heinous plot to overtake my throne."

She grins. "There's the Ty I know and love!"

I roll my eyes.

"You can start with this."

She pulls a folded paper from her pocket and hands it to me. I accept it with a frown.

"What's this?" My eyes widen in disbelief as I scan it over. "You stole a letter addressed to the Duke of Brookeshire?"

Rissa grins like a cat. "How else are we supposed to figure out what he's up to? Now, look that over and get it back to me as quickly as possible. He can't know it went missing. You have an hour at most."

"Fine," I say, setting the letter on my desk and folding my arms across my chest. "Anything else you have lined up for me to do?"

"Yes," she says, with a sharp nod, standing tall. "You are joining me in the Grand Hall tonight for dinner."

I shake my head, backing away from her. "Like Hell I am."

"Like Hell you aren't, Tybalt Adrian Shadowmoss."

I grit my teeth and look her in the eye. "I can't."

"You can."

"If my father hadn't—"

"It is not your father's fault that he got better."

Her words sting and I flinch, glancing away. "I know."

"He's still your father," she says softly. "He still loves you, and you still love him. He may be better now, Ty, but it might not last. It can't last indefinitely, and you know it. One day he will be gone, whether from this disease, old age, or something unrelated, and I don't want you to regret the time you lost with him because you blamed him for things he had no control over."

I take a slow, steadying breath. I hate that she's right.

"Fine. I'll come to dinner."

"Thank the gods. If I have to spend one more evening conversing with that bride of yours, I can't promise I wouldn't stick a fork in my own eye to get away from her."

The corner of my mouth twitches, threatening a smile. "That bad?"

Her eyes widen dramatically. "She's the worst! I thought Penelope Merriworth was droll, but she has nothing, *nothing* on Amarelia. I think when the gods created her, they forgot to give her a personality."

I laugh and Rissa grins. Something settles between us, something settles in me, that feels a little lighter and little warmer. Rissa seems to sense it, too; I can see it in her eyes.

"All right," she says, marching toward the door. "Look over that letter, get it back to me quickly, and I'll see you at dinner."

She goes to leave but I call out to her.

"Where will you be when I'm ready to return the letter?"

She flashes me a wicked grin. "I thought to oversee some of the soldiers training."

I chuckle and her grin grows. "General Harrow hates it when you do that."

"That only adds to the fun." She shoots me wink over her shoulder as she saunters into the hall. "Join me whenever. I know you enjoy it as much as I do."

The door closes, and for the first time in weeks, I feel like things might just turn out okay.

CHAPTER FOUR

RISSA

There are few things I enjoy as much as watching sweaty, reasonably attractive men practicing to kill each other. I can tell their captain isn't exactly pleased by my presence as it seems to be leading several of the aforementioned men to show off, but that only adds to my delight.

"You should probably stop distracting the people meant to protect us," Ty says, walking up behind me.

I hum in response and he rolls his eyes, pulling the letter from his pocket and passing it to me. I put it in my own without even bothering to pull my eyes away from the soldiers.

"So, what did you think?"

"I thought the paragraph in the middle quite meandering and a bit off topic."

"Interesting, because I thought the same."

"I'm assuming it was some sort of code?" he says, pushing for more information.

"I'm assuming."

"Damn it, Rissa," he snaps, drawing a slip of a smile from me. "You wanted me to read the thing and practically begged for my help, and now you're ignoring me to watch a bunch of trainees."

"Oh, please. I did not beg. And can you blame my choice of entertainment? These men are delicious."

"Rissa."

His voice is hard. He's done playing. Since I did force him from his funk, I probably should pay him more attention before I lose him again. I sigh and turn to him.

"Yes, there was some sort of code nestled in the middle of the letter. As to what it means, I haven't quite deciphered. My lessons in espionage were overshadowed by tea etiquette and foreign languages. I believe the references to the weather connect to how their plot is going. Not sure about the bird bit. If you'd like, I can pass on my notes from previous letters and you can see what connections you can find that I've missed."

He arches his eyebrows. "How many have you intercepted, exactly?"

"Exactly?" I shrug. "Enough to know that he's definitely involved in something suspicious, even if it isn't part of whatever is or isn't going on with Amarelia."

"How did you come by so many of his letters?"

"I have my ways, Tybalt," I reply with a smirk.

He makes a face. "Please don't tell me that means what I think it means." I offer him a coy smile and he gags. "Gods, Rissa. A little self-respect can go a long way."

I raise my chin. "I have plenty of respect for myself and for my lovers." I cock my head. "Well, most of them."

He shakes his head with a groan. "I don't need to know this."

I roll my eyes. "I didn't even share any details."

"And I'm good with that. Please, never share the details."

I smile and smooth my hands over my dress. "As you wish."

"Oh, I wish." He pauses. "If your offer to let me look over your notes was sincere, I think I should."

"Consider it done. I'll drop everything by your room after dinner." I meet his eyes and grin. "As long as you keep your promise to dine with us tonight."

"Fine." He sighs dramatically. "I guess I'll see you later then."

"I look forward to it."

He huffs a laugh. "Liar."

I don't even bother to contradict him before he heads off. Once he's gone, I allow myself a small smile of satisfaction because, for the first time in days, I got Ty to leave his room.

After I enjoy the theatrics of the soldiers for a bit longer and have endured several furious glances from their captain, I head inside. I don't have anywhere I need to be, but when I hear Cressida's voice around the corner, I know where I don't want to be. I quickly alter my course and run smack into someone, sending papers flying everywhere.

"Oh! I'm so sorry!" I cry out, immediately dropping to the ground to pick up the papers.

A low chuckle has my attention going to the person I ran into—Ty's priest.

"It's quite all right," he says, his voice low and amused as he squats down next to me to finish picking up the mess. I've never really seen him up close before, but he is incredibly attractive. For a priest that is.

My cheeks heat as I try to straighten the few pages I've picked up into some sort of organized stack. "Should these be in any specific order . . . ?"

He smiles, showing off rows of perfect teeth. "Yes, but it

won't take me long to sort them." He pushes up from the ground and offers me his hand, pulling me up as well. "Thankfully, this particular scribe numbered the pages. I do so love it when they do that. Makes my job that much easier." He looks down at the papers still in my hand. "May I have those? Or have you grown particularly attached to them?"

My eyes widen and my face feels like it's on fire. "I . . . No. Here."

I shove the papers into his arms and he chuckles. It's a glorious sound. Gods, Klarissa. You are better than this. It should take more than an attractive face, a pretty smile, and a rich laugh to turn me into a stuttering fool. I straighten, taking a deep breath through my nose, allowing what I hope is a coy smile to curl my lips.

"I'm sorry I disturbed your day," I say, tipping my head.

"Disturbed? Hmm. From where I'm standing, I think my day got better."

Is he flirting with me? Are priests allowed to flirt? Normally, I'm the one to initiate a flirtatious situation, so this is new on multiple fronts. I think I like it.

"I bet we could make it go even better," I say, dropping my voice and leaning closer as I place my hand on his forearm.

His eyes flash with interest, but there's an undeniable twinkle of amusement there as well. "Are you trying to get into my archives?"

I bite back my laugh. "Maybe." I tilt my head, tracing my fingers up and down his arm as I shift even closer. "Actually, I wouldn't mind learning more about the bonding ceremony and the details surrounding how magic is shared from the royal family to the rest of Elodia."

He grins, his amber eyes crinkling at the corners. "Do you even know my given name, Lady Meadowbridge?"

I'm so lost in his eyes I almost don't register his question.

When I do, I jerk my hand away and take a step back, feeling oddly admonished, though there's nothing harsh in his expression.

"I—I'm sorry. I feel I've misstepped."

Some of his humor vanishes as he closes the distance I created. "It's fine. I promise." He pauses, searching for his next words. "Though, if you don't mind me saying, I know of your—how should I put it—reputation?"

I stiffen. I'm not ashamed of sleeping around, but I don't like being judged for it. However, when I look into his eyes, I don't find judgment.

"Is this where you give a lecture on whoring myself out?"

He barks a laugh. "Hardly. No, as long as your . . . transactions are consensual."

"I would hardly force someone—"

"Not what I meant," he says quickly, holding up his free hand. "I have no doubt that people very willingly fall into bed with you. I only hope that you don't feel obligated to engage in sexual activities if your heart isn't in it."

There's something so genuine in his voice I find myself softening.

"I enjoy sex and other intimate activities," I state plainly. "While it is sometimes transactional, as you say, I enjoy the transaction. Having people at my mercy, weak and trembling and begging for more has a certain amount of power to it, and if I can satisfy my needs while satisfying theirs, all the better. Not every interaction actually ends in sex, anyway. Most of the time it's merely a lot of flirtation and maybe some kissing. People like to exaggerate to make themselves feel accomplished. Also, to be clear, it's less of a transaction and more an exchange of services. People provide me with information, and I give them the night—or if they're particularly useful or skilled, nights—of their lives."

If I didn't know any better, I would say his eyes are definitely shining with lust as he leans closer.

"Night of their lives, huh?" he murmurs. I nod and he grins. "I wouldn't mind experiencing that myself."

I gasp and place a hand to my heart, feigning scandalization. "Father Finnick, are you suggesting that you want me to sleep with you in exchange for knowledge about the bond magic?"

He shrugs, his eyes shining like gems. "To be entirely honest, I will happily share any and all information I have with you free of charge. There's no need for any sort of 'transaction.' However, you are a beautiful and clever woman with many other admirable qualities, and given that I am a man who has not had any sort of intimate contact in quite some time, I'd be remiss to let the chance pass me by."

Now I'm grinning. "Well, perhaps then we could consider it less a transaction and more a . . . gift of appreciation."

He arches an eyebrow. "Appreciation?"

I nod once. "Yes. We chat and you share whatever knowledge you find interesting or of value, and then I show you exactly how much I appreciated your knowledge."

"I find that extremely enticing," he says, his voice rough and low. "I'm unfortunately not available now, but would you be amiable to coming to my room tonight after dinner?"

"I believe I will find it difficult to wait, but if I must, then yes. I have to drop some things off for my dear cousin first, but then I will come directly to your rooms after."

He smiles, shifting the papers in his arms. "I'll see you later then. Unless, of course, you decide against it."

"I don't think you have to worry about that in the slightest."

"Good." He brushes past me but pauses after a few steps, looking at me over his shoulder. "It's Miles, by the way."

"What?"

"My name. If you keep calling me Father Finnick, I'm afraid tonight may be very awkward. I'm not into roleplay."

A laugh startles out of me and I quickly cover my mouth with my hand. He only grins, shooting me a wink.

"I suppose you should likewise call me Klarissa if you'd truly like to be on even footing."

"Klarissa it is then."

The way he says my name sends shivers of delight skirting across my skin. If I don't leave now, I'm likely to make some very foolish decisions, and gods know I've already made myself enough of a fool in this man's presence.

"See you later, Miles," I manage.

"I'll count the minutes . . . Klarissa."

CHAPTER FIVE

TY

I pore over Rissa's notes for the millionth time today, looking for more connections. So far, I've managed to decipher some things and have a few possible interpretations, but it's not enough. I need more. If people are plotting within my castle walls, it needs to be stopped. I jot down more notes, barely paying attention to the servant bringing in a tea cart, fully stocked with one of my favorite brews. I don't remember requesting any tea, but then again, I may be losing my grip on reality. These letters are nonsense, and I think they're getting to my head.

"I've been thinking," Rissa says, barging into my room without knocking, "that we could get Miles to help us out. You know, share some unique insight, check out the crystal."

"Why would you need to check out the crystal?" I pause, looking at her as she fixes herself a cup of tea. Well, that explains the tea cart. "And who the Hell is Miles?"

"Your priest."

"My—You mean Father Finnick?"

She takes a sip of her tea as she settles into an armchair. "Yes, but don't call him that. It makes him sound so old."

"Isn't he old?"

She rolls her eyes. "He's twenty-four, a couple years older than us. He merely looks older because he's going prematurely gray."

"If you say so."

"I do. We should see what he has to say. I know you're convinced that's Bastion's crystal, but Miles—"

"I'm not calling him that."

"—could tell us for sure."

"How would you even go about getting him to help us? March in there and demand his help? I'm not sure we can trust him. He's too intertwined with everything, and my mother likely has him in the palm of her hand. He is the one who confirmed Amarelia would be a good match blood-wise. Who's to say he'd be on our side?"

She shoots me a sly smile over the top of her teacup. "I have ways of getting people on my side, you know."

It takes a minute before I register her meaning, but when I do—

"Klarissa, you can't seduce a priest!"

"That is factually untrue. It is entirely possible."

"Okay, let me be a touch clearer—you *shouldn't* seduce a priest."

Klarissa blinks at me with feigned innocence. "Oops."

"Gods, Rissa!" I groan, collapsing into the chair across from her.

"I don't think he's one of those priests that took a celibacy vow," she counters, waving her hand through the air like it's nothing. "Or, at least I assume so, otherwise he definitely broke that vow last night. And this morning. Repeatedly."

She grins into her teacup as I point an accusatory finger

at her. "It's on you if you muddied our priest so that the gods no longer find him holy enough or whatever and the bonding ceremony fails."

Rissa rolls her eyes. "I'm sure the gods don't mind a little good fucking. In fact, I'm sure the gods themselves enjoy a little—"

I launch out of the chair, slamming my hand across her mouth to cut her off. "For the love of all that is holy, please shut the Hell up before you incite their wrath."

She promptly licks my palm and I yank it back with a gag.

"You're disgusting," I grumble, wiping my hand on my pants. I look back at Rissa with a smirk. "You don't even know where my hand has been or what I was doing with it less than an hour ago."

Rissa fake retches. "Point taken."

I plop back into my chair. "Did your so-called seduction at least turn up anything useful?"

"First, there's nothing 'so-called' about it. I was entirely successful. Or he was. It was very confusing, if I'm honest." I make a face as she rambles on. "Second, yes. Yes it did."

I lean forward, suddenly invested in Rissa's latest venture. "It did?"

"Mm-hm." She takes a deliberately long sip of tea. "Oh, did you want details?"

"If you're going to be annoying, get out of my room."

"Fine. Fine. So I found out some intriguing things about Amarelia's blood-testing."

My breath catches in my throat and I'm not sure if it's from fear or hope. "Was Amarelia not as magical as he said? Is she not a match?"

"It's . . . complicated."

I shake my head, pushing up from the chair. "Get out if you're going to string me along."

"No, it really is complicated. There's a lot to it." She sets her cup down on the side table and stands. "Miles is willing to go over it with you, if you'd like. He also said he can take a closer look at the crystal found in the carriage wreckage and make sure it really is Bastion's. He's free now if you want to talk to him."

I hesitate. The obvious answer here should be an immediate "yes." I should want answers, but it's not so cut and dry. If it's not what I want to hear, it could make things worse.

"Look, Ty," Rissa says, her voice uncharacteristically gentle. "This whole thing is difficult. I know you're still trying to come to terms with everything that's already happened and everything that's still happening, but hiding away in your room isn't going to solve anything."

"I looked at the letters. Well, your copies of the letters. And your notes."

"That's a good start, but there's more you can do."

Guilt and fear swirl in me, and I turn my back to her, not wanting her to see how defeated I feel right now. She gave me back a sliver of hope. Bash and Freya might still be alive. There might really be a plot underway that I can flush out. I may get a chance at a true happily ever after. But if I look too closely and do proper research, that hope could unravel. Sure, I could find the answers I want, but it's just as likely I'll find things I don't.

I startle when Rissa's hand lands on my shoulder, but I don't turn to face her.

"I won't force you, Ty, but if you decide you want to know, that you want to figure this out, I'll be in Miles's room off the library." Her hand falls away. "I hope you'll meet us there."

Rissa leaves without another word, and I stand, frozen to my spot, staring at the door. When I can finally move, I walk over to my desk, but I can't make myself open the drawer. What if it is Bash's crystal? Does that mean that Bash is dead, even if the blood isn't his? Why would Bash leave it behind? I take a deep breath and steel myself. I can do this. I open the drawer and pull the crystal out before I can talk myself out of it. I don't even stop to close the drawer before I leave to meet with Rissa and her priest.

When I arrive, I pause outside, peering into the room through the cracked door. Rissa and Father Finnick are sitting on opposite sides of a round table, a few papers scattered between them. She's leaning forward and he's blushing. Rissa's light laugh reaches me first, followed by a low chuckle. Fucking Hell. She really did seduce my priest. When I push the door open, Rissa grins up at me, straightening, and Father Finnick stumbles to his feet.

"Your Highness," he says, bowing from the waist.

I wave him off. "None of that. Please. Just call me Ty."

"And you may call me Miles," he replies, his mouth cocking up into a lopsided smile.

I frown. "Not sure if I can manage that, but sure. Rissa said you had some information about the blood test that might interest me?"

"Ah, yes. Take a seat, and I'll explain."

He goes over to a stack of books on a nearby table while I sink into an empty chair next to Rissa. He returns, setting an open book in front of me before resuming his seat. I peer down at the book, but other than a random word here and there, I don't understand what I'm looking at.

"I'm assuming that doesn't make much sense to you," he says with a chuckle, "but those are the details behind how the blood checking works. These symbols"—he leans forward, tapping on a set of doodles in the top left corner—"represent different magical markers that we sense in the blood when we do the spell."

I squint at the page, leaning forward, but closer examination doesn't make it any clearer.

"This," he continues, pointing to some notes and scribbles on the bottom right of the page, "shows what the minimum markers need to be in order for the spell to work." He taps his finger in the center of the page where a set of symbols and notes are circled in red. "And this is the ideal formula."

I raise my eyes to his. "I'm still not sure I entirely understand."

"Okay, let's put it in more basic mathematical terms. Every spell has a certain amount of magic that goes into it. Basic elemental spells take little to no magic for someone with control over that element, but larger spells require more particular amounts of magical energy. This formula shows the energy needed for the bonding to work. With me so far?"

I nod hesitantly and he grins.

"Good. So let's assign some arbitrary numbers to the energy levels. A basic spell might need an energy level of one, but the bonding spell would require a combined level of, let's say, fifteen to work. That means that the combined energy of both parties must equal at least fifteen to be effective. Thanks to your father's previous attempts at bonding as well as others before him, we have a relatively firm idea on what those energy levels need to be."

I nod along. "So if my magic registers as a six, I would have to marry and bond with someone who registered at least a nine."

"Correct," he says with a nod. "Of course, magical energies are much more abstract than that, but yes, that's the general idea."

"So it's more than just the color of the blood?"

"Correct once again. Color is one of the key indicators—the magical energy of golden blood is always in the higher range—but there's still a variance of power that can't be determined by color alone."

"Now tell him about Amarelia's blood," Rissa says, grinning at me.

Hope leaps in my chest. "Does her blood not have a high enough magical energy?"

The priest frowns. "Yes and no. This is where it gets complicated. When I first arrived, only days before you, I was asked to test her blood almost immediately. When I did, the primary results showed the correct magical energy needed to pair with yours."

"But?" I press, praying that there is a "but."

"But," he says, making my breath catch, "there was an additional energy I picked up."

I furrow my brow. "What does that mean?"

"I'm not sure." I open my mouth to demand more, but he holds up his hand, silencing me. "Usually it would mean that another source of magic was being detected. This can happen if another spell is being performed too closely to the blood spell. However, I feel quite confident that no one was casting nearby, at least not close enough to affect the spell. Furthermore, the energy I detected in her blood had an odd quality to it. It took longer than usual to register and seemed faint, almost like a shadow of energy rather than energy itself."

I sit up straighter. "Is it possible to fake the blood spell through illusion?"

"It shouldn't be," he says with a shake of his head. "It might be possible for the results to be otherwise altered, however. I've been looking into possibilities, but any definite answer would come from checking her blood again, prefer-ably in a way where she was not aware that her blood was being tested."

"So basically, we need to stab your princess," Rissa says, eyes shining as she leans forward.

Miles rolls his eyes, barely containing a smile. "That is *not* a recommendation I can make."

"But if we manage to get ahold of her blood, you could test it again and figure it out?"

He nods. "It would at least put us one step closer to having an answer."

"How much blood would it take?"

"A daggerful," Rissa chimes in.

I shoot her an admonishing look and she shrugs.

"Honestly?" the priest asks, tilting his head. "I wouldn't need much, but the more the better." He points at Rissa. "Not enough to seriously harm her."

Rissa huffs and collapses back in her seat, crossing her arms. "I thought you were fun."

Miles smirks. "I think I've proven quite well how fun I can be."

"Okay, no!" I say squeezing my eyes shut and shaking my head as if it can clear the images popping into my head. "I don't need to know things like this."

Rissa cackles as Miles mumbles a quick "my apologies" that doesn't sound very apologetic.

I sigh through my nose and open my eyes, focusing on the unabashed priest. "I have another question."

He nods for me to continue, and I pull the crystal from my pocket and set it in the center of the table. Rissa sobers, offering me an encouraging smile. Miles looks from me to the crystal and back, waiting patiently for me to find the courage to voice what I need. I take a shaky breath, pressing my palms against my thighs to keep them steady.

"Would you be able to tell if that crystal had been used for magic, and if you can, would you be able to pinpoint the magic user?"

"Yes and no," Miles says. "I can tell you if the crystal has been used for magic and a rough timeline of when that last use was, but unless I have magic to test it against, I cannot tell you the wielder. I could, however, tell you the type of magic."

I straighten in my seat, my heart picking up its pace. "So you could tell me if the person who used it had air magic?"

He nods once. "Yes. Would you like me to test it now?"

"I . . ."

'Yes' sits on the tip of my tongue, but I can't get the word out. What if it is Bash's crystal? What then? Does that mean he's dead or at least severely injured? Is he captured? Or is a ruse of some sort? And what of Freya?

Dizziness overwhelms my senses and the world shifts out of focus. The air thickens around me and it's hard to draw a breath. My fingers tingle, going numb, and I can't think straight. I hear mumbled voices, but I can't tell who's speaking or what's being said. Someone shakes me, but everything's fuzzy and out of sync. A sharp smell cuts through the haze and I jerk back as the world snaps into view.

Rissa leans over me, holding a potent packet of something strong under my nose. I gather enough of my sense to push her hand away with a groan.

"You okay?" she asks, her voice filled with concern.

I suck in a breath, releasing it slowly as I shake my head. "I don't know." I glance at the packet now resting in the center of the table. "What even is that?"

Rissa grins. "Smelling salts." I arch an eyebrow and she shrugs. "You never know when they'll come in handy. Now, do you want Miles to run the spell or not?"

I swallow, looking over at him. "No."

"Wait, what?" Rissa says. "But if we test it—"

"Then all we know is whether or not it might belong to Bash. I know myself, and if it even remotely appears that it's his, I'll assume the worst."

"But what if we tested it and there's no indication it's his?"

I shrug. "It still wouldn't tell us definitively one way or the other." I meet Rissa's eyes. "I need to not know. Not knowing, hanging onto that little piece of hope that it's not his, is all that's keeping me from giving up again."

She studies me before nodding. "Fine. I think you're making a mistake, but it's your mistake to make. As long as you remain invested, then I suppose, for now, we'll leave it."

Tension seeps from my body as a weak smile flickers onto my lips. "Thank you."

Miles clears his throat, glancing between us. "Is there anything else you need from me?"

"No, I think that's all for tonight," I say, rising. "Thank you for your time and the information."

He offers me a nod. "Of course. I'm happy to help."

Rissa pushes up from her chair, grinning down at me. "Now we just need to go stab your fiancée."

CHAPTER SIX

FREYA

One breath in. One breath out. One breath in. One breath out.

"You don't have to do this if you don't want," Bash says, studying me carefully.

"I want to," I assure him. "We're already here. Can't go back now."

I gesture to the trees around us. We're well hidden off the side of the road the supply cart should be taking. Any minute now, it will arrive, we'll attack, and the *draíochta* will have to find some other way to restock their supplies.

"I can handle it," Bash says. "Say the word, and I'll do it on my own. It wouldn't be the first time I've robbed a supply cart without assistance. I did the last one."

"That was because you didn't think I was ready." I pause, biting my lip. "Do you think I'm ready now?"

"Yes," he says without hesitation. "I think your mission last night proved it. But it doesn't matter what I think. It matters what you think. Do you feel ready?"

"Yes."

He smiles, eyes shining. "Good."

We don't have a chance to say anything else, the rattling of wheels interrupting. Bash tenses, ready for action, and I try my best to focus and steady my racing heart. When the cart rounds the corner, I frown. It's much larger than expected, and the back is completely covered. It's not quite a carriage, but it's definitely more than a simple supply cart. A glance at Bash's furrowed brow tells me he's as confused and concerned as I am.

We don't have time to rework our plans, however, so when Bash raises his eyebrows in question, I shrug and nod. He grins and nods in return. A moment later we're leaping onto the road, daggers drawn. Bash jumps in front of the cart, startling the horses and bringing them to a halt. The driver yells, but I know Bash will handle him. It's my job to check the supplies. While we don't really need anything, we have to make it look as much like a regular robbery as possible. I also need to check for anything that might prove useful in bringing down the *draíochta*. The last couple robberies resulted in a restock of our coffee and information about the house I raided last night. This one brings a whole different surprise.

A knife nicks my ear the moment I lift the flap covering the cart. A second knife flies my way, and I only save my face by reacting quickly. It's dark inside, but before I duck back out into the light, I catch a glimpse of four, maybe five people hiding among the supply crates.

"Bash!" I yell, stumbling back. "We're not alone."

Seconds later, Bash is by my side, the red on his sleeve telling me the driver put up a decent fight. A moment later three men jump from the back of the cart, daggers slashing through the air. Two go after Bash, but the third lunges toward me. He's clearly much better at hand-to-hand than I am, but thanks to training with Bash, I've gotten good at dodging. As the man struggles to land a blow, I work to get him further from the cart and his friends.

"You chose to rob the wrong cart," he snarls, nearly landing a blow on my arm, cutting my sleeve. "At least you made my day a little more fun."

"So glad to be of service," I reply, ducking under his arm and slamming my elbow into his stomach.

His moment of breathlessness is all I need to stick my dagger in his neck. I do it so instinctively, I don't even fully comprehend what I've done until it's over. The man's eyes widen as he falls back, gasping for air. I blink down at him. He's dying.

I killed him.

My dagger suddenly feels heavy in my hand. I barely register Bash stepping forward and driving a sword through the man's heart. It takes me a moment to realize Bash is talking to me, his voice sounding like it's buried beneath a flood of water.

"Did you say something?" I ask, blinking up at him.

He frowns, eyeing me with concern. "I asked if you were okay," Bash says, his voice slow, careful. His eyes fall to the cut on my sleeve. "Are you hurt?

I manage to shake my head, struggling to find my voice. "He didn't cut me." Bash's scowl deepens but I cut him off before he can say anything else, nodding to the cart. "I think there were more. Inside."

Bash studies me a moment longer before nodding. He steps over the body, heading back to the cart. He slips inside while I stand in the middle of the road, useless. My eyes fall back to the man I killed. Bash may have ended his suffering, but I know he's dead because of me. My blow would have killed him—was killing him—before Bash stepped in. I killed someone without a moment of hesitation, but I don't think I feel guilty or any sort of remorse. Should I? After all, I've literally been training for this. Still, shouldn't I feel *something*?

Scuffling and screaming from the cart pull me from my spiral. The sounds silence a moment later and Bash pops out. Blood is splattered on his face and shirt, but he seems uninjured.

"Not much in the way of useful supplies, but I did find this," he says, holding up a bag heavy with coins.

I nod numbly, not quite looking at him, my eyes focused past him on the cart.

He frowns. "Are you sure you're okay?"

"I—" I freeze, a flash of red catching my attention. I brush past Bash and snatch a red envelope sticking out from the cart. I turn it over in my hand, slowly lifting the flap and pulling out a slip of paper.

"What is it?" Bash asks, stepping to my side.

"An invitation," I mumble, staring down at the embossed paper in my hand. "For an initiation ball in five days in"—I lift my eyes to his—"Bellshire."

"Glad you spotted that, Princess. Now, how about we destroy the evidence that we were here and head back?"

A few minutes later the entire cart is ablaze, and Bash and I are slinking through the trees to where we stored our horses. We don't speak the entire ride back, but I can tell by the way Bash keeps glancing at me, his jaw twitching a bit more every time, a serious conversation is in our future. The door's barely closed behind us before Bash turns to me, crossing his arms across his chest.

"Talk." I open my mouth to deny there's anything to talk about, but he holds up a hand, stopping me short. "Don't bother lying again, because I know you're not okay, even if the bastard didn't actually nick you with his dagger. I'm aware more than anyone that not all wounds are physical." Some of his aggravation seeps away, replaced by concern. "Are you okay?"

"I just . . ." I sigh and sink down onto the edge of our bed, looking down at my hands folded in my lap. "I'll be okay, even if I'm not now. I promise. I've never actually killed anyone before, only wounded, and I don't know how I feel about it."

The bed sinks a bit as Bash takes a seat beside me. "You never have to be okay with killing."

He places his hand on my knee, and I startle and look up into his eyes. "I—"

"I mean it." His eyes search my face, whether he's looking for a tell that I'm far from okay or just for any sort of emotion I'm not sure. "I can take care of all the nastier bits of this whole thing. I don't want you to feel forced to kill simply because you feel you have to."

I lick my lips, trying my best to push down the warmth in my chest spurred by the sincerity in his eyes. "It's not that I have a problem with killing, exactly. Not when it comes to the *draíochta*. I'm more than happy to take them out the best I can. It's only . . . I did it so quickly, without hesitation. I didn't even pause."

Bash nods. "You were fighting for your life. It would've been you or him. Your instincts saved you."

"I know. I know. I think that's another reason why I'm okay with it, but I'm worried that it will become too easy. I don't want it to become too easy."

The corner of Bash's mouth turns up a little. "I don't think you have to worry about that."

"Why not?"

"Well, for one, you're too good and kind to develop that

kind of bloodlust. Trust me. I've met a lot of bloodthirsty killers, and you're not one of them."

I pick at the edge of my shirt and Bash reaches over, taking my hand in his.

"For another, even I haven't quite gotten to that point."

"You haven't?"

He shakes his head. "I won't lie and say I don't want every bastard of the *draíochta* to die at my hand, or if anyone ever touches you without your permission I won't hesitate to run them through. I find satisfaction in defending you and those I care for and in taking out the *draíochta*, but I don't relish killing. I do it because it's necessary, because I protect what's mine. I don't seek it out to satiate some dark part of me that craves destruction."

Tension seeps from my shoulders as relief washes over me. I sigh and rest my head on Bash's shoulder. He startles slightly, but relaxes quickly, releasing my hand to slip his arm around me.

"You're a wonderfully decent person, and I don't see that changing anytime soon."

We stay like that for a few minutes before I finally pull away, slipping out the invitation from where I tucked it into my belt.

"What should we do about this?"

"Well," Bash muses, a mischievous twinkle in his eyes, "what would you say to attending a ball?"

"You think we should go?"

He shrugs, standing and walking over to the desk. "We were planning on heading to Bellshire anyway, and this seems like the best way to see what's really going on. Besides, you have your dress."

He shoots me a grin and I groan. As part of the "compensation for my troubles," Queen Lyra gifted me several high-quality dresses along with gold, jewels, and other fancy trinkets. Since I wouldn't need most of it on the run with Bash, we traded the majority of the clothes and trinkets for more practical items like weapons, food, and travel clothes. Bash, however, insisted that I keep at least a couple of the finer items, including one satin dress, saying I never knew when I would need to dress up. That time has come I suppose.

"Fine," I concede with a sigh. "When will we leave?"

Bash sinks into the chair at his desk and looks over at the map. "I think leaving in the morning should work. It shouldn't take more than a couple days to get there, and the ball is five days away. That gives us plenty of time to travel, stake out the location, and make necessary preparations."

I nod, rising from the bed to stand behind him. "Anything we should go over before we leave?"

"It wouldn't hurt to run back through the higher-ups and key players of the *draíochta* and refresh your memory on who to look out for."

I groan, tired of what feels like endless research and memorization. Bash looks up at me and arches an eyebrow.

"Fine," I relent with a huff. "I guess it makes sense to be as prepared as possible."

Bash grins. "Ready for another adventure, Princess?"

Despite my earlier mood, I feel a smile slipping onto my lips as I meet his gaze and nod. His eyes brighten and I swear his whole face glows. Happy Bash is my favorite Bash.

"By the way," he adds, turning back to his notes. "Any idea what the bird references were?"

"I have a theory."

He raises his gaze back to me. "Really?"

"I think they're people. I didn't get a good look inside, but there were a total of five people correct? Not including the driver?"

He nods. "Two women and three men."

"That's what I thought. I think the bluebird was the new recruit, the one who had the invitation to the ball and one of the women. And the robin was the other woman, and the crows were the men."

Before I even have a chance to blink, Bash has risen from the chair. He looms above me, barely inch away, looking down at me with nothing short of wonder. My breath catches in my throat, my heart stuttering as I look up at him.

"Have I told you how brilliant you are?" he asks, his voice low.

"Not enough lately," I manage, going for light but it comes out weak, my voice rough.

His eyes drop to my lips and the world stills. But the next moment he's walking away. Disappoint surges through me as he opens the door, pausing in the doorway.

"I'll get us some dinner to celebrate." He glances over his shoulder and shoots me a smile that's tight around the edges. "Any requests?"

I try and fail at a smile of my own. "Anything will be fine."

He winks. "Got it. Be right back."

The door closes behind him with a click. I sink onto the bed, suddenly feeling very exhausted and drained, and I don't think it has anything to with today's heist.

CHAPTER SEVEN

BASH

F inding the location for the ball is easy once we reach Bellshire. The city might be one of the larger ones in Elodia, but there are few residences large enough to hold a ball. The house itself sits on the edge of the city, a significant presence, though it's levels below any of the estates owned by the upper nobility.

When I arrive to scope it out, the grounds bustle with people setting up and preparing for the ball the following evening. I integrate myself into their ranks and am able to get the layout down fairly quickly. Using a bit of charcoal and a pocket journal, I make a rough sketch of the layout of the house and grounds. When a cart arrives with items to be taken inside, I grab a crate and head inside with the crew. There's enough chaos in the kitchen area that I'm able deposit my crate and sneak off into the main part of the house unnoticed. I know I won't have much time before I'll have to vacate the area, so I work quickly, focusing on finding the exits and quickest routes to get in and out of what will likely be the busiest areas tomorrow night.

The main room that will most certainly be used for the dancing itself is situated near the kitchen and doesn't appear to have any direct exits to the outdoors, though it is connected to several smaller, open rooms which I sweep quickly. While surveying one of the more extravagant side rooms, I notice a dark back hall half-hidden behind a statue in the far left corner. After checking to make sure I'm alone, I slink into the shadows.

The hall isn't long, coming to a dead end a few yards later. I frown, taking in the small area with what little light I have. A portrait of a sour-faced man takes up a large portion of the end wall and two small busts sit on thin, chest-high columns in the corners, but that's it. I feel along the wall and edges of the portrait, looking for a trigger of some sort that might reveal a hidden passage or doorway, but nothing happens. Voices echo from the main room, which is a little too close for comfort. I slink back out of the hall and sneak back through the rooms, careful to avoid the servants on the opposite side of the dancing room. Thankfully, they're too caught up arranging flowers to notice me.

I head back outside and circle the building, looking for any signs I missed that might indicate where the hallway leads. I locate the main room easily enough since it has several windows, but there's no obvious signs of a hidden room anywhere nearby. Maybe it really is a hall and nothing more, possibly meant for stolen kisses and debauchery.

I'm heading back around to the side of the house where the carts are still unloading when I spot a thin, long window at ground-level, half-hidden behind grass. I squat down and try to peer inside, but the glass has been blacked out. I look further down the wall and spot a couple more windows. Stepping back and referencing my map, I confirm that the windows are placed below what would be the room with the hall, the makeshift ballroom, and neighboring room. The hallway likely does lead somewhere, but it's underground.

"You shouldn't be back here," a sharp voice says, nearly making me jump.

I stuff the map in my pocket and turn to find a stout man in sharp clothes glaring at me.

"I'm sorry. I was helping unload and thought I saw a dog head over this way." I cock my head and offer the man a sheepish smile. "I can't resist petting a dog."

The man doesn't seem entirely convinced, but his shoulders relax a bit. "No dogs loose on this property. Get back to work or I'll have you removed."

I tip my head to him. "Of course. I'll hop right back to it."

He follows me as I walk back to the unloading area and doesn't leave until I've picked up another crate. Once he's gone, I take the crate inside and snatch a pair of spare livery from a storage closet before sneaking away and heading back into the city proper. Now that I've been spotted, it's too risky to do more surveillance.

I make a couple stops before returning to the place Freya and I rented yesterday. It's a small room above a bakeshop, but it has a washroom and two beds, which has done wonders for my nerves and emotions after the last space Freya and I shared, which required sharing a bed. When I get up the stairs into the room, I find Freya huddled over the table in the corner, studying the sketches and descriptions I gave her detailing the people and operations of the *draíochta*. She looks up at me, her eyes lighting up as I close the door and cross the room to her.

"You're back earlier than I expected," she says with a smile as I drop the stolen livery on my bed.

"I did what I needed to do," I reply, shrugging off my jacket and tossing it next to the livery. I try to ignore the way her smile makes my heart beat faster. I pull the journal from my pocket and flip it open to the map. "I got a decent idea of the layout. Key exits are marked with an arrow."

She stands, walking my way. I pass the journal to her, pretending the brushing of our fingers doesn't affect me. I hover nearby as she studies the page, her lips moving sound-lessly as she commits it to memory. After a few moments she passes the journal back.

"I also rented a carriage to drop you off tomorrow evening," I say, tossing the journal onto my bed with the other items.

"Why? Shouldn't we take our horses in case we need a quick escape?"

"Yes, because nothing says 'I belong here' like riding up on a horse wearing a gown fit for royalty," I say drily.

Her cheeks color slightly as her lips tip up. "Oh. I suppose that wouldn't work."

"While you're riding in the carriage, I'll follow along at a safe distance on horseback and stash the horse safely at the edge of the property."

She moves back toward the desk, her fingers absentmind-edly shifting the papers around. "And where will you be during the ball if I need you?"

My heart swells with the idea of her needing me, but I push the emotions away, taking a seat on the edge of my bed. "Around." She narrows her eyes at my vague reply and I feign indignance. "What's the matter, Princess? You don't trust me?"

She rolls her eyes with a huff, and I bite back a laugh.

"I'll blend in with the staff as best as possible, so I'll be invisible but conveniently located should anything dangerous go down."

She nods, musing over my words. "And if we do get separated?"

"I'll find you."

"But what if—"

"I will find you," I promise, my voice firm. "I will always find you."

She looks momentarily startled by my reply, turning around to look at me properly before a small laugh escapes and she mumbles something I don't catch.

"What?"

"It's just . . ." She shakes her head. "Never mind."

"What is it? Because I mean it. I'll find you."

She smiles up at me, but her eyes are sad. "It's nothing. Only . . ." She sighs, glancing away. "Ty said something once about you always finding him."

I inhale sharply, not expecting her reply in the slightest. My heart seizes painfully. I remember making that promise to Ty over and over, and I always held true to my word. I always will find him when he needs me, and now Freya is also under that same protection.

She pushes out a forced laugh in my silence, shaking her head. "I'm sure you don't mean it in the same way."

It is the same. It is *exactly* the same, and the urge to make sure she understands that is overwhelming. Before I even make the conscious decision, I'm standing and closing the distance between us. She blinks up at me, her brow furrowed.

"Bash, what—?"

"There is nothing in this life or beyond that can keep me from finding you should you be separated from me. I will destroy any barrier that gets between us and take down anyone who dares to step in my way. Your enemies are mine. I would bathe the world in blood if it meant bringing you home and keeping you safe. I assure you, Freya, the promise I made Ty and the promise I made you are one and the same. I will always find my way to you."

Her lips part on a soft inhale, and I realize with start exactly what I said, what I essentially confessed. I stumble back a step, my panicked breaths coming out in short, sharp spurts. Dizziness disorients me. I have to get away. I have to get out of this room. I turn toward the door but freeze when Freya's hand lands on my arm. My eyes dart to hers and she smiles.

"Thank you," she says, her voice soft, kind. "That means a lot."

I swallow, running my tongue across my lips. My heart still races wildly in my chest, but I can breathe now. She doesn't push the subject, and I don't want to cross any more lines than I already have. I offer her a weak nod.

"There's one more thing I should check before the ball," I mumble, taking a step back.

Her expression falls a little, but she nods, dropping her hand from my arm. "Okay. I'll go back to studying, then."

I manage a weak smile before I stumble from the room. Once the door closes behind me, I close my eyes and lean back against it, praying for my heart to steady. How does she manage to do this to me? She overrides my good sense, and I lose control in ways I've rarely done before.

Falling in love with Ty was a slow, subtle process, shifting from loving him like a friend, gradually tipping into something more before it became all-consuming. With Freya, it started as something entirely different. My affection for her crept up on me, culminating in a sudden overwhelming sensation all at once, and I have no idea how to deal with it. I was a fumbling mess with Ty, but we were still boys, both figuring things out.

With Freya, we're both adults. She might have expectations I might not be able to fulfill, despite wanting to. I have no idea how to navigate a relationship with her that goes beyond what we already have, and I know even less what to do with these feelings. For the sake of our mission, I need to find a way to smother them so I don't damage the casual companionship we've built. I need her like I need air to breathe, so if I have to push aside these feelings to keep her, I will.

CHAPTER EIGHT

RISSA

I'm the first to enter the small tearoom, save for the servant meant to serve the tea. I sigh. I suppose it's to my advantage. This way I can make myself comfortable in the room and finalize my plan. I need to lull Amarelia into a false sense of security and get her to cut her hand or finger or something on a teacup or saucer that will somehow get accidentally broken. Honestly, I highly doubt this plan will work, but Ty refuses to let me stab her. I bet he'd let Bastion stab her.

I take my seat at the small table, looking over the available options to break. The servant offers me a steaming cup of tea, thoroughly distracting me from my treason. I take a sip and wince. It's been over-brewed to bitterness.

"Would you like some cream or sugar?" she asks.

I'm not sure cream or sugar can save this tea, but I offer her a smile and pass the cup back. "A little honey and a smidge of cream would be delightful."

She nods, accepting my cup and making the requested changes. When I receive my cup back, the contents are a little more bearable. I guess I'll suffer through with this tea now and reward myself with a proper cup later. The door opens, drawing my attention, and one of the princess's official attendants from the Rebel Isles steps inside.

"Presenting Her Royal Highness, Princess Amarelia."

I barely contain my eye roll as I stand. It's not completely out of place to have the princess announced—she is royalty after all—but for something as simple as tea between the two of us it seems pretentious at best. I incline my head politely as the princess enters, her attendant stepping back into the hallway to wait until she's ready to be escorted back to wherever they keep her. I allow her to take her seat before I resume mine. Despite the very obvious efforts they've made to make her appear older than her seventeen years, she still looks very small and untested. She bumbles her way through her tea order and makes no sign that she finds the tea bitter. Well, her poor taste is the least of my concerns.

"Is there a reason you wanted to have tea?" she asks, eyeing me warily as she places a couple tea cakes on her plate. If nothing else, her rich accent is delightful.

"You and I are to be placed together quite frequently, I suspect," I answer diplomatically. "I thought it only best to establish a relationship. Ty and I are close, after all."

She nods, taking another sip of tea. She still seems fine with it. Maybe her tastebuds are broken.

"Besides, I did originally come to Rosana to be a member of your predecessor's ladies in waiting. I would be honored to be considered—"

"No," she says abruptly, looking at me with a cold expression that sends shivers down my spine. She straightens and schools her features into something more passive. "I mean, that won't be necessary. I have my own ladies that I brought with me."

"Of course. I only thought that, perhaps, having someone who knows the lay of the land here might be advantageous. I know you have plenty of royal experience given your upbringing, but it never hurts to find the upper hand in a new situation."

She considers me for a moment as if she's searching for the lie in my words. After a moment she relaxes, reaching for a tea cake. "I appreciate your offer, but it is unnecessary. I am fine."

She takes a bite of the tea cake and I take a sip of my poor excuse for tea. The silence that follows is uncomfortable. Even the attending servant shifts from foot to foot like she wants to make a run for it.

"I heard you have the occasional rough day, but it seems I was fortunate enough to catch you on one of the days you feel well," I say in an effort to disperse the silence.

She glares at me over her teacup. "Well enough for tea. It's not exactly a taxing activity."

"Indeed. Well, either way, I'm glad to see you up and about. Perhaps you might enjoy a walk in the gardens. They are lovely this time of year."

"I don't care much for the outdoors."

I frown. "Don't you have earth magic?"

"What? Oh, yes. Earth magic. Yes," she fumbles, her shoulders tensing. Her gaze sharpens in a scowl. "What of it?"

"I also have earth magic and I typically find it refreshing to be outdoors."

"Not all magic is the same," she says sharply. "My magic isn't affected by the outdoors. In fact, given my disposition, I typically fare better inside."

Her defensiveness is off-putting. I've never met someone with earth magic that didn't feel called to the outdoors. In fact, being trapped in this room with nary a plant in sight has my magic itching uncomfortably beneath my skin, and my magic isn't even particularly strong. I can't imagine having magic as strong as Amarelia's and not wanting to spend every second outside.

"Forgive me for my assumption," I manage, offering her a smile. "I was merely seeking a way to bring you comfort. If I overstepped, I do apologize."

"I don't need your comfort." She must realize how childish she sounds, because she straightens, tipping her chin up. "But thank you nonetheless."

Absolutely nothing in her voice says her thanks is sincere, but I smile and offer her a nod of acceptance anyway. As if anyone would actually want to be friends with the brat. Even if I didn't suspect her of being up to something nefarious, she's nowhere near good enough for Ty.

"Since you don't spend time in the gardens, how do you fill your day?" I ask, attempting more pleasantness in the hopes the girl will let her guard down.

She huffs, rolling her eyes. "I read."

"Oh really? Anything you've read recently that you can recommend? I didn't bring nearly enough books with me, so if there's something here that maybe I could borrow—"

"The books I read aren't in Elodian," she says, cutting me short.

I grit my teeth to keep from snapping at her. I can speak and read seven languages, thank you very much, but I don't tell her that. Instead I offer her a tight smile.

"Ah. Well then."

I take a long sip of my tea, wondering how much longer I can drag this out so as not to be suspicious while also keeping myself from actually stabbing her.

Amarelia pushes back from the table. "I just remembered something else I need to do. Please excuse me."

I leap from my seat. "Already? I—"

My foot catches on the leg of my chair and I tilt forward. I could easily catch myself, but instead I decide to lean into the fall, pulling down the table and Amarelia with me. As expected, the teacups shatter against the stone floor, pieces scattering everywhere. I make to get up and "accidentally" shove a shard of porcelain into Amarelia's palm. She hisses in pain, but I already have a cloth napkin ready to soak up her blood.

"Gods! I'm so sorry!" I say, pressing the napkin to her palm. "I can be so clumsy sometimes!"

I shift the napkin, but Amarelia rips her hand away before I can sneak much more. Hopefully whatever I got is enough. She tightens her hand into a fist, clutching it against her chest. Her wide eyes look horrified as she stumbles to her feet. She glances down at her hand, at me, and then back at her hand, squeezing her eyes closed. She wavers on her feet, paling. I quickly push up and reach for her with one hand while I shove the napkin into my pocket with the other.

"Are you all right?" I ask, a touch of genuine concern in my voice. She truly looks unwell.

Her eyes open with a flash as she staggers back a step. "I'm fine. I just . . . don't do well with . . . blood."

She wavers again, calling out in Panbrionese, and the attendant she brought with her rushes into the room, moving quickly enough to catch her in their arms. The princess blinks up at them and they shake their head, looking her over.

"She cut her hand, I think," I offer, nodding to where the girl still clutches her hand against her chest. She's likely to stain her dress.

The attendant's eyes widen a touch, and they move so that their body blocks my view as they check the princess's palm. They sigh and relax a moment later, supporting the girl as they make their way out of the room, barking orders at the other servants. It seems I've been entirely forgotten. Once the door slams shut behind them, I turn to the wide-eyed servant.

"I'll help you clean this up, and then I suppose I'll take my leave as well."

"No, my lady," she says, shaking her head. "I could never allow you to clean it up."

"I made the mess, and I'm not above cleaning up my messes. I assure you."

"I can't—"

"Oh please," I say with a wave of my hand. "If you're worried about anyone finding out, who will tell? Not I."

The servant considers me for a moment before nodding somewhat reluctantly. I kneel on the ground and carefully start placing broken bits of teacups on a saucer that survived with merely a crack. When I discover the shard with blood on it, I freeze. The blood is red. Very red. Carefully, without drawing too much attention to myself, I withdraw the napkin from my pocket. There are two splotches of blood. One is red without any gold and the second smaller sample only has the barest hints of it. I glance at the servant to make sure she isn't watching me as I tuck the bloody bit of porcelain into the napkin and shove the whole thing into my pocket. I'm not sure what I discovered, but I have a sinking feeling it isn't anything good.

CHAPTER NINE

TY

I sit cross-legged on my bed surrounded by painful memories. I started rereading the letters from Cora on a whim in an attempt to ease some of the longing in my heart, but now I'm feeling less sure about the whole thing. Knowing what I do now about Freya's closeness with Cora, I was almost desperate to find some clue of that in the scribbles, some proof that Freya could be out there finding her happily ever after with someone like she'd done before. But, like I assured Freya, there's no hint that they were anything more than friends.

Reading over the letters backfires, hurting in a way they didn't before. I can now see Freya clearly in every passage. I can hear her laugh and smell her skin and feel the warmth of her touch. I wanted to soothe the emptiness left by her departure, but reading the letters only makes me crave her more. I know I should put them back in their box and move on, but I can't. Something in me can't give up. Not yet. Even as much as it hurts, having these little pieces of her is better than nothing.

CHAPTER NINE

My brooding is interrupted by my door flying open and Klarissa flouncing into the room. I frown at her.

"In some cultures, such as ours, knocking is preferred before entering a room uninvited."

"Knocking would just slow me down and get in the way of— What are you doing?"

"Nothing." My face heats as I try to gather the letters scattered all around me, which isn't easy since the pages are spread across most of my bed.

"Wait," she says, perching on the edge of my mattress and plucking up one of the papers closest to her. "Are these letters from—what was her name again? Cora?"

I lean forward, almost tipping over, and snatch the paper from her, placing it into the box with the others I've already rescued. "It's none of your business is what it is."

She gives me an almost pitying look. "Ty, there's nothing wrong with wanting to hold onto Freya." She straightens, smirking. "Plus, it's nice to know I was right about the whole letter thing being a good idea."

I snort. "Actually, Freya wasn't too keen on it when she found out."

The night in the shepherd's shack drifts to the top of my mind and my heart aches. How I wish I could go back to that night and hold her again. Of course, it had ended with Bash's nightmare, but even that turned into a positive experience. Gods, I miss them both so much. I need them to be alive. I need them to be okay. I need them to come home to me. I just need *them*.

Rissa places a hand on my knee, jolting me back to reality. "Ty, are you okay?"

"I'm fine," I snap, snatching more letters and shoving them into the box. "I don't need your pity."

She sighs through her nose, shaking her head. "I'm not

pitying you, but I am here if you want to talk." She leans over and picks up a wayward letter too far from my reach and passes it to me. "As much as I tease you, I really do want you to be happy. You know that, right?"

I accept the letter, gripping far more tightly than necessary. Despite our arguments and disagreements across the years, the core of our relationship has always been camaraderie.

"I know," I whisper.

Rissa smiles at me as I place that last letter in with the rest and close the lid. Her eyes fall to the box.

"Is that the box Bastion gave you for your thirteenth birthday?"

I can't hold back the smile that slips onto my lips. "Yeah. He didn't think it was worthy of a prince and almost didn't give it to me. I'm glad he did."

"Bastion is a good man."

I swallow the lump trying to form in my throat. "The best."

"Anyway, stash that little treasure chest of yours wherever you keep it buried, because you and I need to go see my favorite priest."

I make a face. "I really wish you wouldn't call him that."

"Why? It's the truth."

"Still." I kneel on the floor and push the box back into its hiding spot. Once it's safely stored away, I stand, turning to Rissa. "Why do we need to see him?"

She reaches into her pocket and withdraws a crumpled napkin. "I got your fiancée's blood."

"You did?" I narrow my eyes at her. "You didn't actually stab her, did you?"

She hums, shrugging her shoulders, already striding across the room toward the door.

"No, but really, you didn't stab her, right?" I repeat, chasing after her.

When we reach Miles's room, we find him hunched over a book, wire-rimmed reading glasses slipped down to the tip of his nose. He blinks up at us when we enter, brightening a moment later as he pushes his glasses up.

"Was I meant to be expecting you?" he asks, but he doesn't sound put off, his voice light and cheery.

"You should always be expecting me," Rissa says with a grin. "But no, we didn't have anything arranged. We managed to get some of Amarelia's blood for you to test."

Miles sits up straighter in his seat, his eyes shining. "You did?"

Rissa pulls the napkin from her pocket and passes it to the priest. "I hope this works."

He's almost overly eager as he jolts up from the chair and takes the piece of cloth from Rissa.

"I got two samples. The larger is from right after her hand started to bleed and the smaller a moment later."

He leans forward, studying the blood splatter carefully, his previous delight twisting into a frown. He adjusts the napkin, his frown deepening as he examines the second sample.

"Are you sure this is Amarelia's?" he asks, turning the napkin over in his hand.

"Quite sure," Rissa replies with a sharp nod. "I collected it myself."

Something slips from the napkin, falling to the floor with a soft clatter. Miles bends down and picks up what looks to be a small piece of porcelain.

"That's what she cut her hand on," Rissa explains. "There was a bit of an accident involving a teacup."

The corner of my mouth tips up into a smile against my

will. It's such a Rissa thing to do, inviting someone to tea only to steal their blood by using a teacup as a weapon. She's far too clever for her own good, but I'm never telling her that.

I step to Miles's side, looking down at the items in his hand. "Why are you doubting whether it's Amarelia's blood?"

"Do you notice anything odd about it?" he asks, extending the napkin so I can see it clearly.

I scowl down at it for a moment before I realize what I'm looking at. I raise my eyes to meet his.

"Her blood isn't as golden as it should be."

"Precisely." He sets the napkin and shard down on the table and moves toward the corner of the room where he keeps his supplies. "Tell me, what do you know about how blood works when it comes to human verses Fae heritage?"

I lift a shoulder in a half-shrug as he rummages through his things. "Not much, if I'm honest. I know what you told us before about magical markers, of course. I also know that the stronger the Fae heritage the more golden the blood, but that's it, really. I don't know the details. If I was told at some point, it didn't stick."

"Same here," Rissa says. "I never really had to think on it before. It was something I simply accepted."

Miles nods like this is the answer he expected. He returns to the table balancing an assortment of things in his hands, including a small stone bowl, a stone pestle, and some ingredients in various containers. He sets them down next to the discarded napkin and looks up at me.

"In all honesty, we don't know exactly how the body produces golden blood or any mix of gold and red. We simply know that Fae bodies produce golden blood naturally and human bodies produce red, their hearts pumping it through their veins. When the two species, for lack of a better word, are combined through reproduction, it results in a combination of the two. If someone is half-Fae and half-human, their bodies typically produce an equal amount of each type of blood, creating a type of marbling effect in the veins. If you were to cut them, you would immediately see a mix of both. However, if someone with little Fae heritage were cut, their blood would typically present mostly red, maybe entirely red if the Fae bloodline is weak, and any gold would show only after a moment once the blood starts flowing steadily. The opposite would be true for someone who is significantly more Fae than human with their blood presenting golden right away."

He pauses, concentrating on pouring some of the ingredients into the bowl. His tongue peeks out between his lips as he leans in to get the measurements exact, his glasses slipping down the bridge of his nose.

"So the fact that the blood on that napkin is red means that Amarelia doesn't have the Fae heritage she claims?" I ask carefully, almost afraid to hope.

"Possibly," Miles replies, crushing the ingredients with the pestle. "I'm going to run the blood test again and see if the same markers show up that were in the original test. While it's extraordinarily rare and highly improbable, sometimes the blood can appear significantly more human than Fae even if the Fae bloodline is strong. Though, when I first performed the test, the girl's blood was most assuredly far more golden than this sample."

He adds a few drops of liquid to the mixture and gives it a satisfied nod. My heart beats erratically against my ribcage as he dips the bloody napkin in the mixture, whispering a prayer or spell of some sort. He closes his eyes, almost as if he's absorbing the magic—which I suspect he is. A moment later he opens his eyes and repeats the process with the second sample of blood. I don't dare breathe as I wait for the answer.

When he looks at me, a smile curves his lips. "This blood doesn't even begin to pass the test."

Relief overwhelms me and I barely make it to a chair before my legs give out. Tears fill my eyes as I look up at the priest.

"So I don't have to marry her?"

He shakes his head. "I wouldn't recommend it. I guarantee this"—he holds up the napkin—"will not sustain the bond."

"How did she pass the first time?" Rissa presses, stepping up behind me, not quite touching me but close enough that her presence is oddly comforting.

Miles turns his attention to her and I use his distraction to wipe the tears from my eyes.

"I really don't know. I believe it may have to do with those additional traces of magic I mentioned before. Given these results, I am almost positive she's using a spell of some sort to fake her Fae heritage. Tell me, how did she react when her hand got cut?"

I look at Rissa over my shoulder as she furrows her brow in thought. "Scared," she says after a moment. "She couldn't get away from me fast enough, and then she almost fainted."

Miles's eyebrows shoot up. "She seemed weak?"

Rissa nods. "She said she was bothered by blood, but there honestly wasn't that much. And she was holding her hand in a fist against her chest, so she couldn't even really see it."

The priest nods, mulling over her words. "It's my hypothesis that she is pulling her magic from another source to appear to be the perfect bride."

"How can she do that if she doesn't actually have magic?" I ask.

"Well, there are actually two types of magic. One is what you've grown up with thinking of as magic, but it's known most technically as *Faecræft*. It is essentially control over the elements given to us by our bonds with the Fae. The other is *Naturcræft*, which is something humans have always been able to wield. Though the term is used less today, it is the study of potions and spellwork. It's still often used in many medicines as well as what I do. The elemental magic of *Faecræft* I've been gifted is a rare element sometimes referred to as Spirit or Soul magic. I often use it alongside *Naturcræft* in the form of the spellwork and potions like what I just did."

"So you think Amarelia is using some sort of *Naturcræft* to fake her bloodline?" I ask.

He nods. "I do."

"But how would she benefit from it? If her blood isn't what the bond needs, magic will fail. Why would she want to marry me?"

"I can't answer that as it would only be speculation, but I would assume that she has motives of her own. Perhaps she wants the bond to fail."

My stomach twists uncomfortably as fresh fear washes over me.

"We need to tell the queen immediately," Rissa says, already moving toward the door.

"Wait," I call out, my voice weak. "Not yet." I turn my attention to Miles. "You said she was pulling from an outside source. What could that be?"

He takes a deep breath before answering, his words carefully chosen. "I cannot be entirely sure since my study of this aspect of *Naturcræft* isn't comprehensive, but I would assume she's pulling from another person who actually does have magic. That may very well explain why she seems ill of health some of the time and why she would have been near fainting from such a small cut. The magic would drain her."

An idea starts to take proper form in my head and terror floods like ice water in my veins.

"It would be worse if the person she pulls from is sick, wouldn't it?"

Miles considers me for a moment before nodding. "Most likely. She wouldn't be able to pull the magic alone. She would share everything with the person, so if they were weak or sickly, she would be too."

"And the other person, would they feel the effects of the spell?"

"Perhaps. Once again, this is mostly speculation, but if the spell works like I believe, based on what little research I have done of such subjects, the bond created by the spell would have mutual effects and benefits. So, times when she might be weak the other person might be strong."

I swallow hard and take a shaky breath in a vain attempt to steady my racing heart. "So, let's say she created the spell using someone who was dying, that person might appear to be getting better while she has weak spells?"

"Most likely."

Rissa gasps behind me. "Ty, you don't really think . . ."

I turn and look up at Rissa, tears once again burning my eyes, but these tears are far from the relief I felt moments ago. "Yes, I do." I look back at Miles, whose confused eyes flit between Rissa and I. "I believe she's using my father."

Miles's eyes widen in realization. I swallow and nod.

"She arrived before you, right?"

"Yes. She was already a guest in the palace on the evening

I arrived. I was called in to perform the blood test first thing that same night."

"So she would've had plenty of opportunity to put the spell in place?"

He nods. "It likely wouldn't have taken much. A little preparation beforehand and access to the king."

"But, Ty," Rissa cuts in, "your father is under constant guard. You know as well as I do that there are eyes everywhere. Even if guards weren't actively stationed outside his room, there's never a time he's entirely alone without someone within shouting distance."

"I don't think she's working alone. She has help, and until we figure out who and why, we have to keep this quiet." I push up from the table, ignoring the shaking in my limbs. I have to be strong.

"This stays between us three." I look between the other two and they both nod. I focus my attention on Miles. "I need you to see if you can pinpoint the type of spell used and how to potentially break it without harming my father."

"Of course, Your Highness," Miles says, inclining his head, and it's only then I realize that authority has seeped into my voice.

I straighten to my full height. "Good. Let me know if you find anything helpful." I glance to Rissa then back to the priest. "Actually, if you discover anything, send word through Klarissa. There's no reason you and I should be seen together often. I don't want to risk raising any suspicion that we may be onto something. Rissa coming and going from both your room and mine won't seem that out of place." I turn to her. "You're okay with that, right?"

Her head bobs in immediate agreement. "Of course, Ty. Do you want me to also keep an eye on Amarelia?"

I hesitate, thinking it over a moment before I reply. "Not

obviously. If you show her too much attention, she may suspect something, but if you see easy opportunities, do so with caution."

She nods and I take a deep breath, turning to the door. "Now, if you'll excuse me, I have to go make a plan to find Freya, because if this whole thing truly is a ruse, magic is doomed without her."

CHAPTER TEN

FREYA

The carriage slows to a stop outside the house where the ball is taking place, and I take three steadying breaths before I exit. Despite knowing I have no need to worry, I can't quite push away the nerves swishing in my gut. I have a half-dozen daggers hidden on my person— gods bless Bash and his ability to alter clothes to hold weapons while leaving no trace—and I know that even though I can't see him, Bash is somewhere nearby should I need him.

There's a short line of people at the door waiting to get in. I take my place behind a cheerful couple as they hand their invitation to the doorman. He glances at the paper and offers them what appears to be a genuine smile before waving them inside. I step up next and pass him my stolen invitation. He takes it and his smile falls. He raises his wide eyes to mine. He swallows hard and licks his lips.

"W-welcome," he says, passing the invitation back. "When the gong sounds, head to the eastern sitting room." He forces a smile back onto his face as he motions me inside. "Have a good evening."

I offer him a nod of thanks as I step inside, tucking my invitation into a pocket. His reaction seems a little odd, but maybe he's wary for a reason. He didn't act that way with the couple before me, so maybe not everyone here is a cult member? As I step farther into the house and take in the vast number of people crowding the area, I sincerely hope that the cult hasn't managed to recruit this many people.

I slowly navigate the house, doing my best to remember the layout Bash sketched. The crowd here isn't dressed quite as nicely as I am in my dress, but there are several other attendees wearing nice silks so I don't stick out too much. Honestly, the energy of the crowd puts in me in mind of the dances I attended back home. Only those usually took place in a barn instead of a nice house and the clothing was far more casual.

I skirt around the edges of the room where people are dancing to some lively violin music, and step into a side room where a spread of mouthwatering delights has been laid out. I help myself to a small cake and am sipping sparkling wine form a flute when someone addresses me from behind.

"That dress is truly lovely."

I turn to find a tall green-eyed woman with brown hair tucked into a neat bun on top of her head. I take a moment to look at her dress. It's not quite as luxurious as mine, but the rich blue silk paired with delicate black lace is definitely a notch above what most of the other attendees are wearing.

"Yours is quite lovely as well," I say, offering her a smile. My attention falls on her companion, a smaller woman wearing a pink dress that highlights her bright blue eyes and blonde curls. "I love yours as well."

The blonde practically preens. "Thank you." She leans forward, her eyes taking on a conspiratorial sheen. "I suppose yours also came from a well-to-do patron?"

"I—" I glance to the first woman, whose lips are pursed. I straighten, forcing a smile. "Of course. I suppose you have a patron as well?"

The blonde breaks out in a full grin, turning to her friend. "See, Tabitha! I told you she was one of us!" She turns back to me. "My patron might not be quite as . . . generous as yours, but I'll take what I can get. I can't say I can complain given everything they offered."

"You make it sound like you only joined for the money," the brunette—Tabitha—says, shaking her head.

The blonde rolls her eyes. "Well, I can't say I was all too eager to join for free. Do you think I go around killing people for fun?" She whispers the word "killing," glancing around a little a nervously.

"There is duty and service you know," Tabitha counters, but the other girl waves her off, turning back to me with a smile.

"My name is Francine, but you can call me Francie. This is Tabitha."

I nod in greeting. "Nice to meet you both. I'm"—I hesitate for a second, not wanting to give my real name—"Astrid. You can call me Astrid."

Both girls accept my middle name without question.

"So," I say, looking between them, "I guess you're initiates as well?"

"Yep!" Francie says brightly while Tabitha nods.

"Have you always been invested in the cause?"

Francie laughs. "Gods, no! I hadn't even really heard of it before one of the recruiters came to my village. Even then, it all sounded a little dramatic. If it hadn't been for the generosity of my patron, I'd likely never have considered it. My mother was a little against it, but ever since my brothers and Da died, it's been just us. We needed the money and well"—she shrugs—"it all worked out. We got out of debt and I'm here. Might even find a decent match, though all the men I've met so far aren't really marriage material."

Uneasiness twists in my stomach. They're recruiting people and paying them to join? The only comfort that immediately comes to mind is that filling the ranks with people who haven't been trained since birth might give us more of a fighting chance. Also, maybe it means they're getting desperate? I swallow and turn to Tabitha.

"Did you join for the same reason?"

She shrugs, taking a sip of wine from a glass I hadn't noticed before now. "My cousins have always been involved, and they've been trying to convince me and my brother to join for years. My brother joined a couple months ago when the prince's bride conspiracy was revealed. I considered it then, but I won't lie and say that the benefits offered didn't perhaps seal the deal."

"The . . . bride conspiracy?"

Tabitha nods. "Yes. You hadn't heard about it?"

I shake my head. "My patron didn't mention it." The girls exchange a wary glance and I quickly add, "I had my own reasons for joining. I have a bit of a . . . history with magic."

They nod like this is reasonable explanation.

"Well, you know how the prince suddenly had a bride that was supposedly a lower-class girl that had no noble blood?" Tabitha asks and I nod. "Well, turns out that was all a ruse. The royal family has been sending out magical nobility into villages to breed a new, stronger line for magic. They knew this girl existed all along and they were training her for a rise to power."

I barely contain my laughter, staring at Tabitha in disbelief as Francie's head bobs up and down in agreement.

"But, why?" I manage.

"Because," Francie jumps in, "if they can replace those of us with normal blood with a whole slew of magical descendants, they can wipe us all out! That's their plan. They want all of us normal humans gone so magic can flourish again."

She says it so earnestly, it's all I can do to rein in my shock and denial. I glance at Tabitha, sure that both can't believe the extent of this lie, but she appears to be in full agreement.

"Wasn't the prince's bride sent home?" I ask tentatively.

"That's what they want you to think," Francie says.

"Honestly," Tabitha jumps in, "I find it more concerning that they replaced her with someone from the Rebel Isles. I think that's a sign more than anything that something is wrong with the Crown."

Well, I can't exactly disagree with that.

"Enough politics!" Francie says with a clap of her hands. "This is a ball! And while I hope my patron can get me invited to more events, this may be my last chance to experience something this nice. I want to have a good time before they pull us away for the formal initiation." She glances at Tabitha. "How long do you think we have?"

Tabitha shrugs, looking out over the crowd. "Probably at least a couple hours, I'd think. They want us to blend in with everyone else so we don't call attention to ourselves. The Grand Patron didn't sponsor this event for us to be discovered."

My attention spikes. Who is the Grand Patron? She speaks the name with a certain amount of reverence in a way that sends shivers down my spine. Despite all the studying Bash has me doing, I've never heard of the Grand Patron, and we haven't run across the name in any of the communication we've intercepted.

"Do you know the Grand Patron?" I ask carefully.

Tabitha snorts. "Hardly. My family may have deeper connections than others, but we don't mingle much with lords."

Lords? The Grand Patron is nobility? How has this escaped our notice? Is this a new development? It would definitely explain where the influx of funds has come from. But who is it? Is Ty in even more danger than we originally thought? Ty. Gods. Someone has to warn him. I need to find Bash. No, I need to find out more. If Francie and Tabitha don't know the Grand Patron, maybe someone else here does.

"So, should we go dance?" I say, impressed with how light I keep my tone. "Maybe we can even find a few gentlemen here for the same reason as us to pair up with."

"I know of a couple already. Including that man over there," Francie says, nodding past me to a sour-faced man with brown hair around our age. "He wasn't entirely pleasant, though."

"They can't all be bad," I counter and she shrugs.

Despite her lack of enthusiasm, we do head to the room that seems filled with the most dancing couples. Her and Tabitha point out a couple other gentlemen they know are part of the cult in one way or another. I do my best to catch their eyes and succeed. I'm a little nervous dancing with men who have killed at least one person simply because they had blood like mine, but then I spot Bash along the wall holding a serving tray. With him nearby, I'm safe.

The first couple men I dance with don't have much more information than the girls did. Then I get stuck dancing with several men who are local. They all seem a little surprised—but quite pleased, one notes—by all the out-of-town guests. Finally, I catch the attention of the first man Francie pointed out. He meets my eyes across the room, downing a glass of amber liquid before stalking my way. His leer as he looks me over makes me uneasy, but I force a smile. He leads me to the dance floor, his grip tighter than necessary. When the dancing starts, he jerks me to him and uses the movements of the dance as an excuse to lean close to whisper in my ear.

"You're here for the same reason I am, aren't you?" he says, the smell of alcohol strong on his breath.

I pull back enough to offer him a coy smile. "I believe so."

He grins. "I thought I sensed something dark about you. You're not afraid of a challenge, and don't mind getting your hands a bit dirty. I like that in a woman."

I force my smile to hold, but I don't need to reply because he doesn't really give me a chance to speak. I have a feeling he also likes his women silent.

"Your dress is nice." He fingers trail up my back as if he's feeling the material. "Very nice. I suspect your patron is better off than most."

This time he does pause, looking as me expectantly.

"Perhaps."

His grin sharpens. "Mine too. I doubt anyone has a patron as wealthy as mine."

My breath catches in my throat. "The Grand Patron?"

"Being from Wanesworth has its advantages. It put me in his direct line of notice." His eyes shine and he tugs me closer again, his tepid breath brushing my ear. "I can put in a good word for you. He also has a taste for beautiful young women."

The music stops, not that I could hear it well over the pounding of my heart. He holds onto me a moment longer than necessary, but then takes a wide step back, shooting me a wicked grin.

"Hopefully we can chat again after initiation," he says with a bow.

I swallow and manage a nod, knowing full well I never want this man to touch me again. The dancers reassemble around me, preparing for another dance, and he disappears into the crowd. I stumble from the dance floor and head into the room where the refreshments are kept. I take a glass of champagne from one of the servers and gulp it down. I need to find Bash. I also need to figure out why Wanesworth sounds familiar. It's sitting on the edge of my brain like an itch.

I'm searching for Bash, trying not to be overly obvious, when a loud gong sounds, echoing through the rooms and bringing everyone to a soft hush. A voice calls for everyone's attention from the furthest room, and most of the crowd starts to shuffle that way. I'm about to follow them when I remember the door attendant mentioning a gong. I look around and notice Tabitha and one of the cult gentlemen I danced with heading a different way. I follow them and discover a dozen or so more people heading behind a statue into what looks like a hallway.

I recall Bash's map, but I'm pretty sure that was a dead end. When I turn the corner, however, I can see an open door held open by a man in a black cloak with the hood situated to hide his features. I swallow and glance over my shoulder, hoping Bash will appear, but I only see a couple other revelers pushing along behind me. With no other choice I follow the others through the door.

CHAPTER ELEVEN

FREYA

Torches flicker along the wall, illuminating a spiral staircase that stretches down into darkness. Hand trembling, I grip the banister and make my way down. At the bottom of the stairs stands another man in a black cloak. He's handing deep purple versions of the cloak to what I assume must be initiates. When I reach the bottom step, I accept my own cloak and slip it on.

The room is open and cold, clearly a cellar of some sort. More torches line the walls, casting the room in an eerie orange glow. Several people in black cloaks stand along the edges of the room while those in purple cloaks are taking up positions in a wide half-circle around what appears to be an altar of some sort encircled by large candles dripping wax. Nearby is a pedestal with a large bowl.

As I step closer I realize the initiates are standing on painted X's. When I take up my own position I startle, realizing that the X is made of blood—red with the slightest traces of gold. My fingers twitch nervously at my side, pressing against the hardness of my hidden daggers. The door closes above us with a boom, and I pray Bash manages to find a way inside.

My heart pounds in my chest as a man steps up behind the altar. The candles highlight his features despite his hood. He's not unattractive, but there's something cold and dark in his eyes that makes me want to get as far away from him as possible. My aversion is so strong, the fact that he looks vaguely like one of the many sketches Bash made me study is an afterthought.

"Welcome," he says, his voice carrying clearly across the room. "The fact that you are here is a feat in and of itself. Whether you have been recruited to join our active ranks to take back our beloved kingdom, poisoned by the Fae, or whether you will take on a less active role, you are all equally important to our success. The Crown is eager to disable our cause and has recently been successful in taking down some of our operations, but we will not let it defeat us. As we continue to share the truth of their hate for those of us without magical blood, our ranks will only grow. You are our proof."

A rumble of agreement echoes around the room and the man smiles.

"You have all successfully passed the first test to become part of the glory that is the *cultas draíochta*. Together we will overcome the abomination that is *Faecræft*, which was only ever meant to destroy humans. Using the power of *Naturcræft*, you will become one with us tonight. Bring her forward."

The man motions to someone at the back of the room, but I don't dare turn to look. A moment later, a man steps into my view, pulling along a teenage girl who's bound and gagged. She kicks and writhes in his grasp, desperate to get away, her long black hair slashing through the air. The gag muffles her screams, but they're no less desperate. I chance a glance at some of the other purple-cloaked individuals around me, but none of them seem concerned. Some actually seem excited.

The man gets to the altar and grips the girl's neck, forcing her to stand straight as he presents her to the man at the altar. The girl's chest heaves, her eyes are wide with terror. The man behind the altar reaches out a hand to brush her cheek and the girl flinches.

"Don't worry, my dear. Your distress will be over soon, and all for a good cause." He turns to the altar and picks up a small clay bowl. "Remove her gag."

Another man steps forward and yanks the gag from the girl's mouth. As soon as her mouth is free, panicked words tumble out.

"I'm nobody," she pleads. "I'm not magical. I don't know what they told you or who told you, but I'm nobody. I'm nobody! My blood barely has traces of gold! Please! Let me go!"

Tears trail down her cheeks and her whole body shakes. Nobody does anything to help her. The man holding her smirks, and the man behind the altar gives her a smile that isn't comforting in the slightest.

"It may not be your fault the Fae have cursed your bloodline, but do not fear. It will end tonight." He dips his fingers into the bowl, lifting them to show the thick paste now covering their tips. "This will ease your pain."

The girl whimpers as the man forces his fingers into her mouth. She chokes, struggling against him at first, but then she goes still. He steps to the side and dips his hands in the bowl. It's only then I realize it's water. Water. I call on my magic, but don't release it. It can be very unpredictable, but today it comes quickly. I can feel its comforting hum from the crystal resting between my breasts, hidden well beneath my dress. I seek out the water, finding a fair amount in the bowl. I'm tempted to unleash the full force of my magic immediately, but I can't yet. I have to wait. I can barely take someone in a one-on-one battle. There's no way I could take on this room of people, especially if they're half as well trained as the ones I've seen before.

"Place her on the altar," the man says, drying his hands on a cloth.

The second man lifts the limp girl and lays her on her back, stepping back a moment later. The girl's eyes are still wide and terrified, tears leaking down her face, but she seems unable to move or speak. The first man steps to the altar, towering over the girl as he looks over the crowd of initiates.

"This girl may seem young and innocent to many, but we know she is threat. Her blood bears undeniable traces of magic. You can see the evidence in her brother's blood beneath your feet."

The girl manages a soft whimper, and bile rises in my throat. The blood making up the X's on the floor must be her brother's. This poor girl. Her poor family.

"Tonight we will put her out of her misery while coming together to strengthen our cause." He holds up a dagger, the twisted blade pointed upward, catching the light from the candles. "We will work together to strengthen our ranks and our bonds. I will make the first cut, and then each of you will step forward and plunge this blade into our guest while repeating our creed—*Bás ad faec ræft*. When you have each taken your turn, I will finish her off, and we will have one less threat to our freedom."

I watch in horror as he turns the blade downward, clutching the handle with both hands. My stomach clenches as he raises the blade high in the air. I can't let this happen. I can't let this girl die. I suck in a breath and pull on the full force of my magic, concentrating on the bowl of water. The man has just gotten out the words *"Bás ad—"* before I force my magic outward, shattering the bowl. Pieces of clay fly through the air and he reacts quickly, shielding his eyes with his elbow as the dagger clatters to the ground. A moment later, his attention shoots upward, eyes blazing with hatred as he scans over the initiates.

"Who did that? Who dares summon the magic of the Fae on our holy ground?"

I say a quick prayer to the gods that Bash is on his way. He promised he'd find me, and I can only hope that he can keep his word. *Find me Bash.* I slip my hand into one of my hidden pockets and slip out a thin dagger. Taking a deep breath, I step forward, meeting the man's eyes.

"I can't let you do this."

The man laughs, looking me over. "Seriously? You? And how do you plan to stop me?"

I force what I hope is confident smile and adjust the dagger in my hands. "I guess you're about to find out."

If Bash doesn't find me soon, I'm never making it out of this cellar alive.

CHAPTER TWELVE

BASH

I've lost Freya. I had one job—to be here if she needed me—and I fucking lost her. I had eyes on her until the crowd shifted with most of the people moving into one room. When I arrive in the other room, she isn't there. I scan the crowd over once, twice, but she's definitely not present. Heart pounding, I race from the room, scanning frantically for any sign of where she might have gone. There are no direct exits to the outside. There's only one place she could be.

When I stumble to a stop at the start of the hidden hall, it's empty. There's no sign anyone was here, but this is the only place I can think of that she might have gone. I glance around and make sure no one is watching before I enter the area. I examine the painting at the end of the hall more care-fully this time. I pull it away from the wall and lean closer to look behind it for some sort of trigger. When I do, I catch a voice coming from the other side. Heart beating frantically, I place my ear to the wall. I can't make out anything that's being said, but there are definitely people down there.

Damn it. Freya is trapped with a cult that won't hesitate to kill her.

I realize with a start my hands are shaking. No, this isn't the time to lose it. I can't lose focus. I take a steadying breath and force my thoughts to calm down. Freya will be fine because I will find her. I promised, and I don't break my promises. I take another deep breath and look around for other options. I lift and examine the small bust on the column to the left of the painting. Nothing is amiss. When I go to lift the matching bust on the other side, it doesn't budge. I swallow hard and push it back. It resists little, but gives with a small crack, revealing a hidden door in the center of the wall. Thank the gods.

Not sure what I'll find on the other side, I slowly pull the door open, slipping inside quickly before too much light can filter in and give me away. I find myself at the top of a spiral staircase lit by torches. Thankfully, the stairs are unguarded at this point, giving me full access. I close the door with a soft click and withdraw a dagger. I creep down the stairs, careful not to make any noise, but freeze halfway at the sound of a familiar voice.

Blood rushes in my ears and I can't think. I know that voice. If he's here, things are more serious than I thought. My instincts tell me to run, to get out of here while I still can. Then I hear Freya's voice. Freya. My Freya. I can't leave her here with him.

I quickly make my way down the stairs. There are two guards at the bottom, but their attention is focused on the center of the room. I call on my magic, pleased it's responding, and slice their throats before they can notice my presence. With them out of the way, I'm able to see what's going on. The room is filled with thirteen people in purple cloaks —Freya is one of them—and what looks like twenty others in black cloaks. Freya stands slightly outside of a half-circle, facing down Killian, a man I'd rather forget. There's also a helpless girl on what looks like an altar.

I've barely taken stock of everything when the action starts. Several people rush toward Freya, and I react on instinct, shoving them away with magic. This, of course, draws attention to me, including Killian's. His eyes widen with surprise for a fraction of a second before his mouth turns up into a wry smile. I can't hear his words when he speaks, but judging by the way those closest to him rush forward, malice etched on their faces, he's given the order to eliminate the threat I present.

I take out two people with my dagger almost effortlessly, doing my best to track Killian out of the corner of my eye. Someone else comes at me with a sword, but I duck under their blow and stab up. They stagger and I snatch the sword from their hands. In one swift blow from their own blade, they're dead. I slip my dagger back into its hiding place and use the sword to block another immediate attack from someone else. I dodge and twist, my sword clashing against another attacker's. I push them back and spin to plunge my sword into the chest of my first attacker. They gasp and stagger back. I grab up their sword so I have one in each hand and spin back to my other opponents. I react on pure instinct, not entirely sure what I do, but they're both dead a moment later.

I hear Freya cry out and I see red. I'm not even sure of my exact movements as I cross the room toward her. She's fighting off a couple people in purple cloaks, doing a good job of dodging, but even from across the room, I can tell she's already getting tired. I slash and stab, taking down person after person. Those in black cloaks are clearly more trained than those in purple, but I know better than to assume any of them are harmless.

Several people make a run for the stairs. Dropping one of my swords, I grab daggers back-to-back and fling them across the room, taking out three more people. Whether they're dead or mortally wounded, destined to die slowly, I don't know or care. A couple others manage to get up the stairs before I can retrieve more daggers. We need to hurry in case they raise the alarm.

I turn my attention to Freya. She's managed to get a sword of her own and isn't doing half bad fighting off a lanky young man in a purple cloak. Judging by the bodies near her feet, she managed to take out a few people on her own. Between the two of us, the room is almost empty now, most assailants having either become martyrs for their cause or fleeing cowards. I quickly scan for Killian among the shadows. I feel confident he wouldn't flee a fight, but I have no doubt he'd stand by while others did most of the dirty work.

Before I can spot him, my attention snags on a figure in a purple cloak stepping up behind Freya, a dagger raised in the air. I throw a blast of wind toward them and they stumble back, turning to face me. It's a girl with dark hair. She looks frightened and unsure as I cross to her. She hesitates a moment before pointing her dagger at me. A dark chuckle escapes me. I've just cut down at least a dozen well-trained soldiers and this girl, who is clearly untrained, thinks she can take me?

"S-stop," she says, her eyes darting around. "I don't want to kill you."

She actually sounds like she might be speaking the truth, but she tried to hurt Freya. She's part of the cult, or at least an initiate of some sort, and therefore must be eliminated. In two swift moves she's on the ground bleeding out. Freya must hear her fall and turns to me, ready to strike. Almost immediately, her shoulders relax and she lowers the sword.

"Bash," she breathes out.

I want to pull her into my arms and tell her it will be okay. Then I notice she has a cut on her cheek. She's hurt. I stumble closer to her, stepping over the body between us. I'm lifting a hand to her cheek when a voice cuts in from behind me, chilling me to my core.

"Does Bastion Shamblefoot have a weakness?"

I slowly turn, adjusting the sword in my hand as my other hand withdraws my last spare dagger. I look into the eyes of a man I've despised since we were both boys.

"You've risen through the ranks, Killian," I say through gritted teeth.

"And it seems you've risen from the dead. I knew that tale of your carriage accident was too good to be true." He grins, but there's no joy in it. "I replaced my father. You remember him, don't you, Bastion? You should. You're the one that killed him, the hand that cared for you."

I scoff. "Your father never cared for me."

"He taught you everything," he spits, "and you killed him."

"I killed him before he had a chance to kill me."

"Before he killed your prince, you mean."

"Like he didn't try to end my life as a boy."

Killian shakes his head. "He definitely made a mistake in not killing you then, but today, I'll take his revenge."

I barely have a second to ready myself before he lunges. I block him easily enough, but he pushes me back, making me stumble over a body. I adjust quickly and dodge his next blow, making one of my own which he blocks easily enough. Our swords clash as we make our rounds through the room. Two men, one in black and one in purple, stand off to the side, watching with swords at the ready. Freya remains toward the center of the room, eyes on me, sword still in her hand.

Killian swings low, taking me off guard and slices into my thigh. I hiss and stumble back but keep my footing. I do my best to ignore the sting, but I know my returning blow is weak.

"Losing your edge, eh, Bastion?" He chuckles. "Pity. I thought this would be a fairly matched battle. Seems I've closed the gap a bit since out last fight."

I growl and thrust my sword forward, but it's sloppy. He laughs again. I block two more blows but a third catches my elbow, nicking the skin enough to bleed. Too many more hits and I'll be losing too much blood. I'm probably losing too much now.

"Pathetic," Killian sneers. "I knew my father was wasting his time on you." He glances off to the side briefly then back to me, a cruel grin curling on his lips. "Or maybe the girl really did make you weak. I won't give her the chance to make me weak, I assure you."

He nods to the two men at the edge of the room and they step toward Freya with wide grins on their faces.

"No!" I yell, moving to intervene, but I don't get far.

My leg aches and I feel lightheaded. I call on my magic, but it's even weaker. It took some training to learn to use my magic without my crystal, much like when I first started really using my left hand to fight, but without the extra aid and focus the crystal provides, I don't have the strength I need to use magic while this drained and wounded. I manage enough of a wind to knock the man in black back a step.

Killian clicks his tongue. "That's cheating, Bastion."

I snarl and turn back to face him. I leap forward, calling on every bit of strength I have. My motion startles Killian and he stumbles back. I hear the clashing of swords behind me and I pray to the gods Freya can hold out a little longer. I move quickly, switching the sword from hand to hand between each strike. Killian obviously isn't used to fighting this way and can't quite keep up. I land a hard blow to his right wrist, cutting clean to the bone. He cries out, dropping his sword. The fighting behind me stops and his eyes dart to the other two men before he nods. They come into my line of vision as they make their way to the stairs.

"This isn't the last you'll see of me, Bastion," he snarls, taking a step backward as he clutches his left hand over his wound to slow the bleeding.

"I'll be ready."

He growls before turning and fleeing up the stairs with the other two. Part of me wants to chase him down and end this now, but Freya needs me. Freya. I turn to her. She's hovering by the altar, looking over the girl lying there.

"We need to get her somewhere safe," she says looking up at me as I approach. "That man drugged her with something."

I nod, looking Freya over. "We'll get her out safely. Are you okay?"

She smiles softly. "Yeah." I lean across the altar between us and brush my thumb across the cut on her cheek and she winces. "Just a few minor injuries." Her brow furrows. "You're hurt, though."

I know there's no point in denying it, but I wave her off. "Don't worry about me."

She doesn't look convinced, her brow furrowing. I want to play it off with a light smirk, but the blood loss is starting to make me a little dizzy and the cut hurts like Hell. As if thinking about the problem makes it worse I stagger forward, barely catching myself on the altar.

"Bash!" Freya cries out, crossing around to me.

"I'm fine," I grit out, but I can't even convince myself, let alone Freya.

The world spins and goes out of focus. I sink to the ground, leaning back against the altar. I can hear Freya's frantic voice, but I can't make out any of her words as the world fades to black.

CHAPTER THIRTEEN

TY

I wake in a cold sweat, Bash's name on my lips. It takes me a moment to realize where I am. My room is shrouded in darkness and while I can't quite make out the clock, it must be around midnight. I close my eyes and breathe—*in, out, in, out*—attempting to calm my racing heart, but I can't make myself relax. I don't even remember my dream, merely the terror from it. Fear sits heavy on my chest, and I can't shake the feeling that something is wrong. Very, very wrong.

Pushing back the covers with clammy hands, I scoot to the edge of the mattress. I let my feet dangle for a moment before I ease from my bed and make my way across my room to my balcony. I throw open the doors and the coolness of the night wraps around me. I look at the stars above, seeking their usual comfort, but tonight, not even they can ease my fears.

I go back into my room, leaving the balcony doors open, hoping the chill will drive away whatever terrors still lurk in the darkness. I debate ringing for a servant to bring me something to calm my nerves, but I don't want to wake anyone. Maybe I could rouse Rissa and get her to brew me a batch of her favorite chamomile tea. I wouldn't mind waking her, but the price she would make me pay might not be worth it. All I know is that I'm very unlikely to get back to sleep anytime soon.

After attempting to read over my latest notes from the letters Rissa's been stealing and not being able to focus in the slightest, an idea comes to me. My first instinct is to push it away, but whether it's a mistake made in the throes of my exhaustion or something better and stronger, I can't resist the pull. I don't bother putting on my robe, but I do don a pair of slippers before sneaking out into the hall. The pair of guards set to watch over me for the night raise their eyebrows at my departure, but when I wave them off and assure them I'll be right back, they stay put. After all, I'm not going far.

My father's rooms are often guarded by soldiers stationed at the ends of the hallway, but tonight two men are directly outside the main door. One is a newer man whose name I'm not sure of, but the other is Anton, a long-time royal guard that I remember guarding my father since I was a boy. When I pause in front of the door, he smiles.

"Now, what has you up this time of night, young prince?" he asks. "I assume you're staying out of trouble?"

I offer the man a smile that borders on genuine. "I couldn't sleep and thought I'd check in." I glance toward the doors. "Do you know if he's awake?"

"You're actually in luck," Anton says, grinning. "He just settled in with a cup of tea. You're not the only one having difficulty sleeping tonight, it seems."

"Is he alone?"

Anton nods. "Your mother is still keeping to her separate

quarters as she's done since the king first fell ill. You'll have him to yourself."

I'm not sure if I'm supposed to find comfort in his words, but he's opening the door for me before I can overthink it.

"You have a visitor, Your Majesty," Anton says, stepping into the room first.

"I do?" my father replies, his voice more vibrant and clearer than I've heard in a very long time. "Who would visit at this time of night?"

I step around Anton, nodding to my father who is sitting up in his bed, a cup of steaming tea in his hands. "Hello, Father. I hope I'm not disturbing you."

His face softens. "Ah, Tybalt. I was wondering when you would finally make your way here. I can say that I did not expect it at this hour, but perhaps the night is when we can resist things the least." He looks past me at his guard. "Thank you, Anton. That will be all."

Anton leaves with a bow, the door closing behind him. I stand frozen to my spot, staring at my father. I've seen him only once since my return, the length of the dining hall between us. Now that I'm mere feet away, nothing between us but air, I can see how much better he truly looks. Even bathed in the low light from his wall lanterns, he almost looks like his normal, vibrant self. He looks like the strong hero of a man I looked up to as a boy. I take a shaky breath, doing my best to force away the tears that threaten to spill. My father is okay. He's alive. He's well.

"I suspect you came here to do more than stare at me," he says not unkindly, setting his teacup on the table next to his bed. "Come closer, my boy. I know I haven't been much help to you lately, but perhaps tonight I can make up for it?"

I swallow and manage a quick nod, stumbling closer to the bed.

"I'm sorry I haven't come to see you before now," I say after a moment.

"It's all right, Tybalt. I know the circumstances were less than ideal. I can't say that if I had been in your place I would have reacted any differently. For the record, I do not agree with how things were handled. I would have preferred the girl to stay in case some things did not work out. I do not want you to think ill of your mother, however. She did what she thought was best based upon what little discussion we were able to have at the time."

I frown. "You were part of the decision to change my engagement without any input from me?"

"I was open to the idea, yes. The Panbrio Isles have always been difficult to deal with since their liberation. Having this opportunity presented was too good to turn down without serious consideration. As much as I want you to be happy, there are duties and sacrifices you must make as a king."

"But Freya was perfect," I say, doing my best to keep anger from my voice. "She was everything I wanted, everything I needed."

"If I recall correctly, it was not all that long ago you were in love with someone else you were convinced was perfect."

"He was. He is. Bash was—is—perfect. I still love him. That hasn't changed."

This seems to surprise my father, his eyebrows arching up. "Yet you still fell in love with the girl?"

"Yes." My answer is a mere whisper. A confession. "I love them both, and now, thanks to this new deal with the Rebel Isles, I've lost them both."

"I am sorry for your loss."

His words strike something deep within me and bile rises in my throat. He thinks they're dead. Everyone thinks they're dead. Thanks to that stupid hope from Rissa, however, I can't accept it. I take a step back, shaking my head.

"They're still alive, out there somewhere. I know it." My father gives me a pitying look, but I barrel on. "They can't be dead. I would feel it. Here." I clench my fist over my heart. "I know they're alive. I have to believe they're alive."

"I hope for your sake they are."

"If they were, and I could find them, would you allow them to return?"

It's a desperate plea, and perhaps I should be ashamed, but I'm not. My father studies me for a moment but nods.

"Yes. As I said, I do want your happiness, and I am not convinced that this marriage alliance is the best decision. Having a backup plan would be a good thing. However, I do not want you to get your hopes up that anything would change should they come home."

It's too late for that, but I manage to school my features enough that my father can't see the true joy flooding though me. All I have to do is find Freya and Bash and bring them back while also proving that Amarelia is up to something. I'm tempted to spill everything to my father now, but without any evidence beyond our vague guesses and suspicions, I'd be throwing out useless accusations. No, I'll have to wait until I know for sure what's happening and present my father with actual proof. In the meantime, I have a sliver of hope to hold onto. However, I'd hoped before only for everything to fall apart.

"Father, can I ask you a question and receive full honesty?"

"Of course."

"Why wouldn't you let Bastion and I be together? I know I need an heir, but I can't be the only crown prince in the history of Elodia to love a man."

My father's silence is heavy and I wonder for a moment if he's going to answer. He takes a deep breath, and I steel myself for his denial.

"You are correct."

I start. "What? Then why . . . ?"

"It's complicated, son, but like I said before, being king comes with sacrifices. Yes, there have been kings before who loved men. With one the question of his heir nearly led to devastation and the shattering of the kingdom. Another chose to step down, handing the throne to someone else ill-prepared for it. Others have chosen to marry a woman while keeping their lovers nearby under official titles. However, with magic as weak and at risk as it is, we wanted your path to be as easy as possible despite your sacrifices. We didn't want you to stress over an heir, and, even if Bastion's blood was enough to create the bond and save magic, you still needed someone to produce an heir with enough magic in their blood for the next generation without anyone questioning their right to the throne."

"Freya still could have given me an heir when she was found."

My father arches an eyebrow. "Asking her to enter into a formal engagement with you is one thing, but do you really think it would have been fair to her to ask her to give up everything to come to Rosana for the sole purpose of bearing your child? She would have been trapped at your side without any chance of happiness of her own. You might have had Bastion, but Freya would have been reduced to however many nights it took to bear a child and possibly nothing more. Knowing her as you do now, would you really ask that of her? Would you demand use of her womb and nothing more?"

I swallow, shaking my head. I understand his reasoning as

much as I hate it. Had I been presented with the question even a few months ago, I might have answered differently—I know I would have answered differently two years ago—but now? Now I know how wonderful Freya is, and I know she would have been miserable reduced to nothing more than a breeding mare, forever doomed to live in my shadow. Gods, I would have been no better than the people who treat her poorly because of her low birth. She would have too easily become an object instead of the girl I love.

"I still love him," I confess. "And I love her, but I will never love Amarelia."

"That may be," my father says. "I hope that should this marriage of your mother's arranging go through, you will learn to love the young princess in time. I don't want you to give up all hope of happiness, Tybalt."

I manage a tight smile. I know my father is being honest, but I don't think he fully understands what he's asking. He's trying, but he's always been better at duty than I am. I can only pray that Rissa and I get to the bottom of everything in time so I can get rid of Amarelia and bring back the people I love. I may not be able to have them both in the way I want, but being able to marry one while having the other as close as possible will be enough. I *have* to make it enough.

"Thank you, Father," I say, inclining my head. "I should really let you get back to sleep."

He chuckles. "It's fine. I will ways make time for you, Tybalt, even in the middle of the night. Besides, I think all the sleep I've gotten the past few months has made me restless. Sometimes these rushes of energy hit me at the most inopportune times."

Because Amarelia is sleeping and not drawing on the magic.

The realization hits me full force. Even though I suspected it before, this only seems to add to the evidence.

Amarelia is controlling my father. Something must show on my face because my father sits up straighter, concern flashing across his face.

"Tybalt, what's wrong?"

I shake my head, forcing a smile as I take a step back. "It's . . . nothing. I'm realizing how tired I am."

My father doesn't seem entirely convinced, but he doesn't press the issue. "Of course. You should get your sleep."

I swallow, nodding as I take another step back. "You, too."

I turn and start toward the door, but my father calls out to me. "I hope this means you won't be avoiding me anymore?"

I freeze, closing my eyes for a moment before I turn back to my father, but he speaks again before I can reply.

"I really am on your side. I hope you see that. Should things not go the way you hope, I will help you in whatever way I can."

"I'll visit you again soon," I promise, meaning every word.

He smiles. "Good. Sleep well, Tybalt."

I practically run from his room back to mine. I collapse on my bed and all the emotions I've been shoving aside break free. I cry because I miss Bash and it was never fair he got ripped away from me. I will never believe loving him was a mistake. I cry because I miss Freya. It was never fair to her that she had to uproot her life only to be tossed aside when my mother had no more use for her. I cry for my father who's still unaware he's dying, tricked by Amarelia's hateful magic. He's become a pawn in someone else's game. I cry for myself because I'm not ready to be king. I'm not ready to live my life without my father to run to. Or without Bash to hold me up when I can't stand on my own. Or without Freya to tell me everything will be all right. I cry because it's too much and I feel so very alone.

I don't want to be alone.

I need Bash to come back. I need him to be okay.

I don't want to be alone.

I want Freya back in my arms. I want to marry her and make her mine.

I don't want to be alone.

I need them. I truly hope they're really out there for me to find. Because I'm going to do it. I'm going to find the people I love and I'm going to bring them home even if it's the last thing I do.

I refuse to be alone.

CHAPTER FOURTEEN

BASH

I come to with a start, pain radiating from my leg. I try to sit up but the world tilts viciously, and I fall back onto my pillow with a groan. I rub my face, squeezing my eyes shut as I attempt to orient myself. Memories of fighting Killian crash in on me and panic swells in my chest.

"Bash?" Freya's voice cuts into my spinning thoughts, grounding me. I force my eyes open and a blurry image comes into focus. Freya stands over me, brow furrowed in concern.

"Freya?" I manage, my voice coming out hoarse. I ease up onto my elbows, slower this time, and she visibly relaxes.

"Thank the gods. I was starting to worry. Here, let's get you situated." She leans forward and arranges the pillows behind me so I'm in a somewhat upright position.

"How did I get here? Last I remember, we were in the cellar of that house."

"You passed out and scared me half to death. Your leg was wounded really badly. I managed to bandage it with material torn from the cloak I was wearing. Not well, but enough to stop the bleeding. I took the girl upstairs and apparently some of the people up there recognized her and were grateful enough to help get you out of the cellar and to our horse. How I actually got you here and in bed, I'm not sure. It's a blur, to be honest. I really thought you were dead. You scared me, Bash."

Her voice breaks on my name, her chin wobbling. I swallow, hating I made her worry. Hating I couldn't take care of myself.

"How long have I been out?"

"It's been almost three days."

"What?" I try to sit up, but the dizziness returns and I fall back on my pile of pillows. "Shit."

"You need to rest," Freya says. "And eat. Hold on, I'll warm up some soup for you."

She disappears from my bedside and I close my eyes. I drift off a little, but when Freya returns with a bowl of soup that's mostly broth, I rouse easily enough. She adds another pillow behind my back to help me sit up properly before pulling a chair next to the bed with one hand while balancing the bowl of soup in her other hand.

"Should I feed you or do you think you can handle it?" she asks as she settles in the chair.

My face heats. "I think I can do it myself."

She nods, offering me the bowl. "If you change your mind, let me know. I've been giving you a little broth and water here and there while you slept."

I'm pleased to find that my hands are steady enough I can feed myself. I've only taken a few bites when the heat of Freya's gaze pulls my attention to her. She's watching me closely in a way that tells me she has something on her mind beyond my recovery. I try to shove my worry aside, already able to guess her concerns. In the past few weeks we've been open and honest with each other. I don't want that to end now.

"Go ahead," I say, not able to look at her. "Ask."

"Bash . . ."

I look up at her and force a weak smile. "I know you have questions. I'm fine with sharing the answers, but it's a lot. Give me a place to start."

"That man, he looked like someone from your sketches, but when I looked him up, it was the face of a dead man."

I nod. "His father."

"You seemed to know him."

"He's my cousin, in a way. Not really by blood, but that's how I think of him because that's how he was introduced to me. I was never close to him, but his father, my uncle . . ." I trail off with a sigh, happy I have the excuse of eating to give me a moment to collect my thoughts. "It's a long story."

Freya nods like she truly understands. Silence swells around us as I try to decide how to explain everything, but Freya is the one to break it.

"Your blood is golden."

I take a deep breath. "Yeah."

"Ty mentioned you had fairly golden blood, but I've never seen someone with blood that golden before. Mine doesn't even come close."

I stare into my soup for a moment before slowly lifting my gaze to hers. There's no judgment there, just gentle curiosity.

"My father was a full-blooded Fae."

Her eyes widen as a soft gasp escapes her lips. "You're half Fae?"

"More than half." I swallow, the truth heavy and dangerous, but I know I can trust Freya. "My mother also had strong Fae heritage from both her mother and father. How much, I'm not sure, but from what I remember, her blood was similar to yours, maybe even a touch more golden. She kept it pretty secretive for safety reasons."

"But if that man was your cousin, how does that work? How was someone so magically inclined related in any way to someone who is clearly among the higher ranks of the *draíochta*, even if it wasn't through blood? You still called him your cousin, right?"

"It really is a long story."

She places a gentle hand on my arm and offers me a small smile. "We have time, if you want to tell it. I understand if you need to rest."

I take a deep breath. "Now is as good a time as any, and I'd like to get it out." *I don't want to keep anything from you.*

"If at any point you want to stop or you need to rest, that's fine," she says softly.

I offer her a small smile. "I appreciate it, but I think I can handle at least most of the story now."

She gives me an encouraging nod, and I take a deep breath, steadying myself.

"When my mother was only a few days old, the *draíochta* attacked her village. There were a few magical families there. My grandmother was apparently very beautiful and, when her house was attacked, they stole her away. She promised to go without a fight if they also left her newborn child alive— my mother. For whatever reason, they agreed. My mother was raised in the house of her captors, forced to call the man who stole her mother away 'father' and his sons 'brothers,' even though the man never married her mother and treated them both as disposable things. Her so-called brothers never treated her well, but the middle son, my Uncle Mordecai, treated her better than the rest. My mother always suspected he did it as a way to manipulate her and gain her trust, but she was so grateful she accepted his help and kindness without question. When she turned sixteen, she was married off to someone the cult approved of to 'dilute her bloodline.'"

"She was only sixteen?" Freya asks, eyes wide with horror.

I nod and take another spoonful of soup. "It was a loveless match, as you can imagine. My stepfather was cruel and abusive. My mother was careful to take herbs and whatnot to keep from conceiving one of his children, and he was constantly threatening to get rid of her. She was already looking for an escape when she met my father. She was nineteen and he was twenty.

"She was visiting the market and she tripped, cutting her palm. When my father saw her golden-tinted blood, he was intrigued. When he discovered her living situation wasn't safe, he started helping her plan her escape. He was supposed to pass through and be gone days after they met, but he stuck around. They made the mistake of falling in love, and the plan changed from simply getting her somewhere safe to them escaping together. On the night she went to meet him to make their getaway, she found him dead."

Freya gasps. "Your poor mother."

"She was terrified and frantic. She raced home and discovered her brother had arrived, the one she got along with. He still had my father's blood on his sleeves. At first she assumed he'd found out about their relationship, but it ended up he'd been tracking down and murdering Fae for the *draíochta*—though she didn't know that was who he worked for exactly, only that he hated magic and worked to rid the world of it. Staying at her house was merely convenient. Had my father moved on when he was supposed to, he would have been safe. Staying for my mother killed him."

"Did she know she was pregnant with you yet?"

I shake my head. "She found out a few days later. She, of course, pretended I was my stepfather's child. He was always suspicious since they hadn't been overly intimate at the time, but my mother did what she could to protect me, including getting immediately pregnant again with Rupert so my stepfather wouldn't kick us out when he inevitably discovered I wasn't his child."

"When did he discover it? I think you mentioned before it was your magic that gave you away?"

"Yeah. I think he was a little wary about how golden my blood was, but he didn't know anything about magical heritage, so he accepted my mother's explanation that my blood was only golden because of her. When I was about four or five, I got a kite stuck in a tree. I used my wind to get it down and he saw. After that, he basically knew. Thank the gods he kept it to himself and didn't immediately run and tell my mother's family, or I have no doubt they would have ended my life right then and there."

Freya nods, absorbing everything I've told her so far while I finish off the last bit of my soup.

"That man, your cousin, he said his father trained you?"

I take a deep breath and look away, happy memories that shouldn't really be happy filling my brain.

"When I was about seven, my uncle began showing up every few months. Like I mentioned before, he was kind to my mother for his own reasons. That attention extended to me. He offered to train me, and I accepted. My own father, or the man I called a father at that time, showed me no kindness at all, so I craved my uncle's attention. He would stay for a couple weeks and teach me some new moves and tricks. He was strict, but he always praised my efforts. I never understood why my mother watched our training sessions with such trepidation, but I know now she was terrified I'd get hurt and my uncle would see my blood. She might have been able to lie about my real father to my stepfather, but my uncle knew too much about Fae bloodlines to believe her lie.

"Everything worked well until my uncle brought my cousin with him. I was eleven and Killian was thirteen. I was determined to prove to my uncle that I was skilled, and I fought my hardest. I beat Killian soundly. My uncle laughed, shaming Killian and praising me. Killian was furious and attacked me from behind, wounding me. It wasn't bad, but when my uncle saw my blood, everything changed. He was no longer the loving parental figure I had grown to love. He tried to kill me, and I was only saved by my quick reflexes and by my mother running between us."

I swallow, shuttering my eyes as the memory surfaces, as clear today as it was then. I can still hear my mother's pleas and feel the hot tears on my face. My eyes startle open at a soft touch on my arm. I look up at Freya to find nothing but understanding and kindness.

"You don't have to talk about it."

I force a smile that I'm sure is less than convincing. "It's fine. It was a long time ago. I've moved on and healed. If it weren't for that day, I probably never would have met Ty." *Or you.*

She takes the empty bowl from my hands and stands. "How did you meet Ty?" she asks, carrying the bowl away and setting it on the table in the corner of the room. "And when? I assumed you came to castle earlier than it sounds."

A true smile curls my lips as she resumes her seat. "It wasn't much later actually." My smile falls. "After my uncle confirmed I was very much not my stepfather's child, my stepfather had no reason to pretend to like us anymore. My mother was obviously not going to give him any more children and he had proof of her infidelity. He also didn't have to worry about any sort of retribution from my mother's so-called family, not that I think they would have lifted a finger to help her anyway. He began openly bad-mouthing both of us and treating us like slaves. He wouldn't even let us sleep in the house. Our new room was in a drafty back house that was so close to falling apart it was barely livable."

I pause and Freya takes my hand, giving it a squeeze. It's a small thing, but it comforts me and gives me strength to continue.

"Winter came and my mother got sick. She was bedridden, but my stepfather refused to let her sleep in the warmth of the main house. He also refused to let her have any sort of medication or to call for the doctor. He even denied us extra blankets. I did everything I could, but in the end, it wasn't enough."

My voice breaks and Freya's grip on my hand tightens. Tears fill my eyes as I look over at her.

"She died and left me alone. I buried her myself on the back of my stepfather's property against his wishes. He beat me for it and locked me in a shed. I expected to die there, but a few days later, General Harrow arrived—though he was only Captain Harrow at the time. Apparently during my mother's last days, she convinced one of the kinder servants to post a letter for her to the palace. She told the captain about my skills and my magic and begged him to take me away and train me for the king's army. Thank the gods he came when he did, because his arrival literally saved my life.

"He brought along a boy around my age for me to spar against to show my skills. When they saw my state, they almost left, but I told them I could still hold my own. By some miracle, I did. I didn't actually beat the boy, but I came damn close, close enough to impress them both. That's when the boy looked up at the captain and demanded they take me to Rosana."

"Demanded?" Freya asks as understanding dawns. "The boy was Ty."

"One and the same, though I didn't discover his identity until weeks later." I take a deep breath and release it slowly. "Ty saved my life that day, and I felt like I owed him a life debt. I was determined to become even better in the hopes I could one day return the favor and save his life. At the palace, I was put in training with other boys about my age, but Ty would sneak out and spar with me on a fairly regular basis. Eventually we became best friends, and I was moved to his personal guard once I had proven myself worthy. The rest is history."

Freya opens her mouth to ask a follow-up question, but she stops with a smile when I yawn.

"You need some more rest. You don't want to push it."

I want to protest, but honestly, I'm suddenly very exhausted. I'm not sure if it's from my injury or the fact I just spilled my life story. I manage a nod as another yawn overtakes me. She tucks my blanket around me as I settle back against my pillows. She stands, hesitating a moment before leaning down and brushing a quick kiss on my forehead. My heart flutters at her touch. Her cheeks grow pink as she takes a quick step back.

"Sweet dreams, Bash," she whispers.

As much as I would like to stay awake and talk more with Freya, sleep pulls me under quickly. I'm not sure if I'm still awake or if I'm already in the world of dreams when Freya's voice whispers "I need you to be okay." I'm sure it must have been a dream.

CHAPTER FIFTEEN

FREYA

Bash isn't supposed to get hurt. He's supposed to be stronger than this, invincible, as much as I know that's impossible. The first three days of not knowing whether he would live or die, if I had done enough to save him, were unbearable. I couldn't concentrate on anything besides him. Even now, after seeing him awake and okay, my nerves are still rattled. As he sleeps, I check and redress his wounds, reapplying a healing salve to ward off infection. He wakes on and off, and I offer him water and soup between his naps and help him up to relieve himself as needed.

The conversation about Bash's background, learning how instrumental Ty was in saving Bash's life, has me missing Ty even more. I find myself pulling out the letter he managed to get to me before his mother ousted me from Rosana. The paper is worn from being read probably a hundred times now, but even over a month later, his words make me long for him.

My Dearest Freya,

I told you that you had become my happily ever after and I meant it. Even if my mother succeeds in forcing you from my side, she cannot sever my love for you. No matter the obstacles, I will find a way to marry you. You, Freya, have taken the shattered pieces of my heart and put them back together. In the midst of all the darkness, you are my light.

Please, no matter what happens over the next few days, weeks, months, PLEASE do not give up on us. I am done losing people I love. I will find a way. I don't know how, but I swear it. I love you, and I refuse to give you up.

Forever and Always Yours,

Ty

I force myself to put the letter away. I can't go back to Ty, as much as I wish I could. If Bash's plan worked, Ty thinks we're dead. Everyone does. It's better that way. It has to be. I sigh and busy myself looking over my notes.

It takes me a little while to remember why the name Wanesworth sounded so familiar. Turns out, Wanesworth is one of the neighboring villages to the one I grew up in. I never paid attention to the other villages around me since I seldom did anything on the trading end or any sort of business with our farm. Papa took care of that. Though, I'm not even sure we did much trade with Wanesworth.

I don't want to mark the map Bash drew, so I make a careful copy of my own. My map isn't nearly as neat as his, but it serves its purpose. I label all the villages close to Wanesworth and fill in the leaders and nobility I can recall for each, which honestly isn't many. I cross-check those names against the lists we have of cult members, but none match up. I then comb through the information I have on the cult, looking for Wanesworth, East Hingling, or any of the other places listed as key locations for the cult, but nothing is connecting. It's a frustrating process, but I'm determined to find something.

"What are you so focused on?"

Bash's voice startles me and I jump a little. I twist in the desk chair to glance at him over my shoulder. He's sitting up, facing me, his legs slung over the edge of the bed. I stumble to my feet.

"You should be resting!"

He chuckles. "I think I've done plenty of resting. How long has it been altogether? Even with being awake more, time's a bit fuzzy."

"Five days total," I reply, walking over to him. "Want me to help you up?"

He shakes his head. "Let me see if I can do it on my own."

I nod and step back to give him space. He eases up from the bed with a groan, tentatively testing his leg. He wobbles slightly but keeps upright. He offers me a small half smile before limping to the washroom. Once I'm sure he's not going to topple over, I return to my seat at the desk. I try very hard to concentrate on the papers in front of me and not worry about whether Bash is about to topple over without me nearby to catch him. When he reappears a minute later, tension seeps from my shoulders.

"What are you studying?" he asks, stepping up behind me and placing his hands on the back of the chair. I pray to the gods he can't hear the way my breath hitches when his knuckles barely brush against my shoulders.

"I've been cross-referencing some details." I look up at him, ignoring the fluttering in my heart to have him so near. "I had some interesting conversations at the ball, and I've been trying to put the pieces together."

He hums, moving around the chair so he's standing beside me. "Why don't you show me what you've put together and maybe I can fill in the rest?"

I spread out my notes and map across the desktop so he can easily take them all in as I go over everything. I share the bits I learned about the cult, its new recruiting efforts, what I suspect about the Grand Patron, and the cult's attachment to something called *Naturcræft*—which Bash hasn't heard of either.

"I have a feeling he resides somewhere in this region," I say, gesturing to the circled areas on my map, "but I can't be sure where. None of the notes have any known members of the *draíochta* living in this area."

Bash frowns down at the map. "You're correct, but something about this town, Carrisburg, sounds familiar," he mutters, pointing to one of the towns slightly south of East Hingling. "What do you know about it?"

I shrug. "Not much. We did a fair amount of trade with them, I think. East Hingling is largely livestock country and Carrisburg was known for their vegetables and grain, which worked well for feeding said livestock."

Bash snaps his fingers. "That's it!"

I scowl. "What's it?"

Instead of answering, he moves around me and shuffles through some papers stacked in the corner of the desk. He mumbles under his breath before I catch a "here it is" as he pulls a crinkled paper from the stack.

"Do you remember this?" he asks, placing the paper on top of the map as he leans against the desk, practically sitting on top of it.

"I think so. This was from that first supply carriage we waylaid, right?"

"Correct," he confirms. "Look at the top."

I scan the paper, trying to figure out what Bash saw and when it strikes me, I gasp.

"The town of origin is listed as EH via Carrisburg! East Hingling is the town of origin. Which would fit because this shipment had a lot of food supplies." I pause. "But that shipment also had clothes and other items."

"True, but if East Hingling is the base of operations, it would make sense that other cities and towns would send items there. It's possible it only stopped in Carrisburg to load up on the grain and other food because it was a logical stop on the way out."

I nod. "East Hingling is at the topmost corner of Elodia. Why would that be the base when it's nowhere near being a central location, and why haven't we made this connection before?"

Bash shrugs. "Maybe it's a newer development. I took out a lot of their higher-ups before, so they probably had to relocate and shuffle their ongoing operations. It's also possible this has always been a key location that they managed to keep it quiet and contained for obvious reasons, but the recent hurried expansions have made them careless. Or maybe this Grand Patron is a new member or someone who wasn't as actively involved before because their skill set wasn't needed in the field until recently."

"What do we do now?"

Bash grins. "Looks like you might be going home after all."

Nerves twist in my stomach, a mix of anticipation and something that feels an awful lot like fear. I should be happy to go home, but somehow it doesn't feel like home anymore. Bash frowns, clearly picking up on my hesitation.

"That's a good thing, isn't it?"

I nod, swallowing hard. "It isn't a bad thing."

He opens his mouth to speak, but stops short, wincing as he moves away from the desk and closer to me. I practically leap from the chair.

"You should sit." I motion to the chair between us. "I can't believe I've been making you stand."

He smiles softly, shaking his head. "I'm fine."

"No, you're not. I saw you wince."

His smile falls a bit but doesn't disappear entirely. "I'm still sore, but I really am fine. I've been in that bed too long and I'm a little stiff. I forgot for a moment my leg was hurt and put too much weight on it." I frown at him and he has the audacity to chuckle. "Princess—"

"No," I cut him off sharply, hating the tears that burn my eyes. "No, Bash. I—"

Suddenly all the emotions I've been trying to rein in over the past few days are escaping. My chin trembles and I clamp my jaw shut, turning my head so he can't see the tear that slips free. Unfortunately, I'm not quick enough and Bash reaches out and takes my chin, turning my face to him.

"What's wrong?"

"Nothing."

"Don't lie to me."

I take a shaky breath that turns into a soft sob. Bash pushes the chair out of the way and pulls me into his arms. I give in to my tears and collapse against his chest.

"Hey," he whispers, his breath warm on my ear as his fingers trail a comforting path up and down my back. "It's okay. *I'm* okay."

I pull back enough to peer up at him through my tears. "You weren't, though. I didn't know if you were going to wake up."

"But I did," he says, his voice so soft it hurts. He tucks a strand of runaway hair behind my ear. "I did wake up, and it's because of you. You got me out of there and made sure I was okay."

"But you never would've been hurt if you hadn't come looking for me."

"None of that. If I'd gone into that house on my own, I would've still ended up in that cellar, only I probably wouldn't have made it out alive."

"But—"

He presses a finger to my lips. "No. No more self-doubt." His eyes brighten slightly as a smile tips onto his lips. "You were incredible in there, Princess. Not just when you got my wounded ass out of there, but before. I saw you fighting and you were wonderful. I was so proud of you."

My chest warms. "Yeah?"

"Yeah."

His expression turns to something more intense, and his eyes flick down to my mouth as he swallows.

"Bash," I whisper, the word barely audible over the beating of my heart.

"I'm sorry," he mutters, pulling back, but before he can get too far, I grab his shirt and tug him toward me. I have only a moment to register his wide eyes before I press my lips to his. When I realize he's not returning the kiss, I release him and stumble back, my face burning.

"Oh, gods. I'm sorry. I shouldn't have—"

I'm cut short as he envelopes me in his arms and presses his lips to mine with a ferocity and need I've only ever dreamed of. There is nothing gentle about the kiss—it's desperate and hungry—and yet there's so much care and tenderness in his touch. One of his hands cradles my cheek while the other finds its way into my hair, his fingers twisting into my runaway curls. A small whimper escapes me as he tugs my face up to better meet his, and he releases a rumbling growl in response. I press closer to him, my own hands grasping blindly at his clothes, craving the feel of his body against mine. It's only when he flinches that I remember he's still healing, and I jerk back several steps with a gasp.

"We should . . . That was . . ." I try, words failing me as I work to steady my racing heart.

Bash's lips quirk, his eyes still filled with heat as they meet my own. "Very much." His confidence staggers a bit as he runs a shaking hand through his hair. "I suppose that was all right then?"

A huff of a laugh escapes me, and I take a step closer to him. "I kissed you first."

He chuckles. "I suppose you did." He closes the distance between us, placing his hands on my shoulders as he looks down at me with nothing short of affection. "Though, I confess, I've wanted to do that for quite some time."

"Why didn't you?"

His smile falls as he looks away. "It's complicated, but for one, I didn't know if my advances would be welcome." He looks back at me, his expression heavy. "I thought you might still be in love with Ty."

"I am," I confess.

His hands drop from my shoulders and he takes a step back. "Oh."

"But that doesn't mean I can't feel things for you, too. I do think it's possible to love more than one person, don't you?" His eyes widen a touch, and I rush to add, "Not that I necessarily love you, not yet."

He swallows, hesitating a moment before he nods, a soft smile curving the edges of his lips. "I don't just believe it's possible, I know it is."

My chest warms and I feel lighter. "Because you also still love Ty."

He takes a deep breath before releasing it slowly. "Yes, and I'm afraid I always will. I've loved him too much for so long. He's a part of me."

I smile up at him. "You know, there was one time a family came into the market where we were selling our goods, but they weren't a couple like we usually saw. There was one man and two women with three young children. My mother caught me watching them and she must have noted my confusion because she pulled me into her arms and whispered, 'Isn't it a beautiful thing when a heart has so much love that it can give its affection to more than one soul and for that heart to receive mutual love and respect in return?' I always thought it was wonderful concept, though I never imagined my heart could hold that much love."

"That is a lovely sentiment," he says, his voice low. "I honestly never thought I'd ever find love, let alone someone who would love me back. Imagining having that with more than one person would have been an unattainable dream."

"Well," I say, reaching out and taking his hand in mine, "maybe we both got lucky."

He smiles down at me. "Maybe."

Then he pulls me into another kiss, this one even more searing than the first.

CHAPTER SIXTEEN

BASH

I wake with Freya in my arms. At first, I'm not convinced I'm actually awake. Surely this must be a dream. She releases a soft sigh, her warm breath ghosting across my skin, and I realize that my dreams have become reality. Memories from last night flicker into my brain. We spent hours kissing between researching and planning before we curled up in my bed together. Nothing more physical happened, but being close with her feels right. For the first time in years, I feel almost complete.

She shifts and her eyes blink open. For a moment she looks almost puzzled, and I wonder if she feels the same muddled confusion I felt moments ago. Or maybe she regrets everything. What if she remembers yesterday in a different light? Panic swells in me for a moment until her lips tip into a tender smile, and I recall *she* kissed *me*. Of all the miracles I've ever witnessed, that has to be one of the greatest.

"Good morning," she mumbles, snuggling closer.

I smile and press a kiss to the top of her head. "Good morning."

I give her one more quick kiss and sit up. I start to move from the bed but she groans, grabbing my shirt and holding me in place.

"Where are you going?"

"I thought I might find us some food."

She mumbles something that I don't quite catch.

"What was that?"

She lifts her face to me, a sweet pink lining her cheeks. "I said 'maybe it can wait.'"

I chuckle, placing a finger under her chin to tilt her face for a quick kiss. "Perhaps, but we do need to eat."

"Oh," she says, sitting up. "You probably are hungry. I forgot you're still healing." Her eyes dart to my leg. "How are you feeling?"

"A bit stiff and a little sore, but much better overall."

She nods before pushing back the covers. "I'll get you some breakfast then."

"No," I say and she scowls at me. I laugh. "I'll get *you* breakfast."

"Bash—"

"I won't hear any protests. You've been taking care of me for days. It's the least I can do to repay you."

She opens her mouth to protest, but I cut her off with a kiss. When I pull back, she grins, shaking her head affectionately.

"Fine, but if gets to be too much for you—"

"If I can't handle getting some breakfast, I sure as Hell won't survive a trip to East Hingling," I say, easing from the bed. I'm pleased that it doesn't really hurt too much to stand, but I take tentative steps across the room. "We did agree we'd leave in two days."

"Sure," Freya concedes, but I can sense her concern even with my back turned to her. "You'll let me know if you're not up for it, right? You'll be honest?"

I glance at her over my shoulder. "I promise."

She smiles and my world tilts. I force myself to focus on cutting some fruit for breakfast while water heats for tea over a small fire. I also busy myself making a couple pieces of toast, topping them with jam. I arrange our breakfast on a tray and return to the bed where Freya is reading one of my books. I catch the title and, gods, of all the books I have, why is she reading *that* one.

"I didn't take you for a romance reader," she says, setting the book to the side as I ease down next to her, balancing the tray carefully so nothing spills.

"I read a little of everything," I admit. I hesitate before adding, "That's one of my favorites, though."

She grins, her eyes shimmering with delight. "It's rather detailed."

She takes a bite of toast, her tongue darting out to catch a drop of jam, and my face warms. I look away and busy myself with preparing a cup of tea.

"Yes, well, there's a lot more to the story than . . . details."

She giggles, nudging me with her shoulder. "I know. I've read it before."

I raise my surprised gaze to hers and she laughs. It's such a glorious sound and for a moment I wonder if I can survive on just that the rest of my life. But then her attention turns to the food, and I realize that I'm actually quite hungry. We eat in pleasant silence, and at some point, Freya shifts so she's pressed against me. Despite my racing heart, I don't dare move away from her touch. When breakfast is complete, I move the tray to a side table next to the bed and turn to her. She looks up at me and every thought in my head flies away.

"May I kiss you?" I ask, my voice hoarse. Gods, I sound like an awkward boy again.

Freya grins up at me. "Please."

A moment later my lips are on hers and I'm soaring. The kissing intensifies and Freya eases herself into my lap, wary of my leg. When she releases a soft moan into my mouth and moves against me in a way that should excite me, something snaps in my brain and I pull back. Freya looks up at me, and I offer an apologetic smile.

"Freya," I say softly, carefully. "Can we . . . slow down a little?" I sigh and look away, my shoulders sagging. "I'm sorry."

"Hey," she says, placing a hand to my cheek and drawing my attention back to her. "It's okay. We don't have to go any further if you don't want to. I get it. You're wounded, I was engaged to Ty not all that long ago, and—"

"That's not it," I say quickly with a small shake of my head. "Well, not entirely. I am *very* much into what is happening and where this is going, but what I enjoy sexually isn't quite as straightforward as what you might be used to." I pause, a smile curving my lips. "Right now, I would rather watch you pleasure yourself, if you think you'd enjoy that as well."

Her pupils flare wider as her mouth drops open. Her cheeks flush and she catches her bottom lip between her teeth. Something hot and wicked flares to life inside me and a grin curls my lips.

"Would you like that, Princess? Would you like to pleasure yourself while I watch? While I tell you what to do?"

A small sound escapes her and her flush deepens.

"Yes, I, uh, I would be okay with that," she manages, her voice rough.

Heat sparks through me and my smile sharpens, my normal confidence returning.

"So," I say, leaning closer, trailing my fingers up her arm, "you would be okay with me telling you how to touch yourself? Maybe even making you ask permission?"

She inhales sharply and manages a nod, her pupils so wide her eyes look like black pools of ink. I reach up caress her cheek with barely-there touches. She shivers.

"And you wouldn't mind if I watched as your cheeks turn that beautiful, glowing shade of pink I love so much?"

A soft, desperate sound escapes her lips and desire overcomes me. She ducks her head, but I grab her chin, gently but firmly, and tip her face up so her eyes meet mine.

"Is that what you want?" I ask, my voice a low rumble.

"Please." She sounds breathless, borderline desperate, and it does something to me. Perhaps we should take a moment to cool off, but I can't bring myself to care about anything other than the heat pooling low in my gut.

"Please what, Princess?" I purr. "Tell me what you want."

She lets out a small whimper that's almost my undoing. "Please, take control. Watch me."

I hum, pressing my thumb to her bottom lip. "And you'll listen? Do what I ask?"

"Yes."

"Good girl." I release her with a jerk. "You're not going to do very well sitting up. You should lay down, stretch out across the bed."

She doesn't even hesitate, moving quickly to obey my command, and she looks so beautiful doing it. Somehow I'd forgotten she went to sleep in one of my spare shirts. It's oversized on her enough that it worked well as a night shirt, but now that she's laid out so wonderfully in front of me, I let my eyes rove over the luscious, thick curves of her legs.

"May I touch myself now?" she asks, her voice trembling.

"Hmm," I tilt my head, taking her in and she squirms beneath the heat of my gaze. "Yes. One hand."

Her hand slips up under the shirt—my shirt—exposing more skin. Her fingers find their place and a soft gasp escapes her lips. Gods, I almost want to make her stop and undress entirely, but something about seeing her in my clothes while she pleasures herself has me preening in appreciation. Her head tilts back and she closes her eyes for a moment before looking back up at me.

"What are you thinking about?" I ask. "Are you thinking about me?"

She manages a nod, her breathing heavy.

"Are you imagining that it's my hand bringing you pleasure? Or perhaps my mouth, my tongue lapping you up, tasting you?"

She whimpers, her entire body quivering as her hand moves faster.

"You're not answering me, Princess. If our little game is to work, I need you to reply. Otherwise we may have to stop. Do you want to stop?"

"No!" she gasps out. "I need . . . more."

"Which is it? My hand or my mouth?"

"Mouth!"

I hum and reach a single finger to trace along her cheek. She immediately moves into my touch, her eyes shuttering closed.

"Open your eyes," I say, keeping my voice low as my finger trails down to her lips. "I want you to look at me as you find your pleasure." Her eyes snap open, meeting mine.

"I want you to remember whom it is who has you in this state, who's in control. You remember, don't you?"

"You! It's you."

"Yes, it is." I slip my finger into her mouth and her lips close automatically around it. "Suck."

She obeys, pulling my digit further into her mouth, moaning. I swallow hard, unable to look away from her. I've seen many amazing, beautiful things in my life, but none of them compare to the delicious sight before me.

"Are you nearly there, Princess?" I ask, my own voice rough and raw.

She nods, sucking harder.

"Then come for me."

Almost as if she were waiting for permission—and perhaps she was—her back arches and she comes with a cry, her eyes never leaving mine. I slip my finger from her mouth and lean in to kiss her, swallowing her last desperate breaths as she comes down from her high. I pull her closer so that she's half lying in my lap and half leaning against me, and rest my chin on her head as I wrap my arm around her.

"Are you all right?" I ask once her breathing has steadied. "I know that's probably not what you're used to."

She huffs a laugh and tilts her head a little to look up at me. "No, that was better."

I'm sure I don't keep the shock from my face as I reply. "Better?"

"Mm-hm," she says, nestling closer. "That was amazing." She pauses a moment before adding, "Are you sure there's nothing I can do for you?"

I chuckle, shaking my head. "No. That was as much for me as you, and even if I didn't find completion in quite the same way, I assure you I am entirely satisfied."

"You're sure?"

I trace a finger down her cheek and offer her a small smile. "I'm sure. I'm not always capable of moving as quickly as others or even remaining consistent in what I want, but what we just did was perfect for me."

"Good," she says with smile. "Because I really enjoyed it and I hope to do it again." She hesitates a moment before adding, "And if that's all you ever want to do, I'm okay with that, too."

My heart skips a beat. I love that she can accept that so easily, accept *me* so easily, but I also want to be clear and honest with her. I take an unsteady breath and plunge into the truth before I can talk myself out of it.

"I don't experience sexual attraction and intimacy like most people."

She furrows her brow. "Weren't you and Ty . . . ?"

I nod emphatically. "We were. I'm not saying I never feel sexual attraction—I definitely do. I liked what we just did and there are times when I want a more traditional sort of connection, but it's"—I sigh—"complicated."

She offers me a smile and gives me an encouraging squeeze. "If you want to explain it, I'm willing to listen."

Hope flares in my chest and a smile tempts my lips. "Yeah?"

"Yes."

"Okay, well, for most people, from what I understand, there's a more instant attraction. You look at someone and find them aesthetically or sexually pleasing. In some cases, people will act on that attraction and flirt or make offers and it leads to sexual encounters. For Ty, that's all he needs—that basic attraction—and he can fall into bed with them and find pleasure.

"For me, I can look at someone and see why other people are attracted to them and even see aspects of a person that I find aesthetically pleasing, but I don't feel the desire to become physical with them, not even theoretically. If we develop a friendship, I may develop affection for them to an extent. I may even find myself wanting to be in their presence. The deeper our emotional connection grows, the more of them I want to the point where, on occasion, the affection turns physical. I'll seek them out for conversation or simply to be near them. I enjoy their company and crave more of it. I like when our arms brush, or I can take their hand, maybe even share a kiss."

I press my thumb to her lips, which part beautifully for me. "For most people, that physical touch turns into deeper desires"—my fingers trace lower, down her neck and along her collarbone—"and that desire turns into passion"—my fingers continue their movement down her side and back, making her breath hitch—"and that passion becomes sex."

"But not for you?" she asks, her voice rough.

I swallow and drop my hand. "Not always. Not often, if I'm honest." I shrug, looking away. "I'm content enough to let things go on as they have been. On the occasion that the feelings and emotional connection are deep, I can sometimes give in and find pleasure in the physical, but that's honestly the exception."

She nods, processing everything I've said. "But you and Ty, you were intimate?"

"Ty is the only person I've ever been with in that way where I enjoyed the experience," I confess, my voice heavy.

"You've tried with others?"

I nod, staring up at the ceiling even though I can feel her eyes on me.

"Over the past couple years I tried forcing it, telling myself I would get used to it, but I never did. Those handful of experiences only left me frustrated and unsatisfied and, quite frankly, hurt. They left a bitter taste in my mouth, and I couldn't even stand to look at the person after." I slowly bring my eyes back to hers. "I don't want that with you, Freya. I want to look at you and feel light and free."

"I want that, too. I'm willing to wait to see if you can feel for me the way you did with Ty, and if you don't, I'm okay with that as well. I like what we have now."

"I like it, too. A lot." I smile, but I'm sure it's still a little sad around the edges. "I think I may already be at that point, if I'm honest, but I don't want to push it. And even when we do move forward, what I want to do, how far I personally want to go, may not always be consistent. Even once I'm in a relationship with someone I trust, like I was with Ty, like I want to be with you, my arousal crests and part of me craves that intense physical intimacy, but I don't always feel the urge to actively pursue it to its fullest. It's almost like there's a block there, keeping me from that final step that seems so natural to everyone else."

I take a shaky inhale and glance away. "There were many nights where Ty and I would kiss for hours and never go any further. Part of me wanted more, but sometimes it's hard for me to cross that final line, no matter how many times I've crossed it before. I can be aroused and want sex and intimacy and everything it entails, but that final step that for so many people is the obvious conclusion is not aways the final step for me. But no matter how much I need or want it myself, I will always make sure that my partner is perfectly content and happy and satisfied."

I force myself to meet her eyes, though part of me wants to run from the room, but I want to be entirely honest with her. She's watching me carefully, but she doesn't look put off, thank the gods.

"So, you're okay with that? With me?"

She smiles and huffs a small laugh. "Yes, Bash. I'm more than happy to accept you just as you are."

I press a kiss to her forehead and she sighs contentedly. I trace my hand up and down her back in soothing circles, marveling at how perfect she is. A few more moments pass before she shifts, pulling back to look at me.

"We should probably get out of bed."

"Maybe. Eventually. There's no rush. You made it quite clear last night you weren't letting me near a horse for a couple more days, and I doubt there's little more we can glean from our notes than we already have. After all the chaos and worry we've had the last week, I think we deserve this lie-in. Perhaps even a repeat?"

Her eyes flash with interest and I don't bother holding back my grin.

"Rest up, Princess. I think we may have a busy morning ahead after all."

CHAPTER SEVENTEEN

RISSA

I should have been more careful and left long before now, but slipping out of the barracks at the crack of dawn it is. To be honest, I didn't really do anything last night to justify slinking back to my room at this hour other than drinking too much wine and making myself sleepy. Well, that and the delight I get imagining the horror on my father's face should he hear I was seen at the barracks this time of the morning. Still, I don't want too many people to see me. My reputation is already questionable enough in some circles.

I shuffle around the corner of the building, keeping my head low in the hopes no one notices me. I'm looking down when I stumble into someone who staggers back with an all too familiar "oof."

"We've got to stop meeting this way," Miles says, his voice far too cheerful for this early hour.

I raise my gaze to him. Of all the people to discover me sneaking out of the barracks, it had to be him.

"What are you doing out here so early?" he asks.

"I . . ." I glance over my shoulder and motion vaguely. "I was . . . you know."

His eyes scan me over, clearly noting that I'm wearing the same dress I wore last night when I joined him for dinner. His smile is tight but not unfriendly as he nods.

"Ah." He glances away, a little color rising in his cheeks. "I see."

I bristle, straightening my shoulders. "I can go where I please, when I please."

"I never said you couldn't."

"There was a soldier who had possible information. We were talking."

"Talking."

"Yes. Just talking. Well, not just talking, there were other . . . activities, but you have no right to ask after them."

"I didn't ask."

"We aren't an exclusive thing, you and I."

His mouth tips into a half smile, his eyes taking on a mischievous shine. "I know."

"And, well, I . . . You know that I . . ."

I have no idea why I'm so flustered. I've never felt the need to explain myself before, no matter who caught me, but something about Miles's calm acceptance is off-putting.

He places a gentle hand on my arm. "Klarissa, take a breath."

I suck in air almost against my will.

"I told you when we met that I didn't judge you. That hasn't changed. I don't need to know what you were doing in the barracks this early, who you were with prior to this, or what you did with them. My initial inquiry was little more than an attempt at small talk."

I swallow, wanting desperately to look away from his gentle eyes, but I'm unable to find the willpower to do so. "So you don't care if I spent the night with someone else? With another man? Despite everything that has been happening between us?"

He chuckles, the color in his cheeks rising. "Ah, well, I didn't say I didn't care." He raises his sheepish gaze to meet mine. "I would never try to leash you or keep you from doing what you want, but I can't say I'm not a little jealous thinking of you with someone else."

I open my mouth to speak but he cuts me off. "As you said, we're not exclusive. I have no right to demand anything of you, let alone fidelity. I enjoy what we have."

I take a shaky breath and manage a nod. "Would you want to be exclusive?"

His eyes sparkle as they meet mine. "Would I love to be able to call the wittiest, kindest, most beautiful woman in Elodia mine? Absolutely." A laugh bubbles out of me and he grins. "But I'll never demand it, and I never want you to feel pressured to make any decision that isn't one-hundred percent what *you* want."

Somehow he always knows exactly the right thing to say, and my racing heart calms a little under his reassurance.

"So, may I inquire as to *your* reason for being out and about this early?" I say, happy to turn attention away from myself.

"Ah, well, I was up late researching, and I've found a brisk walk in the morning air a good way to wake myself up."

I quirk an eyebrow. "Some people drink coffee or a strong tea."

He chuckles, his eyes gleaming bright. "I'm sure I'll end up with a good, strong cup of coffee before long, but nothing beats a bit of exercise." He pauses, tilting his head. "I don't suppose you'd like to join me for a cup of coffee? It seems we both may have had late nights."

As much as I want to accept his offer, I shake my head. "I actually need to get back to my room and prepare for the day. Besides, I don't care much for coffee. I'm more of a tea person. I can recommend a good one, if you'd like. A tea that is. I have several brews of my own."

"Perhaps on another morning we can share a cup of tea. Could we could meet later today, though? I have suspicions I'd like to share with you regarding my research."

"Oh?" I perk up a bit. After a few days of not learning much on any front, some useful information would be refreshing. Ty is starting to fall back into his discouraged slump.

"Indeed," Miles says with a nod. "I reached out to a friend of mine who knows more about *Naturcræft,* and he sent me some books from his personal collection. I believe I've found the entries that might appeal to you the most, but I think with a little coffee and a fresh mind, I should have more specific details by, let's say, lunch? Noon, perhaps? Would that work for you?"

I nod. "That would work perfectly. I guess I'll see you then."

He smiles and bows slightly from the waist, never taking his eyes from mine. "I'll count the minutes."

I refuse to acknowledge the way my heart flutters in my chest as he resumes his walk. I will not fall in love with a priest.

THE MORNING DRAGS MORE THAN NORMAL, DESPITE MY BEST efforts to keep myself busy. I catch up with all my correspondence, look over and add details to my ongoing notes, and even manage to finish reading a novel I started a few days ago. Even then, I find myself pacing my room, watching the clock tick down to an acceptable time for me to appear in the priest's quarters for our lunch.

When the clock finally drags its hands to a few minutes before noon, I practically run from my room. I'm so caught up in my thoughts of what Miles has to share—I'm definitely not thinking about the warmth of his lips, always tasting of honey for some reason—I almost run straight into someone.

"Ah, Lady Klarissa," a deep voice says, forcing my attention up into a pair of familiar brown eyes. "I was hoping to run into you."

It takes me a moment to realize that the soldier standing in front of me is the one whose bed I slept in last night. My cheeks heat slightly at the reminder that I snuck out this morning while he was sleeping. I steel myself, ready for his chastisement or questions, though I have time for neither.

"It's good to see you again, but I am actually quite nearly late for a meeting."

He frowns. "Don't worry, I won't keep you. I just wanted to pass this on." He withdraws a few folded pieces of paper from his pocket and holds them out. "We got new reports this morning I thought might interest you."

I accept the papers, hesitating a moment before slipping them into my dress pocket. Part of me wants to look them over right away, but I also want to make this conversation as brief as possible so I can get to my—Ty's—priest. For business reasons.

"Thank you. I'll be sure to look them over as soon as possible."

The soldier nods, glancing around a little nervously. "I'll need them back."

I nod once, sharply. "Of course. I will get them to you this afternoon." He scowls and I add quickly, "Well before dinner, I assure you."

He relaxes a bit and manages a slight nod. "That'll be fine."

I offer him a smile. "Well, if you'll excuse me, I really do have somewhere I need to be."

I offer him a parting nod and brush past him. I don't bother looking back to see if he's watching me. I walk a little faster than usual, so I'm a little out of breath when I arrive outside Miles's room.

"I apologize if I'm late," I say, sliding inside.

Miles gives me an amused look. "You are exactly one minute late."

A glance to the little clock on a side table confirms that it is indeed a minute past noon. "I'm sorry. I was stopped on my way here and—"

He cuts me off with a laugh. "It's fine. I won't hold one minute against you. Our lunch just arrived, anyway."

He gestures to the table behind him and I only then notice the small lunch spread of fresh fruits, sandwiches, cheeses, and a pitcher of juice.

"Why don't we enjoy the delectable dishes sent up by the kitchen, and then I'll share what I learned? It might be best to hear it all on a full stomach."

I smile and nod, taking my seat as Miles passes me a plate. Once we both have plenty of food, he joins me. We pass the next several minutes in light conversation that somehow settles any nerves I have. When we've both eaten our fill, Miles clears the table, returning with a well-worn book.

"Should I prepare myself for good news or bad?" I ask, eyeing the book as he settles into his chair.

"I suppose that rather depends," he replies with a shrug.

"If I'm right about the spell, it's a nasty thing, which isn't good, but then at least you'll know what you're up against."

I hum my agreement. "You're quite sure you've narrowed down the spell?"

"I'm afraid so," he says, something heavy in his voice. "I couldn't find much about it in my own books, but I unfortunately found a good bit of information in this one."

He places the book face up on the table and I squint down at it, barely able to make out the faded title. When I do, I raise my eyes to his solemn face.

"That looks like Old Elodian for 'forbidden,'" I say, tracing the curling letters. "Is this a book of dark magic?"

"It's not far from it," he confesses, opening the text to a bookmarked page. "Magic isn't necessarily evil by nature, but this book focusses on spells and potions that were commonly seen as . . . less than good. The particular spell in question had good uses, but it became too easily twisted into something darker."

He turns the book toward me so I can better see the pages. There's a lot of text in the older dialect of Elodian with a few illustrations, but nothing means much to me. My Old Elodian is rusty at best. Thankfully, Miles is quick to explain.

"The spell was originally crafted with good intent. It's a sharing spell. It allowed the users to share certain aspects such as health, strength, and similar attributes. The main person drawing the energy was referred to as the caster and the person sharing the energy was the conduit. When used alongside magic as we know it, called *Faecræft* here, the spell even allowed the users to exchange and share that magic. It was used by mages and soldiers in battles. The spell would allow soldiers to draw from a magical conduit off the battlefield should the caster's own strength start to wane. It also allowed them to heal faster if they were wounded."

"That really doesn't sound too bad. I suppose it was forbidden because of people who abused it? I assume many people drew too much power and potentially harmed the other."

"Well, it was supposed to be a mutual spell, meaning that both people could draw from each other to help maintain the balance between them. When the spell was cast in two parts, one couldn't take advantage over the other, but the spell was altered slightly so that balance could be thrown off. If the spell was cast without the full consent or knowledge of the conduit, the power lay solely in the hands of the caster. Of course, the flow back and forth couldn't be entirely cut off, but the conduit had no control over when that flow would come and go, often leaving them weak and at risk, suffering the ill-effects with no true benefit."

I pull the book closer, glaring down at the pages. "That does sound a lot like what's happening to the king and Amarelia." I focus on an illustration in the bottom right corner of a what looks like a vial filled with small items. I tap it with my finger. "Is this how the spell is controlled?"

"Yes. The ingredients are all placed in a container of some sort and kept on the caster. They draw their power from this token."

I raise my gaze to meet Miles's. "Does the book say how to break an unwanted bond? If we find the token and break it, does the spell break as well?"

He nods grimly, leaning forward to turn the page. A large skull takes up a good potion of the top left corner, and all the blood rushes from my face.

"Miles," I whisper, working hard to keep my voice steady. "Please tell me this doesn't say what I think it does."

He sighs, looking away. "If the spell is broken by force, if we merely break the token, the conduit whose power is being drawn will face unwanted consequences. In some cases they survive, but they have to be strong."

"But the king isn't strong," I manage, emotion creeping into my voice. "If the spell is broken by force, he won't survive it."

Miles places his hand over mine.

"There are ways to end the spell so harm doesn't come to anyone," he replies, his voice soft. "The spell is not infinite, growing weaker until it eventually fades. It should wear off after a few days if it's not fed."

"Fed? What does that mean?"

"There's a catalyst in the spell contained in the token that ties the caster to the conduit, usually blood, bone, hair, or some other physical piece of them." I make a face and he nods. "It's not pleasant."

"Does that mean Amarelia had been stealing literal pieces of my uncle?"

"She would have to."

I shake my head. "There's no way she could get that close to him. She's a stranger. Even as a fiancée to Ty, there's no way she could gain access to him."

"Then she must be working with someone close to the king who does have access."

My mind spins as I run through a mental list of everyone that could be. Doctor Adbar would be the most obvious, but I can't make myself believe he would commit treason of this level. He treated me as a child. There are guards posted at all times, but they would have a list of approved visitors. Or maybe it was one of the guards. I feel sick, on the verge of hurling up my lunch, when a gentle squeeze to my hand draws me from my thoughts. I look over at Miles and take a shaky breath.

"Are you okay?" he asks, giving my hand another squeeze.

I shake my head. "No. Not even a little bit, but I can't focus on that right now. I need to figure out who's helping her." I take a deep breath and force myself to focus. "Does the book say if the—what did you call it?—the catalyst has to be fresh? Is her accomplice sneaking in on a regular basis?"

"It's strongest if the catalyst is, uh, fresh, for lack of a better term, but it doesn't have to be. It wouldn't take much —a single hair, a drop of blood, a little salvia."

"So somewhere in this castle, someone might be keeping a stash of . . ." I trail off with a shake of my head, unable to actually voice the words.

"It seems like the most probable solution."

"Okay, so we have to find a way to make the spell run its course. Then the king is free, Amarelia is exposed, and Ty can marry Freya, assuming she's actually alive."

Miles takes a deep breath and meets my eyes. My heart sinks and I blink back tears.

"That's it. That's all we have to do. Right?"

"The spell was never meant to be used long-term," he says slowly, carefully. "Long-term use wears down the conduit's body. The only thing that keeps the conduit from . . . fading is the mutual effects they receive. Even if the spell runs its course, the king was already so weak—"

"Don't say it."

"—he's not likely to survive once it's gone."

A small sob breaks free, and Miles scoots his chair closer to mine so I can feel his heat.

"I'm so sorry, Klarissa."

He loops his arm around me, and I allow myself to be

drawn to his side, resting my head on his shoulder. I permit myself a few minutes to gather myself, and Miles doesn't rush me. Once I feel steadier, I straighten and clear my throat.

"So that's it then. We simply must find out who Amarelia is working with and make our plan so everything is in place for Ty to take the throne."

"I'll keep looking through my books and see if I can find a counter-spell of some sort that can help stabilize the king."

"Good. And say a prayer to the gods we can find Freya in time." I stand, smoothing my hands over my dress. The papers my solider friend gave me on my way here crinkle and I withdraw them.

"What's that?" Miles asks, standing and stepping to my side.

"Oh, it's probably nothing just . . ." I pause, scanning the paper. " . . . a report."

I scan quicker, my heart picking up its pace. At least my embarrassment this morning was worth something.

"Klarissa? Is it good news?"

I raise my eyes to meet Miles's. "It might be. I'm sorry, but I really need to go speak to Ty."

I'm already halfway out the door when I turn back to Miles. "Thank you for lunch and for . . . everything."

His smile is sincere as he replies. "Anything for you."

Warmth flutters in my chest as I return his smile and rush to find Ty.

CHAPTER EIGHTEEN

TY

I don't know what the duke's plan is, but judging by his most recent correspondence, he's undoubtedly up to something. I only wish I could figure out what it is. It might be nothing, but concentrating on what he's doing serves as a good distraction from everything else.

My door swings open and I sigh, not even bothering to look up. As much as I could use a break from these letters, I refuse to act like Rissa's presence is welcome. If I treat her interruptions as a good thing, she'll never stop.

"Knock, Rissa. You could at least pretend to respect me."

"Look at this," Rissa says, ignoring me as she crosses my room.

"Why? What have you dug up now?" I mumble, narrowing my eyes at a particularly oddly worded line of text in the letter. It has to mean *something*.

She slaps a random report in front of me on top of the paper I'm studying. "Read it and you'll see."

I glare up at her. "I was working on—"

"Whatever that was doesn't matter." She taps the report. "Read it, Ty."

I sigh and pick up the paper, knowing when she gets in one of these moods, there's no use resisting. Besides, I really do need a break. My brows knit together as I scan the paper, reading over the information. Partway through I freeze, my eyes widening as my mouth drops open. My heart rate picks up, and I read over the details again, sure I'm misreading something. When I'm positive I'm not hallucinating, I raise my eyes to hers. She grins and I swallow, reading it one more time just to be sure it hasn't somehow changed in the last few seconds. When I reach the end again, a laugh on the verge of hysteria bubbles out. I stand, needing to move, and toss the paper on my desk as I wipe tears from my eyes.

"Are you okay?" Rissa asks, placing a hand on my shoulder.

"He's alive," I gasp, leaning forward and bracing myself on the back of a nearby chair as fresh waves of relief wash over me. "Bash is alive!"

She grins. "That's what I thought, too, but there's more to it than that." I shoot her a puzzled look, and she steps around me to grab up the paper. "There was more than one person. It says there were twenty-one people killed."

I wave her off. "Bash could kill that many on his own."

"I know he could, but he didn't." She holds out the paper. "Look again."

I accept the paper, reading back over it. "I don't— Wait!"

"You see it, don't you?" she says. "Most of the people were killed by a trained hand, but some were a little sloppier, and one person seems to have mysteriously drowned, despite no major water source being found in the room."

I raise my gaze from the paper, hope bursting so strongly in my chest it hurts.

"There's also a witness report from the kitchen staff," she says, pulling out another piece of paper, though she doesn't hand it over. "They were surprisingly tight-lipped about the whole thing, but they confirmed a man and a woman were involved in whatever went down."

I laugh again, shaking my head. "They're both alive. They're together, damn it! They faked their deaths, just like you said, and now they're taking out the *draíochta* together." I look over at Rissa. "Where's this again?"

"Bellshire."

The word has barely left her mouth before I'm flying across the room into my bedchamber. She follows and nearly gets hit by a pair of trousers I toss toward the bed.

"What are you doing?"

I pause long enough to give her a puzzled look. "Going to Bellshire to bring home the people I love the most in the whole world—no offense—so I can save magic and live happily ever after." I turn back to my wardrobe. "Either help pack or get out."

Rissa crosses the room and places a hand on my shoulder. "You can't do that."

I tense beneath her touch, jerking away. "Of course I can."

"No, you can't, for multiple reasons." I ignore her, continuing to grab things from my wardrobe, but she keeps talking. "One, Bellshire is several days away and this attack happened nearly a week ago. By the time you get there, they will be long gone. I doubt they're lingering at the scene of the crime. Two, if you leave the palace with no notice, it will raise suspicion. There's no telling how Amarelia will react."

I spin to face her, trying hard to rein in my anger. "I don't give a fuck about how Amarelia reacts."

"Ty," she says softly.

"I have to go to them," I say, practically pleading.

"Ty."

I grab a shirt and shove it into a bag, avoiding looking at her. "They have to know I still love them. I have to bring them back. I have to marry Freya." I pause, looking up at Rissa. "Right?"

She shakes her head and my chin trembles against my will.

"I have to, Rissa. I *have* to."

She takes a tentative step closer. "I spoke to Miles, and he's figured out the details of the spell."

Hope and fear war for dominance in my chest, and I can't breathe. "What?"

"There's a lot to it, which I can explain in a moment, but essentially, that spell may be all that is keeping your father alive. If she breaks it or doesn't replenish it, your father won't survive to the Fae moon, if he makes it an hour."

Fear wins out and pain ripples through me as my chest tightens.

"Amarelia is definitely working with someone in the palace, and until we can figure out who, we can't trust anybody. We have to figure this out before we take any steps to bring Freya back."

I squeeze my eyes shut and focus on my breathing. In. Out. In. Out. Gods, I need Bash. He's the only one who can calm me.

"Additionally, if Amarelia and her supporters suspect Freya is still alive, they won't hesitate to go after her. We draw attention to her, and it could mean her death."

I shake my head furiously, staggering back a step as the world around me spins. I force the fear aside and allow anger to take its place.

"No. No. NO!"

My voice echoes around the room, but Rissa doesn't

flinch, not even when I turn and punch the wardrobe door so hard my knuckles split open. All my previous elation is well and truly gone, and I fall forward, pressing my forehead to the wardrobe door, ignoring the stinging in my hand. My shoulders shake as tears overtake me.

"It's not fair," I mumble. I turn to her. "It's not fair!"

"I know," she whispers, crossing the space between us and pulling me into a hug. I lean forward, resting my head on her shoulder. "At least this is good news. You know they're alive, and we can work on a plan to get Freya back to Rosana before the Fae moon. We still have a few weeks. We'll find a way. We'll figure out who we can trust and come up with an excuse to leave the palace that won't raise suspicion. I promise."

I allow myself my sorrow for another moment before I pull back. "Since I can't hunt them down right now, I need to find something I *can* do. What did Miles discover about the spell?"

Rissa takes a seat on the edge of my bed and I join her. She gives me the details Miles discerned from his book and shares her suspicions. None of it is good.

"Who could be helping Amarelia?" I ask, shaking my head in disbelief that anyone close to my father would be willing to betray him this deeply. "She may have my mother won over, but I know there's no way Mother would harm him. Not if she knew the risks."

"Maybe she doesn't know the risks." I shoot Rissa a glare and she adds quickly, "Not that I believe it's her, but if it was, perhaps she didn't know what she was agreeing to? That could be true of anyone. Maybe whoever is helping Amarelia doesn't know what her plan is. Or maybe she has something over them, forcing their hand."

"Maybe," I concede, but I can't quite bring myself to

believe it. "How did she get that kind of information all the way in the Rebel Isles, though? No, I think whoever she's working with has been on her side for far longer than we suspect."

"Are any of your father's guards new? They would have access to him on a regular basis. Maybe one is a plant."

My shoulders sink as hopelessness and guilt tug at my heart. "I really don't know. I haven't paid much attention to them of late, especially since my return. I know some are newer than others, but they're all vetted heavily before being allowed to take their positions. You don't get assigned to the king on a whim. It's a whole process."

"I'm assuming you trust Doctor Adbar?"

"With my life," I say without a moment of hesitation. "If he were in on anything, it would be against his will. Even then, I'd like to think he'd find a way to tell me."

"What about the duke? His letters are clearly coded and you admitted your interaction with him on your tour was beyond suspicious."

I shake my head. "I don't know why he would want to hurt my father. He has plenty of power and influence. He's one of the most respected men in the kingdom. He's up to something, no doubt, but I don't see any advantages for him to harm my father or magic, especially since he's been granted access to magic. I can't imagine him wanting it to fail. If he were tricking me into marrying Cress, maybe I could understand him doing something like this, but Amarelia? No."

Rissa nods, and starts to agree, but she pauses. "What about that creepy friend of his, Lord Earl what's-his-face?"

"Lord Mayberry? The Earl of East Hingling?" She nods and I shrug. "I don't like the man, and I don't like the way he spoke to or about Freya, but there's really not much to go on.

He's essentially powerless. He doesn't have magic or any sort of standing at court. He lacks influence."

"Well, then, there's always servants. We could make a list—"

I growl and stand to my feet. "This is all so pointless! It could literally be anybody! It could be servants or dukes or earls or . . . any-fucking-body! We have no motive and no real suspects and no time to figure it all out!"

Rissa doesn't seem nearly as upset as I am. She remains calmly seated on the edge of my bed, her face etched in thought as she watches me storm around my room. When she finally does speak, her voice is calm and steady.

"You're right. We need a lot more information. You need to sit down and write a list of people who would benefit the most from magic failing or from your father's death. We both know there are plenty of people who don't see you as a fit king and who were less than pleased with your previous betrothal."

I snort. "That's an understatement."

"I'll do what investigating I can among the guards and servants in the meantime. If we can make any connections between a disgruntled individual and the Rebel Isles, we can narrow our list."

"Will that be enough?"

"It will have to be. For now, at least." She stands in one fluid motion with grace befitting royalty. "I'll enlist help from Miles. I'm sure we can trust him."

"That's fine by me. He's been helpful enough so far. Maybe he can dig up a truth spell or something."

The corner of Rissa's mouth tips into a slight smile. "If anyone could, I'm sure it would be him. He's quite clever."

"You know, I had my doubts about you seducing him, but it seems your wiles are actually working in our favor."

She rolls her eyes, but her smile remains. "He would have helped us either way."

I cock my head. "Perhaps, but I still think he's rather smitten with you."

She bats her hand at me. "Oh, hush. He is not smitten. He's simply a kind mind who wants to help the Crown."

Her cheeks darken almost imperceptibly and my eyes widen in delight. "Klarissa Arabella Meadowbridge! Have you gone and fallen in love with my priest?"

She quickly turns toward the door to hide her face. "Don't be ridiculous, Tybalt. I've known the man for a matter of weeks. I have not fallen in love with him."

"Right," I tease as I follow her out of my bed chamber into my main sitting room. "You blush this hard over all the boys."

"I do not blush."

"Then why is your face darker? You're either blushing or dying, Rissa. Please let me know which one it is so I can properly prepare myself. If you're going to drop dead suddenly, I'd like to ready an alibi, or least get you out of my room so I look less guilty."

She sighs, walking over to the wall and ringing for a servant.

"What are you doing?"

"I'm ringing for tea to drink while we work. You have a list to make. I also think it would be a good idea for us to come up with a reason you need to leave the palace. That way you can go out and get your lovers."

"They're not technically both my lovers anymore." *Even if I wish they were.*

"Either way, you need Freya and Bash back here before the Fae moon. Freya, so you can marry her, and Bash so he can pull you out of your moods and keep you from doing something stupid. Going away will also likely put those who are part of whatever is going on at ease and they might be more likely to slip up with you gone."

"That's not a bad idea. With me gone, you and your priest —don't think the change in subject made me forget you're in love with him—can do some more snooping."

She pointedly ignores my side comment and nods. "Hopefully by the time you return we'll have enough of it figured out that you can wed the girl you love, save magic, and rescue the kingdom from impending disaster."

"Well, when you put it like that, we should definitely get to work."

CHAPTER NINETEEN

BASH

Despite initially planning to leave after two days, Freya manages to convince me to put off our departure for three. We spend most of the first day in my bed, Freya tucked against me as we go over our plan. Against her protests, I spend the next two days moving around the small space, partially to prove to her that I really am fine and partially to prove it to myself.

I'm admittedly stiff the first day back on the road, and it doesn't take Freya long to pick up on it. I guess I'm not as good at hiding my injuries as I'd like to believe. She makes us take more breaks than I think are necessary, but in the end, I appreciate being able to take it easy.

It's not until we're on our third day of traveling with constant breaks I realize Freya is purposefully slowing our journey for more than my healing. My suspicions are confirmed the next day when we she suggests stopping for the night in Copperville, a small town mere hours from her own.

"I'm pretty sure we can make it all the way to East Hingling before sundown," I counter, looking at the sky.

Freya shakes her head, refusing to meet my eyes. "I don't think we should risk it. Your leg is still healing."

"My leg is fine. We've barely had to stop today."

"Still, we'd be arriving so late in the day, and—"

"Why don't you want to go home?"

Her gaze snaps to mine. "What?"

"What are you avoiding?" My muscles tense and my grip on the reins tightens. "Are you safe to go home? Because if there's anyone there who hurt you—"

"It's nothing like that," she says quickly. "I promise. You don't have to go in and slaughter half the town."

"I will if I have to. Just say the word."

She smiles. "I know, but I promise you, it's unnecessary." She sighs, staring off at the road ahead. "It's . . . complicated. I'm honestly just stuck in my head. I'm probably over-thinking everything."

"Want to talk it through?"

She hesitates but ends up shaking her head. "Not right now. Maybe after a little rest and some dinner." She glances over at me. "If that's okay."

"Of course it's okay. I'll give you whatever you need."

Her smile returns, soft and gentle around the edges. "Thank you."

Half an hour later our horses are safely boarded and we're pushing through the crowd at the local tavern. Copperville isn't a very large town known for any sort of commerce, so I'm assuming most of the patrons are locals. This is confirmed when I inquire about renting a room for the night.

"I've only got two," the proprietor says, sounding weary,

"but they're both available if you want them. Only one has a bath, though it costs extra to have it filled and emptied."

"We'll take the one with the bath," I reply, pulling coins from my pocket. "I'll pay extra if you can make sure the water is warm."

The man shifts his gaze between us before nodding and accepting the coins. "Aye. Fine." He pulls a key from a drawer and passes it to me. "It'll take Beth a bit to heat the water and fill the tub, so you might as well eat while you wait."

"Very well. We'll take two meat pies and whatever you recommend to drink with them."

The man nods, taking more of my coins and promising to send us the pies when they're ready. I guide Freya through the crowd to a table off to the side. A minute or so later, a woman arrives with two small meat pies and two mugs of ale.

"I don't suppose you're ready to tell me what's bothering you about going home?" I ask, taking a big bite of my pie.

She sighs, staring off aimlessly into the crowd. "You'll think I'm being ridiculous."

"I promise I won't."

She offers me a weak smile, eating while she considers her words. "I only wonder if I'll be welcome."

I frown. "Why?"

She shrugs, poking at her pie.

"Freya, what is it?"

"My parents were thrilled when my match with Ty was made. My village didn't have a lot of prospects and being allowed marry a prince was obviously a great honor." She raises her eyes to mine. "Going home admits I failed, and I don't want my parents to be disappointed in me."

"Surely they'll understand. None of this was your fault."

"Probably." She goes back to poking at her pie. "They

were always supportive of me growing up. They both wanted a big family, but my mom struggled to have kids. Out of all her pregnancies, I'm the only one who made it, and my birth almost killed her. My father is the oldest son, so the pressure was on him to provide male heirs to take over the farm, but all he got was me."

I tense. "If your father ever treated you like you were any less—"

"No, Bash," she says quickly, cutting me off. "He never did. In fact, he always assured me I was more than enough and was worth more than a dozen sons. He taught me everything about the farm and let me help as much as I wanted. Though maintaining the farm is a job meant to be shared among the extended family, I always felt bad when we had to lean on my cousins for help. We all live close together, my family residing in the main farmhouse with my grandparents until they passed."

I nod as she eats more. "And your mother? Was she supportive?"

"Very." She washes down her food with a swig of ale. "She tended to stay inside due to poor health, content to cook, sew, and other indoor activities. She taught me whatever skills I wanted to learn, but what I enjoyed the most were the times we would sit side by side reading together."

"So your mother is where you get your love of reading?"

She smiles in a way that softens everything about her. "Yeah. Like most small villages, our school only taught us the basics of history, math, and reading until we reached our teens, but my mother always encouraged me to read and learn more on my own. We didn't have a lot of books, but we truly treasured the ones we did."

"From everything you've said, I can't imagine them not being happy to see you home and well."

She takes a deep breath and releases it slowly, focusing on eating and refusing to meet my eyes.

"What aren't you saying?"

She swallows, taking a moment before she carefully raises her eyes to mine. "I haven't heard from them since the palace guards escorted me away. I know there were some instructions from the queen, but I'm their only daughter, their only child. How could they not fight back more? Why didn't they try to reach out after I left? I haven't received a single letter or anything."

"You know as well as I do how unreasonable the queen can be," I offer, hoping I can chase away some of her distress. "Maybe they fully intended to reach out, but never got the chance. You weren't at the palace long before you left on your tour, and you were sent away within days of your return."

She shrugs, poking at her dinner. "Maybe." She sighs and offers me a weak smile. "I'm sure I'm overthinking things. I need to distract myself."

"Maybe I can help with that. Did you ever hear the story about when Ty shot Cressida's father with an arrow?"

Her eyes brighten and I dive into some of my favorite stories of Ty. We've finished our dinner and I'm on my third tale when someone arrives to let us know our room is ready. Some of Freya's nervousness returns as we make our way up the stairs to our room, but I'm determined not to let her get lost inside her head.

Our room is on the right of the creaky staircase, and even though it's large enough to house a metal tub in addition to a bed, side table, and a changing screen, it's not particularly spacious. In fact, there's barely any room left. Freya doesn't seem to care, easing down on the edge of the bed with a groan that shoots straight to my groin.

"I am ready to get out of these boots," she mutters as she unlaces them. She toes them off and suddenly I have the urge to see much more than boots removed. Despite our heated moment a week ago now, we haven't done much more than touch casually with the occasional kiss. I appreciate taking it slowly, but right now I think I want a little more. Then again, she might not.

I quickly remove my own shoes as Freya digs through her bag for bathing supplies. I swallow and slowly start to unbutton my shirt, my heart pounding against my ribcage. I'm over halfway done when Freya looks up, her eyes going wide as her mouth drops open. I work to keep my breathing steady as I finish the last of the buttons, Freya's eyes tracking every small moment. I shuck my shirt to the side and immediately begin to undo my pants, letting them drop a moment later. Only one more piece of clothing, and I'll be entirely naked in front of her for the first time.

"I thought, perhaps, we could share the bath," I say, forcing a confident smile. "If you want, of course. I thought it could make for a nice distraction."

She swallows, her eyes taking me in. "I do. Want, that is. I mean . . . Yes. We can share. I'd like the distraction."

"Good."

I tuck my thumbs into the waistband of my underwear, meeting her eyes, and tug them down before I can talk myself out of it. Freya inhales sharply as she takes me in. A smirk curves my lips, and I place my hands on my hips, practically preening beneath the heat of her gaze.

"See something you like, Princess?"

She schools her features and shrugs. "I've seen better."

A snort escapes me as the corners of her mouth twitch to hold back a smile.

"You don't have to lie. I know I look good." I take a step

closer and notice with delight how her eyes darken. "Of course, if you've changed your mind, I can always get dressed and take my turn in the bath later. What'll it be?"

She takes an unsteady breath, her gaze flicking between me and the tub. For a moment my confidence wavers. Maybe she doesn't want to do this. But then she steps closer to me, her lips parting as her eyes meet mine. My heart stutters to a stop when she places a hand on my chest.

"Help me undress?"

"Gladly."

My hands move almost of their own accord, finding their way to hem of her shirt and pulling it over her head. The rest of her clothing and undergarments are simple and don't take much work to remove and cast aside. Before I've even had time to consider what we're doing, she's as naked as I am. Reality crashes in around me and I stumble back, closing my eyes for moment.

"Bash?" Freya says hesitantly. "Are you okay?"

I slowly open my eyes and take her in. Gods. She's gorgeous. Heat stirs low in my gut. It's not often I feel this way, this intense desire, this . . . need, but I do want this. I really, *really* want this. I cross the distance and pull her to me, my lips crashing against hers. She gasps into my mouth and I swallow the sound eagerly. My hands settle on her waist, fingers digging into the softness of her flesh, desperate to keep her close. My body feels like it's on fire everywhere our bodies are touching, and I need more, more, *more*.

I pull back and look down at her. "Bed. Now," I growl.

"But the bath—"

"—can wait. Get on the bed, Princess, and spread your legs for me."

She whimpers, but obeys, stumbling across the small space to the bed. Once she's in position, I take a moment to admire the work of art before me. Her tangles of red-brown hair spill out across the pillow and her swollen lips are parted as she looks up at me. She's made of thick, luscious curves that I want to bury my face in. How did I manage to resist this woman for so long?

I quickly cross to her and kneel on the bed between her legs, pushing them further apart with my knees. She makes a small sound but doesn't fight me. Gods, she's so ready for me. I lean forward and stop inches from her lips.

"You going to be good for me, Princess?"

She nods and manages a breathy "yes" that sends more heat surging through me.

"Good girl." I press a quick, hard kiss to her mouth. "If you want to stop at any moment say the word."

She nods, and I shift my position, grabbing her waist. In one smooth motion, I sit up, tugging her with me. She inhales sharply as I adjust her position so her legs are over my shoulders. I bury my face between her legs, devouring her heat. Despite the factors fighting against it, she's delicious and I can't get enough. I have little to no idea what I'm doing, but judging by the delectable sounds she's making, I'm doing it well. I press in harder, alternating between sucking and licking and she cries out, attempting to muffle her sounds with her hand as she thrusts against me.

I pull back, running my tongue across my lips as I look down at her.

"I want to hear you. I want you to call out my name so loudly that everyone in the tavern below us knows that tonight you're mine." She whimpers and I tighten my left hand on her waist while my right hand trails down her leg. "You are mine, aren't you?"

She nods fervently.

"What was that? I couldn't quite hear you." I punctuate

my words by slipping two fingers inside her and she cries out. "Who do you belong to right now, Princess? Say my name."

"Bash! Bastion!" she keens, arching into my touch and driving my fingers deeper. "Gods, Bastion!" I crook my fingers and she keens again. "Bastion!"

I grin. "Good girl."

I slip my fingers out and replace them with my tongue. She continues screaming my name, and I adjust my movements according to her reactions. I shift to allow myself better access, and my erection brushes against her lower back, sending desire shooting through me. But now is not the time for my pleasure. Not yet. I push aside the heat pooling low in my gut and move my mouth to suck her breasts while my fingers press inside her. A moment later, she clenches around me, crying out with more force than she has so far as she arches beneath me. I don't still my fingers or my mouth until she settles, trembling and breathing hard.

I slide my hand from between her legs and press a gentle kiss to her lips. I settle back so I'm kneeling over her and I grip my cock, giving it a stroke.

"Now it's my turn."

She watches me, cheeks pink, lips open.

"Do you need help?"

I chuckle and shake my head as I stroke myself. Gods, it's been a while.

"I just need you to lie there and let me look at you." My hand picks up its pace and it's everything I can to not come yet. "Who do you belong to right now?"

"You."

"That's right. And do you know what I do with what's mine?"

She bites her lip and shakes her head.

"I mark it."

A moment later, I'm spilling across her. Her pupils flare and a small moan escapes her as I work every last drop out onto her bare skin. When I'm spent, I'm tempted to collapse next to her, but instead I carefully slip from the bed.

"Time for that bath."

I sweep her into my arms and she squeaks in surprise, instinctively throwing her arms around my neck. I carefully take her over to the tub and set her down in the water. I turn to fetch her soaps and she calls after me.

"Aren't you joining me?"

I smile, glancing at her over my shoulder. "You couldn't keep me out."

CHAPTER TWENTY

FREYA

Today I go home for the first time in months. Last night, Bash provided a decent distraction, but now it's time to face the day. Bash shifts beside me in the bed, his eyes fluttering open. The bed is small, barely big enough for two adults, so I'm pressed right up against him, both of us still naked. It wasn't a problem last night, but maybe he'll feel differently this morning with everything a little calmer. Relief washes over me when a smile curves his lips.

"Good morning," he says, his voice rough from sleep.

"Is it?" He frowns and I add, "A good morning, I mean."

His expression softens as he brushes a gentle hand across my cheek. "I'm waking up with you in my arms, so it's a good morning from where I am."

A soft smile sneaks onto my lips, but Bash must still be able to read my concerns and nerves.

"I know you're worried about your family's reactions today, but I'll keep you safe. If it's even half as bad as you're imagining, I'll whisk you away. We can find the information we need without having any interaction with your family." He slips an arm around me, tucking me against his chest. "I've got you."

I sigh and snuggle closer to him, relishing the comfort he provides.

"I'm sure it'll be fine. I'm just up in my head." I absent-mindedly trace a finger across the line of his chest muscles. "I did appreciate the distraction last night."

He takes an unsteady breath. "I'm glad."

His voice sounds a little unsure. I tilt my head to look up at him, but he's not looking at me. He's staring off toward the tub, which is still filled with water since we never bothered to have it emptied.

"Bash?" I ask, sitting up. "Was last night okay?"

"What?" He looks back at me. "Yes. Of course it was." I keep staring at him and he sighs, shifting into a sitting position. "I very much enjoyed myself."

"But?"

"But I'm not sure I'm up to distracting you the same way this morning."

"Oh," I say, tension seeping from my shoulders. "That's fine."

"Really?"

I nod. "I had a lot of fun last night, and I really appreciated it, but I don't need constant sex. I'm sorry if I made it sound that way."

He shakes his head. "You didn't. I made an incorrect assumption." He cocks his head, the corner of his mouth tipping up into a smile. "You're not the only one who gets inside your own head."

I huff a laugh. "I guess not. I won't say I'd turn you down if you feel up to it another time, though."

He grins. "Good to know. Especially since I didn't really know what I was doing."

"What?"

He shrugs. "I told you I don't really feel sexual desire like most people, so while I've done that sort of thing with Ty and had the occasional misguided attempt at intimacy, you're the first with, well, that particular anatomy."

I blink at him in borderline disbelief. "Seriously?"

He shakes his head. "Ty was the first person I ever wanted to do anything with, and I never really looked closely at the reasons behind my attraction. When I attempted to move on from him, I stuck with what was familiar. It wasn't until you that I realized that I could be attracted to anyone if the feelings and connection were there."

"Well, I'm glad you figured it out, because last night was amazing. I haven't been with a lot of people, but you did extremely well."

"It's not hard to pay attention to what your partner wants and follow through." He shoots me a cocky grin. "I use that knowledge to get better every time."

A shiver runs through me and his grin grows. He leans closer so the warmth of his breath brushes across the shell of my ear as he whispers, "I will make you forget everyone else you've ever been with who didn't pleasure you like you deserve. Any satisfaction you felt with them will pale in comparison to how I will satisfy you."

A small sound escapes me and he chuckles, pulling back.

"Unfortunately, even if I wanted to, we don't have time to explore this morning. As much as I know you want to put it off, we shouldn't wait too long to get on the road."

I groan but know there's no point in fighting it. Neither of us exactly rush to get ready, however. We assume a leisurely pace dressing and packing our supplies before heading downstairs. We take our time eating a breakfast of porridge and hardboiled eggs and don't get on the road until midmorning. Even with our slow start, however, we're nearing East Hingling well before noon.

We've only been on the road a couple hours when pastures of cows start running along the roadside. The farmhouses and barns sit farther from the road, but I can still spot them from here. Bash follows my gaze to one such house.

"Does your family live this far out?"

I shake my head, adjusting the reins in my hands. "No. East Hingling is known mainly for two things: cattle and pigs. The cows need more space and therefore their farms are a little farther out from the village proper. The farms with pigs are closer to the main village. My family owns the latter."

"Do you have much contact with the cattle farmers?"

I shrug. "Some. Growing up, we went to the same school and we'd come together for market days. Beyond that, though, we didn't have much interaction. We were friendly but not really friends."

Bash nods, absorbing the information. "It sounds a fair bit nicer than what I grew up with. Moving into the barracks at the castle was a very different experience from what I was raised with up to that point."

"Were the barracks at least nice?"

Bash shrugs. "It wasn't bad."

I allow him to distract me with stories of his time training, and before I know it, we're riding into town. The road twists between rows of stone buildings. Most of them are businesses such as the post office, general store, and a haberdashery, but some are homes. My hold on the reins tightens, but Bash's steady voice never stops.

The main road widens, spilling into a circular town

square. On market days, this area would be filled with carts, but today it's quiet with only a few people milling about. The lack of a crowd doesn't stop me from being noticed, however. I find myself accidentally meeting the wide eyes of Mrs. Nellaway, the owner of the general store and certified town gossip. I offer her a weak smile, but steer purposefully away from her.

The road narrows again, and I lead Bash off a narrow side path that's even too small to be considered a road. We wind along behind the main buildings, heading out toward the farmhouses. We pass the Rollingcreek farm on the right and veer toward another cluster of homes. The small yard area in front of the main house has several chickens that scatter out of our way as we come to a stop. I take a shaky breath and look over at Bash.

"This is it," I say, my voice unsteady.

"You've got this, Freya," he says, his voice gentle and warm. "But if you decide you don't, if you can't do it, we will leave."

I manage a nod and we dismount, securing our horses before stepping up to the door. I pause, my hand hovering in midair, unable to bring myself to knock. Bash takes my other hand in his and gives it a squeeze. I take another deep breath and rap my knuckles against the wood.

"One moment! One moment!" a familiar voice calls from inside.

I'm tempted to run, but Bash holds me steady. A minute later, the door is thrown open and I come face to face with my mother for the first time in months. She inhales sharply, blinking at me in disbelief. Tears burn my eyes.

"Mama?" I say, my voice trembling.

"Oh, baby," my mother says, pulling me into a tight hug.

Bash releases my hand so I can wrap my arms around her.

I breathe in her familiar scent of woodsmoke and sugar, and suddenly I'm a child again, happy and safe. A small sob escapes me and my mother strokes my hair.

"My sweet Freya," she whispers, squeezing me tighter a moment before drawing back to look at me. "I thought I would never see you again. We heard you were dead."

Her voice cracks on the last word and guilt floods my chest.

"I'm sorry about that, Ma'am," Bash says, stepping forward with his most charming smile. "I'm afraid that was my idea. A lie constructed to keep her safe."

My mother's eyes widen and she blinks almost comically up at Bash. She looks at me, a question in her eyes, before she shakes her head and forces a small smile.

"Oh, well, I suppose we have a few things to discuss." She steps back into the house and motions us inside. "Best to do it over food."

We step inside and she shuts the door behind us. The room is well lit by several windows, but after being outside most of the day, it takes my eyes a moment to adjust. When they do, I follow my mother into the kitchen area. My four-year-old cousin, Malcom, sits in the corner playing knucklebones.

"Malcom," my mother says, already grabbing a kettle from over the stove and preparing cups of tea, "can you run and get your Uncle Jack from the far field?"

Malcom hops up from the ground with a nod and rushes away. Silence seeps over the room as Mama finishes up, heading back to the table with an assortment of light snacks and tea. I take a tentative sip, Bash following suit, but Mama continues to look at me with something akin to awe. I clear my throat, unable to stand the silence.

"So, how has the farm been?" I try.

"Good. Good," Mama says. "The money from the queen helped a lot. It's put less pressure on us and allowed us to expand the back field a bit."

Ah. The money. The reason they cut off contact. I try not to let my disappointment show, but Mama with her observant eye catches the change in my demeanor immediately.

"Of course, we would've rather had you here."

"I thought—"

I'm cut short by the door flying open and my father stumbling through the door.

"Freya?" he says, blinking at me in disbelief. No, he's blinking back tears.

"Hey, Papa," I manage with a weak smile.

He rushes forward and I find myself on my feet, falling into his familiar embrace. He holds me tight for a moment before releasing me and stepping back, his eyes scanning me over. "You seem well."

I nod, swallowing hard. "I am." My father's gaze darts to Bash and I remember we're not alone. I step back and motion to him. "This is Bastion. He's—"

"Her protector," Bash cuts in, standing and extending his hand.

My father grips it firmly. "Nice to meet you, but," he pauses, glancing briefly to Mama, "how . . . why are you here? We heard that, well . . ."

"A misunderstanding of sorts," Bash says. "Perhaps we can sit and share everything we've all been through over the past few months? Clear up everything?"

Bash gives me a meaningful look and my heart warms. My protector indeed.

We sit around the table, and Bash and I take turns sharing the events of the past couple months, starting with my initial arrival in Rosana. Of course, there are some details we leave out, but we give them more than enough information to fill in the blanks. My parents listen with care, never interrupting, but I can tell by their expressions they're concerned. Halfway through the retelling of the attack the night of the ball, my mother inhales sharply and my father takes her hands in his. When we get up to the present, I let out a long sigh.

"So, that's why I'm home. I need to see if there's anyone who has any information about the goings-on at the main estate. Ty could be in trouble."

"You mean you're not home to stay?" my mother asks, a slight tremble in her voice.

I shake my head. "Not yet, anyway. Maybe after things wrap up and depending on how things go, I might come home, if I'm wanted."

"Of course you're wanted!" Mama cries out. "Why wouldn't we want you?"

"You haven't contacted me since I left."

"The queen said you agreed to go no contact. She showed us a document signed by you that first day when they separated us stating that, moving forward, you would be taking your place as royal and leaving everything of this life behind."

My eyes widen. "I never signed anything of the sort. When they separated us all they did was go over a bunch of protocol and safety restrictions. The only thing I signed was an updated version of the marriage contract with the date moved up."

My father scoffs, shaking his head. "I told you she would never do that to us."

My mother lifts her chin resolutely. "I was going to

ignore it anyway once you were married and settled. Even the Crown couldn't keep my only daughter from me." She wilts a little. "Though, we got word you were dead before I could write my congratulations."

I reach across the table and place my hand over my parents' on the table. "Well, I'm alive and okay, and even if I don't settle back here, I want to stay in contact."

"Well, we won't be the only ones glad to have you back," Mama says with a soft smile. "You've been missed. And speaking of people who have missed you, you may want to talk to Cora."

Bash stiffens beside me but doesn't otherwise react.

"Cora?" I ask, keeping my voice steady despite the uncomfortable twist in my stomach.

Mama nods. "Since you've left, she's become quite close with Lady Mayberry."

"Lady Mayberry as in the current wife of the Earl of East Hingling?" Bash jumps in.

"Yes. She's actually quite young, despite the age of the earl."

"I've heard he like his wives young," Bash replies, his voice hard, no doubt remembering our last interaction with the man.

"Indeed," my mother agrees. "Either way, if you need an in with the estate, Cora is your most likely ally."

"We can check in with her tomorrow," I say, not ready to face her quite yet. "Tonight I want to spend time with my family."

My mother's eyes brighten and my father smiles.

"Good." My father's gaze settles on Bash. "We can all get to know your new friend."

Bash meets my father's gaze and grins, something challenging in his expression. "I look forward to meeting everyone."

My mother sighs through her nose, shaking her head, but she meets my eyes with a smile. Somehow, despite everything that's gone wrong, I think this might be going right.

CHAPTER TWENTY-ONE

RISSA

I sneak from the mailroom, four new letters in my hand, though only one belongs to me. To be fair, one belongs to Ty and I'm merely delivering it out of the kindness of my heart. Ty and I are no closer to finding someone with both means and motive to overthrow him, but I'm convinced they'll slip up eventually, which is why the other two belong to suspicious members of the court.

My mind wanders, thinking over possible suspects, so I'm not paying proper attention as I turn the corner. Too late I realize Queen Lyra is in the corridor and her disapproving gaze turns to me. I curtsey and make to run off, but she motions me closer. I discreetly shove the letters into a cleverly hidden pocket on my dress and force a smile as I approach.

"Lady Klarissa," she says, her voice clipped.

"Your Majesty." I dip into a full curtsy and hold it until she gives me a sharp nod. "What can I do for you?"

"I was about to take tea in the Eastern sunroom." She nods to a nearby door. "Join me?"

A refusal sits on the tip of my tongue, but I know my aunt well enough to know the invitation is not optional. I force another tight smile and incline my head.

"Of course, Your Majesty."

I allow myself to be led into the sunroom. Of all the rooms in the palace, this is one of my favorites. Vines climb the stone walls and domed glass ceiling with more plants growing along a pebbled path. Pots and planters are scattered throughout the room, flowers turning their faces to the bright sunlight streaming in. The air is filled with life that makes my magic sing, and it's almost distraction enough to push aside the nerves twisting in my gut as I take my seat across from the queen at the delicate iron table in the center of the room.

"Do you remember how when you were twelve, I believe it was, you crafted a special tea using your magic?" the queen asks as a servant pours a floral tea into her cup.

A small smile tempts my lips as my cup is filled. "I do."

She stirs a little honey and cream into her tea, and I do the same. "It was one of my favorites then and remains a favorite still. I make sure we keep it on hand."

I blink at her in disbelief as she lifts the cup to her mouth and takes a delicate sip. "It brews perfectly every time."

I quickly lift my own cup and sip the brew, relishing the way the delicate flavors of rose, bergamot, and a unique blend of my own creation tumble over my tongue. I've made it myself many times, but to know the queen also enjoys it warms me. I know better, however, than to drop my defenses entirely.

"Thank you, Your Majesty. I am honored."

"As you should be. You were a wonderful addition to the palace in your youth, and not just because you created one of my favorite teas. You were a good companion to

Tybalt all those years, the sister I was never able to give him."

There's something heavy in her voice. Few outside the royal family know how much she struggled to conceive and birth Ty. Even fewer know about her struggles and losses following his birth.

"I was happy to be here for him." I pause a moment before adding, "And I'm happy to be back, here for him now."

She nods once, taking a long sip of tea. "I suspect you were behind him finally joining us in the dining hall?"

"Yes, Your Majesty." She doesn't need to know I had to bribe and threaten him.

"Well, for that at least, I'm grateful, but I do wish you would do more."

And there's the real reason she pulled me in here. I take a moment to sip my tea before asking, "How so?"

"Joining us in the dining hall isn't enough. Tybalt is sulking like an insolent child. People, important people, are watching, and he cannot continue this ridiculous temper tantrum. It will not stop the marriage to Princess Amarelia, and the longer he puts off building a relationship with her, the weaker and more immature he looks. This will not do. I need you to push him to be better."

"What exactly is it you're asking me to do? I've encouraged him to talk to her, but I cannot force him."

"Perhaps if you were more welcoming to her, he would follow your example. You came here originally to befriend that imposter of a farm girl. I imagine befriending actual royalty would be that much easier for you, given your upbringing."

I tense, my grip on my teacup tightening. "I extended an offer of friendship to the princess. She chose not to accept."

"Try again. Try harder. And push Tybalt to try as well."

I open my mouth to speak, but apparently the queen isn't done yet.

"Do not think your reputation"—she spits the word in disgust—"hasn't reached my ears. It causes concern for your father, and it does nothing to help the Crown. Do not think it has escaped my notice that you slip back to your rooms at ungodly hours, often from the halls of our priest in residence."

My face burns, more with anger than embarrassment or shame, but it burns all the same.

"Mi—Father Finnick has been teaching me histories, Your Majesty."

She lifts an eyebrow, looking at me over the top of her teacup. "At three in the morning? I never knew you to be such a scholar. Your tutors here at the palace certainly told a different story."

I bite my tongue to keep from snapping a reply.

"You should make better use of your time here in Rosana. Otherwise, it might be best if you go home. Those associated with any misdeeds, even those of holy rank, may need to be replaced as well. The Crown has a reputation to uphold."

The threat doesn't miss, and I swallow hard, still too afraid to speak lest my unfiltered thoughts come out.

"Do we have an understanding?"

I take a deep breath and manage a tight smile. "Of course, Your Majesty."

"Very good. You are dismissed."

I still have half a cup of tea left, but I don't argue. I set my cup down and leave with a quick curtsy. Guards open the doors for me, and I shuffle out into the hall. I clench my hands at my sides, fighting back tears. I cannot get sent back to Langsworth Manor. If I do, my father will inevitably have me married off. Not to mention I'd be leaving Ty alone in a castle where someone plots against him.

I keep my cool down the long corridor while eyes are on me, but as soon as I can, I slip off to the side to get my emotions under control. Tears flood my eyes, try as I might to hold them back. I lift a shaking hand to wipe one away.

"Are you all right?"

I startle and spin around, coming face to face with Amarelia. Of all the people to find me right now.

"I'm fine," I snap, but the tremble in my voice belies my words.

She glances over her shoulder, and I realize she's not alone. And I thought my morning couldn't get any worse.

"I was about to step into the garden. Perhaps you would like to join me? You look like you could use some fresh air."

I'm on the verge of declining, but the queen's demand echoes through my mind. "Thank you. That would be nice."

I fall into step with the princess and head out into a nearby garden, her usual entourage not far behind. Once outside, she turns to them and says something in Panbrionese. They nod and step back, putting a little distance between us.

"There," she says with a small smile. "Now we can discuss things without being overheard. I imagine whatever has you so upset is something you would rather not everyone know."

"Thank you, but I really don't wish to talk about it right now. It's still . . . fresh."

She nods knowingly. "I understand." She hesitates, looking off over the garden. "Perhaps I was too short with you before, when you extended your friendship to me. You must understand how difficult it is to be here, so far from my home. Everything is quite different—the customs, the language, the food. It's a bit much. I crave things that bring me comfort, such as my ladies in waiting."

She looks back at me, the corner of her mouth tipping up into a smile. "Surely you understand as well?"

I manage a nod. "I suppose I can't say I would choose differently if I were in your position."

She nods. "Also, it is difficult not being wanted by your husband, for him to long for another."

"The whole situation with Ty is complicated."

"It always is for us royals. It is no excuse for the way I have been treated by him."

She sniffs and raises her chin indignantly. I don't bother telling her how much I disagree. Instead I try for a smile, but there's no sincerity behind it.

"I'm sure things will change."

"They should!" She huffs. "After all, his previous fiancée is dead. It is not like she is coming back."

Years of training have me biting the inside of cheek to keep myself in check. "Mm-hm."

"I'll make an excellent queen. Even Queen Lyra thinks so."

She preens and I decide that I may need to ease into this new relationship.

"Speaking of Ty, I am supposed to be meeting with him. I shouldn't keep him waiting."

She sighs and waves her hand. "Very well." I start to step away, but she perks up. "Perhaps you would be willing to meet me later for tea? I heard you like tea. Do not worry; you will not be the only one from your court. I have already invited Lady Cressida."

My nose wrinkles of its own accord, but I quickly school my features. "Cressida?"

Amarelia nods. "She's been kind to me, though I suspect it may have something to do with our arrangement. Well, less my arrangement, more my brother's, but I still feel involved."

I frown. "What arrangement?"

The princess's eyes widen. "Oh, I should not have said anything. I keep forgetting it is not known, that it should be a secret."

I tilt my head, slipping on a smile that has won many people over. I place a hand on her arm.

"Come, you can tell me. I'm *excellent* at keeping secrets."

A light blush rises on her cheeks as she meets my eyes. "I . . ." Her gaze flicks from my hand and back to my face. "I suppose I could tell you, but you must keep it a secret."

"I will lock it away with my other secrets," I promise, giving her arm a slight squeeze before removing my hand.

"All right." She glances around before leaning closer. "My brother and Lady Cressida are engaged."

After I pick my jaw up off the floor I squeak, "Engaged?"

Amarelia giggles and nods. "I know! It is probably unusual for such a match to be made, but the Duke of Brookeshire has been so kind and helpful. It is largely because of his influence, and that of the Earl of East Hingling, that I was brought here before Prince Tybalt could ruin things by marrying that commoner."

My mind spins with the new information so much I feel a little dizzy. "That is . . . something. I can see why you're keeping it secret."

"Indeed. Lady Cressida and I are to be family, even if few people know, so I must get to know her better. And you and I will be family as well though Tybalt, so I suppose I need to get to know you as well."

"We should. We definitely need that." I clear my throat and offer her a smile. "I really should get to Ty, however."

"Of course. I do not need him to hate me more for keeping you."

I offer her one last nod before I leave the garden, trying hard not to look like I'm rushing. The day may have started poorly, but finally, *finally* things may be clicking into place.

CHAPTER TWENTY-TWO

TY

I 'm fourteen pages away from the end of my novel when someone knocks on my door. I fold down the corner of the page with a sigh and push up from the couch to answer.

"Why was your door locked?" Rissa demands the moment the door cracks open.

"Maybe because someone kept coming in unannounced, and I wanted a little privacy."

She makes as face as she pushes inside, looking around. She shoots me a look over her shoulder, narrowing her eyes.

"You don't look like you were up to anything suspicious."

I roll my eyes, shutting and locking the door. "Privacy doesn't mean getting myself off. Not every time."

She crosses her arms and arches an eyebrow. "No?"

"No." I saunter over the couch and plop down, lifting the book. "I was reading." I stretch out over the couch. "And I'd like to finish."

"If that's a book recommendation from Bastion, there's

no guarantee you weren't—" She cuts off with a sharp gasp as I open the book to the marked page, lurching forward and snatching the book out of my hands.

"Hey!" I snap, jerking up and grabbing after my book.

"No. I cannot give this back," she says, putting it behind her back.

"Why not?"

"You *dog-eared* a page."

"So?"

"So? So? So you don't dog-ear pages! You are a prince! Use a bookmark."

I roll my eyes. "I didn't have one handy and didn't want to lose my place. It's not a big deal."

"I'm taking away all your books." She hesitates. "But maybe after I tell you what I discovered."

"I still think you're being needlessly dramatic, but fine. What did you discover?"

"You know how we've been looking for reasons that people might want to help Amarelia overthrow the kingdom?"

"Seeing as how my memory is still intact, yes."

"Well, would you say that becoming royalty is a good reason?"

I frown. "Who's becoming royalty?"

She grins, her eyes far too bright. "Cressida."

"What?" I say, unable to keep the disgust from my voice and likely my face. "How is Cressida of all people becoming royalty?"

"Apparently, she's engaged to Amarelia's brother. Or will be. I'm really not sure of the details."

I feel lightheaded and sink down on the edge of the couch. "That doesn't make sense. Unless . . ." I look up at

Rissa and she nods. "Somehow they roped the duke into helping with whatever this plan is by promising Amarelia's brother to Cress."

"We suspected him all along, thanks to those odd letters, but now we have a motive."

I shake my head, still not fully convinced. "We need more information. When was this engagement made? Before Amarelia came or after?"

Rissa shrugs, dropping into the chair across from me. "Not sure. I didn't really want to talk to Amarelia any longer than necessary. Why does the time of the engagement matter?"

"It could give us an idea of how long the duke has been in her pocket. Did she mention anyone else?"

Rissa pauses in thought. "The Earl of East Hingling."

Just his name makes my blood boil. "I hope he's involved so I have a reason to get rid of him." I pause. "Wait, why were you talking to Amarelia anyway? Surely you're not sleeping with her for information."

The mere thought makes my stomach turn, and judging by the look of disgust on Rissa's face, she agrees.

"Ew, no. For one she's basically a child. I do not sleep with people more than two years younger. For another, you know I don't sleep with women. A little harmless flirting here and there? Sure. But I am not interested in women that way. Everyone else is fair game, but I have enough respect for myself not to force myself into a situation I don't truly desire."

"Okay, fair, but that doesn't explain why you were talking to her."

Rissa's face falls and she refuses to meet my eyes.

"Hey, what's wrong?"

She takes a deep breath, looking down at her hands clasped in her lap. "I was leaving the mailroom when I ran into your mother. She pulled me aside for tea."

"You like tea."

Rissa lifts her gaze to mine, and I don't miss the tears glistening there. Seeing Rissa unmoored unsettles me.

"What did she say and how can I rectify it?"

"She told me I need to spend more time with Amarelia and that I need to bring you along."

"That's not unexpected, but why does that have you so upset?"

Rissa takes a slow breath. "She insinuated that if I am unsuccessful I will be sent home. She also not so vaguely threatened to send Miles home as well."

"I won't let that happen," I insist. "And not just because I need you two to help me figure out this whole mess. You're important to me, Rissa, and anyone important to you is important to me by extension. My mother may have destroyed my hope of happiness, but I won't let her take yours. I swear it."

She manages a small nod. "Thank you, Ty."

I lean against the back of the couch. "You don't have to thank me for being my normal, amazing self." She chokes on a small laugh and I grin. "Find anything interesting in the mail?"

"Actually, I forgot about it until now," she says, digging the mail out of a pocket I didn't even know was part of her dress. Women and their hidden dress pockets. I wish I could have hidden pockets.

"Here, this is yours," she says, passing me a sealed letter. She sets another to the side. "That's mine, and these belong to some of the nobles we were suspicious of, but not the

Duke of Brookeshire." She holds up the last two letters. "Should we even bother with them?"

I shrug, breaking the seal on my letter. "Up to you. I think we should focus our efforts on the duke and earl, but it might not hurt to keep others in our eyeline just in case."

She nods and slips the letters back into her pocket as I scan over mine.

"I'll take them back to my room so I can open them discreetly and seal them back. What's that letter?"

I shake my head, setting it aside. "Nothing important. Just information regarding the upcoming apple festival in Krixwell."

"Are you going?"

I shake my head. "I wasn't planning on it. Someone usually goes to represent the Crown, but with everything going on here, I should probably stick close to home."

"Wait, Ty, that could be your ticket!"

I scowl at Rissa. "Ticket to what?"

"To find Bash and Freya!"

I scoot to the edge of the couch, hope and excitement warring in my chest. "You're right! I could use it as an excuse to leave the palace!" I pause, doing calculations in my head. "If I leave within the next day or so that would give me time to take a longer route to cover more ground while still arriving in time to avoid suspicion."

I jump up from the couch and head to my desk, pulling a map of Elodia from the bottom drawer. I flatten it over the desktop, and Rissa joins me, peering over my shoulder.

"We know they were here, in Bellshire," I mumble pointing to the location on the map. "Krixwell is over here." I tap on the second location, shaking my head. "They're far away, but maybe if we go up this way"—I trace my finger up a path in an arc, veering west before heading back east to Krixwell—"I might be able to find out more information."

"That's good plan. It's highly unlikely they'll still be in that exact area, but maybe you can find where they went next."

I look at Rissa. "I might actually find them." A laugh bubbles out, but my joy is quickly extinguished. "First I have to convince my mother to let me go."

Rissa's face falls. "Want me to accompany you?"

I sigh, shaking my head. "No, especially since you're out of favor with her at the moment. This needs to be me, and I should do it now."

She nods and heads over to my couch.

"What are you doing?"

"I'm going to read your book and then find you a proper bookmark."

"Fine," I say, walking toward the door. "Make sure you put it back when you're done. I'm almost to the end, and I will hunt you down if it's not here when I return."

She waves me off and mumbles something I don't catch. I don't push her, and I head out to find my mother. It doesn't take long. She's tucked away in one of her usual spots—a sitting room off the main garden. When I enter, she looks up at me from a piece of paper covered in writing, her eyes widening slightly in surprise.

"Tybalt, what brings you here?" she asks, setting the paper next to her on the couch.

"I received this reminder about the upcoming festival in Krixwell," I say, handing her the invitation. She narrows her eyes but accepts it.

"I thought it might be a good idea for me to go. You know, to show support."

She frowns. "I am not sure now is the right time for you to go off gallivanting."

"It wouldn't be gallivanting," I say, hoping I keep all frustration from my voice. "It's a political trip, something perfectly normal and expected."

My mother sets the invitation on her desk and folds her hands on top, eyeing me like she can see my plan.

"Why this festival?"

I shrug, trying for nonchalance. "I've been before and enjoyed it. It's not too far from Rosana and would make a nice trip."

"Tybalt, this is not close. It's days of travel."

"There are plenty of festivals that would be much farther. Krixwell is fairly central."

"What is your real reason?"

I hesitate. This is possibly my one chance to get away and look for Bash and Freya. If I answer incorrectly, I could lose it.

"I . . . need to get out," I say, opting for a piece of the truth. "I feel like I've been trapped here since I returned from my tour."

My mother nods knowingly. "I suppose you're right. And, while a tour isn't quite in order yet, this could be a good trip for you and Amarelia."

I freeze. "Amarelia?"

"Yes," my mother says matter-of-factly. "You two have yet to be seen publicly together. This could be the perfect opportunity."

"Amarelia can't come with me."

Her gaze sharpens. "Oh? Why would that be?"

I swallow, my heart pounding. "It's not safe." My mother continues staring at me, and I can feel my freedom slipping away. "You know the chaos and danger we experienced on the tour. If Amarelia comes with me, she'll be a target. It would put her safety at risk."

"So you would be safe, but sending your fiancée with you would be a risk?"

"If you allow me to go alone, I can take a small group of guards. We could ride horseback and draw a lot less attention. Amarelia doesn't really seem like a horseback type of princess. She would require a carriage and a slew of guards. We'd stick out like a sore thumb, and those that wish to take us out could do so easily."

"Tybalt . . ." she says with a sigh.

"Besides," I cut her off, "I've figured out a less traveled path I could take to Krixwell that would require less fancy places to sleep at night. Inns, camping, and the like. Amarelia wouldn't like that very much."

My mother studies me for a moment before she releases another heavy sigh. "Fine."

Hope lights in my chest, and it takes a fair amount of willpower to keep my grin under control.

"However, I have conditions."

The hope dims, but I nod. I can handle whatever she throws at me. I have to.

"What conditions?"

"You are to treat your engagement to Amarelia like a proper royal betrothal, starting immediately. Until you leave, you are to escort her to and from dinner when she attends."

"The path I picked to be less detectable would require me to leave soon. Tomorrow, most likely."

"Very well, that leaves tonight. I expect you dressed in your best, walking into the dining hall with Amarelia on your arm."

I take a shaky breath. "I can do that."

"Good. When you return you will be seen with Amarelia as often as possible. You will walk the gardens, attend events, visit nearby villages. I think a full tour would be inadvisable at this time, but there are plenty of opportunities close to Rosana. You will dote on her, kiss her cheek, treat her like your beloved and your equal."

My stomach twists and I'm not sure which is worse—my disgust or my unease with the whole situation.

"If there is a ball, which there will be soon to celebrate your engagement, you will dance with her and look at her like she is the sun to your moon."

"There's to be a ball?"

"Of course there will be a ball. It is common to host an engagement ball when a betrothal has been finalized."

"You never threw a ball for Freya." The words slip out before I can stop them.

My mother tenses, her eyes flashing. "Freya was a commoner. The fact we allowed her to go on your spectacle of a tour was bad enough. Your arrangement with Amarelia is far more respectable and worth the honor of a ball. Her family is on their way, and as soon as they arrive the date and details will be finalized. You will welcome them as your own, and you will celebrate the uniting of our families. Do you understand, Tybalt?"

My mind spins, absorbing these details. More members of her family are arriving, and with them more possible traitors. Maybe if I told Mother my suspicion of Amarelia's treason, she wouldn't force me to do this. She could end the whole charade right now. But I know my mother well enough to know that she'll need hard proof—proof I don't have yet but will hopefully will soon.

"Do you understand, Tybalt?" she repeats, her voice sharper.

I snap from my thoughts and bow slightly from the waist. "Yes, Your Majesty."

"Good. Do not disappoint me. Now, go. I have other things that require my attention."

I bow one last time and stride from the room, keeping my head high. I will not be defeated. I will find the two people I love, and I will uncover whatever plot Amarelia has up her sleeve before it destroys my kingdom. If disappointing my mother is the price, I will happily pay it.

CHAPTER TWENTY-THREE

BASH

T he smell of breakfast meat pulls me from my sleep. It takes me a moment to orient myself, but slowly the events of the previous night float to the surface of my mind. We're at Freya's family home, sleeping in her childhood bed, which is why Freya is currently sprawled on top of me. The bed was barely large enough for one adult, let alone two, but when Freya gave me the choice between sharing it with her or sleeping in a spare room down the hall, my decision was easy. I was more surprised that her parents were okay with us sharing the room, but from what I witnessed last night, Freya's parents will always be supportive of their daughter's choices, even if I'm one of them.

I brush a quick kiss on Freya's forehead and she shifts on top of me, snuggling closer with a soft sigh. A smile curves my lips as my chest warms. I never thought I could have this, could have her, but now that I do, I will do everything I can to keep her. I close my eyes and tighten my hold. A small knock on the door a few minutes later has me tensing.

"Breakfast is ready if you two are awake," Freya's mom calls through the door. Her voice isn't much above a whisper, but it's enough for Freya to stir. She blinks up at me, and I grin at her sleepy expression. I press another kiss to her forehead before answering her mother.

"We'll be out shortly."

She doesn't reply, but her footfalls trail off down the hall. I turn my attention to Freya, who smiles up at me.

"Morning, Princess."

"Morning," she mumbles, her voice rough with sleep. She pushes up with a grunt, rolling her neck. "Sorry I slept on top of you all night."

I huff a laugh, tucking a hand behind my head as I look up at her. "I can assure you I didn't mind in the slightest."

"Still, it couldn't exactly have been comfortable. Maybe you should take another bed if we're still here tomorrow."

I frown, pushing up onto my elbows. "If you were uncomfortable, I can sleep in another bed, but I really was fine."

She glances away, biting her lip. "If you're sure I wasn't smothering you."

I push up all the way into a sitting position and lean forward to catch her chin, turning her to face me. "I'm sure."

I pull her into a kiss and she's smiling when I draw back, a gentle blush coloring her cheeks. She catches her bottom lip between her teeth, looking from me to the door with a small sigh.

"We probably shouldn't keep my mother waiting."

Reluctantly we slip from the bed and dress for the day. A few minutes later we join Freya's mother in the kitchen. She has trays in the center of the table piled high with sausage, bacon, eggs, and toast with a stack of plates and mugs nearby.

"Good morning!" she chirps with a genuine smile as we approach. "I hope you both slept okay."

"Of course we did, Mama," Freya says, kissing her mother on the cheek before taking a seat and grabbing a plate.

I sit next to her, grabbing a plate of my own. I'm filling mine with food when Freya's mom sets a pot of coffee on the table.

"If you'd rather have tea, Bastion, I can fix you a cup."

"Thank you, coffee is fine."

She smiles and takes a seat across from me. "Very well. If you change your mind, please don't hesitate to ask."

I offer her a nod and dig in. The sausage is by far some of the best I've ever had, and I tell her so.

"One of the advantages of living on a pig farm, I suppose," she says with a gentle smile. "We have an endless supply of meat, even with all the demand for our goods."

"Do you supply the palace?"

She laughs, shaking her head. "No, we don't export our meat quite that far. There are several farming villages much closer to Rosana for that. Though, I suppose if there was ever a shortage elsewhere, we definitely could. No, we mostly supply towns and cities within a few days' riding, though that does include several noble households."

I don't miss the note of pride in her voice.

"Well, Rosana's definitely missing out." I wash my food down with a swig of deliciously bitter coffee. "This meat is definitely fit for royalty."

"Thank you. You're very sweet." She pauses, tilting her had in thought. "Though, now that you mention it, it is possible that royalty might eat some of our meat, just not Elodian royalty."

I glance over at Freya, but she's looking at her mother, frowning.

"What do you mean, Mama?"

"Oh, you know," her mother replies, waving a hand through the air. "That deal Lord Mayberry made with the Rebel Isles. I don't suppose we should call them that, given how they've really helped our farms grow lately and since the prince is now engaged to their princess. Old habits die hard."

"What deal?" Freya asks carefully.

Her mother looks up, scowling. "Didn't you know about it? I'm sure it was well in place before you left. Though, it was only the Brownstone and Riverbrook farms at first. Your father would know better than I exactly when we added our goods to the exports."

"Mrs. Brambleberry," I jump in, working to keep my voice steady. "Have you had any more exports added recently?"

"I thought I told you last night to call me Kathy," she says, her voice a kind scold. "And honestly, I'm not sure. I know we've had an increase in orders over the past couple of months, but so much has happened. Jack would be the one to ask."

I nod, exchanging a worried glance with Freya that Kathy doesn't miss.

"Is there something wrong? Does it have something to do with why you're back?" she asks, her eyes darting between me and Freya. "We aren't in any trouble are we?"

"I'm sure it's fine, Mama," Freya says, offering her a mother a weak smile that doesn't reach her eyes.

"You have no need to worry," I add, my voice firm. "I won't let anything happen to you. I swore to protect Freya and that protection extends to her family."

Kathy relaxes a bit. "Thank you."

Freya shifts the conversation to the books her mother has been reading lately and the air lightens considerably. We're nearly done with breakfast when someone knocks on the door. Freya's mother rises to answer, and I try my best not to tense up. That flies out the window, however, when Freya inhales sharply as voices drift our way. I allow my hand to drop from the table, fingers brushing the dagger sheathed at my waist. A moment later, Kathy leads a young woman into the kitchen. I look over at Freya, trying to gauge how much of a threat this woman may be, but Freya looks almost sentimental.

I frown and turn my attention back to the newcomer, taking her in. She has sun-bronzed skin and golden-brown hair pulled up into a messy bun. She's probably close to Freya's height with similar curves. I imagine most people would consider her pretty, beautiful even. Honestly, she doesn't look like much of a threat, though I know better than to assume. Her green eyes flick to me briefly before settling on Freya.

"I hope it's okay that I came. When Mrs. Nellaway told me she saw you ride through town yesterday, I had to see you."

Freya smiles softly. "Of course, Cora."

The name washes over me like ice water. This is Cora, the woman planted here by Ty. The woman Freya loved. She hurt Freya with her deceit, and while Ty was a key component of that deceit, at least he came clean and was honest about it. He made it right with Freya. Even if Freya has managed to forgive her, Cora hasn't earned my forgiveness for her sins, and I don't trust her not to hurt Freya again.

I straighten in my chair and place my hand over where Freya's rests on the table. Freya startles slightly before shooting me an admonishing look. Cora doesn't miss anything, glancing between us.

"Am I interrupting?"

"No," Freya says before I can answer. "In fact, we need to talk to you."

"I'm going to pop over next door and see if your aunt needs any help," Kathy says, reaching for a shawl hanging on a peg nearby. "You three do all the talking you need."

Freya shoots her mother a grateful smile as she slips from the room. Once we're alone, Freya turns her attention back to Cora.

"Mama made far too much food for just us. You might as well help us finish it off."

Cora smiles and approaches with a nod. "Thank you."

She quickly fills her plate, and I take a gulp of coffee, draining my cup.

"What did you want to talk about?" she asks, taking a bite of sausage.

"Mama mentioned you've grown close to Lady Mayberry."

Whatever Cora was expecting, that clearly wasn't it. She nearly chokes on her food, her eyes widening.

"It's not what you think. Well, maybe. I—"

"It's okay, Cora," Freya says quickly. "We need to speak to Lady Mayberry, and we were hoping you could help get us an audience."

Cora relaxes a fraction, returning to her meal. "I probably can. We're friendly enough. Does the reason you need to talk to her have anything to do with letting everyone think you were dead?"

There's something accusatory in her voice I don't like one bit.

"I don't see how that's your concern," I bite out.

Cora's eyes flash and, for the first time since she entered the room, she seems like a threat. One I could easily take.

"It's my concern because I thought my friend was dead,"

Cora snaps. "I was here when her mother was crying and couldn't eat for days. While you were tearing everything apart, I was holding things together."

"Yes," Freya cuts in, her voice strained. "They're related." She looks over at me, her expression hard. "We need to work together."

I clench my jaw but nod.

Cora sighs. "Fine. But, honestly, Freya, if you're able to give answers, there are a lot of us who want them."

Freya nods. "I'll give them to you later, but right now we really need to get information about Lord Mayberry. Ty— Prince Tybalt—could be in trouble."

Cora's eyes widen. "The prince? You really think so?" Freya nods and Cora hums. "I knew the man was evil, but I thought it was more localized evil."

"Evil? How?" I ask.

"For one, he treats his wife horribly. She's miserable. You know he's had several of them and they all die young?" We both nod, and she continues. "There's a reason for that."

"I thought they all died from natural causes," Freya says.

"Natural causes aren't that hard to fake," Cora says.

"That's what I've been saying," I mumble.

"Even then, you think he would've been caught," Freya protests.

"The man's too clever with far too many dark connections and too much money to get caught. He may only be an earl without any magic, but he makes up for it. He knows how to go undetected, keep anyone from proving anything."

"Can *you* prove anything?" I ask.

"Not exactly," she replies. "But I should be able to point you in the right direction."

"So you can get us inside his estate?" Freya asks.

Cora nods. "Yes. If you can help Eve, I'll do anything."

"Eve is Lady Mayberry?" I clarify and Cora nods. "And you're sure we can trust her?"

"Completely. She wants out of the marriage, but she's trapped. If you can prove her husband is engaged in anything dangerous or treasonous, she can be free."

"Free to run off with you?"

"Bastion!"

Freya's reprimand is sharp, but I don't regret anything. I stare Cora down until she nods ever so slightly.

"If she wants." She shoots Freya an apologetic look. "I was heartbroken when you left and then I found Eve. It seemed like Fate."

"How so?" Freya asks, her voice quiet.

"Orders for the main estate rarely ever come into the general store, but for some reason, one did a couple months ago. Mrs. Nellaway asked me to make the delivery, and I did. I was still adjusting to you being gone, trying to find how I fit here without you, and when I saw Eve, something clicked."

"The lady of the house signed for a delivery?" I ask, frowning in disbelief.

Cora shakes her head. "She was outside getting some fresh air. She seemed so closed off but eager to talk to someone. A week later, I found another excuse to visit and she invited me in for tea, and well, things continued. We became friends and now . . ."

Cora sighs, glancing to me. "Look, I know she's married, but her husband really is horrible."

"I'm the last person to judge you for falling for someone promised to another," I confess quietly. I refuse to look at Freya, but I can feel her eyes on me. "I can only imagine how much worse it would be to see that person being treated poorly instead of loved how they deserve."

"Exactly," Cora says, nodding. "So, I'll help you, but not today. Lord Mayberry may be away, but his steward, Mr. Kingsley, is equally vile and unfortunately present. He's in charge while the earl is away. He'll be there today and tomorrow, but the day after that he'll be gone to deal with business out of town. I can take you to meet Eve then. Is that acceptable?"

I give her a single nod. "We can make do with that."

"Good." Cora pushes back from the table, standing. "Well, I should probably get back to town. I convinced Mrs. Nellaway not to gossip about your return yesterday—I figured you had a reason to play dead—but she's likely to let something slip if I'm not there to watch her."

Freya stands. "I'll walk you out."

I wait in the kitchen as Freya escorts Cora to the door. They pause in the doorway, and while I can't quite hear their exchange, I see the emotion on both their faces. Cora launches forward, pulling Freya into a tight hug that lasts a moment too long for my taste. I'm debating accidentally throwing a dagger when she finally releases Freya and steps outside. When Freya returns, tears mist her eyes.

"I told her I knew why she was my friend," Freya explains. "She said she really did love me."

The corner of my mouth tips up. "Of course she did, Freya. How could anyone not love you?"

Her eyes widen a fraction. "You said that before. Surely you didn't—"

"I did." I take a step closer to her. "I very much did."

She swallows, keeping her eyes locked on mine. "So when you said you understand falling in love with someone who was taken, you didn't mean Ty?"

My heart races in my chest as I shake my head. "Not *only* Ty." I chance taking another step closer, putting me well within reach of her. "I love you, Freya. I have for a while. Far longer than I had any right to."

Her lips part on an inhale and I swear her eyes get bluer. "Bash . . ."

I take a half-step back. "It's okay if you don't feel the same. If you need more time."

"I don't think I do. Need more time that is."

My heart leaps into my throat, but I don't dare hope. "Really?"

She laughs lightly, shaking her head. "You're not nearly as unlovable as you might like to believe. I do love you, Bash."

I surge forward and crash my mouth to hers. It takes her a moment to return the kiss, but once she does, she puts as much energy and longing into it as I do. My hands settle on her waist, and she presses closer before pulling back to look up at me.

"My mother will be back soon," she says, glancing over her shoulder briefly. "We should probably stop."

I sigh and press my forehead to hers, closing my eyes. "You're right." I draw back, keeping my hands on her waist as I brush one more kiss across her lips. "Maybe you could show me around the farm?"

Her eyes light up and she nods. "I'd like that."

I drop my hands and opt to hold her hand as she pulls me toward the door.

"I think you'll really like it."

I hum and nod my agreement, knowing I'll like it simply because she does. I don't need any more reason than that.

CHAPTER TWENTY-FOUR

TY

"You're sure you can handle things without me?" I ask Rissa as we walk toward the stable where my guard detail waits.

She rolls her eyes. "You might find it hard to believe, but I am perfectly capable of surviving without you moping about."

"After things with my mother—"

She waves me off with a heavy sigh. "Don't worry. I can handle the queen. This isn't the first time she's been . . . displeased with me, and I'm sure it won't be the last."

I look over at her as we round the corner to the stables. "There's a lot at risk this time."

She comes to a stop, and I halt with her. She glances around before leaning in. "I'll find something condemning before you get back. I *will* find the evidence we need to keep the duke in his place."

"That's the least of my worries, Rissa," I confess.

She frowns, her perfect eyebrows knitting together. "What else could you possibly be worried about?"

"You."

Her frown deepens. "Me? What about me?"

"Well, you and Miles." I make a face, but her frown doesn't disappear. "Look, Rissa, I know something is going on between you two, and I really want you to be happy with him."

Her frown loosens a bit, but she looks away, refusing to meet my eyes. "I don't need a man to be happy."

"I never said you did, but if he would add to your happiness, I want you to have that."

She looks back at me, crossing her arms and cocking an eyebrow. "Are you seriously trying to tell me you want me to be happy? You, Tybalt Shadowmoss? The boy who has tried his best to make me as miserable as possible most of his life?"

I grin. "I've hardly made your life miserable. Challenging maybe. But yes, I want you to be happy. Don't tell anyone, though. You'll ruin my reputation."

She smiles. "I'll let it slide this one time, but if it continues, I'm making you see the palace healers."

"Maybe I'm turning into a romantic."

"You've always been a romantic, Ty, and don't let anyone tell you otherwise. It's one of the better things about you." Rissa huffs a laugh, shaking her head. "And now I'm complimenting *you*. We're clearly both very ill."

"Clearly," I say with a laugh before sobering. "I do mean it. I appreciate your help, but don't jeopardize your happiness."

Her expression also turns serious as she meets my eyes. "Ty, if this whole thing is half what we think it is, everyone's happiness is at risk."

"But you still matter," I insist. "I know I've been very focused on myself lately—"

"You usually are."

"—*but* I really do want you to be happy, too. I've seen how you are around him. He makes you happy, Rissa."

"Ty—"

I hold up my hands in surrender. "I know. Not my place. I'm probably the least qualified to give you relationship advice, but don't let my mother get between you and whatever it is."

She sighs heavily, glancing off. "Fine." I start to smile and she shoots me a sharp look. "Not that I'm saying there's anything actually going on between me and Miles beyond an exchange of services, but I'll keep it in mind. Now, we need to get you on the road."

We resume our walk, entering the stables through a side door. My horse is saddled and ready to go, as are the four horses for my guards. I only recognize one of the four guards, but given I had to argue with my mother to get my escorts down to only four, I wasn't allowed to choose who got to go with me. At least the one I know—Cooper, if I'm remembering correctly—seemed to get along with Bash on our last trip. The other three look like they're going to give me trouble, and I don't have to wait long to find out I'm right. We've barely left the castle grounds when the oldest guard, whom I assume is the one in charge, suggests we alter our path.

"There doesn't seem to be much need, Your Highness," he says, "to go this far off course when a more direct path would prove safer."

I straighten on my horse. "I have chosen this path specifically."

"May I inquire as to why?"

I chose it based on cross-referencing possible locations for Bash and Freya with the help of Rissa, but this asshole doesn't need to know that. Instead, I shoot him what I hope is a charming grin.

"I like the scenery."

He cocks an eyebrow, clearly unconvinced. "If I may recommend some changes—"

"You may, but I'll choose to ignore them."

"Your mother—"

"Is back in the palace, and if you wish to kiss her ass, I suggest you head back now."

Cooper snorts, quickly attempting to cover it with a cough. The guard in charge glares at him before turning his attention back to me.

"There is no need for such hostility."

"Maybe, maybe not, but my mother did allow me to pick my route, and this is the way I chose."

"Your Highness, when the queen assigned me the task of overseeing your journey, I assured her I would do my absolute best to ensure your safety. I am a sergeant for a reason and have additional training in threat assessment. I ask that you respect my appointment and skillset."

"And I ask, Sergeant, that you respect my decision as your Crown Prince to take the path I have planned out."

The sergeant's jaw twitches, but he gives me a sharp nod. "As you wish, Your Highness."

The remaining guards exchange impressed looks, and I feel slightly victorious. However, I feel this is merely a battle won and the war between me and the sergeant has yet to be fought. This theory proves true when he refuses to let us take a decent break for lunch, insisting that if we are to stick to my path, we need to travel longer days. When I suggest he clearly doesn't care about the horses, he gives me a nasty look.

"If your concern is for the poor beasts, Your Highness,

then perhaps we should shift our path to one that harms them the least."

In the end I relent to riding longer, but swear if the horses are harmed, I'll take it from his flesh. He doesn't seem worried. I spend the rest of the day coming up with ways to kill him and hide his body. It makes the trip much more enjoyable.

When we stop for the night, the sergeant offers to take the first watch while the rest of us pair up to sleep. I end up with Cooper, who seems the most decent of my companions.

"You might want to be careful making an enemy of Sergeant Hallowcane," he says, keeping his voice low as we lay out our bedrolls, Cooper positioning his at the edge of the camp.

"Why? He's an ass."

"Very true," Cooper says, not bothering to hide his grin. "But he also has important ties in the palace."

"More important than mine?"

Cooper shrugs. "I suppose it depends on what you're wanting."

I grunt my agreement, stretching out across my bedroll and tucking a hand behind my head. "I suppose that's true for anything. What connections does he have?"

Cooper stretches out next to me, turning on his side to face me. "Not sure, if I'm honest, but everything he wants, he seems to get. Including this trip."

Now that has my interest. I turn over to face Cooper.

"Why did he want to escort me? What does he get out of it?"

"Once again, not sure, but I heard he basically begged to lead it."

"What about you? Did you volunteer?"

Cooper chews on his lip, clearly debating his answer before he nods, almost reluctantly.

"Why?"

Cooper seems uneasy and he glances around a little before answering. "Because I have a feeling I know what you're up to, and I want to help."

My heart picks up its pace a bit, but I refuse to give anything away. "What makes you think I'm up to anything?"

"Look," he says, scooting closer, "I know that your cousin has been looking into something. What, I don't know, but she's trying to figure out something."

"What Klarissa does or doesn't do is of little concern to me."

"Then I find it very curious that she spends so much time with you and the priest."

"She's my cousin, and who she is friends with is none of my concern. You're looking for something where there's nothing."

"So this unplanned trip, taking an unusual winding path, has nothing to do with you looking for Bastion Shamblefoot?"

My heart leaps into my throat and something on my face must give me away because Cooper's mouth turns up into a smug smile. However, despite his glee, Cooper just made himself a threat, and threats are something I can handle. I reach for the dagger hidden in my boot and have the point of it at Cooper's throat before he's even registered my movement. His eyes go wide and flick behind me, but thanks to our position at the edge of the camp and our closeness, none of our companions notice.

"You have about two minutes to convince me not to kill you for being a traitor and a spy."

Cooper swallows. "I'm on your side."

"Prove it."

He nods, taking shaky breath. "I like Bastion and I respect him. He more than earned his place at your side as your guard, and he proved that day after day. I also know that nothing as simple as a carriage ambush would be enough to take him out. I was there on your tour when we were attacked. I saw how he reacted, how he fought. He was the only one who saw the fallen tree as the threat it was. He and I were the only two to survive. His instincts were spot on, and I refuse to believe that those instincts suddenly failed him."

"What makes you think I'm looking for him?"

"Because you care for him."

I press the blade closer to his neck and he inhales sharply.

"You can kill me if you need to, Your Highness, but I know it's the truth. I don't judge you for it."

It's a trap. This has to be a trap. Yet, there's something sincere in Cooper's eyes.

"He's my best friend," I say, my voice breaking slightly enough that Cooper might not have caught it.

"I know," he says, his voice kind. "If my best friend were missing, assumed dead but more than likely alive, I would look for him, and I would want at least one person on my side who I knew I could trust."

I scoff. "You want me to believe that you're that person?"

"I could be. I want to be. I've seen enough of you to know you'll be a great king and enough of Bastion to know that he deserves a position of honor. In all honesty, Bastion saved my life. Maybe not directly, but if he hadn't been there when your carriage was attacked, I have no doubt I would've died along with everyone else.

"I know you have no real reason to trust me, but I hope you will. The sergeant has his own agenda, and he'll do whatever it takes to keep you from fulfilling your secret mission. With my help, you might be able to follow whatever trail you think you can find."

I take a shaky breath and remove the dagger from his neck, not putting it away but pulling it far enough away that Cooper knows I'm not going to slit his throat between one breath and the next.

"Who else knows?"

"About what exactly?"

"Any of it. Bash's possible survival, Rissa's snooping, me."

Cooper shrugs, shifting on his bedroll. "Anyone who knew Bastion suspects he went down too easily, but there's no proof that he lived. As far as Lady Klarissa goes, she's known for, well . . . finding information."

His cheeks redden and I snort.

"No one knows what she's doing or what she's looking for, though," he continues. "They care less about what she's actually seeking or even who she gives the information to and more about hoping she comes to them next, if you know what I mean."

I roll my eyes. "I know. Believe me I know. What are the rumors surrounding me?"

"That you're mourning and angry and irrational, though no one can figure out why."

I barely hold back my laughter. "No one can figure out why?"

I must have spoken a little too loudly because Cooper looks past me, concern crinkling his brow. A moment later, footsteps crunch our way, and I quickly slip my dagger out of sight.

"Is there a problem?" Sergeant Hallowcane asks.

I flip over onto my back and grin up at him. "Not over here. Is there a problem with you?"

He frowns. "Go to sleep, Your Highness."

He walks away, and I take a moment before I turn back over on my side.

"The two people I care the most about in the world were tossed from the castle by my mother, and now I'm forced to marry a stranger who is far too young to be my bride, and people wonder why I'm upset?" I hiss, struggling to keep my voice low.

"You've played the part of a spoiled prince well," Cooper answers somewhat hesitantly. "Your father, who everyone knows you love dearly, is showing marked improvement, but you've barely shown your face in the dining hall. Your bride is beautiful, and you haven't shown her any interest. Even when Freya was in the palace, you treated her with disdain. From where most people sit, you don't care about much."

"And from where you sit?" I grit out.

"I see a prince who cares and loves and wants what's best for his kingdom. That's why I want to help you."

I take a deep breath and release it slowly. "Fine. I can't give you all the details, but I will say you're not entirely wrong. You help me do what I need to do on this trip, and I'll make sure you find your reward. Deal?"

Cooper grins. "Deal."

"Good. Now we should probably get some sleep, or the lovely sergeant may make us pull double duty."

I turn over on my back and close my eyes. I wasn't expecting to have an ally on this trip, but I'm almost relieved to know that I might have found one. Now, here's to hoping that Cooper is as trustworthy as he seems.

CHAPTER TWENTY-FIVE

FREYA

I smooth my hands over the front of my dress, hoping I look presentable enough to meet with the wife of an earl. One advantage to being home with nothing much to do the past couple days was being able to wash all my clothes, including my dresses. I honestly haven't had many opportunities to wear the couple I brought—sabotaging carriages is easier to do in pants or leggings—and now I almost feel out of place in a dress.

"You're beautiful," Bash says, stepping up behind me, his hands settling on my waist as he presses a kiss to my cheek.

A smile tempts my lips, and I lean into him. "Thank you."

"I mean it. You look beautiful and more than worthy of meeting with an earl's wife."

How Bash knows my thoughts, I'm not sure. Either way, it warms me to think of him understanding me so well. I turn around and look up at him.

"Can I kiss you?"

His mouth twitches into a smile. "Please."

His lips catch mine, but unfortunately the kiss is quick. I sigh and he gives me a knowing smirk.

"We have plans today." His hands fall from my waist and he takes my hand. "Shall we go see if Cora is here?"

I force a smile and nod. My mother is busy in the kitchen, a small spread of food on the table, but my stomach is twisted in too many knots to eat anything. I nibble on a piece of toast until Cora finally knocks.

"Good morning," I say, throwing the door open.

Cora stands there in a nice dress, the green material matching her eyes almost too perfectly. For a moment I almost forget how to breathe as memories flood around me. Bash's arm slipping around my waist steadies me.

"Ready to go?" Cora says, glancing between us.

"As ready as we'll ever be," I reply, forcing a smile. "Lead the way."

Even though it takes over half an hour to walk the distance to the main house, we go on foot. When we arrive, Cora leads us around the side to a back door. The maid that answers must be expecting Cora, but she shoots me and Bash a nasty look before allowing us inside.

"Her ladyship is having a poor day," the maid explains as we wind through back hallways.

"I was afraid that might be the case," Cora says, her voice heavy. "She's had too many good days lately, and the bad days always catch up."

We step out into a main hall and the maid pushes a door open, revealing a sitting room that would be cozy if it weren't filled with so much gray and brown. A young woman sits in an armchair in the center of the room, a woven blanket draped over her lap. Her skin seems unnaturally pale, but it could be exaggerated by the long, ink-black hair framing her face. The poor lighting doesn't help, either.

When we step into the room, her eyes fall on Cora and she brightens a bit.

"Hello, love," Cora says, crossing the room to drop a kiss on the woman's cheek. "You got my message about me bringing guests?"

"Of course." Lady Mayberry looks toward me and Bash and nods. "Welcome."

Before I reply, she breaks off in a vicious coughing fit.

"We can come back if you need us to," I offer.

She shakes her head, wiping her mouth with a handkerchief bunched in her hand. "Wouldn't do you any good. I'm like this more often than not. But that doesn't give me an excuse to be rude. Please, come in. Make yourselves at home. There's tea over there on the cart if you'd like some."

Bash and I decline the tea, but we take seats side by side on a small couch across from Lady Mayberry while Cora settles on the arm of the chair, her arm draped across Lady Mayberry's shoulders.

"From reading between the lines of Cora's note, you two aren't here on a social visit."

I shake my head, but Bash is the one to speak.

"We're interested in some of your husband's dealings. We think it may not be quite above board."

"Oh, I can assure you it isn't, but I'm not sure I could point you to any evidence needed to bring him down. Believe you me, if I could, I would hand it to you with a neat little bow."

I frown. "Is he that bad?"

A small, bitter laugh escapes her lips. "Have you met him? Like honestly sat and talked to him?"

"Once, somewhat briefly," I admit with a nod. "He wasn't pleasant."

"And he gets worse the more you know him."

"Lady Mayberry," Bash starts, but she cuts him off with a wave.

"Please, call me Evangeline or Eve. I don't want his name associated with me any more than necessary."

Bash nods. "Eve, why don't you start by telling us why you hate your husband? There are several things we're looking into, and any input you may have could help."

She sighs, nodding. "Fine. To begin, I knew practically nothing about the man before I married him. He was traveling through my town on the opposite corner of Elodia on some sort of business. I probably couldn't have pointed out East Hingling on a map at the time. He took to me and made an offer of marriage. He seemed like a creepy, sick man, but all my parents saw was a shiny new title. They agreed to the marriage and before I knew it, I was wed and being whisked off to the farthest corner from my home."

"When you say 'sick,' what do you mean exactly? Disgusting?" I interrupt.

She shakes her head. "No, I literally mean sick, as in ill, as in how I am now."

"How you are now? You weren't sick then?"

Eve shakes her head. "No, I've always been healthy. I started to feel a little off while we were traveling, but I thought it was likely traveling fatigue since I wasn't used to it. It got worse after I arrived here, but I thought it was the new climate. It's a lot cooler here and the air's damper. Lord Mayberry called for a doctor after I begged him, but the doctor barely looked me over before giving me a bitter tonic that's done nothing."

Another coughing fit overtakes her, and Cora hops up to get a glass of water from the tea cart. Once the coughing subsides, Cora places the glass on an end table and resumes her perch.

"When I arrived, most of the servants avoided me. He made sure I was shut off from practically everybody. It took me weeks to learn I was his fifth wife, all of us young. I found it suspicious, so I began looking for any information on what happened to his previous wives. No one would talk to me, and I couldn't find any records beyond the dates of the marriages and deaths in a ledger in his office. Then, one day I dropped something and it rolled under my bed. When I went to retrieve it, I noticed the corner of a floorboard sticking up. That's where I found this."

She reaches under her blanket, pulling out a small, brown journal. She holds it out, and I take it from her hands, opening it to reveal a curling script.

"Judging by the dates, I assume it belonged to the wife a couple before me. She was from a town a little to the south, not nearly as far away as me, but she started to feel ill as well. She documented her experience very thoroughly. The more I read, the more I realized that her experience matches mine eerily well. Every couple of weeks, I'm hit with a particularly bad bout of illness followed by patches of good and bad. Over time, the patches of good grew shorter and shorter. The exact same is happening to me."

I inhale sharply. "Do you think your husband is poisoning you?"

She looks down at her hands clasped in her lap. "It looked that way, and that's what she initially believed. She began tracking all her meals and documenting whether she felt ill afterwards. She even went as far as to go into the village when she could to obtain her own food. It didn't affect her good days or her bad days." She slowly raises her eyes to mine. "Toward the end of the journal, the entries got a bit . . . erratic. It was obvious she was searching for a way to end her suffering, but some of her claims were odd at best. I thought she might've been going mad."

I flip toward the end. The flowing script from the earlier pages has been replaced by sharp, scrawling words. The sentences are short and choppy. It's like a different person writing.

"Did she?" I ask, looking back up at Eve. "Go mad, that is?"

She sighs, shaking her head. "I don't know. I don't think so. She claimed, well, she suspected magic. But the earl doesn't have magic. He's very bitter about it, too. I thought she must have been reaching for any answer, so I decided to do a little research on my own before my mind went as well. I figured if I couldn't save myself, I could continue what she was doing and help whoever came after me."

Cora tenses and tightens her grip on Eve's shoulders. "There will be no one after you because we're going to figure this out."

"Cora's right," I say with a nod. "At least we can try. Did you find anything?"

Eve looks around before nodding slowly. "One night, shortly before the earl left for his most recent trip, I snuck into the library. I'd been going through his books, looking for answers. I always seem to be a little stronger at night, and he was usually asleep, so it felt safe. On this particular night, however, he was up later than usual. I found books and papers scattered across a table, though he wasn't there. There were several letters bearing wax seals I didn't recognize, not that I normally recognize many. I didn't have time to really read them, but the one I picked up rambled and didn't make much sense. The books were written in a language I didn't know, but there were translations in the margins. I think they were dark magic of some sort that required ingredients and spells."

Eve starts coughing again and Bash and I exchange a look. That sounds too much like the *Naturcræft* that the cult uses to be comfortable.

Eve continues with a frustrated shake of her head. "I didn't get to take in much more because he returned. He was furious —angrier than I'd ever seen him. He locked me in my room for three days without any food or water. He never apologized, but he made it very clear I had crossed a line and my insubordination would not be tolerated. He left a few days later on his trip. I've tried finding those books and letters again, but I haven't had any luck. He must have either taken them with him, which seems a bit unlikely, or he has a hidden room somewhere."

She falls quiet, and Cora looks over at me, meeting my eyes. "Can you help her?"

I glance at Bash and he gives me a nod.

"We can definitely try," I say.

"So you don't think I'm going mad?" Eve asks, something close to hope burning in her voice.

"Definitely not," Bash answers before I can. "I've met the earl, and he's a vile snake. If I'd had my way, he'd already be dead. I have no doubt he's into some dark things, and if he's associated with the people I fear he is, he has some evil connections. Poisoning wife after wife with dark magic is exactly something I would expect of him."

"We can start looking immediately if you show us the library," I offer.

She starts to nod, but then hesitates, biting her lip.

"What is it?" I ask, leaning forward. "You can trust us."

"It's not that. If Cora can trust you, I feel like I can trust you. It's the others in the house I don't trust. Mel, the maid that led you in can be trusted, and there are a couple other servants I think I can trust, but I'm not sure about the others. Some are loyal to the earl and the rest are afraid. I can send some of the more suspect away for the day on errands and whatnot, but you'll still have to work quickly and quietly. You definitely have to be finished by noon tomorrow. Mr. Kingsley will be back then, and he has eyes everywhere."

Bash nods once. "We can work with that."

"Good." Eve sighs and relaxes back in the chair as she looks up at Cora. "Can you get Mel for me?"

"Of course, love," Cora says, pressing a quick kiss to Eve's forehead before slipping from the arm of the chair.

Half an hour later, the house has been cleared of most of the staff and Bash and I are alone in the library. It's not very large and a good third of the shelves aren't full, but it will still be a lot of work. Bash goes to the desk along the far wall to sort through the correspondence and whatever he can find while I start sorting through the books. I'm determined to figure out what's going on, even if it takes us all day.

CHAPTER TWENTY-SIX

BASH

Freya busies herself going through the earl's collection of books shelf by shelf while I search the contents of his desk. I skip right past the neat rows of paper and ink and go straight to the locked bottom drawer. The lock proves to be nothing for a man of my skill and soon I have the contents spread across the desktop. There are several letters, what looks to be a ledger, and an official seal with the earl's crest. I ease into the chair and start sorting.

The letters are nothing particularly suspicious. They're little more than basic correspondence. I'm not even sure why he had them locked in the drawer. The ledger provides a little more information, but it takes me a while to sort how it works.

From what I gather, the earl tracks every transaction, taking note of which farm supplied the products, how much was brought in by the sale or trade, and how the rest of the funds from the sale were distributed. At a glance, some of the funds go back into the farms, keeping them running. Other funds go to running his estate, travel expenses, and other things. A few of the transactions have odd marks here and there that I can't quite figure out. I'd almost think they were accidental if they didn't reoccur on almost every page. I'm able to confirm the sale of meat to the Rebel Isles, but it looks like a relatively basic transaction.

I snap the ledger shut and go through the remaining drawers, finding nothing more of note. The bottom of the last drawer seems to be covered in a dusty dirt, the smell of which gives me a bit of headache. It probably explains why it's otherwise empty. I'm putting everything back in their place when Freya inhales sharply.

"What is it?" I ask, already halfway across the room to her.

"Just a paper cut," she says, holding up her finger to show me the bead of gold and red on her fingertip.

"Do you want me to burn down the library?" I ask, gently taking her hand in mine to examine her small wound.

She snorts. "I hardly think that's necessary."

I hum. "I think I've made it clear that nothing is allowed to hurt you."

She rolls her eyes. "You're being dramatic. There's no—"

She drops off with a sharp gasp as I lean forward, closing my lips around her finger. I lick away the blood, running my tongue across the length of her finger for good measure, before slipping her digit from my mouth. I allow my eyes to meet hers, a smile curving my lips.

"Better?"

She swallows, pupils blown wide. "Some people would just kiss it to make it better."

A low chuckle rumbles in my throat. "I am far from most people, Princess."

The corner of her mouth tips up. "I know."

I capture her mouth in a hard kiss. This isn't the time or the place, so after a moment, I pull back with a sigh, forcing myself to step back despite the fact that this is one of the few times I want more.

"Finding anything?"

She takes a moment to collect herself before shaking her head. "No. This has to be the dullest collection of books I've ever seen. I haven't found a single trace of anything remotely interesting, let alone anything dealing with magic."

"Do you think maybe the previous wife *was* going mad?"

Freya shrugs. "I don't know, but given what we've seen and heard, I doubt it." She pauses, tilting her head in thought. "You know, we might be looking in the wrong place."

"Do you think he keeps his books somewhere else? Another office or his room?"

"He could, but I doubt he would haul everything here to look through. No, I think there might be a hidden room."

I grin, pulling her in for another kiss. She laughs against my lips.

"What was that kiss for?"

"A reward for being clever."

Her eyes brighten. "I get kisses as rewards now?"

"You get kisses for simply existing. Giving you a kiss as a reward just gives me an excuse to kiss you more."

She laughs softly, shaking her head. "You're ridiculous."

"And you're intoxicating."

I pull her in for another kiss, pressing her against the bookshelf behind her. Something is driving me to consume her. I need her like I've never needed her before, like I've never needed anyone before. I grind against her and she gasps into my mouth.

"Bash, wait," she says as my hand finds the back of her

neck, fingers twisting into her hair. But I don't wait. I press closer. Every moment I taste her, I crave more of her. The need pushes through my veins. Each pulse of my heart beats her name. I cannot be satiated. I am addicted and she is my vice.

"Bash," she says again, her voice changed, different.

But still I continue, mouthing down her neck, licking along her skin. I'm dizzy and drowning and she is keeping me afloat. Her palms press against my chest.

"Bastion, stop." Her voice trembles, and if I didn't know better, I would say she's afraid.

Afraid.

Something in me snaps and I jerk back. My breath comes out in short, violent bursts. Freya stands mere feet away, lips swollen and eyes wide. My hand flies to my mouth, fingers tracing my lips. What was I doing? Why was I doing it?

"Bash, are you okay?" she asks, taking a tentative step closer.

"Stop!" I hold up a hand and she freezes. I squeeze my eyes shut, shaking my head. "I—I'm not thinking clearly. Oh gods." I stumble back a few more steps, nearly tripping over the leg of a chair. "I'm so sorry, Freya."

"It's okay," she says, her voice a little steadier. "What do you need?"

"It's not okay. It's not. I don't know what happened. Gods, what even . . . The desk! There was some sort of dirt in the drawer. I think I must have inhaled it."

"Do you think it's a spell of some sort?"

"I have no idea."

She starts to move toward me, but then hesitates, giving me a wide berth as she crosses to the desk. My heart aches at the purposeful distance, though I agree with her choice.

"Which drawer?"

"Bottom left," I reply, not trusting myself to join her. "Be careful."

She nods, taking a deep breath and covering her nose and mouth with her left elbow as she slides the drawer open. My heart doesn't cease racing the entire time she's looking inside. She slides it shut and takes a couple steps away before dropping her arm and taking a deep breath.

"I think it is some sort of potion. If you inhaled it, maybe some fresh air will help." She makes her way over to a window and works it open. "There. Come breathe in some fresh air, and it might leave your system."

I nod and take a step, but stop. "Move away. I don't want to hurt you."

"Bash—"

"Please, Freya," I plead.

She nods and goes back over near the desk where she'll be safely away from me. I quickly cross to the window and suck in several breaths of the cool air. Slowly my mind begins to clear, and I feel more in control. I take a few more deep breaths to be sure before I slowly turn back to Freya.

"Better?" she asks, her brow still furrowed in concern.

"I think so. Maybe give me a little distance for a bit."

She nods. "Okay."

"Freya, I'm—"

"Please don't apologize again, Bash. If anything, add this to the list of reasons the earl deserves to die."

A huff of a laugh escapes me and her smile returns. "It's getting to be a long list."

"It really is. Now, let's find that hidden room."

Still not trusting myself, I keep distance between us, focusing my efforts on the opposite side of the library. If there truly is a hidden room, it's likely on the far left wall or the far right, given the layout of the house, but the trigger could be anywhere. I'm wondering if maybe we should refocus our efforts elsewhere when Freya makes an excited sound. I turn to find her standing on her tiptoes as she reaches up behind a stack of books.

"Did you find something?"

"I think so," she grunts. "I just need to get this to shift and—"

A moment later there's a loud click and the shelf juts forward. Freya grins, her eyes bright. I cross the room and help her pull back the shelf to reveal a hidden room. There's no window to let in light, so I push the door open a little more so we can see properly. I step inside, taking everything in. It's barely bigger than a closest, but every inch of space is being put to use. Overflowing bookshelves line the walls, most bearing books crammed and stacked at awkward angles, but others contain vials, jars, bowls, and various storage containers. A small desk is stuffed in the corner, its surface littered with papers, more books sitting in a stack on the floor next to it.

"Wow," Freya whispers in awe, pushing past me to peer up at the books. "This is a lot."

She pulls a dusty volume off the shelf and flips through. I still don't dare get close to her again and lean against the desk to put as much distance between us as possible in the small space.

"Is it magic of some sort?"

She nods, snapping the book shut and turning it over to look at the cover. "*Naturcræft por Heileighis.* Sounds like a riveting read." She slides the book back onto the shelf and stares up at the books above her. "Where do I even start?"

"Maybe with these," I reply, giving the teetering stack on the floor a tap with my foot. "I would guess that those are the books he references the most."

I straighten and turn around, gathering things off the desk. "I'll take this out into the main room and see if I can make sense of them."

"I'm okay if you want to stay in here with me," Freya says, her voice quiet.

I shoot her what I hope is convincing smile over my shoulder. "I know, but if I go out there, you'll have more room to work in here and I can spread out."

I shift the things in my arms, realizing I'll need to make multiple trips, especially if I'm going to go through the desk. A few minutes later, I'm settled at a reading table in the main library, sorting things into stacks while Freya is seated at the desk in the room thumbing through books. The first few letters I examine don't seem to be in code, but they're very cryptic, bearing no names, only initials. Details are vague. Soon, however, I begin to catch patterns like what we saw in the letters we intercepted. By the time I reach the bottom of my stack, I have no doubt that the earl is involved.

The letters, however, aren't the most interesting thing I find. The desk had another ledger. At first glance, it appears to contain much of the same information. At closer inspection, some things seem off. I carefully extract the original ledger from the desk and compare the two. I discover discrepancies here and there on all the entries with the odd mark. Most of them are minor, barely noticeable changes, but when I look at the account where they're being put, they add up to quite a large number. The transactions take a little longer to figure out, most of the notes made in shorthand I can't quite decipher, but I'm almost positive most of them are bribes.

I flip to a new page and notice a huge discrepancy, and my heart stills. In the original ledger, a sale to the Rebel Isles is listed as making a normal profit, but the duplicate entry shows ten times the amount. I scan down to see how the funds were distributed and have little doubt the funds went to recruit new members for the cult. This seems confirmed when I find a large transaction that went to Brookeshire around the same date as the ball. The earl is working with the Rebel Isles to fund the *cultas draiochta.*

I rise from my seat and almost plow into Freya, who's rushing my way, a book open against her chest.

"I think I know what the earl is doing to Eve," she says, walking past me to set the book down on the table. "This book was toward the top of the stack, and this page was bookmarked."

I look down at the book, but I'm not sure what I'm seeing. The main text on the page is written in a language I don't know and even the sketches and diagrams don't mean much to me. There's text scrawled in the margins, but I can't quite make it out.

"What is it?"

Freya takes a deep breath and releases it slowly. "It's a spell or potion—I'm not really sure what the term would be —that links two people. It allows one person to steal energy, magic, and health from someone else."

"Wait," I say, stepping closer to the book and glaring down at its pages before looking back at Freya. "You're saying that the earl has been using magic to drain the life force from his wives?"

Freya nods, biting her lip. "I'm afraid so. That's why he keeps marrying young, healthy women. They're the most likely to be able to give him the health he needs. The spell also needs to be refreshed every couple weeks or so, which is why Eve's health dips around that time."

"But the earl is gone. Can he still be using the spell on the other side of the kingdom?"

"I think so. As long as he has the supplies he needs to complete the spell—including her blood, hair, or something physical from her—he can refresh the spell as often as needed. I also found some other entries detailing how to strengthen spells, so it's possible he might be using additional spellwork to make it work across the distance."

Her eyes fall to the open ledger on the table. "Did you find anything?"

"I did and it's not good, either." I step over to the ledger and Freya follows. I tap on the suspicious transaction with the Rebel Isles. "Any chance pigs cost that much?"

Her eyes widen before she shakes her head. "I don't even think our whole farm is worth that."

"That's what I thought."

I quickly explain my suspicions to her. When I finish, she sinks into a nearby armchair, shaking her head.

"So we have pretty clear evidence that a despicable man has access to ancient spellwork and that he's working with a cult we know for a fact is trying to bring down the Crown and he's using funds from what was an enemy kingdom mere months ago?"

I sigh and drop down into the chair across from her. "That seems to be the sum of it."

"Does that mean that Amarelia is a plant of some sort, meant to help take the Crown?"

The air in the room thins and I find it very hard to breathe. How had I not considered that before? I suspected the earl and duke were up to something, but I hadn't considered Amarelia could be part of their plans.

I leap to my feet. "We need to get back to Rosana. Now."

"Wait!" Freya says, springing from her chair and grabbing my arm before I can get to the door. "We need to think. We can't just charge back into Rosana. They think we're dead."

"Ty's life is in danger and you want to wait?" I snap, jerking my arm from her grasp. "Do you want him to die?"

She inhales sharply, stumbling back a step. Hurt flashes across her face for the briefest hint of a second before she schools her features into hard determination. Guilt swirls in my gut, but she speaks before I can apologize.

"Of course I don't, but I also don't want to miss an opportunity to fix things while we're here. You asked me to come with you to take down the cult, and while we've been doing some dismantling through our ambushes and the ball, we now have an opportunity to further scramble things. We have actual evidence of the earl's misdeeds. We probably shouldn't take his whole ledger, but we could get away with sneaking a few pages. We can make copies of the rest of the information and send out missives that will disrupt the flow of funds. It will take us days to get back to Ty in Rosana, but if we take advantage of what we know, the resources we now have, we can save lives while creating a bit of a protective bubble around him."

I swallow. "You're right." I shake my head and attempt a smile. "See, you're clever. We do make a good team. I'm sorry I was short with you."

She takes a step closer, her smile sad around the edges. "I know your instincts will always go to Ty and how to protect him."

"And you," I amend quickly, cupping her cheek. "My thoughts go to protecting the people I love. Always."

She smiles, leaning into my touch. I brush a quick kiss across her lips. When I pull back, I shift my attention back to the papers on the desk.

"I can find the most damning information to take and copy, but I'm not sure my missives would be convincing."

Freya grins. "Luckily for you, I know someone who can

copy any handwriting and mimic any voice. Even luckier, she's in this building and she wants to see the earl go down as much as we do."

I cock an eyebrow. "Cora?"

Her grin grows. "Cora."

CHAPTER TWENTY-SEVEN

FREYA

"That son of a bitch is doing *what* to Eve?" Cora yells, her voice echoing off the edges of the library.

"Be quiet!" I hiss, my eyes darting nervously toward the door.

Cora doesn't seem worried about being overheard and only smirks. "You know I've never been good at that."

My face heats and Bash growls beside me. Cora rolls her eyes.

"Fine. I'll be quiet, but I cannot believe that selfish bastard has literally been killing her for his own health. At least he hasn't forced his way into her bedroom like he's done to previous wives."

"Wait, he used spells to get his wives to do things with him?"

Cora nods. "That's how it seems from the journal Eve has, anyway. She has no proof beyond that."

Bash and I exchange a quick look. That might explain the weird powder we found in the desk drawer. This man definitely needs to be taken down a notch or two. I direct Cora to the table where we've laid out all the papers and information we could find in the hidden room. She settles in the seat at the head of the table.

"These are the people we think we should contact first," I say, setting a list in front of her. "I've written down who they are, what they do, and what we need said."

I set another page of text next to the list. "This is a sample of the earl's handwriting and this"—I set down a page in my own handwriting—"is a list of some of the code words and phrases they typically use. Can you handle it?"

Cora purses her lips, her eyes trailing over everything in front of her. After a couple minutes, she nods. "Yes. I can handle it."

"You're sure?" Bash says. "Because if you're not, if you get caught—"

"I've got it, Bastion," she says, drawing his name out in a way that I can tell annoys Bash. She waves him off. "You go do your thing, and I'll do mine."

He mumbles something under his breath I don't quite catch before taking a seat at the opposite end of the table with his ledgers, map, and address book. I sigh and take a seat near the center of the table. Bash decides to go through and try to figure out the major places of operations throughout Elodia to assess the largest threats while I comb through the correspondence looking for any more codes. When I finish, I'll help copy the information of all the traitors and their locations as Bash finishes with his notes.

We haven't been working for too long when Mel arrives with a light lunch. She assures us that Eve is sleeping. After lunch, I decide to take a break from the letters—they don't seem to be yielding any new information—and I look through the books on magic. As I suspected, the magic isn't bad in and of itself. In fact, some of it is quite useful, and I jot down a few things here and there. I even find a couple spells that might prove handy for Eve to use to block the magic being performed on her.

By the time dinner comes, all of our hands are covered in ink. Bash has a comprehensive list of people, Cora has a stack of false correspondence ready to send out, and I have plenty of spells and information to weaponize as needed.

We quickly pack up everything, but I decide to use my knowledge to prepare something to help Eve. Cora follows me into the room and watches me mix together the potion.

"Don't you have actual magic now? Or did they remove your access when they sent you home?"

I nod, crushing some bay leaves with a pestle. "I keep my crystal hidden in my pocket so I can access it if necessary."

"And Bastion? He has a crystal as well?"

I pause, looking up at Cora. "Bash's situation is complicated."

"Oh?" Her eyebrows shoot up. "How so?"

I shake my head, going back to my mixture. "He used to have a crystal, but we had to leave it behind when we faked our deaths."

"So he doesn't have magic anymore? He gave it up to keep you safe? Wouldn't you be safer if he had his magic?"

I turn my back to her and mix together more ingredients. "He still has his magic."

She huffs. "Not without a crystal he doesn't."

My silence must speak volumes because she swears and I wince.

"Freya, are you telling me that man out there is powerful enough he can perform magic without a crystal?"

I sigh and turn to face Cora. "You can't tell anyone. His

magic without the crystal isn't perfect, anyway. He's still learning—well, re-learning—how to use and access it."

"Holy. Shit. That's . . . incredible." Her eyes widen. "Is he Fae?"

"Not full-blooded." I shake the vial in my hands, the brownish liquid inside turning a sparkling blue. I hold it out to Cora. "Take this and have Eve put a couple drops on her tongue every morning and evening. It should work to block some of the magic."

Cora accepts the vial, turning it over in her hand. "Thank you. You have no idea what this means to me."

My lips turn up into a half-smile. "I have an idea."

Cora smiles and looks over her shoulder to a brooding Bash watching us with crossed arms and a sharp glare. She turns back to me with a laugh.

"I wasn't sure about him at first, but I like him for you."

I smile. "Thanks. I like him for me, too."

"I know you weren't too keen on the prince, but I'm glad you and Bastion found each other. I guess maybe Fate had a plan for you after all."

My smile falls. "I did love Ty. I still do."

"Oh. Gods, Freya, I'm sorry."

I attempt a smile but fail. "I'm fine. Or I will be. I do have Bash, and I'm happy about that."

"Well, who knows, maybe Fate will turn out to be even nicer and bring you all back together. I really do want you to be happy."

My smile turns more sincere. "I want the same for you."

After another round of hugs, the room is locked up and Bash and I are on our way home. The night is cool and the fresh air feels nice after being inside a dusty library all day. We walk in silence for the first few minutes, but I get the feeling Bash has something to say.

"So, what's the plan? Did you figure out where we need to go?"

He nods, staring off to the path ahead. "I think we should head to Krixwell. They have a big festival every year to celebrate the apple harvest, and judging by the earl's ledger, the cult is funding it this year. We might be able to take out some more of their leaders if we get there in time, maybe even stop some recruitment."

I hum my agreement and we fall back into silence. After a few more steps I sigh. "Bash, what's wrong?"

He shakes his head. "Nothing. Well, not nothing. I'm worried about about a lot of things, but nothing you need to fret about."

"We'll get to Ty in time."

He comes to a stop and turns to look at me. "But what if we don't?"

I place a hand on his arm. "We will. You always find him and keep him safe. You've never failed him before, and you won't fail him now. *We* won't fail him."

His jaw twitches but he manages a nod. I'm not sure he's entirely convinced, but he resumes walking.

"There's something I'm wondering about, though, now that we know the earl is basically leading the cult. Why didn't he try to kill me when I was still living at home, so close to him?"

"Well, Ty didn't leave you unguarded. There were soldiers here."

"True, but there were soldiers when the carriage was attacked and at the ball."

"Maybe things weren't far enough along. If he had tried to go after you too early and failed, it would have exposed his plans. Maybe he was lying low, waiting for something. Or maybe he was waiting for you and Ty to be together so you could be taken out at the same time. Taking you out was only half the puzzle, and if you were assassinated, Ty would have been ten times harder to get to."

A thought crosses my mind and I laugh, pushing it away. Bash looks over at me.

"What are you thinking?"

"Nothing just"—I laugh again—"what if all those lovers of Ty that tried to kill me were actually working for the cult?"

Bash chuckles. "That is an amusing thought."

We fall back into silence, the gravel road crunching beneath our feet. Off in the distance I can see the glow of candles inside my home.

"I'm still sorry, by the way, for attacking you in the library," Bash says, his voice so low I barely hear him.

"Bash, you were under the influence of something. I don't blame you."

"I forced myself on you," he says, his voice filled with pain.

"Hey," I say, placing my hand on his arm and bringing us to a stop. "I'm fine."

"But what if—"

"No. No what ifs. You didn't. Even under the influence of something foul, you found yourself. You kept me safe."

He exhales slowly. "You really don't hate me?"

"No." I step closer to him. "Not even a little."

I press a gentle kiss to his lips, and he sighs, looping an arm around me.

"Good. Because one day I may want to go further with you than what we've done and don't want what happened today to get in the way."

"Further, hmm? I like what we've done already, but I'm down for whatever else you have in mind."

He chuckles. "I have so many things in mind, Princess. I

can think of a dozen different ways to have you screaming my name."

I shiver and it has nothing to do with the coolness of the night.

"Yeah?"

"Yes." He leans forward and nips at my lips. "I want to have you every way possible." His mouth finds my neck and I inhale sharply. "I want you begging." He catches the lobe of my ear in his teeth. "I want you in ways you've never dreamed of."

I whimper and he presses his mouth to mine, swallowing the sound.

"Tonight?" I ask breathlessly.

He chuckles again. "Maybe not tonight."

He pulls back so we aren't as pressed together but keeps his arm around me.

"Because we're in a house with my parents?"

"Well, there's that, but also, I'm not sure I feel up to anything tonight."

I nod. "Do you want to sleep in another room?"

He hesitates a moment, considering my offer before shaking his head. "No. I like sharing a bed with you. I honestly don't think I'll ever pass on that."

"Good. I like sharing with you, too."

We resume walking and Bash slips his arm from my waist, taking my hand instead. We walk in silence the rest of the way back to my house, but this time the silence doesn't feel so heavy.

CHAPTER TWENTY-EIGHT

RISSA

I will never admit it to his face when he returns, but I miss Ty. Without him here to bother, I'm lonely. Well, not lonely. More bored. I'm especially bored right now, listening to Cressida, Nadia, and Amarelia discuss dresses for the upcoming ball. If I have to hear Cressida talk about how soft shades of blue make her eyes pop one more time, I'm going to stab her with a teaspoon. I don't care if it's blunt; I can make it work.

"I just can't believe no one told me before how much yellow washes me out!" Cressida says, sounding like she's been truly scandalized. "Blue is so much better for me."

My hand tightens around the neck of the spoon. This will be messy, but worth it.

"I think you would also look lovely in the red and gold of the Panbrio Isles," Amarelia says. "It would make your hair look like gold as well."

You know, if I work quickly enough, I might be able to take them both out. It would solve Ty's whole marriage problem.

Cressida preens. "Do you really think so?"

Amarelia nods assertively. "Most definitely. I'm sure my brother would agree."

"The prince!" Nadia cries, practically swooning. "You're so lucky to marry a prince!"

Despite her jovial tone, I catch the jealous undercurrents in her statement. If I play this right, I might be able to incite a bit of violence and get Nadia to off Cressida for me. Keeping my hands clean has its perks.

"I would agree on her luck if it were not my brother. For that, she has my pity," Amarelia says, smirking.

"Oh, I'm sure he can't be that bad," Cress says with a grin. "He must have many winning attributes."

Amarelia shrugs. "I suppose."

"Do you think I should wear red and gold when I meet him?"

Oh, good. We're back to talking about dresses.

Amarelia tilts her head, looking Cress over. "Maybe." She turns to me. "What do you think, Lady Klarissa? You have yet to give your opinion."

"Well, I think Cressida would look lovely in anything," I lie, giving Cress the fakest smile I can muster.

Cressida's answering smile is tight. She stopped caring about my opinion a long time ago, and we both know it.

"Maybe I'll ask Liege Greengrass, if I can get them to see me. I tried stopping by to make an appointment for a fitting on my way here, but they couldn't be bothered to chat even for a second."

I straighten in my seat, my attention piqued. "Liege Greengrass is back at the palace?"

Cress nods. "The queen had them brought back to prepare things for the upcoming ball."

Amarelia scrunches her nose. "The queen asked me to go

to them and get fitted for some new dresses, but I was wondering why. I have my own designers. Why would I need this Liege Greengrass?"

"Oh, but you must go to them!" Nadia chimes in. "They are simply the best! A true eye for design!"

Cress adds in her praise, but I'm already checked out of the conversation, rising from my seat.

"If you'll excuse me, ladies, I just remembered I have somewhere I need to be."

Amarelia gives me a somewhat suspicious look, but Nadia waves me off as Cressida ignores me. I try not to leave the room too quickly, but once I'm out in the hallway away from their prying eyes, I quicken my pace, rushing toward where Gregorian stays when they're in Rosana. It's an area of the palace that's not quite a common area, but still far from where the rest of the nobility resides. When I asked one time why they didn't request a full guest room they shrugged.

"I have a bed and a washroom right off my workroom. What more could I ask for? Besides, I like being away from everyone else. It gives me a chance to work in the quiet."

I never bothered to ask again. If they were content, there was no need for me to interfere.

When I get to their room, the door is open. I peek inside. Gregorian is definitely here, as evidenced by the chaos of material strewn across every surface, but I don't see them anywhere. I rap my knuckles on the door.

"I'm sorry, but I'm not doing any fittings right now," a voice calls out from the attached room. "I'm terribly busy. Try again later."

I smile. Despite having worked with nobles and royals for the better part of seven years, they still have the heavy drawl common among those living in the southeast corner of Elodia.

"Too busy even for me?" I call out, stepping inside.

There's a crash in the adjoining room, a bit of swearing, and then Gregorian appears. As always, they're dressed impeccably in a style all their own. The top half of their outfit mimics a typical male jacket and waistcoat made from the finest green silk and sewn with shining yellow threads while the bottom is a sweeping skirt made of several shimmering layers. Most people assume Gregorian is older due to their fame throughout the kingdom—someone of their skill must surely be someone with decades of experience—however, the attractive individual blinking at me right now reached notoriety and fame at the young age of sixteen and is currently only a few months shy of twenty-three. Nary a wrinkle mars their flawless bronze skin, and gray hairs wouldn't dare impose on the ink-black locks woven into the long braid draped elegantly over their shoulder.

"Rissa!" they say, rushing to pull me into a hug. "I always have time for you." They pull out of the hug, brown eyes darting around the room. "I actually have some deep blue silk around here somewhere that would look flawless on you, especially if I pair it with the lace I had imported from Northern Galloway."

I laugh, feeling lighter than I have in weeks. "I actually didn't come for a fitting."

"No?" Gregorian says, arching a perfectly manicured eyebrow.

"I've already had enough conversations about clothing today to last a lifetime."

"Well, that leaves either a friendly chat over some tea or something more salacious, though I thought after that night we agreed we work better as friends than lovers."

"We do," I say with a nod.

They flash their perfect teeth in a grin. "We really do." Their grin turns into a smirk. "Besides, I'm taken now."

"G! Who is it that finally wormed their way into your heart?"

"His name is Calix. We crossed paths several months ago. It was supposed to be a one-time thing, but it seems I may have caught feelings. Turns out they're not as despicable as I always thought them to be. Who knew?"

My smile falters a little. As much as I'm happy for Gregorian, I can't help but feel a little jealous. I quickly push the pesky, unwanted emotions aside.

"Anyway, I assume that means you came for tea." They glance around. "Seems you forgot it, though."

Another small laugh escapes me and I shake my head. "We can definitely ring for tea, but I mostly came because I need your help."

"Oh?"

I nod, stepping closer so no one walking by might overhear. "There's a bit of treason sneaking through the castle, and I think you might be able to help me suss it out."

"Well, this sounds like a conversation that might require something stronger than plain tea. You ring for some while I dig out some brandy to add a little extra flavor."

A few minutes later we have a full service of tea spiked with the kingdom's finest brandy, the door is locked, and we're deep in conversation. Gregorian listens attentively as I fill them in on the details surrounding Freya's departure, Amarelia's arrival, the cult's latest efforts, and the possible coup. I avoid any specifics for their safety—the fewer people that know the exact details, the better. When I finish, they stare at me for a moment before letting out a low whistle.

"And this is exactly why I'm happy to take the title of

'liege' and all it entails while staying on the outskirts of noble life. Y'all make things messy."

"Sometimes I wish I could escape as well. So, can you help?"

They tap their chin. "I think so. You basically want me to encourage a little gossip here and there among the right people, find out who knows what and whom they support. Correct?"

"If you're comfortable with that."

"Darling, I've been waiting for the day this particular skillset would come in handy. Do you know how much rubbish I've endured for no reason? Now, don't get me wrong, some of it is delightful, but often it's all I can do not to let a pin or two slip."

I chuckle. "Well, I appreciate your willingness to help. If you could also find out exactly how much Cressida is involved, that could be useful. I suspect she's more a pawn than anything, but even a timeline of when her engagement was arranged could be helpful."

Gregorian makes a sound somewhere between a sigh and a groan. "I guess this means I'll have to fit her in after all."

"Sorry."

"The things I do for Kingdom and Crown." They shoot me a grin. "And you. Because I love you dearly."

I return the grin. "I am very lovable."

"You are, darling. You are. Which brings me to asking whether or not anyone has managed to earn your affections?"

I narrow my eyes at them, my heart picking up a touch. "What have you heard?"

Their eyebrows shoot up. "Nothing, but that reaction tells me there's a story."

I shake my head. "No story."

"Lies."

"No, not a lie." I sigh. "It's complicated."

"Love always is. Or so I hear. I'm new to the whole love thing, and while I've actually found it wonderful, I've seen the ill affects it can have."

"You weren't even here to watch Ty fall apart."

Any amusement falls away and Gregorian sobers. "I heard about the accident. He loved her then? Or is it just Bastion he's grieving?"

"Both," I answer honestly. "He loves them both."

"Loves?"

"Did I forget to mention we're pretty sure they faked their deaths?"

They smack my arm gently. "Um, yes! This means that if you prove the coup that magic won't die because Tybalt can still marry the girl."

I nod. "That's where Ty is right now. He's using his trip to Krixwell as a cover to find Freya and bring her back."

"That's a relief."

Their fingers toy with the chartreuse crystal around their neck. Sometimes I forgot part of their honor and title allowed them to receive permission to access their air magic. I'm not sure how much they actually use it for what they do, but I know as well as anyone that once you get used to magic, it's inconvenient to be without it.

"I also rather liked Freya," they confess. "She was clever, kind, and down to earth. She's a good match for your cousin. As someone who grew up a commoner, I'm of the firm belief a commoner queen is exactly what this kingdom needs."

"I agree. I think she and I could be good friends. Amarelia on the other hand . . ." I pull a face and Gregorian chuckles.

"Well, let's pray to whatever gods are listening that things work out the way we want them."

We toast with our teacups and finish off their contents. Gregorian sets theirs down with a sigh, running a hand down their face.

"Well, if I'm to play spy for you, I should open shop." They scowl at the closed door. "The sooner I get orders in, the sooner I can get the work done. Hopefully, my workload won't increase too much."

"I'm sorry," I say. "I can help you out if you need."

Gregorian looks at me, horror flashing across their face. "Absolutely not! Not after last time!"

I wince. "That was a tiny mistake."

"You keep telling yourself that. It took me days to fix that dress. *Days.*"

"It also wasn't entirely my fault. If I recall correctly, you had a little too much to drink which was why I was helping in the first place."

"It was enough for me to learn my lesson and keep you far from my work. I make masterpieces, darling, but that was a master mess."

I cross my arms in a faux pout. "Fine." I look over at them and smile. "But I can come and chat with you and keep you company."

"Now that's an offer I'll accept." They push up from their chair and stroll toward the door. "But for now, why don't you go fill your priest in on your progress?"

Heat rises in my cheeks as I stumble to my feet. "I don't . . . Why would you . . ."

Gregorian gives me knowing look as they unlock the door. "I've known you long enough to read between the lines, Rissa."

I shake my head. "There are plenty of things I didn't tell you."

They pause, their hand on the door handle, and frown at me. "He sounded like a good man, an ally."

"He is," I rush to assure them. "He's a good friend."

"Rissa . . ."

I hold up a hand. "It's complicated. It really is. I don't want him to get hurt."

"Don't you think he should get a say?"

"What makes you think he hasn't already?"

They arch an eyebrow. "Has he?"

I sigh and shake my head. Gregorian sighs and places their hands on my shoulders.

"Rissa, you deserve love just as much as everyone else. If you don't want a relationship, that's fine, but you shouldn't run from one out of fear of the unknown. You deserve a happily ever after, however you choose to find it."

I blink back tears. Sometimes it's eerie how seen Gregorian makes me feel. They press a quick kiss to my cheek before dropping their hands and opening the door.

"Now, go," they say, giving me a gentle push through the door. "We'll chat later."

I offer them a small smile. "Thank you, G."

"Always, darling. Now go."

I'm halfway to Miles's room before I stop, shaking my head. I can't do this. I can't talk to him. Not yet. Not now. Even though I didn't have much brandy, I can feel it buzzing in my brain. I need to wait until my head is clear to talk to him. I take a deep breath and force myself to change course. I will speak to him. I will work things out soon, but not today.

CHAPTER TWENTY-NINE

RISSA

The door in front of me might as well be a wall ten stories tall. Despite putting off visiting Miles for four days, I can't make myself go inside, let alone make myself knock. I'm frozen, heart racing, staring at it.

"Is my door doing tricks?"

I startle and spin around to face a grinning Miles, his arms loaded with books.

"I thought you were inside."

"Nope. I had to grab some things from the main library." He nods to the books in his arms. "But if you'll open my door for me, I'll be happy to meet your expectations. I'd be even happier if you'd join me inside."

"Miles, I . . ."

His smile falls away. "Is everything okay?"

"I'm not sure."

"Well, you're still welcome inside. Unless of course that's why you're here, to tell me you don't want to spend time with me anymore." He laughs humorlessly, shaking his head. "You'd think your avoiding me the past few days would be evidence enough, but despite my clever brain, I can be a bit slow to grasp things sometimes."

"Miles, no, that's not it."

He shifts the books in his arms. "Either way, would you mind?" He nods to the door. "These are quite heavy."

"Oh, of course."

I fumble with the doorknob and open the door, stepping aside so he can walk through first. I follow, somewhat hesitantly, closing the door behind us. He sets the books on the table and turns to me with a heavy sigh.

"Are you here to tell me whatever we had is over? You know, even if it is, I'll still help you. You can be honest."

I swallow, looking away. "I should be here to tell you that, but no." I look up at him. "I like what we have. I really do. The queen, she . . . threatened you."

His eyes widen. "What? How? Why?"

"Because of me. She knows I'm up to something, though she has no idea what. She's never really liked me, and now she thinks I'm encouraging Ty away from her plans."

"Well, to be fair, you are, but with good reason." His forehead scrunches. "What exactly does that have to do with me?"

"Well, she made it clear that she didn't like me having a relationship with you and basically threatened to send you packing if I don't do everything she asks. I'm sorry."

Miles chuckles. "I'd like to see her try to send me away."

I blink at him. "What?"

"Do you know how many people are trained and qualified to do the blood uniting marriage ceremony?" I shake my head and he grins. "Five."

"Five? Only five?"

"Yep. Only five. Well, actually three. Last I heard two were technically still in training, and out of those three, I was the only one willing and available to travel here. Do you even know what it takes to be qualified to perform the ceremony?"

I shake my head.

"First, you have to be born with spirit magic, sometimes called holy magic. It's extremely rare, only appearing a few times a generation. Second, you have to train with that magic for a few years until you became a master. Third, you have to study the historical and holy texts until you know them backward and forward. It's no easy task and not something simply anyone can do. If the queen wants me gone, she's a bit out of luck."

He takes a step closer, and my heart starts racing for a different reason.

"So, if that's your only reason for avoiding me . . ." He trails off and I look away.

"That's the main reason."

"And the other reasons?"

I take a deep breath and dare to meet his eyes. There are no expectations there, merely gentle curiosity.

"I've come to care for you. Deeply."

He doesn't say anything, waiting for more. When I don't elaborate, he huffs a laugh.

"I care for you too, Klarissa, a good bit more than I've ever cared for anyone else. I would even go as far as to say I—"

I flinch without even meaning to, and he hesitates only a moment.

"—cherish you. I *cherish* you, Klarissa."

I breathe out, relieved he didn't say something I'm not sure I can echo.

"I told you before I'd never try to hold you back or tie you down. I meant that."

I take a shaky breath, fighting back tears. "I know. Things shouldn't be this complicated. *I* shouldn't be this complicated."

"I don't mind complicated."

"What if I wanted something different?" I ask, my voice barely a whisper.

"What?" He takes another tentative step closer. "Are you saying that you want to be exclusive?"

"Maybe?" I shake my head. "I don't know."

"What's holding you back? Is there anything I can do to make you more comfortable?"

I take a deep breath and release it slowly. "I grew up with Ty, who believed through most of his childhood that Fate would hand him his perfect match and they would live happily ever after. I never had anyone telling me I had a perfect match out there, but I did have a father trying to marry me off to anyone who even glanced my way. I decided to foil his plans at every turn, flirting and doing whatever I could to push those suitors away while still having fun of my own. I don't regret anything, though I figured it would be temporary, that one day I would discover love and that would be that.

"Then I saw Ty fall deeply in love with the wrong person. I saw how much he hurt, and I knew I never wanted to feel that way. I decided that I would never let myself get close enough to someone to fall in love. I honestly wasn't even sure I could feel love like that. Sexual attraction, sure, but romantic love? That wasn't something for me. But now? I'm not so sure. I met you and I'm considering things I've never even wondered before. I'm a mess and I'm broken and I'm too complicated. You don't really want me."

He takes another step closer and reaches toward me.

When I don't move away, he takes my hands in his, meeting my eyes.

"First of all, you are not broken. It's okay if you don't feel attraction, romantic or otherwise, the same as other people. Everyone moves at their own pace and has a right to feel however they feel. Maybe you need more of connection with someone before you can develop those romantic feelings. Maybe you have things you need to work through to overcome preconceived ideas you have in your head. Whatever the reason, you are not broken, and it's okay to feel the way you do.

"Secondly, if given the chance, I would happily call you mine. You and your happiness mean the world to me. I want this. I want *you*. If you're ready to take this step, I accept, and if you ever feel trapped and need things to return to the nonexclusive way they are now, I accept that as well. I accept you exactly as you are. You are perfect."

I'm not exactly sure when I start crying, but my cheeks are damp and I'm a weepy mess.

"I'm not perfect. I'm very flawed."

"Hmm. Are you? Maybe. But I'm also flawed. Quite flawed, actually. Do you care about my flaws?"

I manage to shake my head and he grins. "See? Flaws aren't a dealbreaker when you . . . cherish someone the way I cherish you. I cherish you because of your flaws, not in spite of them, because they they make who you are. You are incredible, Klarissa, and I very much want to keep you in my life. If you need to step back and just be my friend, then so be it. But I need you. You fill the pieces of me I thought would be empty forever. You are smart and clever and you complete me. I'll take you however I can. Just let me know what you need."

"I think I want this. You. Us. Only us. No one else."

His whole face glows. "Yeah?"

"Yeah."

His eyes flick to my mouth then back up. "May I kiss you?"

I answer by kissing him first. It's simple and chaste, but there's an undeniable fierceness and longing behind it. When I pull back, his eyes are shining.

I sigh and close my eyes, pressing my forehead to his.

"I cherish you, too."

He huffs a small laugh before pressing another quick kiss to my lips. This time when he pulls back, he puts enough space between us to look me in the eyes.

"So, we're good?"

A smile curves my lips. "We're good."

"Excellent. Not to break the mood, but would you like to hear some of the results of my research?"

I laugh. "Of course."

He takes my hand and leads me over to the table. Even after we take our seats, he keeps his fingers tangled with mine, sorting the books on the table with his spare hand.

"I haven't found a counter spell," he explains, opening one of his notebooks, "but I think I have some ideas on how to sustain the king's magic and fight some of the symptoms. Nothing I've found would be a permanent solution, but it could work like a salve to prop up the king should something go wrong. Give us enough time to maybe find something else."

I nod, pulling the notebook in front of me, looking it over.

"There's nothing more definitive?"

He shakes his head. "Not that I've found. Unfortunately, there aren't that many books on *Naturcræft* that are easily accessible. We would almost need to find the library of someone actively studying and using it."

"But those people are likely involved in the cult."

He nods. "Precisely, and if they think we're sniffing around, it could put them on alert."

I sigh and frown down at the notebook. I feel so useless. Miles gives my hand a gentle squeeze, and I look up at him.

"We'll figure something out. I promise. Even if I have to explore new facets of my magic, I'll do it."

"What do you mean? What exactly can your magic do?"

"Well, spirit magic in general is connected more directly to the flow of magic. You have earth magic which connects you to plants, soil, and the like. From what I understand, your specialty is over plants."

I nod and he continues.

"Freya had water magic, so water would call to her and she could manipulate it. Bastion could do the same with air, and Ty can control fire. I have that same pull and control in a sense, but my element, if that's what you want to call it, is the spirit of magic. Most of the time I use it for things like testing magic or the binding ceremony, but there are other lesser known uses."

"Like what? Could you manipulate someone's magic enough to stop or control it?"

"In theory, yes. There's supporting evidence that spirit magic can hinder or aid the flow of magic in others. However, with magic as weak as it is . . ." He trails off with a shrug. "I'd also likely need more training. I'm still relatively young and untested despite my years of practice. I may have been studying since my magic was discovered at age fourteen, but when it comes to my branch of magic, ten years is hardly anything."

Something in my face must show the hopelessness I feel

seeping over me, because he gives my hand another squeeze and traces his thumb over my knuckles.

"It doesn't mean I won't try my damndest to figure out if and how I can help."

I offer him a weak smile but it's sincere. "Thank you, Miles. I really appreciate it."

He leans over and brushes a kiss on my cheek. "Anything for you. Always."

I hold his eyes for a moment, relishing the comfort his gaze brings, before forcing myself to look away.

"Maybe I can help you look through the things you've found?"

He grins. "Excellent idea. First, why don't we ring for some tea?"

A small laugh escapes me. "Tea sounds perfect."

I think, perhaps not for the first time, when Miles is involved, most things feel rather perfect.

CHAPTER THIRTY

BASH

Freya lands a blow with her dagger and immediately spins to block another blow. She pushes the person back into my sword. I grin at her as their eyes go wide. I jerk the sword out, and the body falls with a wet thud.

"Is that all of them?" I ask, looking around.

"One tried to escape off that way, but I stopped them with a throwing dagger."

Pride swells through me. "You're getting really good with those daggers."

She grins. "I had an excellent teacher."

I chuckle and step closer, tucking a stray piece of hair behind her ear. "You get more credit than I do. You've worked hard on your precision."

"I am pretty amazing."

"You're incredible."

I pull her into a kiss so fierce it leaves me lightheaded. She grins up at me and attempts to wipe a smudge of blood from my cheek, but I'm pretty sure she only ends up smearing it more.

"We should really get cleaned up and back on the road," she mumbles.

I nod, sobering a little as I look down the road. I'm still eager to get back to Rosana and check on Ty, but our current path has allowed us to take out three supply carts since leaving East Hingling. I can't deny the progress we've made in taking out the cult. If we make good time, we should arrive in Krixwell by nightfall. How long we'll stay there is still undecided.

"Ty will be fine," Freya whispers, pulling me from my thoughts. "We'll get to him in time."

I sigh and attempt a smile. "I'm sure you're right." I glance over my shoulder at the supply cart. "Let's figure out what to take and burn the rest."

She nods her agreement and we make quick work of it. We're soon back on the road. When we arrive in Krixwell, the streets are still flooded with people even though the official festival doesn't start for another couple days. The inns and available spaces are mostly booked, but we manage to find room above a tavern. It's small, but we've worked with less before. At least it has a dividing screen for some privacy and a tub we can use to wash up. As a bonus, there's a back entrance that will allow us to come and go as needed without having to go through the tavern area every time.

We have a quick dinner in the tavern before returning upstairs. I kick off my boots and stretch out across the bed.

"What's the plan?" Freya asks, settling next to me on the mattress.

I slip my arm behind her and pull her closer so she's lying on my chest. I love how perfect she feels there.

"We stake out the most likely areas for cult activities. The records didn't indicate whether the earl here was directly involved or whether he's simply been turning a blind eye. We can stake out his residence and see what we can find. There are also a few businesses I'm positive are involved. We can observe them tomorrow and see which ones are fronts for more direct cult activity and which are more passive."

She nestles closer, tucking her head under my chin. "Should we split up? You could take the main residence, and I'll check out the businesses. We can meet back here in the afternoon to compare notes."

I tense, but relax a moment later. "I would rather stick together but we could cover more ground if we split."

"Would it make you feel better if I promised to be careful?"

A chuckle rumbles out of me. "Maybe, if I thought you'd stick to that promise."

"Hey!" she says, pushing up to scowl down at me. "I'm careful."

I grin and she rolls her eyes. "Let's not forget that you're the one that sent me into that cult house with half the information I needed. If anyone here is careless, it's you."

Guilt washes over me. "You're never going to let me live that down, are you?"

"Nope," she says, collapsing back on top of me.

I kiss the top of her head. "You know, I was terrified when I realized that the house wasn't as empty as I thought it would be, but I also knew you were strong. I had faith in you. I still do. Do you realize how far you've come? How incredible you are?"

"I'm not *that* incredible," she mumbles against my chest.

"Oh, but you are. You really are, Freya."

The use of her name has her sitting up again. When I look up at her there's nothing but admiration shining in her eyes. My heart stutters and I hope she sees the same in my gaze.

"I love you. So much."

A soft smile twitches on her lips. "I love you, too, Bash."

I smile and reach a hand to cup her cheek. She sighs and leans into my touch, her eyes fluttering shut. I shift my position so I can press my lips to the warmth of hers. It's meant to be a brief kiss, but she moves into it, almost as if on instinct. It heightens quickly and heat pools low in my gut. I pull back but don't move away. In one smooth motion, I flip our positions so she's flat on the bed and I'm braced above her. She looks up at me and the heat in her gaze is enough to melt away the rest of the world.

I lower myself down and capture her mouth in a kiss that leaves every other kiss far behind. A small sound escapes her as my body presses against hers. I groan, grinding against her almost involuntarily. The friction is delicious and I need more. She moves her body with mine, making pleasure and need ripple through me. Our breaths quicken with our movements and I need more. More. More. *More.*

My hand slides up under her shirt and the feel of her skin beneath my fingertips has me aching for her. She must sense my need, or maybe it's a need of her own, because a moment later she's working her shirt and undergarments over her head, throwing them to the floor. I don't hesitate to join her, casting my own shirt aside. I resume my previous position and gaze down at her.

"Look at you," I say, tracing a hand down her body. She quivers under my touch. "So beautiful."

"Bash," she breathes. "Please."

"Please what, Princess?" I say, circling her breasts. "I need you to tell me what you want." She whimpers and I grin. "What do you need?"

"You!" she gasps.

"How do you want me?" My touch trails back up her body, back over her breasts, the tips of my fingers brushing over her peaked nipples. She moans and arches into my touch. "Do you want me to use my hands or my mouth?"

To punctuate my point, I lean down, pulling one of her breasts into my mouth and running my tongue across her nipple. She cries out, back arching. I smile against her skin. I linger a moment, relishing the taste of her, before I push back up, meeting her eyes.

"Well, Princess? What do you want?"

"Can you . . . Can we . . ." Her eyes dart lower to where my cock is straining against my pants.

I freeze, holding her gaze as I register what she wants. She quickly shakes her head.

"Never mind. Your mouth. Your mouth is fine."

I swallow, glancing away for a fraction of a second. "You want me inside you."

It's not meant to be a question. Not really. But I want to be sure before we take this step.

"Only if you want it too."

"I . . ."

Do I want it? The ache in my groin says yes. The desire pulsing through me says yes. But there's still that small echo of doubt in the back of my mind wondering if I want this for me or if I'm only considering it because it's what is expected.

"Bash," she says, reaching up to cup my cheek. "I honestly only want it if you do."

I nod slowly. "I think I do." A smile breaks out across my face as I realize that I mean it. "I do."

She hooks a hand behind my neck and pulls me down into a kiss.

"If you change your mind—" she starts but I cut her off with another kiss.

"Then I'll use my mouth instead, but I do want this."

I pull back enough so we can rid ourselves of the rest of our clothes. When I straddle her again, she looks up and takes me in properly and I do the same. This isn't the first time we've seen each other naked, but it feels wrong not to properly appreciate her. I love watching her body react to mine. Her eyes trace up my muscular thighs to my heavy cock, leaking and ready. She doesn't stop her appreciation there, allowing her gaze to travel over the hard planes of my abdomen and chest, which I may or may not purposefully flex. When her eyes finally get to my face, I'm smirking.

"Done looking, Princess?"

She returns my smirk. "Are you?"

I grin, leaning down so my lips are directly above hers but not quite touching. "Never. I will never have my fill of looking at you."

Before she can reply, my mouth is on hers. Her body shifts below mine, our bodies lining up. I don't insert myself yet, but I press slightly against the heat of her entrance.

"Bash, please," she begs, moving against me.

Gods, I love hearing her beg. I tease her entrance and she makes a sound somewhere between a moan and a gasp.

"Patience, Princess," I say, moving my mouth to her neck.

"Bastion!" she cries out and I chuckle at her desperate eagerness.

"So needy." I nip at her ear. "I like that."

I reach down between us, my fingers brushing her clit. She whimpers and I allow my touch to linger a moment more before I line myself up properly and slide inside her. She gasps and I could come from that sweet sound alone. I'm not even in all the way and I'm already overwhelmed by the feel of her. It's bliss and I need more. A second later I'm pushing deeper, slowly but effectively filling her. When I bottom out, I pause. I wonder if I'm giving her a chance to adjust or myself. It's so much and yet not enough.

"Okay, Princess?" I ask, my voice rough.

"Never been better," she manages, her voice breathy.

I chuckle and start moving. Each thrust brings with it a new wave of pleasure. The sounds that escape her mouth are pure ecstasy, driving me. My want and need overwhelm my senses when she starts moving with me to create as much friction as possible.

"So good," I gasp out. "So perfect for me. Such a good girl."

She makes a sound between a whimper and a moan and I thrust harder, eager to draw sounds from her lips. My climax is approaching too quickly, however, and I force myself to slow down. I will not end this before she gets her pleasure.

She clenches around me and I can tell she's close. I lean down and whisper in her ear.

"Come for me, Princess. Come for me."

As if spurred by my words, her climax shudders through her. She cries out and I continue thrusting as she tightens around me. She finally stills beneath me, breathing hard. I realize I'm not far behind her.

"Can I finish inside you?" I ask, voice tight.

She manages a nod and my own pleasure crashes through me a moment later. I empty out into her, breathing hard. I wait a moment before slowly sliding out and collapse next to her on the small space between her body and the wall. I breathe in and out slowly, staring up at the ceiling as what we did fully sinks in. What we've done up to this point still qualifies as sex, but this was the first time since Ty I've attempted this particular level of physical intimacy where I didn't feel dirty or sick afterward.

"Are you okay?" she asks, her voice timid, almost afraid.

I turn my head to meet her eyes. "I'm much better than okay." I push up on an elbow. "Are you okay?"

"Bash, that was incredible. Yes, I'm very much okay."

"Really?"

"Really."

A smile twitches on my lips. "Gods, you're perfect." I collapse back on the bed and shift to slide my arm behind her, pulling her against me, craving her touch. I kiss the top of her head. "How did I get so lucky to call you mine?"

She snuggles closer. "After what we just did, I'm pretty sure I'm the lucky one."

"I guess we're both pretty lucky." I sigh, tightening my hold on her. "You know, I never thought I would get to have this. Not just with you, but with anyone."

My confession is quiet, barely above a whisper. I'm afraid if I say it too loudly, my fear will manifest. Freya shifts closer, pressing a kiss to my bare chest. It's simple, but comforting, encouraging me to continue.

"After Ty . . ." I shake my head, pushing aside the pain that rises. "After Ty I figured Fate had her fun with me and decided I wasn't worth her time. Sometimes I wonder if I'll wake up and find everything with you has been a dream, something I made up to get past everything else I've been through."

"If that's what Fate really thinks, she's wrong," Freya says, her voice insistent but calm. "You're worth it, and you deserve the world. Despite what happened before, I'm here now with no plans to go anywhere. You're stuck with me, Bastion Shamblefoot, and you're not getting rid of me."

My fingers trace lazy circles on her side, but I don't

speak. I'm not sure there are words to describe what I'm feeling right now. The hope. The fear. The longing. The terror. After a moment she pushes up enough to look down at me.

"Did you hear me? I'm not going anywhere. I promise."

My smile is sad as I meet her eyes. "I want to believe that, but my experience has proven I seldom get what I want."

"Well, fuck Fate and everything she's thrown your way. I thought I was supposed to marry Ty and save the kingdom's magic with my blood, but that supposed Fate fractured and shattered. This thing between us is the fortune of fractured Fate. We survived what was thrown at us, and now we're here, together and happy. We deserve this."

My smile turns more sincere. "We do, don't we."

"We definitely do."

I blow out a breath, looking up at her with nothing short of admiration. "I love you."

She kisses me, chaste and quick, but there's so much meaning behind it. "I love you, too."

She settles back down, cuddling against me. I resume trailing my fingers along her skin and slowly we drift off, feeling happy, safe, and content.

CHAPTER THIRTY-ONE

TY

We're only a day or so out from Krixwell, and I haven't found a single shred of evidence that Bash and Freya are alive. One innkeeper claims he saw a couple potentially fitting their description, but they arrived late and left early so he wasn't really sure. Despite Cooper's help, I'm not getting nearly enough chances to ask around thanks to the sergeant's hovering. Tonight we're camping alongside the road and it's cold enough we break out the tents. Sergeant Hollowcane immediately separates me and Cooper, assigning himself to share my tent.

"I don't know what you're up to, Your Highness," he says, his voice low as I lay out my bedroll, "but when we arrive in Krixwell, I expect you to act like the prince you are."

I sit down on my bedroll and look up at the sergeant, feigning a look of innocence. "I'm just here for the festival."

"You and I both know that you have alternative plans. Your mother also knows."

"What would those plans be? What could I possibly have

planned for the literal middle of nowhere and an apple festival?"

"As I said, I do not know. What I do know is that you are putting yourself and the kingdom at risk."

I scoff, shaking my head. "I'm not the person you need to worry about putting the kingdom at risk."

"Perhaps your cousin, then."

I clench my jaw and glare up at the man. "You keep Klarissa out of this. She's done more for Elodia than you ever will."

Now he scoffs, shaking his head. Before I even fully realize what I'm doing, I'm on my feet. I grab his shirt and jerk him closer. I relish the shock on his face before he twists his mouth into a sneer.

"You work for the Crown," I growl. "Which means you work for me."

He has the audacity to laugh and my grip on his shirt tightens.

"I work for the Crown, indeed, but not for you. I work for the king and queen. Gods help us when your father dies." His eyes dart down to my fists still gripping his shirt. "This does nothing but prove to me how unfit you are."

"Get. Out." I throw him back, and he stumbles but unfortunately does not fall. "Get out of my tent."

"Your mother assigned me to your detail, not you. I'm assigned to protect you, and you cannot override your mother's orders."

"Let me make myself perfectly clear. You are welcome to stay in my tent tonight, but I cannot guarantee that I won't slit your throat the moment you fall asleep."

He narrows his eyes. "You wouldn't dare."

"Try me."

He studies me for a moment before huffing. "Fine, but

when you get yourself killed, the blood will not be on my hands."

He snatches up his things and storms from the tent. A few minutes later Cooper slips inside, giving me a curious look.

"Why is the sergeant on a rampage?"

"He's a treasonous ass who doesn't know what he's talking about," I mumble.

"Right. Okay." Copper glances over his shoulder before dropping his things with a sigh. "We should get some sleep. I have next watch."

I nod and settle on my bedroll while Cooper lays out his and does the same. Despite the rush from arguing with the sergeant, my nerves calm and I fall asleep relatively quickly. That rest doesn't last long however, and I'm woken by yelling. I blink into the darkness of my tent, taking a moment to orient myself. Once I do, I'm on my feet, my sword in hand. I rush out of the tent, Cooper on my heels.

We're under attack.

Our attackers are dressed in all black, making it difficult to tell how many there are, but if I had to guess, there are at least a dozen. What I know for sure is we are very much outnumbered. Having taken us by surprise, one of the guards that was on watch is already down and the sergeant has blood dripping from a nasty wound on his arm. I leap into the fray, taking down a masked attacker relatively easily before turning to another. This one puts up a little better of a fight, but this group doesn't seem to be as trained as previous groups I've encountered. I take down two more before I realize they're moving me away from camp. Shit.

Suddenly I'm surrounded by even more people, completely separated from the rest of my group. I pull on my magic. It's weak right now, just like it has been the entire trip, but I manage to find a flicker of a flame and bring it forward. I allow the flame to sit in my palm for a moment before I throw it forward, setting the person closest to me aflame.

I push my magic into the fire wide, and push the flames outward, probably wider than I should given how the surrounding brush catches. At least my error in judgment works to my advantage, sending my attackers scrambling away from the flames. Unfortunately, my magic is too weak to control the flames effectively, and I struggle to rein the fire in. I'm vaguely aware of Cooper joining me and beating back the remaining attackers while I focus most of my energy on controlling the flames. By the time I've reduced them to wisps of curling smoke, the battle is done.

I look around to scattered bodies, some bloody, some burnt, taking in the damage. Cooper groans beside me, and I turn to him. His hand grips a wound on his forearm, blood seeping between his fingers.

"Let me see," I say, dropping my sword and taking a step closer.

Cooper releases his arm with a wince, and I nearly gag at the gash in his arm. I've seen a lot of wounds but this one is bad. Really bad. He meets my eyes, and I can practically taste his fear.

"I don't—" He wavers on his feet, his eyes rolling back in his head. I lunge forward and catch him before he hits the ground.

"Cooper," I say, giving him a shake.

He mumbles something incoherently, but his eyes don't open. He's losing so much blood. I look around frantically, but there's no one around. Is anyone else even alive? I force myself to focus, putting pressure on the wound, but that does nothing. The hot blood seeps between my fingers, coming entirely too fast.

"Fuck!" I scream. "Don't die on me. You can't die on me! I will not allow it."

I consider ripping material from his shirt to tie off the wound, but I know that won't be enough. He needs the wound properly sealed off. He needs it sewn up in some way. He needs . . . I freeze.

He needs fire.

I take a deep breath and reach for my magic. My hold on it is even weaker than before, but I don't need a full flame this time, only heat. I breathe in and out slowly, centering my energy. Smoke curls outward from my palm as it heats and glows. I carefully press my hand against Cooper's wound. The smell of burning flesh floods my nostrils, and I cover my nose with my elbow. I wait another moment before removing my hand. The smell is still overwhelming, and I turn to the side and retch. Once I'm able to steady myself, I focus on Cooper. It worked, thank the gods. The gash is sealed over. A burn in the shape of my hand mars his skin, but at least he won't die now.

I stand, sheathing my sword and hoisting Cooper with me. I stumble back to our campsite with him in tow and find even more carnage. Among several dead from our attackers lie the rest of my guard detail, including the sergeant. Even as much as I hated the man, I didn't want him dead. Not really. I swallow and force myself to stay on task. I need to get myself and Cooper out of here. I lay Cooper down off to the side and quickly pack up one tent as well as my and Cooper's supplies, attaching everything to our horses, which, thank the gods, didn't run off in the chaos. I do release the extra horses in the hopes that maybe they'll return home. I dig out medicine from the sergeant's pack and fetch some water, heading back to Cooper. I splash some water on his face and he startles, opening his eyes with a groan.

"What happened? Did I— Shit!" He inhales sharply when he goes to move his arm. His eyes drop to his wound and widen.

"I'm sorry," I say quickly. "There was a lot of blood, and I didn't know what else to do."

He swallows hard. "Thank you."

I nod. "Of course." I glance around. "We really need to get out of here." I look at him. "Do you think you can ride?"

He pauses, considering my question before nodding slowly. "I think so."

I pass him the medicine I found. "This should help with the pain, but it may take a while to work."

He downs the medicine without hesitation, and I help him to his feet. He winces as he mounts his horse, but he seems steady enough. He cradles his arm, steering his horse with one hand but seems overall capable.

We ride for a few hours, putting as much distance between us and the attack as possible. I insist we take a break and tell Cooper I'll take first watch. He doesn't protest, falling asleep immediately. I only make it a couple hours, however, before I'm waking him. I make him take another dose of medicine before I fall asleep.

When he wakes me, dawn is kissing the horizon. I offer to let him get some more sleep, but he argues that getting on the road would be the best option. We change out of our bloody and smoke-scented clothes so we don't draw attention should we meet anyone on the road. Once we're ready, I check over his wound in the daylight and my stomach twists at the obvious handprint marring his skin.

"Gods, I am so sorry."

"It's fine," he says, his voice weak but firm, pulling his sleeve over the scar. "I'm alive. That's the important part."

I nod, wanting to believe him. I have to believe him.

We make good time despite our exhaustion, arriving in Krixwell midafternoon. The streets are overflowing with people in town for the festival, so much so we're forced to board our horses at the first available stable to navigate the streets.

"Do you already have a room?" Cooper asks as we elbow our way through the crowd.

"Technically, I'm an invited guest of Lord Crawhill, but I think accepting the invitation to stay at his estate would put more of a target on my back. I think laying low tonight might be the better option. Let the cult think their attack worked."

Cooper nods his agreement. "I can try to find us somewhere to stay, though we may not have any luck, as busy as it is."

"Can't hurt to try. If we don't find a place, we can try the estate. We'll just have to remain alert the entire time." I pause, looking around. I nod to a fountain in the center of the main square. "Why don't you see what rooms are available, and I'll meet you there in an hour?"

"Deal."

He disappears into the crowd and I try to blend in as much possible. It doesn't take long for me to realize I'm being followed. I bob and weave through the crowd in an attempt to lose whomever it is. When I accidentally duck into a dead end alley, however, I have no way out. I sigh, rolling my neck, and turn around. My muscles ache from riding all day and exhaustion pulls at me, but I'm sure as Hell not backing down now.

"I know you're following me," I call out, my voice echoing off the walls. I slide my sword from its sheath. "Might as well show yourself so we can get this over with."

At first, no one appears and I wonder if my exhausted

brain is playing tricks on me. Then a shadow shifts and someone steps into the alley.

"Bit risky wandering around alone, you being a prince and all."

I blink, sure my brain is playing tricks as the person grins. "Hello, Ty."

CHAPTER THIRTY-TWO

FREYA

Ty seems as surprised to see me as I am to see him. Of course, I've had more time to adjust since I've been following him for several minutes. I didn't want to confront him, however, until we could be a little more alone. A side alley seems to work well enough.

"Freya?" he asks, disbelief filling his voice. He stumbles forward. "Is that really you?"

My grin widens and I move nearer, closing the distance between us. "In the flesh."

He takes a shaky breath, reaching to trace along my cheek in a barely-there touch. "You're really not dead."

Guilt swishes in my stomach. "Sorry about that. It was Bash's idea."

Ty startles, dropping his hand as he looks around. "Is Bash here, too?"

"Yes, well, not *here* here, but here in Krixwell, yes. He's been staking out the earl's house most of the day while I checked out the shopkeepers, but he's probably in our room by now. I was heading back myself when I spotted you in the crowd."

Some of the shock finally seeps from his features and he smiles that half-cocked grin that makes my stomach swoop.

"I'm glad you found me. I've been looking for you."

"You have? Why?"

His smile falls away, a shadow crossing his face. "Well, for one I missed you. It was never right of my mother to treat you that way. I meant what I said in my letter. Every word." He rubs the back of his neck. "But as much I wish that was the only reason, a lot has happened since you left, and I need your help." He hesitates, glancing around. "It's sensitive information."

I nod knowingly. "Bash and I have a lot to share as well. Let's head back to our room and we can compare notes." I pause, frowning. "Are you here alone?"

Ty's eyes widen. "Shit. I almost forgot about Cooper."

"Cooper?"

"Yeah, he's my guard detail. My mother sent me with a few others, but we were attacked last night. Cooper and I were the only two to make it out. He's looking for a place for us to stay. We were supposed to meet back at the fountain."

"Why don't I take you to the room first and then Bash or I can get Cooper? Everywhere is pretty much booked, so I doubt he'll be able to find anything anyway. We need to get you off the streets before you're recognized."

Ty nods, looking a little dazed. I cock my head, looking him over.

"Are you okay?"

"Huh? Yeah. Sorry. I'm just tired. I didn't get much sleep last night."

I laugh. "Poor little tired prince."

He grins and my heart melts a little. "Take me home and tuck me into bed?"

Conflicting emotions crash over me, and I opt to bury them with a smile.

"Come on."

I'm even more grateful now that our inn has a back entrance. It makes it ten times easier to sneak Ty upstairs without being spotted. When we get to our room, I hesitate a moment outside the door, listening carefully for any sign of Bash inside. Unfortunately, the door is too thick and the noise from the tavern below too loud for me to pick up on anything definitive. Ty gives me a curious look, but before he can say anything, I steel myself and open the door. Bash is indeed inside, apparently in the middle of changing his shirt. My breath catches at the sight of his bare chest and he grins. However, his cheerful expression vanishes, replaced by parted lips and wide eyes.

"Bash!" Ty cries, rushing into the room and pulling Bash into a hug.

Bash doesn't react at first, shooting me a look of startled confusion, but he snaps out of it and slowly returns the hug. I carefully close the door as Ty releases Bash, practically glowing.

"I found you. I really found you both!"

Bash glances to me, then back to Ty, before releasing a laugh and shaking his head as he pulls on a shirt.

"What are you doing here?" Bash asks. "And why are you alone?"

Ty waves Bash off. "I'm not alone. Cooper is here somewhere trying to find a place for us to stay tonight. I could stay at the earl's estate since I'm here as a guest to celebrate the festival, but I want to keep a low profile given that I was attacked last night."

AMBER D. LEWIS

Bash's amusement falls away. "Ty, what the fuck?"

Ty grins. "I survived."

I roll my eyes. "Obviously. I think Bash was wondering more why you're here in the first place."

Ty frowns, looking between us. "Because I was looking for you." He sighs, rubbing the back of his neck. "Look, a lot of stuff has happened, and it turns out Amarelia isn't who we thought at all. In fact, she's more than likely using some sort of outdated magic on my father, and there's no way she could be doing it without help from someone close. Klarissa and I suspect Lord Vanderhof and Lord Mayberry."

Bash and I exchange a look. We have pretty damning evidence to support that theory.

"But none of that matters right now." Ty's smile returns and he steps toward me, taking my hands into his. "Because one reason I had to find you was because Amarelia's blood test was faked, which means we still need to get married to save magic."

My heart leaps into my throat as Ty cocks his head and grins.

"What do you say, Freya Brambleberry? Will you marry me?"

"I—"

I look past Ty to Bash, all words evading me, but he's no help. He's gone lethally still. I'm not even sure he's breathing. I look back to Ty, whose smile is slipping.

"Ty, I—"

He drops my hands and takes a step back, shaking his head.

"I'm sorry about everything my mother did, but I won't let her get in the way again. I love you and I want to marry you. Even if Amarelia was an actual match, I would still want to marry you. If I hadn't thought you died in that carriage

274

attack, I would've started searching for you sooner. You believe that, right?"

"Yes, I believe you," I manage.

"So you'll marry me?"

"I—"

I glance to Bash, and he gives me an almost imperceptible nod. I'm not sure if what I feel is closer to disappointment or relief. Either way, my world is crumbling around me and there's no way to win. I look back to Ty to find him studying me.

"Freya, what—" His eyes widen and he stumbles back a step, his eyes darting between me and Bash. "Shit. I should've guessed. I—" His legs hit the edge of the bed and he sits, putting his head in his hands. "I fucked up. Shit. Shit. Shit."

I look frantically to Bash for help, but he's still frozen, his jaw clenched and his hands in fists at his side.

"Ty, I—"

His face jerks upward. Tears shine in his eyes as they meet mine. He attempts a smile, but it's a mocking, sad thing, barely turned up in one corner.

"I missed my opportunity. You two are . . . something. Right?" He lets out a humorless laugh before I can attempt an answer, shaking his head. "I can't blame you. I've fallen in love with both of you—I'm *still* in love with both of you—so I can't say I don't see the appeal. I thought—" He sighs, everything about him drooping like the life has seeped from him. "I thought you'd be happy you'd get to marry me after all."

The last part is said in such a broken whisper it shatters a bit of my heart. I quickly cross the room to him, taking a seat next to him on the bed.

"I am happy, Ty," I say, placing a hand on his knee. "It's just all a bit of a surprise."

He scoffs. "You don't have to lie."

I open my mouth to speak, but before I get a chance, Bash cuts in.

"We're both happy to see you, Ty," he says, his voice a little too stiff. "You two should really talk this out. I'll go find Cooper. I'll be back soon."

Bash goes to leave and I catch his gaze before the door closes. A little of his practiced resolve slips and I glimpse how brokenhearted he is. A little more of me shatters, but I force myself to hold it together, focusing on Ty. We sit in heavy silence for a while before he wets his lips, allowing his tear-filled eyes to meet mine.

"Do you . . . do you still love me?" he asks, his voice barely above a whisper. "Because I still love you."

I glance away. "I thought maybe I had started to get over you. I knew I still loved you deep down, but I was moving on and was becoming more and more okay with how things ended." I look up and meet his eyes. "When I saw you in the street, all those feelings came crashing back in. I realized I wasn't getting over you at all; I only figured out how to ignore the part of me that fell in love with you."

Hope flares to life in his eyes. "So you do want to marry me?"

"I do, but . . ." I glance away again.

"But you fell in love with Bash."

He sounds defeated and I nod guiltily, though I know I have no reason to feel guilt. Tears burn my own eyes and my heart aches.

"I love you both," I confess, my voice trembling. "Gods help me, but I love you both."

A tear escapes and Ty brushes it away with his thumb without a moment of hesitation. I lean into his touch, and he lets his hand linger.

"I can't say I blame you," he says softly, caressing my

cheek. "I'd be a hypocrite if I told you it wasn't possible to love two people at once."

I take a shuddering breath. "What are we going to do?"

"I don't know, Freya. I really don't know. I almost wish that Amarelia was a viable match so you and Bash could go off and live your happily ever after together. That way at least the two of you could be happy, and I could save my kingdom and maybe eventually fall in love with Amarelia."

"You'd really want that? To give us both up so we could be together?"

He sighs, dropping his hand as he looks away. "For you and Bash I would do anything. If I could find another suitable person to marry before the Fae moon, I would give you both up so at least you two could have happiness. You both deserve that."

"You deserve it too."

He lets out a bitter laugh. "The gods clearly disagree. But it doesn't matter."

"Because it's not an option," I say softly, my voice barely above a whisper. "Amarelia's blood won't work, so we're back to where we started."

He shakes his head and weaves his fingers with mine. "No, it won't work, but we're not back at the start. We're in a whole new mess, and I'm not sure how to navigate it. Quite frankly, even if we had time, I'm done looking for someone else. I need you in every way, Freya, and I'm terribly selfish. I *want* to marry you. I only hate that it will hurt Bash because I love him just as much and want him to have the happiness he deserves. If I could keep you both and have you both and all of us could have and be with each other, then I would take it in a heartbeat."

I still. "Can we have that? Is it possible? Could we all be together? All three of us?"

"I don't know. Maybe? It's complicated. Everything is always so fucking complicated." He sighs. "Kings and queens before me have had companions beyond their marriages, but I don't know of any examples where the king and queen shared their companion. I can't believe we'd be the first in all the history of Elodia, but if there's precedent, I'm unaware. History's never been my strong point. I promise I'll try to find a way, though, if it's what you want. I'll do everything in my power. I swear it."

I nod solemnly and we fall silent again for a moment before he whispers, "But you will marry me?"

I huff out a small laugh. "Yes, Ty. I'll marry you."

He pulls back enough to look down at me. "And not only because we *have* to get married to save magic?"

My heart flutters in my chest at the vulnerability in his gaze. Gods help me. I really do love this man, but even with that knowledge I can't bring myself to say that saving magic isn't a factor. Because I do love Bash, and potentially leaving him behind to marry Ty wouldn't be a decision I'd make so quickly if magic wasn't a factor.

Ty must sense my hesitation because he adds, "Assuming I succeed in finding a way to keep Bash, and I'm not making you choose between us."

I smile up at him. "I'll marry you to save magic and because I love you and do want to be with you and Bash." I pause, frowning.

"What is it, Freya?" Ty asks, scooting back to look at me properly. "Whatever it is, tell me and I'll do what I can to fix it."

His gaze is so earnest, I have to make myself look away.

"Just . . . if you do find a way for you, me, and Bash to be together, how will I know you won't regret me being part of your relationship? After all, you and Bash were together long before I came along. I messed everything up for you."

"I love you as much as I love Bash," he insists.

"But you don't. Not really. Everything you feel for Bash has been happening for years. It's tried and true. It's proven the test of time and separation. What we have is new and fresh. It's very possible that whatever you feel for me might fade while what you feel for Bash will only continue to grow."

"Freya, no." He drops down to his knees in front of me, placing a hand on my cheek and guiding my gaze to meet his. "No. I love you. So much. You have no idea how betrayed and distraught I was when my mother sent you away. I was inconsolable when I thought I had lost you. I didn't even dare hope. When Rissa presented the idea you were alive, I didn't want to believe it because I didn't think I could stand losing you again. I would have searched the world over to bring you back to me. You took hold of my heart and never let go."

"But you and Bash have a history."

"That doesn't mean you and I don't have a future. I'm in this, Freya. I don't know what the future holds, and I know that sometimes people drift apart, but I swear to you, I will wake up every day and choose to love you."

His thumb gently traces over my cheek, and I relax into his touch.

"Do you believe me?"

I nod, fighting back tears. "I do."

He smiles and resumes his seat on the bed. "Good, because I mean every word."

I sigh and rest my head on his shoulder. It's comfortable and calming and I can't ignore how it feels so right to be pressed against him like this. We stay like that for several minutes until Bash returns with Cooper.

CHAPTER THIRTY-THREE

BASH

It doesn't take me long to find Cooper, but I take us the long way back to give Freya and Ty more time to talk. I also need a little more time myself to adjust to the idea that the person I love, the person I was beginning to plan a future with, has been ripped away from me once again. My utter shock at seeing Ty quickly turned to relief at him being alive and then to soul-crushing devastation when I realized why he had come. When I saw Ty realize Freya and I are together, I had to get out of there. Even now as we approach the room, Cooper jabbering away in my ear, I dread what I'll find when we open the door.

Despite everything I worked up in my head, I'm surprised to find Ty and Freya simply sitting side by side on the bed. Yet, as simple as their position may be, it might as well be an arrow through my heart. They both straighten when we walk in, but I purposefully avoid meeting their eyes.

"Bash!" Ty says, hopping off the bed. "Can we—"

"Cooper said you two barely got any sleep last night thanks to the attack," I say, cutting him off. "Why don't you two take the bed and catch up on your sleep while Freya and I compare notes from our surveillance today?"

"Oh, sure," Ty says. I don't miss the disappointment in his voice. "I could use some sleep."

Cooper gives me his thanks as he and Ty lay down on the bed, Cooper taking the side along the wall and Ty putting as much space between them as possible so he's practically hanging off the bed. I take a seat on the floor against the far wall, and Freya joins me, pulling out her own notes. I quietly compare them against the notes I made from the Lord Mayberry's records, pretending not to notice Ty's eyes on me as he drifts off to sleep. Once he's out cold, Freya finds her voice.

"Bash, Ty and I talked and—"

"And you're going to marry him," I mumble, not looking up from the papers in front of me. "Which you should. Not only is it the right thing to do, but also you love him and deserve happiness."

I look up at her and force a smile. "I'm happy for you two. You're a good fit. I think you're good for each other."

"Ty returning doesn't take away my feelings for you."

"No, but it might as well negate them. Your feelings for me or the way I feel for you no longer matter."

Hurt flashes across her face and I swallow, looking away.

"I mean, it matters—you matter—but we can't let that interfere with what's best for everybody else."

"Bash—"

"No," I say, my voice coming out harsher than I intend. I sigh and try again. "I love you, Freya, and I love Ty, but I can't deal with this right now. I need time to process. So, can we please focus on this right here?" I motion to the papers in front of us. "Because this is something I can control, something I can plan and put into action, and I really need that sense of control right now."

Freya still looks upset, but she forces a tight smile and nods. "Sure. Absolutely. As long as you promise to talk to Ty eventually."

"I promise. Now," I say, turning back to the notes, "what did you discover in town today?"

It doesn't take long to confirm my suspicions. There are several vendors and shopkeepers in Krixwell that seem to be working directly with the cult, while several others merely turn a blind eye to their activities. Lord Crawhill seems less an active participant and more someone who's been bribed to overlook any suspicious activities.

We've begun constructing possible plans when Ty wakes up. He blinks at us bleary-eyed for a moment before he sits up with a groan, rolling his neck. He casts a glance at Cooper over his shoulder before sliding off the bed and sitting cross-legged on the floor across from me. He frowns down at the papers, twisting his head to read some of them.

"Are these actual records of some sort?" he asks, pointing to one of the pages I tore from the earl's ledger.

"That is," I confirm with a nod. "A lot of these are notes and copies we made based on evidence we found at Lord Mayberry's estate."

Ty lifts wide eyes to mine. "So you found evidence that Lord Mayberry is involved in illicit activities?"

"That and more," Freya says. "He's definitely directly involved with the cult, and it looks like he's using money from the Rebel Isles to fund it."

Ty shakes his head. "I knew he was involved somehow. Rissa and I intercepted some of his letters and Lord Vander-hof's letters, but we haven't been able to make any firm connections. This, however, may be exactly what we need."

We take the next few minutes to fill each other in on everything we've discovered. It's almost eerie how Ty and Rissa's discoveries line up with mine and Freya's. When he tells us about the spell Amarelia is most likely using on the king, Freya and I exchange a look. It can't be a coincidence that Lord Mayberry is using the same spell on his wives. He clearly provided the information and potentially the means to harm the king and gave Amarelia a way in. The plan to overthrow the Crown is well underway, and I don't even want to consider how easily they might have succeeded had Freya and I not been hunting down the cult.

Cooper stirs as we finish, easing up to sit on the edge of the bed as Ty organizes the notes into stacks.

"I'll lean on Lord Crawhill and let him know that we're aware of his involvement. Better to cut him out of the cult's plans before he can sink any deeper," Ty says.

"Do you think you should even let him know you're here?" Freya asks. "Shouldn't you lay low?"

Ty shakes his head. "I'm the Crown Prince. I have a duty to my kingdom. I need to protect my people. Lord Crawhill is corrupt, and even though he may not be as directly involved as Lord Mayberry and Lord Vanderhof, he's contributing to everything. I can't stand by silently while treason is happening."

"Wait," Cooper says, leaning forward. "Did you say Lord Vanderhof is involved in something treasonous?"

I tense, narrowing my eyes at Cooper. "Whatever you hear in this room, you keep to yourself."

Cooper raises his hands in surrender. "I will. I promise. I have no desire to get on your bad side or the Crown's. I'm loyal." I give him a sharp nod and he relaxes a fraction, lowering his hands. "I was only wondering because Lord Vanderhof has several guards and soldiers in his pocket."

Now that has my attention. "Which ones?"

"I don't have an exact list on me," Cooper says with a shrug, "but I could get you something more definitive when we get back to Rosana. I can also get you a list of soldiers you can trust to have your back should things get bad fast."

Ty smiles a little too easily at Cooper. "That would be appreciated. We'll need every protection we can get, especially if we're going to perform a secret wedding and bonding ceremony under Amarelia's nose."

Reality rushes back in and I tense. Somehow in our planning and sharing of information I'd managed to forget our current circumstances. Ty is going to marry Freya, and I'll lose both of them all over again. Freya tries to catch my eye, but I look down at the stacks of papers, jaw clenching.

"There's going to be a wedding?" Cooper says brightly, obviously not noticing the thick tension that's seeped into the room.

Ty swallows, glancing between Freya and me before settling his attention on Cooper. "I'll have to marry Freya at the next Fae moon or we risk losing magic. Thankfully, the priest on is on board. We'll also need approval from a royal. Hopefully all this"—he motions at the papers—"will be enough to get my mother or at least my father on board."

"And if it's not?" I ask, cautiously meeting Ty's eyes.

"Then we'll figure it out," he says with a sigh. "It's not a perfect plan, but it's all we have."

Before anyone can say anything else, Cooper's stomach growls, and he chuckles.

"Guess I'm hungry."

Freya pops up from the ground. "You know what? I'm hungry, too." She steps over the papers and pulls a confused Cooper to his feet. "Cooper and I will go find some food."

She tugs him toward the door, and he has no choice but

to stumble along with her. She opens the door and pushes Cooper out into the hallway.

"You two talk," she says before slipping out herself and closing the door with a click.

Silence falls and I can't bring myself to look at Ty, through I can feel the heat of his gaze on me. I begin gathering up all the papers, shoving them back into my bag.

"Bash," he starts, sounding unsure.

I shake my head and push to my feet. "No."

Ty stumbles to his feet. "We need to talk."

I scoff, still avoiding looking at him. "What do you need to say? That you need to marry Freya? I know. That the world is unfair? I know that better than anyone. What can you possibly have to say that I don't already know?"

"Maybe that I love you and Freya and I want to find a way for all three of us to be together."

A bitter laugh chokes out of me, and I finally meet his eyes. "That can never happen."

He crosses his arms. "Why not? I'm the crown prince, the future king. I can make things happen. I can change things."

"That's exactly why. You're going to be the king, Ty. You have expectations to meet. You have to marry Freya and save magic and create a line of perfect little heirs."

"I wouldn't be the first king to love someone besides the queen. There are titles and positions—"

"No," I cut him off, turning my back to him. "I can't do that, Ty. I just . . . can't."

His boots scuff the ground as he steps closer. "Can't what? Be my consort? Be *our* consort?"

"I can't . . ." I take a deep, steadying breath, my hands clenching into fists at my sides as tears burn my eyes. "I can't be in the shadows anymore. I've spent my whole life in the shadows, always second best."

"You aren't second best," Ty says, his voice firm.

I spin to face him and he staggers back a step. "That's how everyone would see me. That's how everyone has always seen me. The man I called a father most of my life never saw me as his. I was always the other son, the unwanted bastard, the extra. Even when you and I were together, we couldn't be seen as anything more than friends to the public. I loved what we had, I loved dreaming with you, but dreams are different than reality. In reality, I was no one, and when everything came to light, I became the extra again."

"I'd make sure—"

"Ty." I sigh. "You can't control how other people see me. You can't fix everything with a wave of your hand. Even as your official consort, I'll never be seen as equal to you and Freya. When your history is recorded, it will show you married to Freya. A portrait of you and Freya will hang in the palace for generations to come. History books will list your heirs and accomplishments. I'll be lucky to be mentioned at all. I'll be a forgotten footnote in your history."

"No," Ty says, closing the distance between us. "You will never be a footnote in my history. You won't be a footnote in anyone's history. If anything, I deserve to be a footnote in yours."

I scoff, looking away, but Ty grabs my chin and forces my eyes back to his.

"I mean it, Bash. Everything you've done, everything you've survived? You deserve the world, and I'm going to give it to you. I love you. You were never a footnote to me. You're not a footnote to Freya. I will do everything in my power to make sure that the history books list you alongside us, as our equal companion. Fuck anyone who tries to erase you. Fuck anyone who tries to make you anything less than what you are."

"And what am I?" I ask, hating the way my voice trembles.

"You are Bastion Shamblefoot, soldier, assassin, protector, lover. You are mine. I claim you and I will keep you. I will forfeit my throne before I let someone take you from me again. Do you understand me?"

A sob catches in my throat and he places a hand on the back of my neck, steadying me. His eyes peer into my soul and I can taste his determination.

"I love you, Bash. Freya loves you. You love us. We will find a way to make this work."

"What if you can't?"

"I will."

"But—"

"I. Will."

My eyes shutter closed and for a moment I let myself hope. I let myself dream. When I open my eyes, Ty is watching me carefully.

"So, what of it, Bash? Will you give us a chance?"

"If if doesn't work out—"

"It will."

"But if it doesn't, I don't think I can go on."

Something close to fear flashes in Ty's eyes. "What do you mean?"

"Losing you the first time almost destroyed me. You were right before. Me leaving to go after the cult the first time was a suicide mission. I wanted to die, but I wanted to die with some sort of honor. If I give into hope again, and it doesn't work out . . ."

Ty's grip on my neck tightens. "I will not let you fall. I promise." When I don't say anything he adds, "Give me until the Fae moon at least. If I haven't found a satisfactory solution by then, one that you feel is fair, then I won't mention it again. You can stay, you can leave, just please give me a chance."

I take a shaky breath. "And between now and then?"

The corner of his mouth tips up. "Until then you give things a try. You, me, and Freya. Together. We get a taste of happiness, so even if it can't last, we at least have the next several days. Deal?"

I run my tongue across my lips, carefully considering his offer and everything it means. Even though my instincts are telling me to be careful, pushing me to run, I find myself nodding.

"Deal."

Ty brightens and my heart somersaults.

"Thank you, Bash. I—" His eyes flick to my lips. "Can I kiss you?"

He doesn't get a chance because I kiss him first, and it's as perfect as I remember and more. It's fierce and gentle. Passion and care. He makes a small sound, his hand sliding into my hair to angle us better together. My hands find his waist and I press our bodies together. It's familiar and new and wonderful.

I push him back until we fall onto the bed. I press him down into the mattress and continue to kiss him senseless. We don't do more than that; kissing is enough. We continue until we're both breathless, lying facing each other, our legs tangled together and our hands clasped between us. Ty's lips are beautifully swollen and he's so perfectly debauched. The look in his eyes as he takes me in is nothing short of adoration, and I know in this moment that I'll do everything to hold onto him this time. I'm not letting him go again.

I'm going to fight for him and Freya. I'm going to find my way to happiness and the rest of the world can fuck off. I deserve this. *We* deserve this, and with the gods as my witnesses, we're going to find a way to make this work.

CHAPTER THIRTY-FOUR

RISSA

I'm surprised to see the king sitting next to the queen when I'm called before her. He smiles at me, and I can't help but notice the queen herself looks a little more at ease as she sits on her throne.

"You summoned me, Your Majesties?" I say, pulling up from a curtsey.

"Yes, we wanted to commend you on the effort you have made to include Amarelia," the queen says.

I incline my head. "Of course, Your Majesty. It has been my pleasure."

Her tight smile tells me she doesn't believe me in the slightest.

"I assume your friendship will continue once Tybalt returns?"

"Yes, Your Majesty."

The queen nods sharply. "Good. The rest of her family should be arriving in the next couple of days."

I still and barely manage to hold my calm expression.

"Her family? As in the queen and king of the Re—Panbrio Isles?"

"Not the king himself, but the queen and the prince along with some other nobles." She arches an eyebrow. "Will that be a problem?"

My mouth goes incredibly dry, but I still manage to force my lips into a smile. "No, Your Majesty. Of course not."

"Good." She straightens on her throne. "In Tybalt's absence, you will help represent the royal family. I hope you are up to the job, Klarissa."

Tension tightens my shoulders and jaw, but the king chuckles. My attention snaps to him, and I swear he has a twinkle in his brown eyes.

"Now, now, my love. There's no need to doubt Klarissa will be anything other than a shining example. She's never given us reason to believe she might disappoint." His shining eyes meet mine and a small bit of relief courses through me. "I have every confidence she will know exactly how to handle the situation."

"I appreciate your faith in me, Your Majesty."

"Of course, my dear."

The queen sighs through her nose, but she smiles nonetheless. "Very well. That is all. You may continue about your day."

I incline my head and turn to leave, but I don't get far before the king calls out to me.

"Lady Klarissa, if you would not mind, I can walk out with you."

A true smile curves my lips and I turn to find the king descending the throne platform, a winning smile on his face.

"I would appreciate the company," I reply.

As he approaches, his guards fall into place behind him. My attention catches on one member of his detail, a young man with a sharp jawline, dark hair, and dark eyes. There's something familiar about him I can't quite place. I don't get long to dwell on it, however, because a moment later the king is at my side and we're resuming our exit from the throne room. Once the doors have closed behind us, the king turns to me.

"I wanted to thank you in person, Klarissa."

"For what, Your Majesty?"

"For always being there for Tybalt." I open my mouth to protest, but my uncle holds up his hand, keeping me silent. "I know my son fell into quite a stupor after his previous bride was sent away, and I know you helped pull him from it. This isn't the first time you've been there for him, and it will likely not be the last. In many ways, you are the sister he deserves."

Another protest sits on my tongue, but the sincerity shining the king's eyes keeps it in place.

"It is my pleasure. There are times when Tybalt repays the favor ten times over. I'm very lucky to have him as my cousin."

My uncle chuckles. "Indeed. I also wanted to thank you for a lovely tea I had this morning. I was told it was one of your special blends."

Delight heats my cheeks, and I duck my head. "I'm pleased you liked it. I put together a few blends that typically help with different ailments."

"Well, my dear, I truly believe it is that tea that helped me get up and about today. It has been a while since I have felt this much energy, even if it is fading quickly."

I startle to a stop. "My tea?"

"Yes, my dear." He also pauses in his stride. "Is that so shocking? I've found that sometimes a good tea can help turn the tide just as quickly as a bad meal can sour it."

I blink at him a moment before regaining my composure. "I'm happy to have helped."

We resume our stroll though the castle and I swallow, carefully considering my next question. "I don't suppose it was a sour meal that started you down this path of affliction?"

I half-expect his denial, but instead he hums, keeping his attention fixed ahead. "I did start to feel weak shortly following a meal, but there were no traces of poison, if that's what you're thinking. No, I'm afraid this illness is a bout of terrible luck, which makes me all the more grateful when something as simple as a tea can help."

I manage a small nod as we near a splitting of corridors. "I'm truly happy to have helped, even if temporarily, but if you'll excuse me, I have a meeting elsewhere."

The king inclines his head. "Of course. Thank you for walking with me this far."

I wait a moment to give the king and his entourage time to put space between us before rushing to Gregorian's chambers. My mind is spinning as I throw open their doors. An older court lady whose name I don't recall stands in the center of the room with them. Gregorian looks at me and cocks an eyebrow.

"Lady Klarissa, did we have an appointment?"

I force a smile. "No, but I was hoping you could fit me in."

They nod, ignoring the annoyed huff of their current client. "Give me five, maybe ten minutes, and I'll be available."

I nod, swallowing, my mouth suddenly very dry. "I appreciate it. Perhaps you could meet me near the library when you are done?"

They study me for a moment before nodding slowly. "Of course."

"Thank you, Liege Greengrass. I appreciate it."

I quickly back from the room, closing the doors behind me, and rush to Miles's rooms. When I throw his doors open, I find him in an armchair next to the fireplace, an open book spread across his lap with his glasses slipping down his nose. He looks up at me and smiles, but that smile quickly fades as he takes in my appearance. He stands, dropping his book into the chair and rushing to me, eyes scanning me over.

"Are you okay? Is something wrong?"

I shake my head, not really sure which of his questions I'm answering.

"You've studied a lot of the details of magic. Is it possible for someone to infuse their magic into something else?"

He frowns, his brow furrowing. "I'm not entirely sure what you're asking, but yes? Any time you use magic, you're infusing your magic into whatever element is being used. For example, anytime you use your magic to make a plant grow, you're transferring little bits of your magical energy into the plant."

I nod absentmindedly. "Would it be possible for me to put my magic into a tea that, in turn, could pass on magical qualities to someone else in a beneficial manner?"

Miles's frown deepens. "I suppose it might be possible, depending on the circumstances." He studies me for a moment. "I have a feeling this isn't hypothetical. What are you trying to figure out?"

I take a deep breath and release it slowly. "The king told me a brew I created with my magic helped him fight whatever his illness is."

"Ah," Miles says, relaxing a little. "Well, you and the king do both have earth magic and are related by blood, so I suppose the magic you infused into the tea could help him. I'm guessing there's something else you're wondering?"

"Would it be possible for you and I to use our magic together, with what we know of healing potions and spells, to create a type of antidote for what Amarelia is doing to the king?"

His eyes widen, his mouth curving into a full smile. "You're suggesting combining what we know of *Faecræft* and *Naturcræft* to create something stronger than we've already discovered in the texts." He stumbles over to his table, strewn with books, and snatches up one of his notebooks. He adjusts his glasses and starts flipping through it. "Mixing *Faecræft* and *Naturcræft* isn't a new concept, but I'm not sure if it's been used quite how you're describing. That doesn't mean it can't be done, however."

He's practically giddy and a small laugh escapes me. Miles's bright eyes meet mine.

"What?"

I shake my head affectionately. "Nothing. I love when you get excited over your studies."

He grins. "I didn't devote my life to learning simply because I had spirit magic, you know."

"I know."

My joy fades as I remember the second part of what I came to ask. He immediately notices and steps my way.

"What else?"

"The king said he fell ill shortly after a meal but that there was no poison. Could a poisoning via *Naturcræft* go undetected?"

"It's very possible. Unfortunately, there are almost too many ways to do it that I've discovered, and anyone with knowledge of *Naturcræft* probably knows a dozen more. Like any poisoning, without knowing the source, I'm not sure how to combat it or even pinpoint it."

I sigh, sinking into a nearby chair at the table. "That's what I was afraid of."

He takes the seat next to me and draws my hands into his. "That doesn't mean we can't try."

I look up into his kind eyes, but before I respond there's a knock on the door.

"Are you in there, darling?" Gregorian drawls.

"Yes, come in!" I call out.

A moment later, they sweep inside, their eyes trailing over the room as they close the door with the heel of their boot.

"Bit dreary in here," they mumble.

"Too much light can harm some of the older texts," Miles replies, not put off in the slightest.

Gregorian hums, stepping farther inside. Their gaze settles on me and they smile.

"Thank you for interrupting my fitting with Lady Mallory. She would have talked all day if I hadn't had a reason to hurry things along. But I assume you didn't come to me to hear me complain."

I smile up at them. "No, I did not, though with as much as you've heard me complain, I can lend you an ear whenever you need it."

They smile and their eyes dart to an empty chair to my left. "May I take a seat while you ask what you need of me? I've been standing for hours."

"Of course!" Miles says, jumping to his feet. "I'm sorry not to have offered you a seat before."

Gregorian waves him off as they glide to the chair. They settle into the seat and fold their hands on the table, looking to me as Miles plops back into his seat.

"Now, what do you need from me?"

I take a deep, steadying breath. "Have you been able to

assess a timeline of when Cressida's engagement was struck?"

"From what I was able to ascertain from her endless babbling about her upcoming fiancé and nuptials, it's a rather recent development."

I sink in my seat and Gregorian arches an eyebrow.

"Why does that seem to disappoint you?"

"Whoever is the key behind the plot to take the throne has likely been at it for a while. I think they may have even gone as far as to poison the king to make him appear ill to move up Ty's marriage. If the engagement was a recent development, I'm not sure why the duke would be willing to betray the king. There wouldn't be a good incentive for him to commit treason."

"Ah, well that would be—" They pause, eyes going wide. I sit straighter.

"What is it, G?"

"It may be nothing."

"Tell me," I press.

"Several months ago, when I was fitting Cressida for the winter solstice ball, she was going on and on about how she hoped that the rift between her father and the king didn't get in the way of her plans to marry the prince."

"Wait, what rift?"

They shake their head. "I'm not entirely sure. I'm not sure *she* knew, but either way it seemed like a significant falling out. I, of course, thought her ridiculous and may have questioned the magical qualities of her blood. She waved me off, saying her blood was the least of her problems because her father had ways to ensure it wouldn't be an issue. She rambled on a bit about her father's connections and network, but something that struck me as odd was that she was sure her father's proximity to the king was all she needed."

"Proximity to the king?"

Gregorian nods once. "Yes. That was exactly how she phrased it. I remember because I thought the word choice odd. I assumed at the time she meant proximity as a means to refer to the closeness of their relationship, but now I wonder—"

"—if she meant literal, physical proximity," I finish for them and they nod again. "The winter solstice ball lines up with when the king first started showing signs of his illness."

"I don't know Cressida or her father," Miles interjects slowly, "but is this something they would do? If they thought they could get the throne by poisoning the king to move up the marriage, tricking the blood test with Cressida as the bride, and then having Cressida be queen, would they risk treason?"

"I doubt Cressida would knowingly do something of the sort, but the duke might," I answer.

"The duke definitely would," Gregorian agrees. "I've fitted that man dozens of times and all he ever wants is to be perceived better than anyone, and he never fails to brag about his connections."

"But why change the plan? Why have Amarelia take the throne instead?" Miles asks.

I shake my head. "Maybe he found out some of the risks of the whole thing and decided against it or maybe someone higher up vetoed it. A marriage to a foreign prince is a good consolation prize."

"So is the duke stealing the catalyst for the spell directly?" he asks. "Or is it someone in his so-called network?"

"I don't—" I stop with a sharp gasp, my eyes widening. "That's where I've seen him!"

AMBER D. LEWIS

Gregorian glances around, puzzled, while Miles frowns and asks, "Who?"

"One of the guards that was with the king earlier. I knew he looked familiar but I couldn't place him."

"Well, who is he?" Gregorian presses, leaning forward.

"When we first suspected the duke of misdeeds, I looked into all his servants and guards. Most of them came with him directly from his estate. A couple were already stationed at the palace, but I didn't think much of it. The palace recruits from neighboring areas all the time. What I didn't realize was that one of the duke's regular guards was also a guard for the king, at least on occasion."

Gregorian gasps dramatically. "So he's had an in the entire time!"

"But is it the duke performing the spell, one of his other contacts, or the guard?" Miles counters.

I shake my head. "I honestly can't be sure. No matter how he's accomplishing it, the duke is most certainly guilty of treason, and I'm going to unravel his plot and hang him with it. And I'm going to need help from both of you."

Gregorian nods. "Whatever you need, darling, count me in."

Miles leans forward. "Me too."

I take a deep breath and smile. The duke won't know what hit him.

CHAPTER THIRTY-FIVE

TY

Lord Crawhill is awfully sweaty for being in such a cool room, but I suspect most people might get a bit nervous if the crown prince suddenly showed up. It's not like I didn't have a literal invitation, though. We're currently in his office, sitting across from each other on very uncomfortable sofas, and the man has yet to meet my eyes.

"Are you sure you won't have a nip of brandy?" he asks for at least the third time since I entered the room.

"Quite positive, but if it will calm your nerves, than by all means." I wave my hand to his drink cart.

He shakes his head a bit feverishly. "No, I'm fine as well."

"Great. Well then, I suppose I'll get to it. I'm sure you're aware I'm here on your invitation?"

His eyes meet mine for a couple of seconds before darting away again. "Of course, Your Highness! We always welcome the Crown!"

"Were you aware that there was an assassination plot in place for me?"

His gaze snaps to mine so intensely it's as if he's afraid to look anywhere else, his eyes widening to near comic proportions.

"No! Of course not! I would never— The people— My city—"

I hold up my hand and he stumbles to a stop.

"While all your stuttering is very reassuring, I think it's only fair I let you know that I have intel proving some very disturbing, rather treasonous things." I hold up a single finger. "One, you've been accepting funds, likely bribes, from a known member of the *cultas draíochta*, an organization that seeks to eliminate magic by destroying the royal line."

He opens his mouth to speak but I cut him short, holding up a second finger.

"Two, there are several members of your illustrious city who are members of the cult. They are actively recruiting and supporting the cause right under your nose, which I'm sure you know is treason."

"Please, Your Highness, I do not support them. I am loyal to the Crown."

"But not loyal enough to turn over the cult members or to reject a bribe?"

Oh, he's really sweating now. "I . . . Please, Your Highness, if you would allow me to explain . . ."

"I'm not sure how you can explain your way out of this, but go on."

He runs his tongue across his lips, nodding. "Thank you. I had no idea it was going on for quite some time. I knew that, perhaps, some of the shopkeepers were participating in less than legal activities, but I had no idea what. When I was presented with the extra source of income to keep my silence, I accepted, believing my actions to be more or less harmless. When I very recently learned what was happening, I decided I would tell you once I had sufficient evidence."

"Is that so?"

"Yes, Your Highness."

"And you maintain you had nothing to do with the attempt on my life barely a day outside your city?"

He pales and shakes his head so hard his hair flops every which way. I study him for a moment and, while the man is incredibly nervous, there's no obvious sign he's lying. I release a heavy sigh and relax against the sofa, spreading my arms across the back and crossing my legs.

"Well, in that case, the most I suppose you're guilty of is aiding and abetting a cult trying to kill me and accepting bribes that you don't pay taxes on. The second isn't punishable by death, not entirely sure about the first."

"Please, Your Highness, what can I do to fix my error in judgment?"

I quirk an eyebrow. "What makes you think you can fix this?"

His breathing is coming out in short, choppy bursts. I shouldn't be enjoying his distress nearly as much as I am.

"Please, Your Highness, I'm begging you."

"You don't look like you're begging."

He immediately falls to his knees, clasping his hands in front of him.

"Please, I have a wife and two sons who know nothing of this. At least spare them."

I sigh and wave a hand through the air. "Very well. I will allow you to live and remain out of the dungeons on a few conditions."

"Name them. I'll do whatever."

I sit up straighter. "One, you provide me with a room tonight in your home. I'm tired of sleeping in inns."

"Done. I already prepared my grandest suite with

multiple rooms should you need your guards with you as well."

"Very good. Condition number two, you tell no one we had this conversation. You won't be tipping off anyone in the *cultas draíochta* that we're on to them. That will be undeniable treason, and I'll have no problem making an example of you and your family."

I didn't think he could get any paler, but somehow he manages. "My lips are sealed, Your Highness."

"My next condition is that you pay taxes on every cent you received in bribes. I have ledger records, so don't even try to get away with paying less."

He looks mildly disgruntled but nods. "Consider it done."

"And my final condition is that you track and report every single transaction or activity of the *draíochta* that occurs in your town or any attempt further made to bribe you, along with any other evidence you manage to collect. If you want to prove you are truly on my side and the side of the Crown, you will prove your worth."

"Yes, Your Highness. I will happily do so."

"Excellent." I push up from the couch in one smooth motion, and Lord Crawhill stumbles to his feet. "Now, if you don't mind, I'd like to be shown to my room so I may bathe and relax for the rest of the evening."

"You're sure he's not actively involved?" Bash asks the moment he, Freya, Cooper, and I are alone in my suite. Cooper and I basically had to sneak Bash and Freya in so as not to let anyone else know they're alive.

"I'm pretty sure he wasn't. He was nervous and a little terrified, but I seemed to hit the nail on the head with my accusations," I say, collapsing onto a couch that is thankfully much more comfortable than the sofa I was on earlier.

Bash nods like this is the answer he expected. "I think it might be safe to assume that the other nobility with similar payouts were also accepting bribes to look the other way."

"That's a fair assumption. I—"

The sound of cheering outside stops me short and I hop up from the couch and head over to the balcony. The doors are open a crack, letting in the sounds from the streets below. Unlike so many other noble estates, Lord Crawhill's is in the center of town. More cheers erupt and I push the doors open and cautiously step outside. Sheer red and blue curtains float in the breeze around the edges of the balcony, obscuring me from the world below, but allowing me to see what's going on. I step up the balustrade and peer down, realizing I have the perfect view of a group of fire dancers wowing the crowd.

"Be careful," Bash warns.

I sigh and look over my shoulder. Both he and Cooper stand at the entrance to the balcony but neither has stepped outside.

"I know it's not safe, but I really wish I could enjoy the festival. I did come all this way."

The corner of Bash's mouth tips up and I wonder if he's remembering the time he came with me to the festival as part of my guard detail. It was a newer appointment and one of the first trips we made together. I still remember the way his eyes lit up when he took his first bite of a candied apple. He steps out onto the balcony, stopping a few inches away, his eyes looking past me to the crowd below.

"I suppose as long as you go unnoticed, you can enjoy some of it from here."

A breeze blows across the balcony, twirling the curtains

and bringing with it the aroma of delectable delights from below. My stomach rumbles.

"I can go down and get you some treats, if you'd like," Cooper volunteers with a grin.

"Well, I won't say no to that," I laugh, placing my hand on my stomach as it rumbles again.

"Should I go with you?" Freya asks, stepping up behind Cooper.

He shakes his head. "Nah. I can probably handle it on my own. You three stay here; I'll be right back."

Cooper scampers away while Bash, Freya, and I make ourselves comfortable on the floor of the balcony, peering down at the activity below through the decorative spindles. It doesn't take too long before Cooper returns, his arms laden with food. We haul some cushions and blankets out onto the balcony and spread out, eating, laughing, and enjoying ourselves.

When the evening finally fades into night and it gets too difficult to see properly, we filter back inside. Music floats up from the streets, and I turn to Freya with a bow.

"Dance with me, milady?"

She giggles, placing her hand in mine. "As long as you promise not to step on my toes."

"I would never!" I say with an offended gasp.

She lets me take the lead as we dance around the open space in our suite. Cooper claps along to the beat and Bash watches with a grin. The music changes below and Bash steps forward.

"My turn."

I grin at him. "Which of us would you prefer?"

He pretends to consider his options, a wicked gleam in his eye. "Well, I heard you step on people's feet."

A laugh barks out of me. "Bloody false rumor! Fine, you dance with Freya, and I'll dance with Cooper."

Cooper's eyes widen. "Me? I'm not— I don't dance."

"Don't worry, Cooper. I won't step on your feet, and I won't steer you wrong either."

He glances nervously to Bash who shrugs, before Cooper stumbles my way. I grab him and pull him close and the dancing begins. The four of us dance song after song, switching partners between each one. Cooper is most definitely the most awkward of us all, but his lack of skills doesn't hinder the fun. Finally, after hours of dancing, Freya and I collapse onto the couch, grinning. Cooper, who was dancing with Bash, takes step back and glances from person to person.

"Well, I'm pretty tired, so I think I might turn in." He nods to one of the three rooms off the main area. "Is that one mine?"

"If that suits you, then sure. We'll take one of the others."

He gives us one last nod before disappearing.

"So, the three of us will share a room tonight?" Bash asks, not quite meeting my eyes.

"Yes. If that's all right with both of you." I glance between my partners.

Freya nods, her cheeks glowing and her eyes bright. "Fine by me." She looks up at Bash. "Are you okay with that?"

Bash lets out a slow breath and slowly lowers his gaze to meet Freya's, then mine. My heart catches in my chest, afraid that he'll change his mind about wanting to give this a try, but after a moment he nods, his mouth tipping up into a small, almost nervous smile.

"Yeah. I'm okay with that."

He offers me his hand, and I allow him to pull me to my feet. I hesitate only a moment before closing the distance and pressing a quick but firm kiss to his lips. As I'm drawing away, he places his hand on the back of my neck and pulls me back in. He leaves me breathless, and I feel like I'm floating when he finally pulls back. He hesitates a moment before he extends his hand again, this time to Freya. She glances between us before accepting. He pulls her into a kiss that has my heart rate speeding up. When they pull apart, Freya turns to me and presses her swollen lips to mine.

"Should we go to bed?" Bash asks, his voice rough.

I manage a nod as a grin overtakes my mouth. "Yeah, bed sounds perfect."

CHAPTER THIRTY-SIX

BASH

I wake in a tangle of limbs, warmth and contentment buzzing through me. It takes a moment for the events of last night and my current position to surface, but once they do, that contentment increases. I'm in an oversized bed in a nest of blankets with Freya and Ty. I'm on my side facing Ty, who's in the center of the bed curled with his back against my chest, my arm slung over his waist. His arms are wrapped around Freya who's snuggled against him, but her hand is in mine. I don't remember falling asleep this way, so our hands must have found each other in the night. In so many ways it's perfect. However, I have business I need to take care of.

I carefully untangle myself from Freya and Ty, easing off the bed. Ty mumbles something and flops over on his back, occupying the space I was in moments ago, but he doesn't wake. Neither does Freya. I slip from the room and relieve myself in the attached washroom. When I reenter the room, Freya is awake, lying on her side, watching me through heavy-lidded eyes. I smile and opt to ease down on her side of the bed, lying down so we're face to face.

"You seem concerned about something," she says, not quite whispering, but keeping her voice low enough not to disturb Ty. "I thought you might feel better now that you know Ty is okay and you can be sure that nothing is going to happen to him."

"I do feel a little better."

"There's something else bothering you."

She says it so plainly. Perhaps I should find it startling that she can see so easily past my mask, but maybe that's why she and I work. She can see the parts of me that I try to hide. I sigh and find her hand where it lays between us, weaving our fingers together.

"I want this."

Her eyebrows scrunch together. "This as in you and me and Ty?" I nod and she frowns. "You have us."

"Do I?"

She shifts on the bed, putting us closer so that I'm almost cross-eyed looking at her.

"You do. If you want us, that is. Neither Ty nor I will force you into anything." She pauses, eyebrows arching. "Is that it? Are you feeling forced? Because I know everything between us is new, and the idea of any sort of commitment is . . . a lot."

"No," I say quickly, giving her hand a squeeze. "That's not it. Maybe it should be, and perhaps if it were, I would feel better about being hesitant. But, no."

"Then what is it?"

"It feels too right." The words tumble out and Freya blinks at me. I take a deep breath and try again. "All my life I've wanted to belong, and a few times, I've found a place where I thought I accomplished that goal. At first it was at my uncle's side, training. Even though I wasn't his son, he made me feel more like a son than the man raising me ever did. Then I found a place among the palace guard. Then Ty and I started our relationship. We planned for the future and everything felt like it was falling into place. More recently, it was with you, on the road, hunting down and destroying the *draíochta.*"

She smiles softly, giving my hand a squeeze.

"But every time I found a place where I thought, 'Yes, this is it, this is where I'm meant to be,' my world shattered again. My uncle tried to kill me. Most of the guard turned against me. I lost Ty. I lost you."

"You haven't lost me," she cuts in quickly.

"Not yet, but I can't shake the feeling that this is all about to go wrong again. Whenever I let myself consider a future with you and Ty at my side, I feel happier than I ever have in my life, but I'm afraid to let myself concentrate on that feeling for long because the higher I let myself soar, the farther I'll fall when it all goes wrong."

"I can't promise that nothing will go wrong, but I can promise to do whatever I can to make this happen."

I nod, tearing my eyes away from the intensity in her gaze to look at our clasped hands. I trail my thumb over her knuckles.

"Ty told me not to give up hope until at least the Fae moon."

"Then trust Ty."

I pull my gaze to meet hers and my heart stutters at the affection in her gaze.

"I love you, Freya."

"I love you, too, Bash."

Ty snorts behind Freya and jerks upright. He blinks rapidly, his attention snapping to me.

"Wait, weren't you"—he looks to his other side—"here?"

He looks back at me and I chuckle, pushing up onto an elbow. "Morning, Ty."

A slow smile curves his lips and his eyes brighten, pushing away sleep. "Morning, Bash." He looks down at Freya, his grin growing as he leans down to brush a kiss across her lips. "Morning, Freya."

"Morning," she replies, grinning up at him.

"No kiss for me?" I tease, arching an eyebrow.

Ty smirks mischievously. "Nah, your morning breath is killer."

I shoot upright, grabbing a pillow and throwing it at Ty. He bats it away with a laugh and it lands on Freya.

"Hey! Leave me out of your domestic squabbles!" she says with a giggle, pushing the pillow away.

Ty grins. "Sorry, my love. Can you ever forgive me?"

She rolls her eyes. "Maybe. If you can arrange for breakfast, I'll consider it."

"On it."

Ty slides off the opposite side of the bed and plods toward the bedroom door. He pauses halfway and turns back, rushing across the room to me. Before I can fully register what's happening, he's pulling me into a kiss. When he pulls back, he meets my eyes with a wicked grin.

"I will always have kisses for you."

He winks at me before sauntering off, leaving me winded and elated.

Several minutes later servants bring up a full breakfast spread that Ty, Freya, Cooper, and I fully enjoy. We don't linger long, however, eager to get back on the road. With the Fae moon only a week and a half away, we don't have time to stay in one location for too long. Despite the wandering way Ty took to Krixwell, we take a more direct path back. Instead of splitting the shifts four ways, we double-up to decrease our chances of being ambushed. We switch off who is paired with whom each night, but it doesn't give Freya, Ty, and I many chances to work out our situation without Cooper hovering nearby. That doesn't stop the casual intimacy between us—knowing glances, gentle touches, and occasional kisses. Everything between us seems so natural and entirely too easy, but the closer we get to Rosana, the more I start to doubt whether what we have will be able to last. I want to fight for this, for us, but I'm terrified of getting my hopes up.

On what is hopefully our last night on the road, we stay up late, chatting around the campfire, making sure everyone is on the same page.

"You'll have to stay hidden until the full moon," Ty says with a sigh. "I don't like it, but if Amarelia gets even a hint at our plan, she might kill my father."

"Where will we go?" Freya asks. "Is there someone in the city that might be willing to hide us?"

"Klarissa might know someone," Ty says.

"I might have a solution," Cooper says hesitantly, looking between the three of us. When none of us object to his input, he clears his throat and continues. "A couple years ago, a small cabin became available right outside the city limits and a few of us guards went in together to purchase it so we could have somewhere private to go if needed. It's not much, but it would be close without being under any sort of palace surveillance."

I arch an eyebrow. "You want us to stay in your rendezvous house?"

Cooper turns bright red as Ty snorts and Freya covers a smile with her hand.

"It's not only for that!" Cooper sputters. "Sometimes we

like to get away from the barracks a night or two for personal time."

"Right," I say. "And how would we know none of the guards would pop by for a quick jerk-off?"

I didn't think Cooper could get any redder, but he does. "It's mostly only used at night, so if we arrive midafternoon, which we should, I'll have plenty of time to tell the others the house is occupied."

"Can we trust them? The other soldiers?"

Cooper nods. "I'd bet my life on it."

"You better be able to bet your life on it, because that's exactly what you're doing," I say, my hand settling on the hilt of my sword as a waning.

Cooper's eyes widen, but after a moment he straightens, lifting his chin defiantly. "They're all good people. I swear it."

"I trust Cooper," Ty cuts in. "If he says we can trust them, I believe him."

Ty's confidence is enough to convince me, and I relax, giving Cooper a nod.

"If you're sure, then we'll welcome their assistance. Knowing that Lord Vanderhof and Lord Mayberry are part of the plot against the Crown isn't enough. We need them under surveillance so they can't disturb our proceedings, especially on the night of the ceremony."

Ty nods along, leaning forward. "Can you take care of that, Cooper?"

"Definitely. I know several soldiers you can trust, and I can spread the word among them."

I offer him one sharp nod. "Get me the list so I know who to kill if something goes wrong."

Cooper eyes me for a moment, probably trying to figure out if I'm serious, but in the end he agrees. We hash out a few more details, and even though Ty promises to check in on us as often as possible, I can feel him slipping through my fingers.

We approach the capital early afternoon the next day as anticipated. Ty offers to go with us to the cabin, but I refuse to let him put himself at risk. It will be safer for him to take the normal path into the city while Freya and I head to the cabin on our own. Each step I take away from Ty, every bit of distance, feels more and more like a hole stretching between us that I'll never be able to cross again. Opening the door to the cabin only seals the deal. It's simple, one room with a bed shoved in one corner, a table near a fireplace, and a scattering of other household objects. It's made for commoners. It's made for people like me. Ty will forever be royalty with responsibilities. Ty will always be needed at the palace and other royal engagements. But me? This is what I'm meant for, and the sooner I let that sink in, the better.

"Shall I make us some tea?" Freya asks, pulling me from my stupor.

I look up and find her hovering near the fireplace, a kettle in her hand.

"I think I spotted a well outside. I can get some water, but you'll have to help me get the fire started. I've always struggled with that."

I manage a nod and head her way. She carries the kettle outside while I work with a piece of flint to get the fire going. By the time she returns, a proper fire is flickering away. She smiles and goes about setting the kettle over the flames and digging out the things we'll need for tea. As I watch her from a seat at the table, my chest aches at the domesticity. I would have loved to marry her. I could have been very happy with her.

"Here," she says, taking the chair to my left and setting a

steaming cup in front of me. "Drink this while you tell me what has your forehead so scrunched up."

"I don't know what you're talking about," I mutter, taking a sip of the tea.

"You do too. Are you worried we won't be safe here or are you already giving up on us?"

I take another sip of tea to avoid answering. Freya sighs, but she doesn't sound exasperated with me.

"You promised Ty you'd give him until the Fae moon to work things out. Don't you have faith in him?"

I look down into the amber liquid. "I have faith in him. It's the rest of the world fighting against us that I don't trust."

"You don't think Ty can take on the world and win?"

I look up at her to find her eyes bright.

"Because I think when it comes to you, Ty will do everything he can to win."

Rather against my will, I find myself smiling. "You might be right."

She scoffs. "Might be? Haven't you known me long enough to know I'm always right?"

I laugh and she grins a moment before sobering.

"I'm only saying not to give up yet. If the Fae moon arrives and we haven't found a solution that you're okay with, neither Ty nor I will force you stick around. But it will be a Hell of a lot harder to find you a way to stay if you're already running away."

I take a deep, steadying breath and meet her eyes. "You're right. I'm sorry."

She waves me off. "Nothing to be sorry about. Now, drink your tea before it gets cold."

I smile but do as she says. Freya is the calm confidence I need, and I really hope Fate lets me keep her.

CHAPTER THIRTY-SEVEN

RISSA

I'm beginning to dread summons from the queen. This time, the king is not in attendance, but she is far from alone. She's standing in the center of one of the main sitting rooms with Amarelia, a sharp-faced man with dark hair, a tall, sour-faced woman, and a slew of what look to be foreign guards.

"Ah, Lady Meadowbridge, how pleasant of you to join us."

I barely hold back a cringe at my formal title. I don't remember the last time my aunt referred to me as "Lady Meadowbridge." I force a smile anyway, inclining my head.

"Of course, Your Majesty."

"I would like to introduce you to our new royal guests, Queen Helena Poshswallow and Prince André Poshswallow of the Panbrio Isles."

Queen Helena seems entirely disinterested, but André's jaw tightens as he looks toward me with something I can only place as disgust. I smile wider out of spite and dip into a curtsey.

"A pleasure to meet you both."

André says something rapidly to Amarelia in Panbrionese and she replies. I'm not sure what they're saying, but I have a feeling Amarelia is not listing all my amazing qualities. When he turns back to me, he looks me over from head to toe.

"A pleasure indeed," he says, his accent much thicker than Amarelia's.

His mother turns to the queen. "It has been a long journey. Perhaps we rest away from"—she sends a sneer toward me—"the nobility?"

"Of course!" my aunt says with a smile. "I'll have someone show you the way." Her smile falls away as she turns to me. "Could you fetch someone on your way out?"

I'm not sure if it's worse being oddly titled or so carelessly dismissed, but I agree, happy to escape the room. Luckily there's a servant right outside the room who's happy to assist so I don't have to go far. I quickly make my way to my room, determined to hide until Ty returns, hopefully with good news.

I DO A FAIRLY GOOD JOB AVOIDING OUR NEW GUESTS. THEY seem to want to keep to themselves anyway, and far be it from me to push in. Of course, this means I have to rely on other sources for information, but given I've decided to keep things exclusive between me and Miles, I can't resort to my usual methods. Thankfully, I have backup.

"Hello, darling!" Gregorian drawls, strolling into my room after knocking once.

I look up from a book as they collapse into the armchair across from me.

"Now I see where Ty was coming from."

They arch an eyebrow, and I laugh, marking my page with a bookmark and setting the book aside.

"Are you already done for the day?"

They sigh, settling back into the chair. "Not *done* done, but I have a bit of a break, which I deserve after spending all morning fitting the new prince and his entourage for the upcoming ball."

"Did you learn anything?"

They roll their eyes. "Hardly. All they did was glare at me and talk in Panbrionese. I'm pretty sure they spent half their time insulting and misgendering me."

Anger roils through me. "They're assholes. Don't let them get to you."

Gregorian waves their hand through the air. "I know. I am above gender and its constraints and beyond being bothered by people who actively choose not to respect me. They're probably jealous of my freedom and confidence. Their opinions don't mater to me." They sigh. "It still hurts a bit, though."

"I'm sorry, G. Anytime you need to get away, you're welcome to hide out with me."

A little light returns to their eyes. "Thank you. I do truly appreciate that. Oh, by the way, your cousin returned home."

I perk up. "Ty's back?"

"Yep," they say, popping the "p." "He and a guard were seen returning not that long ago. Pretty sure the queen summoned him right away."

I hop up from my seat. "Come with me."

Gregorian doesn't hesitate to follow. "Where are we going?"

"Ty's room."

I hold the door open for them and they step out into the hall, arching an eyebrow at me.

"Okay, not arguing with you as to why, but, well, why?"

I close the door with a sigh and start toward Ty's room, Gregorian falling into step beside me.

"Because I need to talk to him as soon as possible, and I'm afraid if I'm not there the exact moment he steps into his room, the queen will find some way to keep us apart."

"Ah, well, that's logical enough. Do you think he was successful?"

I shake my head. "No idea, but hopefully, for the sake of this whole kingdom, he was."

Thankfully, Ty's room is both unguarded and unlocked. I pace while Gregorian pries around the room, opening drawers and peeking into books. We don't have to wait long, however, Ty arriving a few minutes later, a bag slung over his shoulder. He startles halfway through the doorway when he spots me. I expect him to admonish me for being in his room, but instead he practically slams the door before rushing to me, a wide smile on his face.

"They're alive, Rissa! I found them! Well, they found me, but I brought them home."

I still. "Wait, they're here in the palace?"

He shakes his head. "They went to a safe house just outside the city. Cooper is helping to watch out for them."

"Cooper? Who's Cooper?"

"The guard that went with me to Krixwell."

"You took multiple guards to Krixwell."

"The rest died."

"What? How?"

Ty sighs, rubbing the back of his neck. "Look, a lot happened while I was away, but the important parts are that I found Bash and Freya and I have evidence that Lord Mayberry, Lord Vanderhof, and Amarelia are all tied up with the *draíochta* and are part of a treasonous plot."

This gets Gregorian's attention and they wander over. "What kind of proof?"

Ty startles, clearly having not seen them yet. Once he recovers, his grin returns and he reaches into his bag, withdrawing a stack of papers. He hands it to me and I settle on the couch with Gregorian at my side. Ty doesn't protest them looking as well, choosing to stand behind us and look over our shoulders as we sift through the papers. As we read, he explains what Bash and Freya have been up to. A lot of the papers simply contain notes and copies, but there are a few ledger pages that are pretty damn condemning.

"When my mother sees this, she'll have to approve my marriage to Freya and hopefully Bash."

Gregorian draws a sharp breath through their teeth while I shake my head, still looking down at the papers. "I don't think you can risk showing these to your mother."

"Why not?"

I look up at Ty who's glaring at me. "Because since the arrival of our foreign guests, your mother almost always has some of the Panbrionese guards nearby if not the queen herself or some other person of nobility. I also haven't discovered every servant and guard we can trust. You are so close to achieving your goal; you can't risk them finding out."

Ty frowns. "In order for the marriage to be official, we have to have the formal royal blessing of my mother or father, and while I know my father has been faring better, do you think he might be able to oversee and bless the ceremony?"

I brighten. "Actually, I have good news on that front. Miles and I figured out a way to infuse magic into tea to boost your father's health. It fights the magic Amarelia is using. It's not foolproof, but he usually has a little extra energy after he has his afternoon tea which is usually around"—I glance at a nearby clock—"now, actually."

The light comes back to Ty's eyes. "That's amazing! I bet Miles can do even more with the notes Freya took from Lord Mayberry's books. You can get them to him?"

"Of course she can," Gregorian answers for me. I kick them, but they only grin in response.

"Great!" Ty looks at the clock. "Let's go talk to my father."

I push up from the couch and Gregorian follows my lead. I set aside the papers I need to give to Miles and Ty takes back the rest.

"If you can give me a few minutes, I'll call Prince André in for a second fitting to make sure he and his people are occupied," Gregorian offers as we head toward the door. "I can't promise to keep them for long, but I'll do what I can."

I brush a quick kiss on their cheek. "You're the best, G!"

They shoot me a wink. "I'm aware."

They swish off and we give them a few minutes before heading to the king's room. I'm relived to see his normal guards standing outside the door and not the few I now suspect being under the duke's influence. When we enter the room, my uncle is seated at his desk, a steaming teacup in his hand. He looks up at us with a smile.

"To what do I owe the pleasure of this visit?"

"I need your blessing to marry Freya and Bash, in whatever capacity I can," Ty blurts out. I barely contain my eye roll at his lack of tact.

The king frowns, setting down his cup. "Tybalt, you know that's not possible. As little as you might like it, your mother has arranged a deal with the Panbrio Isles. There's no backing out. I'm sorry."

"What if I told you we uncovered a plot orchestrated at least partially by the *cultas draíochta* that's aided by several members of the nobility, including the Duke of Brookeshire and the Earl of East Hingling?"

The king's frown deepens and he looks to me. I take a timid step forward, inclining my head.

"It's true, Your Majesty. Mi—Father Finnick confirmed Amarelia's original blood test was faked, and we're pretty sure your current health fluctuations are linked to Amarelia's use of old magic called *Naturcræft.*"

Ty stumbles forward, holding out some of the papers he showed me earlier. "We have proof."

His father accepts the pages and looks over a couple before his eyebrows rise and he looks up at us.

"Explain."

And explain we do. We go into as much detail as needed. I share everything Miles and I have linked and discovered, and Ty adds in everything he learned from Freya and Bash. The king listens to every word, occasionally looking down at the evidence in his hands. When we finish, he sighs.

"So, to sum it all up, I'm living on borrowed time, and if things continue as planned, we lose magic and likely the kingdom in one fell swoop."

"Unfortunately, it seems that way, Your Majesty," I say. "Though Father Finnick and I are working to create more things like your tea in the hope we can fight whatever magic is being used against you."

He nods slowly before turning his attention to his son.

"I will back your marriage on the Fae moon."

Ty straightens. "You will?"

"Of course I will, Tybalt. I want you to be happy as much as I want you to be able to save the kingdom's magic. It seems you've found a way to make it work, and I won't get in your way. However, I'm sure you understand how delicate this situation is. Do you have a way to contain the information and make sure that the ceremony can go off without a hitch?"

Ty nods. "One of my guards, Cooper, can be trusted and he's creating a team of soldiers that can be trusted as well. By the end of the day, they'll be keeping an eye on everyone we even remotely suspect of treason."

"They'll be on duty the night of the ceremony?"

"That's the plan."

"Where will this ceremony take place?"

"I think it might be safest to have it at the house where Bash and Freya are staying. Father Finnick already has everything he needs, including the crystal for the ceremony, so all we have to do is get everyone there."

The king nods like he's mulling it over.

"One problem," I say, looking over at Ty. "Your mother has planned your engagement ball for the night of the Fae moon."

"Don't worry about that," the king says. "I'll make sure you have a way to leave, and then I'll follow along behind."

I nudge Ty with my elbow. "At least the ball will give you a reasonable excuse to get a proper outfit for your wedding."

Ty rolls his eyes. "Because that was my concern in all of this. My clothes."

"In the meantime, don't mention anything to anyone who is not already involved, including your mother," the king warns.

"You're not going to tell her?" Ty asks, clearly as shocked as I am.

The king shakes his head. "I think she would be on your side as well given this evidence, but with the Panbrionese officials always so close, it might be best to keep it to ourselves. If you need anything else, come to me."

Ty inclines his head. "Thank you, Father."

He sighs, a smile turning up the corner of his mouth. "I really am happy for you, son, and I sincerely hope this works out."

Ty smiles. "Thanks." He glances over to me. "We should probably go. You need to get the information to Miles."

"Right." I dip my head to the king. "We'll speak soon, Your Majesty."

He dismisses us with a smile and a wave of his hand. As we leave the room, I feel for the first time there's an actual chance for everything to work out.

CHAPTER THIRTY-EIGHT

TY

Mother arranged for entertainment tonight after dinner as a sad attempt to impress our guests. As amusing as the juggler is, no one blinks an eye when I slip away claiming a headache. I meet Rissa's eyes with a meaningful look before slinking from the room and sneaking away to the small house where Bash and Freya are hiding. When I arrive, I pause outside the door, fresh nerves swishing in my gut. Tonight, we finalize the details. Things will fall into place, and I'll get to marry the people I love. I'm raising my hand to finally knock when the door swings open.

"I was wondering how long you were going to stand out there," Freya says with a grin.

I roll my eyes and push inside. "I wasn't out there that long." I pause, glancing around. "Wait, where's Bash?"

I turn to face Freya, but she's very purposefully not meeting my eyes. I take a step closer.

"Freya, where's Bash?"

She slowly raises her gaze to mine. "He said he needed some fresh air."

"Will he be back soon? Miles and Rissa . . ." I trail off at the look on her face. "He's not holding out hope, is he? He thinks this is the end of us, all of us."

Freya bites her lip and nods. "He claims he doesn't want to intrude on our plans, but I think he's trying to create distance now to avoid facing the full brunt of separation and disappointment later."

I try not to take it personally, but it still hurts. "But I want this. I want him. And you."

She steps closer, placing hand on my arm. "I know, Ty. I want it, too, and I know Bash wants it as well." There's a knock on the door, drawing her gaze away. "Let's get through this meeting and see what Miles can offer. We can talk to Bash later." She looks back at me and offers a weak smile. "Okay?"

I nod somewhat reluctantly. "Okay."

I take a seat at the table as Freya opens the door. Rissa slips inside, Miles following behind with what looks like a heavy satchel full of books. He settles across from me, offering us a weak smile. Rissa sits to his right and Freya takes the last seat next to me.

"Where's Bastion?" Rissa asks, looking around.

My shoulders sag. "He's unavailable."

Rissa gives me a sympathetic look, but I do my best to avoid meeting her eyes.

"Shall we get right to it, then?" Miles asks.

I nod and motion vaguely for him to continue. He clears his throat and opens a thin book, placing it on the table before pulling out a spare sheet of paper, a quill, and a jar of ink.

"All right. The ceremony itself will be fairly straightforward. It has two parts: the ceremony with the bonds and the marriage vows. I'll introduce you and a royal member will step forward to bear witness of your oaths and give their blessing." His eyes dart between me and Freya. "I assume you have that worked out?"

"My father agreed."

Miles's head bobs up and down. "Excellent. Once that's done, you'll swear your oaths to each other and your loyalty to Elodia, and then you'll repeat '*Faecræft ardú ón Natur, breite do sciatháin an ár bann und stärken ár Ríocht*' before adding your blood to the stone." He jots the words down on the paper and passes it my way for Freya and I to look over as he continues. "Of course, I'll have a special ceremonial dagger for you to use made from a magical crystal and magically enhanced silver. I'll complete the spell with a few phrases of my own, and the magic will transfer to you and your bond."

"Is that it?" I ask.

Miles shrugs. "More or less. Some couples seal the bond with a kiss or light a candle or exchange rings or other tokens. Since this is a private ceremony, those things matter less since they tend to be for show more than anything, but there are other options we can add in, additional oaths and whatnot."

"Unless you have an option in your spellbook to marry and bond three people instead of two, I think that will be all," I mutter, unable to keep the bitterness from my voice.

Freya reaches over and places her hand on my knee, giving it a small squeeze. I place my hand over hers but can't bring myself to look at her.

"Are you . . . are you serious?" Miles asks hesitantly, his attention darting between me and Freya. "Because that may actually be an option."

My heart stills as my breath catches in my throat. I blink helplessly at Miles as Freya's grip on my knee tightens almost painfully.

"What do you mean?" Freya asks carefully, voicing the words I can't find.

"I'm saying," Miles mumbles, digging through his bag, "it's not unprecedented. It's been done before with great success. I think I have the book I need in here somewhere."

I glance to Rissa to see if she knew about this, but her attention is fixed on me, surprise registering on her features. She had no idea either.

"Ah, here it is," Miles says, setting a crimson book on the table and flipping through. He stops on a page that shows an image similar to one I've seen before of the bonding ceremony, only this version shows three figures instead of two— one man wearing a crown and two women. I snatch the book and pull it in front of me, staring disbelief.

"Who is this?" I demand, thrusting my finger at the man.

"That, Your Highness, is King Victor. He ruled Elodia a little over two centuries ago, probably closer to two-and-a-half if I recall correctly. And these lovely women are his brides."

"What . . . ? How . . . ?"

Miles chuckles, his eyes shining. "King Victor was born in the time when arranged marriages were already quite common to keep the blood line strong, but also in a time when the Fae were growing disgruntled with the kingdom in general. There was a particularly powerful clan of Fae in the south of Elodia that had significant influence over the majority of the Fae population dwelling in the kingdom. In order to appease them, King Victor's family arranged a marriage with one of their noble families. Much like your own arrangement, however, the young woman, Kailia, was to remain on her land until closer to the wedding. With such distance between the betrothed, the king fell in love with someone else, a young woman by the name of Jada, and he considered breaking off the engagement.

"When the Fae heard of his plans, they immediately sent Kailia to the palace without any notice. Victor was clever and knew that the Fae had likely done so not only to harm his relationship with Jada but also to show their strength. Instead of shunning Kailia like many expected him to do, he accepted her with open arms, introducing her around the court and to his lover. To the shock of many, Jada and Kailia became fast friends and allies, and, if the rumors and records are to be believed, lovers themselves. It was rare that any of the trio was seen alone without the company of at least one of the other two. When the time came for the bonding ceremony, Victor refused to leave either of his loves out of the ceremony and the priests of the time reworked everything to include a triple bond."

"And it worked?" I ask, my voice hoarse and barely a whisper. "It really worked?"

Miles smiles. "Very well. Magic surged and flourished, stronger than it had been since that first bonding centuries before."

"You have record of what they did to make the bond work?" Freya asks beside me, her voice holding the same strained optimism that I feel pulling in my chest.

"I do," Miles says with a nod. "I never thought I'd need it, but I keep it handy because I find it interesting. The ceremony itself doesn't vary much, and I could easily perform such a ceremony if you'd like."

Hope flares in my chest but I push it away. I can't give it

air. Not yet. If this had been an option all along, then surely I would've known. My mother was willing to let me marry a farmer's daughter and then a princess from a traitor kingdom. If a triple bond could work, it would have been tried. It's not possible. Miles must be mistaken.

"If a triple bond worked to make magic strong, why wasn't it tried again when magic started failing? Why wasn't I taught about this king and his wives?" I shake my head. "It can't be true."

Miles's smile slips as a shadow crosses his face. "I promise you, it is true, but there are a likely couple reasons it hasn't been made public knowledge or offered as a viable option. For one, magic is a living thing, born from nature itself. While the bonding ceremony can weave magic together in a useful way to spread magic throughout Elodia on its own, it works best when there is an actual connection or relationship between the two creating the bond."

"It needs love to work?" Freya asks.

"Love is of course the strongest influence, but even true desire to make the bond and connection work is enough to uphold it. If love or some sort of emotional connection comes later, it helps to sustain and strengthen that initial bond. Creating such a bond of magic is risky enough with two people, but if that bond were to stretch between three people who didn't have a strong enough connection or interest, it could put the whole spell at risk. It would become too delicate and shatter, taking magic with it. Because of that, no priest would have mentioned it as an option, not with magic already so weak."

"But if the three really love each other, like these three," Freya says softly, nodding to the book, "then the bond is possible?"

"Yes," Miles says without hesitation. "Which is why I'm willing to mention it now."

"What's the other reason?" I ask, still not ready to place my hope in something so fragile. "You said there were a couple reasons."

"Unfortunately, this particular bond is what led to the civil war that wiped out the Fae."

All the air whooshes from my lungs as I stare at Miles. "How?"

"Well, as you can imagine, the Fae were less than pleased that the alliance they built through the marriage arrangement was altered somewhat by the triple bond. They felt they'd been tricked. They further felt jilted when the human queen produced two female heirs before the Fae queen gave birth to her one and only child, a son. They believed that the Fae child should be the rightful heir and were furious when the crown passed to the oldest daughter. The son did his best to smooth the path between them, agreeing to an arranged marriage of his own to a Fae woman from the same clan, but the Fae were still less than pleased.

"The prince was a general in Elodia's army, and when the Panbrio Isles went to war for their independence, he led the charge to get them back, despite his wife being with child. He was, most unfortunately, lost in battle. His wife died less than a month later in childbirth. The clan of Fae swept in and offered to raise the orphaned child. Since the kingdom was dealing with the recent loss of the Panbrio Isles and other upsets, the queen didn't fight it and didn't think to check in on her nephew. The Fae took advantage of her distraction and poisoned the child with a hate for the ruling family, raising him to believe that the crown was rightfully his.

"When he reached adulthood, he led a charge for the

throne. Having so recently lost the Panbrio Isles and with magic once again in flux, the ruling king at the time struck back hard and fast. He easily overtook his cousin and, to ensure no further rebellion, wiped out what remained of the Fae clans."

Miles stops speaking and a thick silence settles over the room. I'm barely even breathing as his words sink in. Now that he's told the story, I remember vaguely learning about King Victor and his reign of magic. I remember hiding from my tutor as a boy and stumbling across a painting half-hidden in the back of the magical archives of a king flanked by two queens. I remember hearing how there was a link between the loss of the Panbrio Isles and the slaughter of the Fae. All along my answer was all hidden between the lines of histories. I know without a shadow of a doubt that every word Miles has spoken is true. I can have Bash, I can have Freya, and they can have each other. We can all be together.

"Ty?" Freya whispers, squeezing my hand gently and drawing me from my thoughts.

I raise my eyes to hers and realize she's crying. I realize *I'm* crying. I choke on a laugh and lift a hand to wipe the tears from my cheeks.

"Freya, would you be okay if—"

"Yes," she says, breathlessly.

I laugh again and pull in her for a kiss. It's a simple kiss, barely more than the press of lips, but it's filled with fire and promise. When I pull back I meet her eyes and smile so wide it hurts.

"We have a groom to find." I jump up from my seat, pulling a laughing Freya with me. As we race from the house, I yell over my shoulder to Miles. "Prepare whatever you need for a ceremony for three, Father, because in a couple days, we're having a trio wedding!"

The cool of night embraces us as we tumble outside. There aren't a whole lot of places for Bash to go, and we find him easily enough, wandering alone a few yards from the cabin.

"Bash!" I call out, racing toward him.

He turns to me with a frown. Another laugh breaks out and I stumble to a stop in front of him, Freya not far behind. He looks between us, his brow furrowed.

"Aren't you two supposed to be working out the ceremony details with Miles?"

"Wouldn't do to finish up the details with one of the grooms missing."

His frown deepens and he takes a step back, shaking his head. "Ty . . ."

"Miles figured it out! He has a way for all of us to be together as equals. We can be united though marriage and through the bond."

Bash's lips part and he looks past me to Freya.

"It's true, Bash," she says, smiling wide as she steps to my side. "There's precedent and everything."

Bash takes a shaky breath, running a hand through his hair. "So, you're saying we can all be married and together as—"

"King, king, and queen. Yes," I say with a nod. "All I need is for you to agree." I drop to my knee and look up at Bash. "Bastion Shamblefoot, will you marry us?"

Bash blinks several times, his eyes darting between me and Freya while I wait for his answer, breath caught in my chest. Slowly, a hesitant smile appears and a huff of a laugh escapes his lips.

"Is that a yes?" I ask, standing. "Please say that was a yes."

He laughs, his gaze meeting mine. "Of course it's a yes."

I cheer, pumping my fist in the air as Freya laughs, stepping forward to kiss Bash's cheek. I reach out and pull Bash into a kiss. Unfortunately, that's all we get to do because I have to head back to the castle before anyone notices I'm missing. I bid them each goodbye with one more kiss each, and walk back to palace, feeling like I'm floating on air.

CHAPTER THIRTY-NINE

FREYA

The days between the finalizing of the details and the night of my wedding drag. Ty hasn't had a chance to visit, but Klarissa has managed to slip out a few times to keep us updated. So far, no one seems to suspect anything, and the queen's plans for the ball keep everyone busy. Still, I'm afraid that someone may barge in at any moment and attempt to take Bash and I out, but somehow we make it to the Fae moon without incident.

Gregorian arrives first with a few helpers, bearing a dress for me and formal attire for Bash along with a full-length mirror and a slew of supplies. They set up a series of changing screens down the center of the room, shooing Bash to one side and me to the other.

"Is this necessary?" Bash growls from his side.

"You cannot see the bride before the ceremony," Gregorian states.

"That's bollocks and you know it."

"Tradition is what it is, sweetheart, and I won't have you tempting Fate."

Bash mumbles something that sounds a lot like threats, but Gregorian seems entirely unbothered. The helpers leave to go back to their stations, and Gregorian sets about dressing me first. They used my previous measurements to create my dress, but it fits perfectly. It's a flowing, floor-length white gown with sheer silver layers over the skirt and intricately woven lace over the bust. They do my hair up into an intricate braid, weaving in delicate white and silver flowers created by Rissa.

Once I'm dressed, they flit over to make sure Bash is ready. Apparently, he must look decent enough, because Gregorian returns a moment later.

"It's a pity practically no one will witness these master-pieces," they lament with a sigh.

I run my hands over the lace. "This dress is stunning."

"No, my dear," they say, stepping to my side and turning me to take in my reflection in the full-length mirror. "The dress is not the masterpiece. *You* are."

I don't get a chance to respond before there's a knock on the door. Bash starts toward it, but Gregorian yells at him.

"The door is on Freya's side and you will not cross!"

"I'm not letting her open that door!"

"I will get it," they reply, already halfway there. "If it's anyone bad, I'll stab them with a large sewing needle."

The needle isn't needed however, as it's only Klarissa.

"Ty and the king aren't far behind me. We should— Oh!" Her eyes fall on me and she rushes to my side. "You look beautiful!" She adjusts one of the flowers in my hair. "Ty won't know what to do with you."

"Pretty sure he has plenty of ideas, darling," Gregorian says with a smirk, stepping to her side as she makes a face.

There's another knock on the door and Klarissa looks

over her shoulder. "That should be Miles. I told him to come get us once Ty and the king were in place."

Sure enough, a moment later Miles steps into the room, looking very nervous. His eyes fall on Klarissa in her full ballgown, and a slight blush rises on his cheeks before he looks away, focusing on me.

"We're ready for you whenever."

I nod, nerves swishing in my gut. "What do I need to do again?"

Miles smiles softly. "I have the altar set up with the stone and the ceremonial blade. Your prince is already waiting. All you need to do is join him. Once you're in place, Bastion can join you as well."

"You hear that, solider boy?" Klarissa calls out.

"These screens aren't so thick they obscure voices," he snaps. I wonder if I'm the only one who catches the nerves in his voice. Knowing Bash is equally nervous calms me a bit.

"I'll head on out," Klarissa gives me a quick hug. "Join us when you're ready."

I nod and Miles, Klarissa, and Gregorian make their exit. I shutter my eyes and take a deep breath, releasing it slowly.

"You okay?" Bash asks.

"I think so," I reply honestly. "It's just now hitting me that I'm getting married."

He chuckles. "I know what you mean." He shuffles closer to the screens. "You're sure about this still? Sure about . . . me?"

I step closer to his voice and place my hand on the screen. "I've never been surer." I hesitate a moment before asking, "Are you sure about me?"

"I've never been surer," he repeats back to me.

I smile and release another slow breath. "I should probably head out then."

"Freya?"

"Yes, Bash?"

"I love you."

"I love you, too."

I can practically feel his relief through the screens as I cross the room and exit. I head around to the back of the house where Klarissa and Gregorian set up our wedding area. There are a few chairs, but the only guests in attendance are the two of them and a couple guards. It's obvious Klarissa used some of her magic to add more greenery and flowers to the area, including an arch covered in flowering vines. I, however, don't care about any of the decor right now because beneath the arch next to an altar and Miles stands Ty in a stunning silver suit. When he sees me, he straightens and his lips part in a smile. If I had any doubt I loved him, those doubts would perish at the adoration in his eyes. My heart flutters and threatens to beat out of my chest. I'm thankful Gregorian paired my dress with a pair of flat, slipper-like shoes, because I'm not paying any attention to my steps as I float toward Ty.

"You look beautiful," he breathes, tears shimmering in his eyes.

I manage a feeble smile. "You look half-decent yourself."

Ty grins, but before he can reply, Miles clears his throat, nodding past us. We both turn our heads to find Bash striding toward us. My heart stutters to a stop and races to catch up. While Ty has been fitted in a silver suit, Bash has been dressed in a shimmering deep gray that sets off his eyes. I've never had any doubts about my attraction to him, but in this moment, I can't imagine never loving this man.

He comes to a stop between Ty and I, standing across from Miles. His jaw twitches as he attempts to hide a smile as he looks from me to Ty.

"Are we ready?" Miles whispers, giving us each a reassuring smile.

"Never been more ready," Ty answers as Bash and I nod.

Miles gives us one last nod before stepping back and up onto a small platform that puts him slightly above us so he can address the crowd.

"Ladies, lords, and lieges, we are gathered here on this Fae moon to unite these three in the bond of marriage, both in the eyes of the gods and in the eyes of the kingdom. Tonight you will bear witness to this union and see firsthand the history of the future King Tybalt, King Bastion, and Queen Freya unfold. Before we continue, is there any among us who object to this union?"

My heart seizes in my chest, knowing that there are many throughout the kingdom who would object. I relax after a moment when Miles's question is met with nothing beyond silence.

"Very well," he continues. "I now ask if a member of the royal family will give their blessing."

"I will."

I turn my head only slightly to watch the king stand and walk forward. He's a little unsteady on his feet but he's nothing short of regal. He steps up to the podium and Miles extends a piece of paper and a quill.

"I, His Royal Majesty King Frederick Julian Shadowmoss, standing King of Elodia, do hereby give my blessing to the union of His Royal Highness Tybalt Adrian Shadowmoss, Bastion Tobias Shamblefoot, and Freya Astrid Brambleberry."

The king signs with a flourish. Once that's done, Miles produces a candle dripping red wax and the king adds his royal seal. When he pulls his hand away, he meets Ty's eyes with a gentle smile.

"May their union be as happy and fulfilling as my own."

With a nod from Miles, the king returns to his seat.

"As a representative of the gods, I am happy to unite these three in a union as one. Though it may not be common, the gods bless this union, as I do. Together, we all bear witness."

He turns to Ty. "Do you, Tybalt Adrian Shadowmoss swear loyalty to your companions and promise to love and cherish them until the end of your days, no matter what comes?"

Ty looks from me to Bash. "I do."

"And do you, Freya Astrid Brambleberry, swear loyalty to your companions and promise to love and cherish them until the end of your days, no matter what comes?"

I take a deep breath, my heart pounding against my ribs as my stomach swirls. "I do."

Miles nods and looks to Bash. "And do you, Bastion Tobias Shamblefoot, swear loyalty to your companions and promise to love and cherish them until the end of your days, no matter what comes?"

He meets Ty's eyes for a moment before he looks to me. The corner of his mouth tips up as he holds my gaze. "I do."

"Then with the power gifted me by the gods, I unite you as one, husband, husband, and wife."

Joy surges though me. I'm married to the two men I love most in the world. But we aren't done yet. Miles turns his attention back to Ty.

"Tybalt Adrian Shadowmoss, as Crown Prince your duty is first and foremost to the kingdom of Elodia and the magic therein. Today, as a symbol of both your union with your partners and of your service to Elodia you will be united together with magic. Your love and companionship will shine through and fuel the magic of the kingdom. The blood of the kings and queens of old and of the Fae runs through your veins. In the memory of King Harraque and his beloved Queen Vascha, we continue the tradition of sharing Fae magic with your people."

Miles places a silver bowl containing the crystal from the Temple of the Divine on the altar. He gingerly lifts the crystal and holds it up for everyone to see.

"This bears not only the blood of every generation since that first ceremony, but it also stands as a sign of unity. Tonight, these three will add their blood to a promise that has been held for the last several hundred years. How the magic works, exactly, no one is sure, but we know that as long as those that make the bonds have both the heritage of humans and Fae, the promise made all those years ago holds strong and magic flows throughout the kingdom."

He pauses, withdrawing a diamond dagger with a silver hilt that gleams in the moonlight.

"Part of the bond requires trust. You will each use this danger to draw blood from one of your partners."

I startle slightly. I knew that I would have to use my blood for the bond, but I somehow missed the part where I'd be the one drawing the blood from someone else. Miles, however, is unfazed, continuing with the ceremony.

"Once your blood has been drawn, add it to the stone and repeat the phrase 'Faecræft ardú ón Natur, breite do sciatháin an ár bann und stärken ár Ríocht,' which loosely translated means 'Magic rise from nature, spread your wings on our bond, and fortify our kingdom.'"

Miles passes the dagger to Ty first. Ty swallows, looking down at the dagger before lifting his eyes to meet Bash's. Bash offers him a weak smile and holds out his hand, palm up. Ty carefully slices the dagger across Bash's palm, the golden blood showing immediately. Bash holds his hand over the crystal and repeats the words. As his blood hits the crystal, it glows faintly.

Ty passes the dagger to Bash who turns to me.

"I'll be careful," he promises, his voice a low whisper.

I smile. "I know."

Without fear I hold out my hand and Bash slides the dagger across my skin. It doesn't hurt as much as I expected. I take a shuddering breath and add my blood to Bash's.

"*Faecræft ardú ón Natur, breite do sciatháin an ár bann und stärken ár Ríocht.*"

My mouth trips over the strange words, but it must do the trick because the stone's glow increases. I take the dagger from Bash and look across the bowl to Ty. He offers me a half-cocked smile, extending his hand.

"Be gentle with me. I cry easily."

A small laugh huffs out of me and a couple others chuckle. I steady Ty's hand with my still bleeding one and let the dagger slice his skin just enough for his blood to appear. He winces slightly but doesn't hesitate to add his blood. The Fae words sound almost natural coming from his lips, and I briefly wonder if he had to learn Old Elodian as a child. The crystal hums, pulsing bright with magic. Miles takes the dagger from me and holds it over the bowl, point down. He closes his eyes and says something in Old Elodian that sounds very much like a prayer. As he speaks, the coolness of his spirit magic winds around us and the glow from the crystal increases with every pulse, flashing out in a blinding light as he finishes speaking.

The magical pulse that accompanies the flash is so powerful I'm knocked back, only saved from falling by Bash's hand. My magic hums through me in response, so strong it's almost overwhelming. The blood in my veins might as well be water pushed through my body by the flow of magic. I look over at Bash, wondering if his magic feels like mine, but before either of us can say anything, Klarissa laughs behind us. I turn to look at her as she stands, holding out her hands. The vines in the arch above us twist under the effects of her magic, hundreds of blooms bursting to life and exploding. The petals shower down over us and Bash grins, sending a flick of his magic into their midst, making the petals dance around us.

"I think it's safe to say that magic has been more than restored," Miles says with a grin.

Ty laughs, plucking a petal from Bash's hair. "I never knew magic could feel like this. I almost wish I had something I could set on fire."

Bash rolls his eyes. "Maybe after the ceremony."

Our glee is cut short, however, as a snide voice calls out, "Looks like we're late to the party."

We all turn to find Bash's cousin, Killian, standing at the edge of the ceremony area flanked by Lord Vanderhof and a sharp-faced man I assume is Prince André. Behind them are dozens more.

"Lord Mayberry sends his regrets. He's been feeling under the weather as of late."

The king stands, glaring at our unwanted guests. "You are not welcome here."

"Pity," the duke says. "But not unexpected. It almost saddens me to do this."

He snaps his fingers and André lifts a small glass vial between two fingers. The moonlight glints off the vial, blocking the contents, but I'm assuming it's the catalyst for the spell on the king. He grins wickedly and throws it to the ground, crushing it beneath his boot. A breath later, the king collapses like a rag doll.

CHAPTER FORTY

BASH

I watch in horror as the king collapses. Ty cries out and races to kneel at his father's side with Miles close on his heels. I unsheathe my sword. It's meant to be ceremonial, but that doesn't mean it's not a proper weapon. I step between Ty and our guests, pointing my sword toward Killian.

"My wedding is not the one you want to interrupt," I growl. "And I'm positive none of you were invited."

Killian gasps dramatically, placing a hand over his heart. "Oh, how you wound me! I thought we were family."

"You are no family of mine."

All amusement slips from his face. "Agreed."

"How are you even here?" Ty demands, standing to his feet and drawing his own sword.

Killian chuckles. "Oh, little prince, did you really think your meager handful of guards were enough to stop the *cultas draíochta*?" He makes a tsking sound, shaking his head. "Like every other royal, you were so focused on the nobility you forgot that the little people existed. Taking out a few guards to free your duke and foreign prince was easy."

Ty turns his attention to Lord Vanderhof, who's grinning. "Why?" he asks, his voice trembling slightly. "Why would you betray my father? My father was good to you."

The duke scoffs. "Your father was a horrible king. He had his own agenda and didn't think twice about leaving everybody behind, even those like myself of high rank. He used magic as a tool to manipulate and control. I was already doubting his ability to rule fairly when I approached him about getting a crystal for Cressida. He practically laughed in my face, even going as far as threatening to remove my access to magic. Yet, he lets the riffraff have magic."

He gestures to me and I growl, stepping forward. He shrinks back only slightly before remembering he has an entire army with him. He straightens and glares at Ty.

"You father was failing the kingdom. When I learned about the power of *Naturcræft* and all it could do, I chose the winning side. I would've been a fool not to. *Naturcræft* is better than no magic at all."

"You're a fool all right," Ty says. "Why are you even here? Shouldn't you be hiding like the coward you are?"

"And miss watching the fall of the Shadowmoss line first-hand? I think not."

"Enough!" Killian shouts. "Tonight the reign of *Faecræft* comes to an end."

Ty readies his sword, looking over his shoulder at Miles. "Get my father out of here."

"Of course, Your Highness," he replies.

Out of the corner of my eye, I see Klarissa use her magic to lift the king with vines and the two head off toward the castle. A few of the cult start to follow, but Klarissa doesn't hesitate to shove more vines directly through their hearts, blood dripping from their leaves.

"Ignore them!" Killian yells. "The king will be dead soon enough. Focus on killing the prince."

He lunges forward, swinging his sword toward Ty. I immediately leap into action, blocking the blow.

"Nobody touches my husband."

Killian narrows his eyes at me, grinning. "You'll have to kill me to keep me away."

"That I can do."

I swing hard, pushing him back a step, but I can't concentrate on him yet because the rest of his crew is edging forward. We are severely outnumbered. It's just me, Ty, a couple of guards, Gregorian, and Freya. Gods. *Freya.* Fear pounds in my chest as I glance over my shoulder to where Freya still stands near the altar. Her gaze is set and full of anger and hate. One hand is clenched at her side but the other is gripping the ceremonial dagger. I'm about to call out to her to tell her to run back to the castle with Klarissa and the king, but my eyes fall on several more figures approaching from behind.

"Behind you!" I yell, fear so thick I'm practically choking on it.

Without a moment of hesitation, Freya spins around, leaping forward to stab the closest attacker in the neck. Blood sprays the white of her dress, but she doesn't seem bothered, turning toward the next attacker. I send a blast of air magic at the rest of those advancing on her, knocking them back, but that's all I can do because I have my own attackers to worry about. Before I know it, Ty and I are surrounded. This time they haven't bothered to obscure their faces with masks. They undoubtedly have enough faith that they can take us out without any repercussions. However, they weren't expecting magic to be so much stronger.

Calling on my wind has never been this easy. I use it effectively to push back dozens of attackers at once and have no problem slitting several throats. However, even with it easily accessible, it's hard to concentrate on using my magic while also beating back Killian by sword. He's extremely skilled; I don't forget that last time I went up against him, I nearly died. It doesn't help that, thanks to the ceremony, my left hand hurts too much to wield a weapon effectively. The crowd pushes between me and Ty, but he seems to have mastery over his fire. He throws up a circle of flames, blocking the majority of our attackers. A quick glance over my shoulder proves Freya is also within Ty's circle, holding her own against those cult members trapped inside with us. Gregorian and one of the other guards are at her side. I can't remember what kind of magic Gregorian has, but I'm hoping they know how to wield it in battle.

"You know, she's almost too pretty to kill," Killian sneers, snapping my attention back to him. "Maybe I'll let her live. She might be a grieving widow, but I know plenty of ways to keep her compliant."

My brain travels back to the earl's library when I was under the influence of whatever drug had been created with *Naturcræft*. I hated that I lost control. I hated myself for what I could have done, what I almost did. Like Hell am I letting this man harm Freya. With an angry growl I lunge forward, but Killian only laughs, dodging out of my way.

"Still such an emotional little boy, I see," he taunts, swinging hard. I move out of his way, but his sword tip catches the sleeve of my shirt, scratching the skin beneath. He grins. "You're making this too easy."

Anger roils through me and I hold out my hand, calling

on my magic. I take hold of the air around him and everyone near him and siphon away it away. Several of the others' eyes go wide, but Killian only grins. Before I can fully register his movement, he leaps forward and strikes with a small dagger he had hidden in his sleeve. The tip of the blade barley skims my hand, but I feel like the wind has been knocked from my lungs as my magic is cut off. I stumble and fall to my knees, gasping for breath.

"Bastion!" Ty screams. I use every bit of energy I can to hold up my hand to stop him from rushing to my side.

"What did you do?" I grind out, glaring up at Killian.

"I made you properly human, you filthy Fae bastard," he snarls, eyes flashing. He holds up his dagger, the end of it coasted with black liquid. "*Naturcræft* has ways of stripping you of your dark Fae magic. Granted, this blend is only temporary, but it won't matter because I am going to end you."

He raises his sword and everything in me wants to grab mine up and fight back, but I can't. My body is still reeling from the loss of magic. Instead, I jerk out of the way, barely escaping his blow. I roll on the ground and stumble to my feet. If I can avoid him long enough, maybe I can get my strength back. He strikes again and I dodge, stumbling slightly.

"Stop. Being. Difficult!" he roars, lunging forward.

His sword grazes my arm, drawing blood. The cut isn't too deep, but given my already weakened state, it affects me more than I care to admit. Around us, Ty's wall of fire wavers. If his wall falls before I get my energy and magic back, we're dead. Killian must sense it as well and his grin returns. He strikes again and I dodge, tripping over my own feet, slamming to the ground. My head hits hard and my vision blurs. Killian towers over me, grinning.

"And now we witness the end of Bastion Shamblefoot. May you not rest in peace."

He raises his sword and I close my eyes, accepting my fate. When the blow doesn't come, I open my eyes. Killian wavers above me, eyes wide, blood dribbling from his mouth, and a diamond dagger sticking from his throat.

"That's my husband, you son of a bitch!"

A laugh bubbles out of me, and I twist around to look at Freya. She still stands a few yards away, glaring at Killian. Her left hand is held out behind her and she's managed to construct a wall of water that's holding her remaining attackers back. I look back to Killian as he collapses in a puddle of his own blood.

"Bash!" Ty calls out. I look over at him. He's managed to kill his attackers and has both hands extended in front of him, controlling his flames. "I don't know how much longer I can hold the rest off!"

I push to my feet. I'm still a bit unsteady but whatever poison Killian used is starting to fade. I pluck up my sword and take Killian's as well. My left hand stings when I grip the hilt of his sword, but I've fought through worse.

"He took my magic," I shout to Ty. When his eyes widen I add quickly, "Temporarily. I can still fight."

"Wait," Ty says. He reaches one of his hands into his pocket and pulls out my crystal, tossing it to me. "Thought you might need it."

I grin and slip it over my head. My magic buzzes beneath my skin, and while I can't quite grasp it yet, I can feel my strength returning.

I look back at Freya and Gregorian, over at Ty, and then to the two guards whose names I will definitely need to find out later.

"Ready?" They all nod, and Freya plucks up a discarded sword from the ground. "Let's take these bastards out."

Freya and Ty drop their walls and the battle starts fresh. Our remaining attackers, frustrated by being kept back until this point, rush in with fresh vigor. Several of them appear to be using *Naturcræft* to create explosions, making them even harder to fight. Try as we might, for every person we manage to take out, five more rush to take their place. They push us together, circling around us.

Just when I'm about to admit that we might not make it out alive, a vine wraps around the neck of the soldier nearest me, snapping his neck. I watch wide-eyed as more vines appear, taking out several more. I'm baffled as more magic washes over the attacking crowd in various forms, including fire and wind. That's what I see them. Klarissa has returned and with her is practically an entire army, including Cooper.

"Sorry, we're late," Cooper calls out with a grin. "Got a bit ambushed, but we're here now."

"Better late than never!" Ty calls back with a laugh.

The fighting resumes, but this time everything is in our favor. It seems that the ceremony didn't only give magic to those of us who already had it, it spread magic to almost anybody willing to use it. Even though most of the palace soldiers now attempting to use magic know little about what they're doing, it's enough to give us the upper hand. With our combined efforts, it's not long before we've thinned out the remaining members of the cult. Klarissa uses her vines to bind the survivors together as Ty steps to my side, leaning on my shoulder.

"You okay?"

"Just dandy," he says with a huff.

I laugh and press a kiss to his forehead. I look back at Freya to find her sitting on the ground, rubbing her ankle.

She must feel my gaze because she looks up at me. I frown and she offers me a tired smile.

"I think I sprained it. Otherwise I'm fine."

"You're sure?"

"Yeah."

Gregorian offers Freya their hand and pulls her up. They loop an arm around her waist and help her to my side. When she's close enough, I hook my arm around her waist and allow her to lean on me for support instead. Ty straightens and looks past me to where Klarissa approaches.

"Quite a wedding to remember, huh?" she says, stopping a couple feet away. "It will definitely make the history books."

"My father . . ." Ty starts. "Is he . . . ?"

"He's alive," Klarissa confirms with a nod.

"Thank the gods," he breathes, sagging against me.

"Miles's magic, just like our own, is ten times stronger. That combined with his own research and the information about the healing aspects of *Naturcræft* Freya and Bastion found has allowed him to keep the king stable. He feels relatively confident that with the help of Doctor Adbar, the king will make a full recovery."

Ty takes a shaky breath. "Full recovery as in . . . ?"

Klarissa smiles. "As in more or less back to normal."

Ty lets out a small sob, leaning even more of his weight on me.

"So, what now?" Gregorian asks, looking around. "What do we do with those miscreants?"

They nod to where Klarissa's vines are securing the captured cult members, including the duke who hung back during the worst of the fighting.

Ty straightens. "They get locked in the deepest darkest parts of the dungeon to await trial for treason. Don't forget to get Lord Mayberry and any other nobility on our list."

He nods to Cooper. Cooper returns the nod and turns to the group of nearby soldiers, giving more orders. Even though Cooper isn't a captain or in any position of authority, they don't hesitate to obey.

"And us?" Gregorian asks.

"I'm going to go wait by my father's bedside, but the rest of you should head back to the castle and get cleaned up and rest. You may be needed as witnesses for whatever comes next."

Gregorian nods. "I will help in whatever way I can."

Ty gives them a sincere smile. "Thank you." He turns to me. "Can you take Freya to my—our—room so you can both get some rest?"

"Are you sure you don't want us to come with you?" Freya offers.

Ty shakes his head. "No. I have a feeling my mother will be joining me, and there are some things we need to discuss." He attempts a weak smile. "It's not the wedding night I was imagining, but it will have to do for now."

"Don't worry," I say, my voice low. "We have the rest of our lives to make up for it."

His eyes brighten and a small laugh huffs out. "You're right about that."

Without warning, I scoop Freya into my arms. She squeaks, throwing her arms around my neck.

"Bastion!" she says. "You're wounded!"

"I'm fine, and like Hell I'm letting my wife walk on sprained ankle."

She smiles softly. "I am your wife, aren't I?"

"And mine," Ty says, leaning over to kiss her cheek. "Now, go rest. I'll be with you both as soon as I can. I promise."

CHAPTER FORTY-ONE

TY

I pick at the dirt and grime on the front of my shirt. The night started so perfectly, so how did it end in such chaos? I sigh and sink into one of the oversized chairs my father keeps in his sitting room and stare off toward his bedchamber where he's under the care of Miles and Doctor Adbar. I startle when the doors are thrown open and my mother storms into the room. She's still wearing her opulent red ballgown, her face set in a fierce expression. I stand and her eyes fall on me.

"Tybalt," she says, her voice lined with frustration as she marches my way. Her eyes flick over me and take in my disheveled appearance. "What is happening? We were in the middle of a lovely ball when soldiers came in and arrested your fiancée and all her associates! They also dragged away other members of nobility! Hearing it was under your orders was a shock, but imagine my further surprise when I was informed you had been hurt, your father had been attacked, and the visiting prince, an earl, and a duke were all already in the dungeons. I'd like an explanation."

I take a deep breath and look away from my mother's concerned eyes. "If I tell you, will you actually listen this time?"

It's petulant and childish of me, I know, but in this moment, I can't help but think that if my mother had listened to me before, all the horrors of tonight could have been avoided. I could be in bed right now with Bash and Freya, celebrating our wedding night properly.

"Tybalt Adrian Shadowmoss," my mother bites out. "What is happening, and how you are involved?"

I set my jaw and meet her eyes, straightening to my full height. I cower before her so often I forgot I have a good two inches on her. Her eyes widen and she looks startled for a moment before she schools her expression, her sternness returning.

"I'll tell you," I say, my voice hard, "and you will listen, really listen. I can prove everything, so there's no point in denying it. To start with, Amarelia is *not* my fiancée. Not anymore." She opens her mouth but I hold up my hand, silencing her. "I'm married to Freya and Bash."

"How? That's impossible. You'd need—"

"The blessing of a king and a priest. Done."

She shakes her head. "Marriage to both of them is impossible."

"Turns out, it's not. Everything was done to the letter of the law. We're married, and as I'm sure you can feel, magic has been restored ten times over."

She falls silent, studying me for a moment before her shoulders droop. "What else have I missed?"

I meet her eyes. "Are you really ready to listen?"

She nods and I motion to the pair of nearby armchairs.

"Sit down and I'll tell you everything."

I don't know how long it takes, but I don't hold back any

details. I share everything that happened on the tour up to what happened tonight. I tell her about all the betrayal and how the cult managed to infiltrate the nobility and even the palace. Her face pales more with each word, and she doesn't dare to interrupt except to ask for the occasional clarification. When I wrap up with the events of tonight, she nods solemnly, lips pursed.

"I suppose an apology would not go very far, would it?"

I scoff. "No, it would not, but I would like to hear you admit that you were wrong."

She takes a deep breath and meets my eyes. "I was wrong. I was very, deeply wrong. I could use the excuse that I am only human. I was in no way ready to rule on my own when your father fell ill, and I made many mistakes, it seems."

"You never approved of Freya, even before father fell ill, so don't use him as an excuse."

"I wanted the best for you, Tybalt, and I still do. I grew up in a noble household with noble expectations."

"Stop using other people as a scapegoat. You were biased and petty and classist because you chose to be that way."

"Tybalt . . ." She sighs, shaking her head. "I was raised to believe—"

"No," I cut her off with a firm shake of my head. "I was raised with you as my mother, and I still found compassion for Bash and Freya because I chose to look past their standing."

"That is likely because of your father's influence," she admits with a small shrug, her gaze trailing toward his bedchamber. "Your father has always been a good man and a better person than I." She looks back to me. "I am pleased you found your way to happiness despite my actions, despite my errors in judgment. Fate, it seems, knew what she was doing, and I suppose I am grateful for that. Now that things are perhaps settling, I give you my blessing and wish you continued happiness."

"That doesn't fix things."

"No. No, it does not, but I hope you can forgive me."

I clench my jaw, straightening as I meet her eyes. "Maybe one day I'll forgive you for everything you put me through, everything you put the people I love through, but tonight I honestly don't feel very forgiving. If you want my forgiveness, then you're going to have to earn it."

"Very well then." A sad smile turns up the corner of her mouth. "Somehow in the middle of all of this, I missed when you turned from a boy to a man. The boy you were needed my protection, but the man you are now is strong enough to stand alone."

I shake my head. "Not alone. I have Freya and Bash. I even have Klarissa and Miles. Even Liege Greengrass showed up for me. I'm not alone. I wouldn't want to do this alone. But you are correct that I don't need your protection any longer."

She nods once and we fall into silence. We remain that way as the hours tick by. Finally, as the first hints of dawn are showing through the windows, Miles and Doctor Adbar exit my father's bedchamber. They both look exhausted, but Miles offers me a small smile as they approach. My mother stands first and I follow suit.

"Is he—" my mother starts.

"He will recover fully," Doctor Adbar says with a reassuring nod.

"Thank the gods," I whisper.

"It seems that our resident priest had a few tricks up his sleeve that made all the difference," the doctor says, smiling at Miles.

Miles shrugs. "It was nothing really. Klarissa—er, Lady

Klarissa—helped me realize a few things about how my magic works and some of the circumstances surrounding the current ailments of the king. Using that knowledge along with some of the research brought back by Lady Freya and Bastion, I was able to remove the ill effects of *Naturcræft* put on the king by his enemies."

"It was more than that," Doctor Adbar says with an affectionate shake of his head. "I've never seen anything like it. Father Finnick's ability to diagnose and extract the magic without harming the host was incredible."

Miles shakes his head, a blush rising on his cheeks. "It was only half me, and a good bit of what I did was simply a combination of my spirit magic and *Naturcræft* which, despite the kerfuffle it's caused, isn't all bad."

"Either way," Doctor Adbar says, looking between me and my mother. "The king is recovering quite well. Father Finnick not only fought back the most recent spell on His Majesty but also removed the ill effects of a much earlier spell that caused the king's illness in the first place."

"So, he really will be fine?" my mother asks, her voice cracking.

"The spells had an effect on his body, there's no denying that, but when he wakes he will no longer be on the verge of death. I daresay he has many years left in him."

My mother lets out a small sob.

"May we see him?" I ask, my own voice trembling.

"I have him in a magically induced sleep," Miles says. "It will help to restore his magical core to its full strength."

"It will also allow his body to recover better," Doctor Adbar adds.

"Speaking of his magic, is he still tied to the magic of Elodia?" I ask, looking at Miles.

"Technically, yes," he replies. "Until he passes, his magic

and bond with the queen"—he nods to my mother—"will continue to help uphold the magic, but now that you are bonded and have sworn loyalty to Elodia and your partners, the magic recognizes you as the primary source. It is now you and your partners that feed the magic. That's why magic is so much stronger now. The vast amount of Fae blood that runs through the veins of the three of you has been recognized and celebrated. As long as you reign, magic will undoubtedly flourish. According to the laws of magic, you are the ruler."

Relief washes over me, but I feel the pressure of his words. Magic now sees me as Elodia's leader.

"What of an heir?" my mother asks, and I frown at her.

Miles also frowns. "What do you mean?"

My mother's jaw twitches. "The heir. With two potential fathers, how can we be sure the line will continue properly?"

I tense but Miles grins. "Ah. That's not problem. You see, when a pair, or in this case a trio, is bound through magic and swears their oaths, the magic considers them all the reigning entity. Any child born from Freya, whether fathered by Bastion or Tybalt, would be recognized by the magic as the proper heir. You have nothing to fear when it comes to the succession of magic." He pauses, looking thoughtful. "In fact, there is some precedence for a special anointing ceremony when a child couldn't be conceived the natural way."

My mother doesn't look entirely reassured, but I feel lighter and somewhat vindicated. Though, if I had known about the anointing ceremony bit, that could have saved me a lot of pain and trouble. However, that might mean I wouldn't have Freya, so maybe Fate knew what it was doing all along.

"Thank you, Father Finnick, Doctor Adbar," I say,

AMBER D. LEWIS

nodding to them each in turn. "I'm sure you're both exhausted."

Doctor Adbar offers me a smile. "Very. I'll be back to check on him in a few hours."

"I as well," Miles adds.

"Thank you for all you've done," my mother says, offering them a nod. After they leave, she turns to me. "Are you going to stay with me by your father's side?"

I pause before shaking my head. "No. I have a husband and a wife waiting for me."

My mother smiles and for the first time in I don't know how long, it seems gentle and sincere.

"Go then," she says, placing a hand on my arm. "Be with them."

I return her smile and leave. I don't exactly run to my room, but I don't take my time either.

When I throw open the door to my bed chambers, Bash and Freya are curled together in the center of my bed under the blankets. From what I can see, they've both changed into fresh clothes, but they don't look like nightclothes. Bash startles, sitting up, but Freya remains asleep, shifting slightly.

"Ty?" Bash says, blinking at me. He glances toward the window. "What time is it?"

"Barely dawn," I say with a smile, working my shirt off. "Plenty of time left to sleep."

I slip off my pants and Bash lifts the edge of the blankets for me to slide underneath. He lies back down, and I snuggle against him with a sigh.

"How's your father?" Bash asks once I'm settled.

"Alive," I breathe out. "Miles and Doctor Adbar saved his life. He's going to be okay. Like really okay." I tip my head back to look at him. "I assume everything else went well? Mother said she received word about the arrests."

"Cooper got everyone rounded up. He checked in with me once it was done, figuring you would be busy with your father. We should really see about getting him promoted."

"I agree. We owe him a lot."

Bash nods. "Anyway, the duke flipped on others that we didn't know about in a vain attempt to win favor. We still have a lot to do to clean up the kingdom and finish dismantling the *draíochta*, but with all the information we have, it shouldn't take too much. Now that magic is back, they'll have less hold over people."

I push up and look down at him. "Wait. Magic really is back? For everyone?"

Bash nods. "It seems so. It's only been a few hours, but from what I've witnessed, almost anyone can access magic to some level. I think—"

He drops off into a yawn and I chuckle, settling back down. "Let's get some more sleep. We can finish changing the world tomorrow."

He huffs out a small laugh and slips his arm around me, pulling me closer. Everything feels so right, so perfect, and for the first time in a long time, I'm actually looking forward to what the future will bring. I'm finally living my happily ever after.

EPILOGUE

FREYA

Two Months Later

"Is this cape thing really necessary?" Ty asks, frowning at his reflection in Gregorian's full-length mirror.

Gregorian gasps, placing a hand over their heart. "It is a royal mantle! Not a 'cape thing.' And of course it's necessary!"

"Forgive him, G," Rissa says, rolling her eyes. "You forget he's entirely uncivilized."

"I'm not uncivilized!" Ty grumbles, adjusting the way the mantle sits on his shoulders. "It's just a bit much."

I step to his side, and he smiles at me in the mirror. "I think it suits you."

He grins wickedly. "You also enjoyed me spread naked on the bed this morning."

"No, no, no!" Rissa shouts, covering her ears as heat rushes to my cheeks.

Ty's grin grows but thankfully he doesn't elaborate.

"You're hopeless," Bash says, from his stool on the other side of the fitting room.

Ty rolls his eyes. "You didn't seem to mind this morning either, but whatever."

"As for the *mantle*," Gregorian says, stepping up behind Ty and smoothing their hands over the fur lining sitting on Ty's shoulders to examine the pins they placed a moment ago, "it is a customary garment for a crowning ceremony. Now, slip it off and I'll make the final adjustments. Careful of the pins."

I move out of the way as Ty gingerly removes the mantle.

"It's not a proper crowning," he mumbles. "My father is still the ruling king."

"Yes," I counter, "but you know the magic recognizes you as the primary ruler now. This ceremony is your father announcing that fact to the kingdom as well as the plan for him to slowly relinquish more ruling power to you bit by bit over the next few years until you officially take the crown for yourself. It's as important as a typical crowning ceremony would be."

Ty grins and turns to me. "We. When *we* take the crown. We're equals here, remember." He pauses, looking over at Gregorian who's putting the mantle on a mannequin. "Hey, does Bash get to wear one of those cape things?"

Gregorian's eyes flash as they glare at Ty. "Call it by its proper name and I'll tell you."

Ty sighs dramatically. "Does Bash get to wear a mantle as well?"

Gregorian grins and goes back to arranging the mantle on the mannequin. "I wasn't instructed to make one for him."

"I don't need one," Bash says quickly.

"Nuh-uh," Ty says, crossing the room and pulling Bash up, linking his arms behind Bash's back. "We're equals. That means you get a mantle."

Bash huffs a laugh, looking into Ty's eyes. "I don't want a mantle."

"Too bad," Ty whispers, kissing Bash's protests away.

"Ugh, stop being gross," Rissa whines, but she's smiling.

Gregorian sighs and looks at me. "Do you want a mantle as well?"

"Yes!" Ty answers for me, eyes bright. "She does. She most definitely does."

I laugh. "I don't need one if it will be trouble."

Gregorian smiles. "For you, sweetheart, I will happily do anything. Do you want a mantle?"

Ty extends a hand to me, and I step over to him, allowing myself to be pulled into a kiss. When he pulls back, he grins down at me, leaning forward to whisper in my ear.

"Tell them you want the mantle."

I laugh and shove his chest. "You just don't want to wear the mantle alone."

"True," he confesses with a solemn nod. "And as spouses, we should support each other in our desires."

I laugh again and roll my eyes, looking over at Gregorian who's watching us with amusement. "I guess I'll take the mantle."

"Very well," they say. "I'll make sure all three of you look as royal as ever."

A knock on the door has us all turning. Bash answers, his hands twitching at his side like he wants to draw his sword. The door opens to reveal Miles and Cooper. Cooper's wearing his new captain uniform well. They step inside and look around as Bash closes the door behind them.

"Ah, you're all here," Miles says. "Excellent. It means I'll only have to tell everyone once."

"Is something wrong?" Ty asks.

Miles shakes his head. "No, I merely came to report that

the survey of the kingdom has concluded, and magic has indeed reached the farthest corners. Everyone has magic."

"Really?" I ask, warmth spreading through me. "We managed to restore magic throughout the whole kingdom?"

Ty takes my hand, weaving his fingers with mine. "Seems the three us were exactly what Elodia needed."

"Indeed," Miles confirms with a nod. "Of course, magic is strongest in the families that embraced their Fae heritage."

I frown. "What do you mean?"

"I'm sure you've noticed there are two types of surnames popular throughout the kingdom—those that sound like nature names, such as Shadowmoss, and those that do not, such as Vanderhof. Those nature surnames came from the Fae. Families that respected the Fae heritage and accepted the Fae names tend to have more magic," Miles explains.

"Oh, I guess that makes sense."

"And along those lines," Cooper says, drawing our attention to him, "we have plans to start implementing magic in our training." He looks at Bash. "I was hoping you could help with that."

Bash nods. "Of course. I'd be happy to."

"All right, go discuss this somewhere else," Gregorian says, making shooing motions. "I have work to do if you're all going to be properly dressed for the ceremony in a week."

We start filtering out and reconvene in one of the gardens, Miles and Cooper joining us. We settle in the grass, Rissa curled against Miles and Bash between me and Ty. Cooper stretches out on the other side of Ty, comfortable in our presence.

"I heard from Cora," I say once we're situated.

"Oh?" Bash says, doing a poor job of hiding his continuing dislike for her. "How are her and Eve?"

"They're good. They've decided to make their relationship official and public and get married."

"Wait," Rissa cuts in. "Will that make them both countesses now? Eve inherited the title and lands when the earl died, didn't she?"

Ty nods. "Yes. After all Eve had to put up with, she deserves the title and can share it with whomever she wants, Cora included. The earl never had children, so there's no one to argue the inheritance."

"Thank the gods," I mutter under my breath. "Can you imagine him raising a child?"

Ty shivers dramatically. "That man was despicable. I'm happy he died all alone in the dungeon, though I do wish it hadn't been quite so quickly."

Rissa nods. "He deserved to suffer more."

We all mumble our agreement. Without access to the catalyst that tied him to Eve, the spell wore off and he faded quickly. Thankfully, Eve recovered just as rapidly, suffering only minor lingering effects that Miles is working hard to find ways to offset. At least we all got to attend the execution of Lord Vanderhof and several of his minions for their treason, though even I felt a little sorry for Cressida despite the fact she literally attempted to murder me. Losing her father and her status all in one fell swoop must have been difficult, though we'll never know to what extent since she left Rosana to live with a cousin in the southernmost part of Elodia with no intent to return.

"Speaking of what people deserve," Ty says, turning his attention to Rissa with a mischievous grin.

"What do you want?" she asks with a heavy sigh

"Who says I want anything?"

She levels him with a stare and Cooper snorts while Ty rolls his eyes.

"Fine. I have a little favor to ask."

"I figured as much." Rissa waves her hand. "Out with it."

"Once the ceremony is over, I need you to create a distraction so I can get away."

"Why would I do that?"

"Because you love me."

Rissa barks a laugh. "Try again."

"Because I'm taking a good and proper honeymoon far away from prying eyes so I can have endless sex with my husband and wife."

My face heats and Bash rolls his eyes, a little color rising in his cheeks. Miles and Cooper suddenly become very interested in their surroundings, Cooper examining the grass while Miles plucks a leaf from a nearby bush.

"You have official responsibilities now," Rissa reminds him.

"If I've learned anything, life is too short not to shirk responsibility every now and again. I've spent my whole life yearning for a happily ever after, and now that I have it, I'm going to cherish it." He looks over at Rissa and shoots her a wink. "Don't worry. I'll back before you know it, bugging the Hell out of you."

"Fine, but when I decide to escape with Miles and give him a tour of the kingdom, you have to help me get away."

Miles startles, sitting straighter. "You want to take me on a tour of the kingdom?"

Rissa grins, pressing a kiss to his cheek. "Yes. I want to show you off to the world."

Miles ducks his head, blushing. "I think I'd like that."

Ty looks at me, then to Bash, and the warmth in his gaze could have melted me ten times over. He takes each of our hands, intertwining our fingers.

"Is this what happily ever after feels like?" I ask, meeting his eyes.

"No," he replies, grinning. "Whatever this is, it's better."

And when he pulls me in for a kiss, I'm inclined to agree.

THE END

ACKNOWLEDGMENTS

As always, I have to thank my beautiful wife for standing by my side and cheering me on. She had to listen to me brainstorm and complain and yell at my characters more than anyone, and yet she didn't divorce me. That's love.

Big shoutout and thank you to Ariel Rae, my author bestie. Not only did you read my trash of a first(ish) draft and give me crucial feedback on my story, but you were there at midnight helping me figure out where to take my story next. You also helped to give Miles his name. I don't even remember what his name was before you helped me come up with "Miles," but I know it was horrible. So thank you for being my ride or die buddy on this book and kind of life in general.

Also a thank you to one of my other earliest readers, Lana. You helped me make this book into a story others would want to read.

Thank you to Rebecca, Konstantina, Roz, Mandy, Melissa, Kim, Autumn, Megan, Kara, and Jessica (I think that's all of you) for being my Beta readers and helping to form what would become the final version of the story.

Of course, I must say a big thank you to my editor, Andi, for helping me polish the final version of this book. You definitely make my words shine.

And I end with thanks to you, the reader. Thank you for

your support. I can never describe just how much it means to me that you picked up my book. I hope you enjoyed it.

Keep reading for a peek into the
FIRE AND STARLIGHT SAGA

THE NIGHT THE
STARS FELL PREVIEW

PROLOGUE

My name is Astra Downs, and in three days I may destroy the world.

I'm a twin, which might seem insignificant, but, in reality, very little about my existence is insignificant. After all, my brother Kato and I are the only twins ever born in our kingdom. Some say we're blessed while others claim we're cursed. I believe we are both.

The night we were born quite literally shook the foundations of Timberborn, the village we call home. But the earthquake was only one thing that marked that night as unique. Not only was it the final night of celebration for the annual Kriloa festival, but also the night the stars poured down, streaking across the night sky. That night set everything into motion, fulfilling prophecies we never even knew existed. The plans of the gods were at play.

Now, Kato and I alone bear the secret of a power prowling beneath our skin. It's volatile and growing in strength. When we turn eighteen I have no doubt this power will break free, bringing with it destruction.

Perhaps I'm overreacting, overthinking. After all, magic has been dead for centuries. How can I possibly know that some power dwells inside me? The truth is I don't know anything for sure, but I

know *something* isn't right. I am a scholar, and I've studied everything given to me in search of an answer. Of course, my village is small and my resources limited, but I know that my brother and I are different from everyone else.

From the moment we were able to form coherent thoughts, we could communicate with one another, no matter the distance between us. Through Kato's eyes I could sense the strength he had when training to become a village soldier, and I begged him to teach me. In return, he wanted to learn more about reading and writing than the basics offered to boys with his skill. In secret, he trained me in the art of weapons best suited for my small form, and I shared with him all I learned. In many ways, it felt like we were one mind and soul with two hearts.

At a glance, we look very different. Kato is gifted with dark hair, black and shiny as raven wings, that spills off his head in loose, uncontrollable, shoulder-length curls. He has broad shoulders and naturally tan skin like our father and strong, handsome features that most envy. Even as a small child he towered over most our age and now stands a full head taller than many full-grown men. I, on the other hand, am the stark opposite—small and dainty to the point of looking almost frail with pale, porcelain skin and sharp yet feminine features. It doesn't help that my hair is whiter than freshly fallen snow. And, while I am not uncommonly short, I am shorter than the majority of the other village girls my age. The only thing Kato and I have in common when it comes to appearance is our eyes—a perfect shade of amethyst.

From a very young age we felt a keen restlessness, more so than other children in Timberborn. It couldn't be satiated with sword drills or tomes. Whenever we felt traces of our power, we spoke of them to only each other and never aloud, only ever speaking in our minds, communicating in the way that only we could. It was far beyond our understanding and knowledge, so we chose to bury it. Hide it. Ignore it. All in the hopes we were imagining it and it would someday fade.

In three days we turn eighteen. Our power has been growing inside us, biding time. It's getting stronger, making it harder to ignore, to push down. While I have no proof, no precedent, I know that in three days, it will finally be revealed. Once we turn eighteen, there will be no going back. There will be no more hiding. I just hope we, along with everyone we love, make it out alive.

THE NIGHT THE STARS FELL PREVIEW

CHAPTER ONE

T he streets already buzz with merchants selling their
wares for
Kriloa, even though the festival doesn't officially
begin until sundown. Kriloa is considered a celebration of
life and being; therefore, everyone wants to be a part. From
where the festival originates, no one knows for sure. It is one
of those things that is simply ingrained in our culture and
has always been celebrated for as long as anyone can remember. The festival starts on the first night of the spring
solstice, ending three nights later when the night finally
gives way to dawn.

Workers gather in the center of town, preparing the large
bonfire that will burn all three nights as the center of most of
the activity. Smaller fires will burn throughout the village
and along the outskirts with more personal gatherings, but
any fire will be welcome to anyone.

The first night is marked with performances galore.
Some of the performers are practiced and planned while
others are impromptu. I glance toward an array of brightly

colored carnival carts not far from the bonfire and wonder who waits inside, ready to perform in the hopes of gathering coins from those drinking more heavily than usual. A voice calls my name from behind and I turn to see a girl my age with wavy brown hair and bright hazel eyes rushing toward me.

"Astra," she calls. "Please tell me you've gotten your nose out of your books enough to have heard the latest news!" She rushes up to me almost breathless, her eyes shining.

"Heard what, Mara? Were you spying on your father's business again? Do we have a new export? Something fun?" I ask with enthusiasm.

Mara rolls her eyes. "I don't spy on my father. Sometimes I just accidentally overhear things."

"Or, perhaps, you've found an amazing present for my birthday? Is my present the new, fun export? Have you finally gotten me a pony?"

"When have I ever *not* given you the best present? But no. The prince is coming to one of the festival nights!" She links her arm through mine, guiding me toward the center of the square to examine the tents and carts.

"What prince?" I ask, scowling.

Timberborn is a wonderful place to live, but we are little more than a small village that serves as a stopping point for occasional merchants traveling throughout the kingdom. We have nothing of real interest to attract a prince or any other sort of nobility. We barely attract these merchants.

"*The* prince, of course! Prince Ehren? The crown prince of Callenia? Surely you know what prince." Her whole face glows. "Anyway, he was on an official mission in Bugharion and won't be able to make it back to the capital for the royal Kriloa festival."

"So he's coming here? To Timberborn?" Mara nods and

my scowl deepens. "But why? There are dozens of cities more suitable along the border between us and Bugharion. Why would he come here?"

Mara shrugs. "I'm not entirely sure and, quite frankly, I don't care if it means I might get to meet the prince. All I know is that my father received word to prepare for the arrival of Prince Ehren and his entourage of guards. Oh! What do you suppose is in that tent?" She breaks off from me and wanders toward a bright red tent with a rainbow of ribbons above the door.

I follow her and send a quick message to my brother through our twin bond. *Kato, have you heard news about the crown prince coming?*

A few moments of silence pass before his voice echoes through my head. *Yes. We just received word to prepare extra sentries and guards for the festivities once he arrives.*

Why didn't you tell me?

Commander Jetson literally just informed me. Besides, when did you care about the movements of royalty? Do you even know the prince's name?

Yes. Of course I know his name. I don't live in a cave, Kato.

Fine. What's his name?

Ehren.

A pause. *Mara told you. I was going to ask how you knew the prince was coming, but that would explain everything.*

"Astra?" Mara's voice breaks into the conversation. "Are you all right? You look distant."

I force a smile and nod. Even as close as Mara and I are, I've never told her of my twin bond with Kato. It's too personal. Kato, likewise, has never told anyone either, including his closest friend, Pax. Yet talking to him in my head seems so normal I often forget my surroundings.

"I was just looking at that cart over there," I cover,

pointing randomly, my finger inadvertently landing on a worn, wooden cart with blue chipping paint. "Is that the man who performed the fire dances last year?"

Mara squints. "I don't remember what his cart looked like but he was one of the most talented fire dancers. I hope he's back this year." We turn and weave our way through the carts. I see my youngest brother, Broderick, weaving through the carts opposite me, heading my direction. His face is red and his hair is sweaty, as if he ran all the

way from the house.

"Astra!" he yells, breathing hard as he approaches. "I've been looking for you everywhere!"

"Why? What is it?" I scan his face, worried. "Is something wrong?"

"Father's home."

Despite the warmth of the day, a chill rushes down my spine. Our father is a merchant who deals in forbidden or questionable goods and rarely makes it home due to his constant traveling. When he is home, he often stays drunk which, in turn, makes him cruel. He hates the fact that I was born before my brother, making his eldest child a girl. If there hadn't been so many witnesses to our twin birth, it's more than likely he would have just gotten rid of me shortly after birth and claimed my brother as the only child born that night. I avoid him as much as possible.

"What does he want?"

Broderick opens his mouth to answer, but closes it again, shaking his head. "I don't think I'm supposed to say. He just wants you home as soon as possible."

I turn back to Mara, but I don't need to say anything. Sad understanding shines in her eyes. "Go. I'll see you later tonight?"

I nod and force a smile. "I'd never miss a night of the festival."

I turn and quickly follow Broderick as he weaves back through the gathering crowd toward our home at the opposite end of the village. I try to push down my concern and panic as I reach out to Kato.

Father's home.

What? I thought he was supposed to be gone for several more weeks. A month at least.

Broderick disappears behind a wagon, no doubt taking some shortcut to get home as quickly as possible. I try to follow him, unwilling to give Father any excuse to take out his frustrations on me.

Well, regardless, he's home now. Rick found me in the square with Mara and told me I'd been ordered home.

I don't like that he's home so early. I'll wrap up what I'm doing and get home immediately.

You don't have to leave training on account of me. Don't get yourself in trouble.

I won't leave you alone to deal with him, Ash. We're basically done for the day, anyway. It is a holiday, you know.

Thank you.

I'm about to add more, but a nearby worker slips from his unsteady stool, the banner in his hand flying toward me. I duck out of the way in time to avoid injury, but stumble hard into a bystander, pulling him down with me as I fall.

"Oh! I'm so sorry," I say, scrambling up. "I wasn't paying enough attention to my surroundings."

I turn to the man I just knocked to the ground. He stands, brushing himself off, scowling. He's a little older than me with dark brown hair and eyes. His face is marred only by a small, almost imperceptible scar on his left cheekbone. His clothes, despite being a simple white shirt and dark blue pants, look slightly nicer than what the average villager might wear, indicating he has a specific reason for visiting our town.

"It is quite all right," he mumbles, glaring down at the dirt now smeared across the front of his white shirt. "I don't believe it was entirely your fault." He looks up me and forces a smile. "I suppose if one must be knocked into the dirt, a lovely girl is not the worst way to go down."

Heat rises in my cheeks, but I manage a smile. "Most people prefer not to be knocked down at all."

"I suppose." He grins. "Are you from this village?"

I nod. "I am, but I take it from your question that you aren't? Are you one of the performers?"

His eyebrows shoot up. "Do I look like a performer?"

My cheeks grow redder. "I don't suppose so, but is there any one look for a performer?" I gesture to the many people shuffling around us.

He shrugs, his smile genuine. "I suppose not. But, no, I am not one of the performers. Just someone passing through. I am from another village, much like this one, and I thought it might be fun to enjoy the festival before continuing on my way. I am hoping to get a room at the inn, if your town has one."

It's only then I notice the bag at his feet.

"We have a couple of inns, just down that way," I reply, pointing in the opposite direction. "I would show you the way, but I'm afraid I'm expected at home. You can't miss them, though. They're right off the main road. The Briar Hog is the better of the two, if you can get a room there."

"Thank you. I appreciate your help." He reaches down and grabs his bag as I turn to resume my path home.

"Will I see you tonight around the bonfire?" he calls out to me. I glance over my shoulder but keep walking. "Perhaps."

He smiles and I can feel his eyes on my back as I turn my focus ahead. If I didn't have other concerns weighing on my mind, I would smile.

Our little house is nestled among others toward the end of town opposite from most places of business. It's a simple dwelling made mostly from split logs. The doorway and windows are open, save for a large cloth serving as a door and some basic curtains over the windows. Today, it's warm enough that those cloths have been tied back to let air circulate through the house.

Despite running the last few yards to our house, Broderick beat me home by several minutes. He sits outside with my younger sister Tabitha drawing in the dirt with a stick. They both pause in their play and look up at me as I approach, their faces etched with worry too deep for their young faces. I give them a weak smile before ducking through the doorway into the house.

The small main room of the house is filled with the smell of cooking spices, bread, and meat. Most people will eat small dinners tonight and then eat specially prepared treats and breads around the bonfire, but Father must have insisted on a full meal. My mother and eleven-year-old sister, Beka, are busy in the corner of the room cooking that dinner. My father sits at the table in the center of the room with a man I've never seen before. I force myself to focus on my father as he rises from the table, an unsettling grin on his face.

"My beloved daughter, Astra!" he says, placing his hands on my shoulders and kissing my cheek with forced affection. My initial reaction is to jerk away, but I smell mead on his breath and know better than to fight against him. "Come! Meet our guest!"

He ushers me toward the table and gestures to the strange man. The man is younger than my father but older than me by at least ten years. He isn't what most people would consider handsome, but he's not entirely horrible to look at. He has rough, hewn features with dark, curly hair and a matching beard. His thick eyebrows knit into a scowl as his dark eyes scrutinize me.

"This is Marco," my father says proudly.

I manage a small nod and force a smile. "Pleased to meet you, Marco. Welcome to our home."

He grunts in response and then looks at my father. "This is your eldest daughter?" There's something akin to disgust in his voice. "She's a waif! And it looks as if her skin's never seen sunlight."

"Now, now," my father counters, taking his seat next to Marco at the table. "She may be on the more . . . petite side and a bit pale, but she is hardy and has enough skills to make you a decent wife. I swear by it. She does carry my blood, after all." He chuckles to himself.

"Wife?" I choke out, the color draining from my face.

My father glares over his shoulder at me, narrowing his eyes, daring me to defy him.

"Yes. Wife. Marco needs a wife, and you'll be of marrying age in just three days. It's a perfect match."

He follows his declaration by gulping mead from his nearby mug. I swallow hard and fight the urge to run or cry. I'm determined not to let him see my fear. I glance toward my mother, but she purposely has her back turned as she prepares dinner.

"But, Father—"

"Now is not the time for discussion," my father cuts me off with a dismissive wave, not even bothering to face me. "Go help your mother and sister finish dinner. Prove to my good friend that you do indeed have some worth."

Fighting tears, I make my way to the corner of the room.

My mother avoids eye contact as she hands me vegetables to chop and then turns away to go back to whatever she was doing. My sister, at least, is kind enough to shoot me an occasional glance of sympathy.

For a few minutes we work in silence while Father and Marco talk in low voices at the table, gulping mead from their cups.

"I'm home!"

I spin to see Kato waltzing through the door, a smile on his face and his arms spread wide.

"Father! You're back!" he says, acting perfectly surprised. "I didn't think we were to expect you for some time yet!"

Father rises and pulls Kato into a back-slapping hug. "Ah, the Southern winds carried me home early! Come, come! Meet our guest!"

Kato eyes Marco, who stands and reaches out his hand to shake Kato's. Kato is a good head taller than Marco with a more muscular build. I'm pleased to see how noticeably uncomfortable Kato makes him.

"And who's this?" he asks as he firmly grips Marco's hand.

My husband-to-be.

Kato's eyes widen and the shock registers on his face for a fraction of a second before he schools his features, looking to our father for his response.

"Marco is an exporter based out of . . . well, I best not say. Security reasons, you understand." Father chuckles like he's just told a masterful joke. "But he does well for himself. He will make an excellent match for your sister. He plans to marry her once she turns eighteen."

Kato surveys Marco with a cold stare that would make a wiser man shrink away in fear. Out loud to Marco he says, "Well, I'll need to get to know you better then, I suppose!" To me he says, *No way in hell, Ash. I'll talk to Father. I'll find a way out.*

I release a sigh and go back to the dinner preparations. Within the hour we're seated around the table, eating our meal. Father and Marco entertain us with stories from the road, the majority of which are laced with illegal activities, loose women, alcohol, and a lot of swearing. Father makes it clear throughout the meal that I'm expected to keep both his and Marco's cups full of mead and I do my best. The more Marco speaks the more I grow to hate him.

THE NIGHT THE STARS FELL PREVIEW

CHAPTER TWO

B y the time dinner ends, darkness has started to fall. Kato glances out the nearest window and grins as he pushes up from the table.

"Well, now, if you would be so kind as to excuse us, Astra and I need to attend Kriloa."

My father scowls. "Don't you think Astra should stay and get to know our guest some more?"

I shudder. His words are more a challenge than a question. One, that if answered incorrectly, could mean consequences.

Kato forces one of his most charming smiles. "Come, Father, we always celebrate Kriloa together. If Astra is married off, next year I may not see her. Consider this a birthday present. After all, we'll only turn eighteen together once."

Marco glances from Kato to me and to my father, a confused scowl on his face. Suddenly, his eyes grow wide and he shoots to his feet. "What? Twins? You didn't tell me she was the twin!" He shakes his fist at my father. "You have tried to trick me, Baffa!"

I wince. All my life I've been treated as an oddity. While I have drawn a few glances from the village boys, most see me as little more than a curiosity to be explored.

"Now, now," my father says, rising and holding up his hands defensively. "She is a twin but she'll still make a fine wife."

"Everyone knows that twins are cursed! That's why the gods have forbidden them to be born! They have put a curse upon your family!" He makes a religious sign with his hands that seems oddly out of place for his character.

Come, Astra. While they're distracted.

I glance back at my brother. His worried eyes lock with mine and he motions his head ever so slightly toward the door.

Come.

I nod and quietly slide away from the table as my father flies into a full argument with Marco. Kato grabs my hand and pulls me out the door into the night before they can notice I've risen from the table. We hurry along the street, drawn toward the main square by the glow of the bonfire, the smells of festival food, and the cacophony of joyous sounds. Neither of us speak until we are safely away from the house, nearing the throngs of celebrating people.

"Never. I will never let that man marry you and take you away," Kato says, stopping to look down at me.

I look up at him and let the tears I've been holding in for the last hour break free. "It seems the deal has already been struck."

My brother's lips tighten into a firm line, and he shakes his head with determination as he takes both my hands in his own, pulling me to face him. "No, Astra. I don't care what bargain father has made or, more likely, what debt he's trying to get out of, but I won't let some stranger with no regard for the law whisk you away. I will kill him with my bare hands if I need to. Do you understand?"

I smile weakly and nod, wiping away my tears with the back of my hand.

"Good." He pulls me to his side in a quick hug. "Now, let's get to this festival. What are the chances a few girls have had enough mead to find me charming and be willing to sneak off for a few kisses?"

I laugh. Truth be told, most girls in our village have their eye on Kato, mead or no mead. "You mean, you wonder if Mara has had enough."

Kato chuckles. "One day she will see my charms!"

"Speaking of charms, what do you know about the visit from the prince?"

"Not much. Just that he's arriving sometime tomorrow, and we're to be on alert and ready to aid as needed."

"But why is he coming? It doesn't make sense. He's never bothered with our village before. Why now? Surely he could find much better celebrations elsewhere."

Kato shrugs. "No idea. Pax heard that the prince is looking for a commoner wife."

"What? Why? Daughters of nobles can't be that bad to look at."

Kato laughs. "I hardly doubt that's the true cause. However, if it's even remotely true, I'm sure the prince has his reasons for wanting a commoner wife. Pax isn't necessarily the most reliable when it comes to information."

We reach the edge of the main celebration, and Kato pauses to scan the crowd.

"What do you want to see first?"

I shrug and grin. "All of it. Let's just make our way through."

Kato nods and we wend our way through the people, watching the performances. Little pockets of performers are woven throughout the crowd, each with their own audience. Kato seems particularly enthralled with a small group of scantily clad belly dancers and wants to linger longer than I do.

"I'm going to go find some fried snacks," I yell to him over the crowd. He nods but keeps his focus on the dancers. I roll my eyes and follow my nose to a small booth selling an assortment of delicious fried doughs covered in a variety of spices and sugars. I've just settled on a delectable piece covered in pink sugar and twisted into the shape of a heart when a hand reaches in front of me and plops coins down for the vendor.

"Allow me," says a smooth voice. I turn to fins the man from earlier standing behind me. "And I will take one as well."

The vendor nods, handing us each our treats and slipping the money in a little pouch. We step out of the way for the next customer.

"You didn't need to do that," I protest before taking a bite of my heart.

"Perhaps. But you did guide me to the best inn in town, so, then again, perhaps I owe you." He offers me a soft smile. "I never got your name."

I swallow my food quickly and answer. "Astra."

"Astra," he muses. My name sounds different on his lips. Different in a way that makes my cheeks feel suddenly warm. "A lovely name."

"And your name? Is it lovely as well?" I say before I can think of a better response. I immediately regret my words, but he chuckles, putting me at ease.

"Not quite as lovely as yours. You may call me Bram."

"Bram," I mumble. "I like it."

"I am glad my name pleases you," he says, grinning as he takes a bite of his heart. "Mmm. This is quite excellent."

"Mm hm," I agree, taking a bite of my own. "The food is one of my favorite things about festivals."

He nods his agreement as we stop to watch a performer juggling with fire. We both watch in silence for a few moments as we finish our fried dough hearts. When we're done, he looks down at me as I lick sugar from my fingers in a very unladylike manner.

"Perhaps you could show me where to go for the best drinks." "Um, sure." I stand on my tiptoes and look through the crowd, but it does little good. It's times like these when I hate being so short. "The Mastons make the best honey mead, if you like that sort of thing. They usually have booth set up in the northwest corner."

"Excellent. You have yet to lead me astray. Show me the way," he says, gesturing with his hand for me to take the lead.

We begin once again weaving through the crowd toward the Mastons' small booth near the edge of the main crowd. We get distracted several times by various performers along the way. As we finally near the booth, Mara cuts us off.

"There you are! I've been looking for you for a good thirty minutes! I heard that—" She stops suddenly, realizing I'm not alone. She eyes Bram and arches an eyebrow as if to ask, *And who is this?*

"Oh, uh, Mara this is Bram," I say, with an awkward motion to the man at my side. "And Bram, this is Mara."

Bram inclines his head toward her. "It is a pleasure to meet you, Mara."

"What brings you to Timberborn?" she asks with a smile bordering on flirtatious.

"Business, mostly."

"Oh! How nice that business brought you here during Kriloa! Our town may be small, but we can celebrate with the best of them. I don't know how exactly they celebrate in the big cities but I can't imagine them outshining us by much! Are you from a village like ours or from one of the larger cities?"

Sometimes I envy how easygoing Mara can be with people, especially complete strangers. She always seems to know what to say. I can barely string together coherent thoughts half the time, let alone make pleasant conversation.

"I am from a small village much like this one further north, but business has brought me into more cities in recent years," Bram replies with an offhand shrug.

"The best of both worlds!" Mara laughs.

"I was just about to introduce him to the Mastons' honey mead," I cut in, selfishly wanting to draw Bram's attention back to me.

"Oh, yes! You must try their mead! My father is the head of the merchant guild here in our village. Really, he oversees everything, and their honey mead is one of our most sought-after exports!"

She begins leading the way toward the booth, linking her arm with mine.

Where are you? Kato's voice echoes in my head as Mara rambles on about exports, imports, and mead.

Done with the half-naked girls, are you?

For now. I can hear the smile in his voice. *But I may need to check on them again later.*

I'm sure you do. I'm getting honey mead with Mara and . . . um, at the Mastons' booth.

Who's "um"? No one.

Astra, are you trying to seduce one of the performers? A juggler perhaps? Don't settle for anyone less than a fire juggler.

Gods, no. Just—just come meet us. I roll my eyes.

Fine. Be there in a minute.

I sigh and focus on what Mara's saying as we take our place in line.

"Of course, he's been busy of late in preparations for the visit from the crown prince."

Bram, who's been casually listening at best, suddenly sharpens his gaze on Mara. "The crown prince? What is this about a possible visit? What have you heard?" His voice is harsh and sharp. Mara seems unusually rattled.

"Um, not much. Honestly. My father just received word he was to visit."

"When?" Bram's gaze is intense and the air around us suddenly feels thin.

Mara backs away a half-step. "I—I don't know. Not really."

"You know nothing of when he is to arrive or leave or where he will be staying?"

"No," Mara gulps.

"And even if she did, why would she tell you?" Bram's gaze snaps to me, the intensity slowly leaving his eyes as I add, "She did only meet you a few seconds ago."

Bram lets out a long sigh and nods, running a hand though his hair. "You are right. I am quite sorry. I did not mean . . . I am sorry if I sounded rude." The line moves forward, making it our turn to order.

"What can I get for you tonight?" a bubbly, pink-cheeked Mrs. Maston asks.

Bram turns to face her, a winning smile replacing his scowl. "Three honey meads, if you please."

"Better make it four," I add. "My brother will join us soon." Bram's smile widens as he gives me a wink. "Four then."

Mrs. Maston nods and busies herself filling four tankards with mead. Bram turns back to Mara, his expression much softer.

"I sincerely apologize if I seemed . . . intense. I am afraid it has always been one of my shortcomings. Growing up, my siblings never ceased to let me forget it."

Mara offers him a small smile, but I can tell she's still a little flustered. "It's all right. We all have our faults. I tend to babble endlessly sometimes."

Mrs. Maston places the four full tankards on the counter of the booth and Bram pays her. I grab up one for me and one for Kato while Bram and Mara grab theirs. Bram takes a sip as we step out of line.

"This is quite excellent." He glances at Mara. "I can indeed see why it would be one of your main exports."

Mara begins to respond but is distracted by Kato emerging from the crowd. I wave him over. He smiles shyly at Mara before sliding his eyes to Bram. I'm used to Kato being the tallest in the crowd and am surprised that Kato and Bram are almost perfectly eye to eye.

"Bram, this is my brother, Kato."

Bram offers his hand and Kato gives it a hearty shake. "Pleased to meet you, Kato."

"And you. How do you know my sister, if I may be so bold to ask?"

Kato!

Tall handsome strangers get vetted by twin brothers. I don't make the rules, Ash. I just follow them.

You most certainly do *make the rules.*

I roll my eyes while Kato continues grinning. Bram, however, doesn't seem startled or put off by Kato's somewhat rude question.

"We met earlier when she knocked me over."

Bram glances toward me, eyes twinkling, and I feel slightly mortified.

"Yes, that sounds like my sister," Kato laughs, earning a glare from me. "And, now, I suppose she's indebted to you and must show you around to make up for her clumsiness?"

"On the contrary. She directed me to a pleasant little inn, and I have found her judgment to be quite excellent. I am actually quite lucky she has agreed to put up with me."

Kato laughs again. "If you say so! However, if you'll trust *my* judgment, I saw a performance on the way over here that seems worth checking out."

"Oh! What is it?" Mara asks, eagerly.

"He's a magician, but not the boring kind with predictable tricks.

I'm pretty sure this guy is using actual magic."

"Magic died out over a century ago, Kato," I mutter, rolling my eyes.

Kato shrugs. "Believe what you will, but you really should check him out with me." He glances between the three of us. "What do you say?"

Kato has the energetic eagerness of a puppy, making it hard to say no. As we sip our mead, he leads the way to the bright red tent with rainbow ribbons that attracted my attention earlier. Standing just outside the tent is a handsome young man with high cheekbones, shocking emerald green eyes, and almost unnatural red hair pulled back with a thick black leather strap. He's dressed in a pair of black pants striped with silver, with a matching jacket over a slate blue shirt. A couple yards away, Bram freezes, his jaw set and his eyes cold. His eyes are locked on the performer, barely concealed rage flashing in his eyes as he clenches his fists by his sides. I furrow my brow in confusion, and his gaze falls to me. He forces a tight smile, but I can sense something has shifted.

"Actually, I think I may head back to my room at the inn for a bit of rest. I traveled most of the day, and I am afraid my journey is catching up with me," he speaks to us but his eyes drift back to the performer. After a moment, he tears his gaze away and looks down at me. "Hopefully, we will meet again tomorrow?"

I smile softly, nodding. "I would very much like that."

"Excellent! Well, a good night to you all," he says, glancing to each of us with a nod before he makes his way back toward the inn, disappearing into the crowd.

Well, he was a little odd.

I don't think so. I pause. *Was he odd?*

Kato laughs out loud. Mara doesn't even seem to notice, she's so entranced by the performance.

Well, he wasn't what I would call "normal," Ash. But he did seem like a good guy. Better than that Marco guy for sure.

My heart sinks. Somehow in the last hour or so I'd managed to forget about the horrible man sitting in my home, waiting to drag me away to gods know where to be his wife. Kato notices the shadow cross my face. He reaches an arm around me and draws me close.

Don't worry, Ash. We'll figure it out. I promise. For now, just enjoy the show. After all, it's not every day you get to witness real magic.

I laugh and Kato grins. Mara glances back at us. "What are you laughing at?"

"Nothing," we say together. She eyes us suspiciously before turning back to watch the performer.

I lean into the safety of my brother's arms and watch the magic tricks. And, I have to admit, they truly seem like real magic.

CONTINUE YOUR ADVENTURE

READ AN EXTENDED PREVIEW OR PURCHASE YOUR COPY ON MY WEBSITE.

ABOUT THE AUTHOR

AMBER D. LEWIS is a highly combustible combination of caffeine, mismatched coffee mugs, and shiny things. In her spare time (and, quite frankly, when she's supposed to be doing other things) she writes fantasy and other stories. She currently lives in upstate South Carolina with her wife and three kids.